MOONLIT EMBRACE

Logan stared at Brenna's face, delicately draped in the silvery web of the moon. Finally he spoke. "What am I?" he asked, repeating her question. His reply was thick with laughter as he dipped his head closer to hers, his breath teasing her cheek. "In case you can't tell, girl, I'm a man." He caught her hand in his and guided it close to his chest. "Perhaps you'd like for me to show you."

He gently eased her to the ground so that she was lying on the soft grass and he was leaning over her. Brenna thought about stopping him, but her body was truant; it whisked her good intentions aside as if they were of no consequence.

Logan brushed his lips back and forth across hers in light, teasing motions. Seemingly of its own accord, Brenna's mouth clung to his. As the kiss deepened, her arms slid around his hard, muscular back. She couldn't think straight. She simply wanted to surrender to the wonder of his touch. . . .

FIERY ROMANCE
From Zebra Books

SATIN SECRET   (2116, $3.95)
by Emma Merritt

After young Marta Carolina had been attacked by pirates, ship-wrecked, and beset by Indians, she was convinced the New World brought nothing but tragedy . . . until William Dare rescued her. The rugged American made her feel warm, protected, secure — and hungry for a fulfillment she could not name!

CAPTIVE SURRENDER   (1986, $3.95)
by Michalann Perry

Gentle Fawn should have been celebrating her newfound joy as a bride, but when both her husband and father were killed in bat-tle, the young Indian maiden vowed revenge. She charged into the fray — yet once she caught sight of the piercing blue gaze of her enemy, she knew that she could never kill him. The handsome white man stirred a longing deep within her soul . . . and a pas-sion she'd never experienced before.

PASSION'S JOY   (2205, $3.95)
by Jennifer Horsman

Dressed as a young boy, stunning Joy Claret refused to think what would happen were she to get caught at what she was really doing: leading slaves to liberty on the Underground Railroad. Then the roughly masculine Ram Barrington stood in her path and the blue-eyed girl couldn't help but panic. Before she could fight him, she was locked in an embrace that could end only with her surrender to PASSION'S JOY.

TEXAS TRIUMPH   (2009, $3.95)
by Victoria Thompson

Nothing is more important to the determined Rachel McKinsey than the Circle M — and if it meant marrying her foreman to scare off rustlers, she would do it. Yet the gorgeous rancher felt a se-cret thrill that the towering Cole Elliot was to be her man — and despite her plan that they be business partners, all she truly de-sired was a glorious consummation of their vows.

PASSION'S PARADISE   (1618, $3.75)
by Sonya T. Pelton

When she is kidnapped by the cruel, captivating Captain Ty, fair-haired Angel Sherwood fears not for her life, but for her honor! Yet she can't help but be warmed by his manly touch, and secretly longs for PASSION'S PARADISE.

Restless Flames
Emma Merritt

ZEBRA BOOKS
KENSINGTON PUBLISHING CORP.

ZEBRA BOOKS

are published by

Kensington Publishing Corp.
475 Park Avenue South
New York, NY 10016

First printing: November, 1987

Printed in the United States of America

To Martha and Hortense and Pets
with love

Chapter One

Austin, Texas
January 1843

Blending with the blackened shadows of night, two men rode into the sleeping town of Austin and dismounted in front of Bullock's House. They tied their horses to the rail and entered the two-storied building. They walked so silently, they passed the dozing clerk without awakening him. Up the stairs and down the dimly lit hall they moved until they stood in front of the room they sought. One of them rapped softly—a coded knock.

The man who opened the door studied the visitors for a moment by the light of the candle he held. Their faces were concealed by broad-brimmed hats that dipped low in the front. Each wore a fringed and open-necked buckskin shirt tucked into the waist of his trousers. Around their waists hung two holstered revolvers. Attached to each belt was a sheathed bowie knife.

"Come on in, boys," a husky voice invited as the door swung open. "The president's been expecting you." Jim Hardee, captain of the Texas Rangers and personal aide to the president of Texas, ushered the two men into the presence of Sam Houston, who sat at

7

a table writing.

The president glanced up as they entered. For a moment the three men stared silently at each other. Unobtrusively Jim moved out of the way, returning to his chair in front of the opened window on the other side of the room. Houston dropped his pen, stood, and moved around the desk. He wore a dark vest and coat and black-and-white checkered trousers tucked into the tops of knee-high boots. A smile softened the craggy hardness of Sam Houston's face as he looked at the two young men.

He spoke in Cherokee. "Thunder-of-the-Storm, eldest son of Antelope Hunter, I welcome you to my humble rooms. Thank you for coming to listen to my words."

The older of the two men, a Cherokee brave, smiled and acknowledged Houston's greeting. "Thank you, He-who-is-called-The-Raven. I am willing to hear your words. You have always been true to your blood brothers, the Cherokees."

Sadness clouded the president's eyes as he remembered Mirabeau Lamar's extermination of the Cherokees on July 15, 1839. "I have been true, my friend, but I was unable to help my people, the Cherokees, in the hour of their greatest need." Houston turned and addressed the other man, still speaking in Cherokee. "And you, Logan MacDougald, adopted younger son of Antelope Hunter, I also welcome."

"Thank you, He-who-is-called-The-Raven," MacDougald replied, also in Cherokee, his steady tone evincing no emotion. "I am willing to hear your words."

Reverting to English, Houston waved his hand to the two chairs in front of his desk. "Thunder"—he addressed the Cherokee by his Anglicized name— "Logan, we're up against a hard one, so I had Hardee

8

send for you because you're the best rangers I have."

"I won't insult you, General," MacDougald said in a low, dry tone, removing his hat as he sat down, "by saying that your memory is failing. I know better. And you know better. But in all respect for your high office, sir, I remind you that we are no longer rangers."

Houston looked at the younger of the two men, and when he spoke it was as if he hadn't heard a word MacDougald said. "Would you consider drawing yourself an assignment?"

"No" was Logan's quick and flat refusal.

For a long moment Houston said nothing. He reached into his vest pocket, pulled out a small gold locket, and cradled it in the palm of his hand in such a way that no one else in the room could see it. Looking down at the delicate piece of jewelry, he said, "If memory serves me right, your maternal grandmother was named Flanna, was she not, Logan?"

Logan tensed. He knew Houston was playing with him. The general might be fifty years old, but he was as alert now as he had ever been. Quietly Logan answered, "Yes."

"And your sister was also named Flanna," Houston said, deliberately building suspense and savoring every moment of it.

Logan didn't speak, but his eyes narrowed and glinted dangerously. He respected Houston as a man, a soldier, and as president of Texas, but he would allow no one to trample on his emotions.

By now Houston stood directly in front of Logan. "What if I said I might have information about your sister?" Houston was a shrewd politician who had learned the art and value of bargaining, and he knew of Logan Andrew MacDougald's relentless search for his sister, who had been kidnapped by the Comanches twenty years ago.

9

Houston dangled the locket in front of Logan. "I recently acquired this."

Mesmerized, Logan stared at the gently swaying locket. He blinked several times as if he were seeing a hallucination, but the pendant didn't disappear. Slowly he extended a large, callused hand to clasp the fragile piece of jewelry which Houston readily relinquished. Like a man in a trance, Logan moved to the candle. With clumsy, shaking fingers he turned the golden disc over to read the delicate engraving.

His lips moved as he silently mouthed the date, 1792, then the inscription: Flanna, my love. Tears stung Logan's eyes as he dropped his hand to his side and tightly clenched his fingers around his grandmother's locket—the locket he hadn't seen since the day the Comanches killed his parents and kidnapped his older sister. From the day of her sixteenth birthday, when his mother had given it to Flanna, she had never taken the necklace off.

No one spoke. Every man in the room, acquainted with the kind of grief Logan was suffering, allowed him a moment of quiet vulnerability. Patiently they waited; they knew how important dignity and integrity were to a man. More, they knew without vulnerability, a man can have neither.

"Where did you get it?" Logan finally asked, his voice husky with unshed tears.

"Rhem Sommers, a settler a few miles out of Austin, close to Brushy Creek. Comanches attacked his place a few weeks ago. He managed to pull this off the neck of one of them."

"I'd like to speak to Sommers," Logan declared.

Softly Houston said, "You must hear me first."

Logan turned around, moving so that he was between the president of the republic and the lamp. His face was shadowed so that none of his features were

10

discernible. "You would use me?"

Again Houston nodded, his eyes never wavering from the younger man's face. "For Texas I would use you . . . but you will also be gaining. You will be using me for your own purpose." He paused, then resumed speaking. "This much you owe yourself, Logan MacDougald."

"Speak," Logan said, his voice once again dry and unyielding. He dropped the locket into his shirt pocket and returned to his chair. "I will listen."

"As you and the entire world know, my one greatest desire has been to make Texas a state in the Union. Three times we have offered, and three times the United States has rejected our offer." Pacing back and forth in front of his desk, his hands laced together in back of him, Houston continued. "Again, in this year of 1843, I will make the fourth offer."

"General," Hardee said with a shake of his head, "that don't make much sense to me. At first we were all for statehood, but not now, not after being rejected three times. We've suffered enough humiliation as it is."

"And," Logan added, his tone slightly mocking, "we are now divided into two camps: those in favor of annexation and those who favor an empire. The Annexationists against the Imperialists, and those who favor an empire are growing daily and increasing in political power. In fact, sir"—Logan's eyes gleamed speculatively as he looked at the president—"there are many who say you are also espousing Imperialism."

Houston threw back his huge head and laughed, the warm, rich sound filling the small room. "Ah, yes," he finally said. "These of whom you are speaking would be referring to my dealings with England." Again he chuckled. "I'm merely giving the people of the United States some food for thought," he explained. "I want

11

them to understand fully that Britain isn't as foolish with regard to Texas as they are. The British would be quick to ally themselves with us to spread their influence across the western portion of this continent."

Houston's face grew solemn. "This year I shall offer Texas to the United States a fourth time." His voice lowered to a whisper. "This, gentlemen, will be my last offer. If the United States should reject us this time, I'll join Clarence Childers and the Imperialist Movement and, if need be, by myself forge the Empire of Texas from here to the Pacific Ocean. I shall guarantee that Texas will be bordered by none other than the United States, Canada, Mexico, and the Pacific Ocean."

Logan laughed softly. "If I know you, sir, half as well as I think I do, you're sure the United States will not reject us this time."

In reply to Logan's comment a cunning grin spanned Houston's face. "By the time I get through with my machinations, men, the United States will be inviting us to join her glorious union." He lowered his head and straightened some papers on his desk. In a quiet, almost detached manner, he said, "The United States has two basic reasons for denying Texas statehood, and both of these arguments come from the North. The first is that we will add strength to the South. That, of course, cannot be denied. The second is the bone of contention. They say, and rightly so, we have two thousand miles of wilderness frontier which will need defending. But they also say this frontier will demand too many soldiers for protection and will drain the coffers of the United States government.

"They are so shortsighted!" Houston exploded. His huge fist landed on the desk with a thud that resounded through the room. "They cannot see beyond the moment. We shall defend our own frontier." His voice lowered to a burning hatred. "But they laughed at me

12

and reminded me of the Comanche incursions on our settlements." He dropped his hand to his side and clenched his fist even tighter. "Incursions which are becoming more frequent, gentlemen, and more daring. With great cunning a small band gets the attention of the rangers and lures them away from the line of settlement on a wild-goose chase while the main body of Comanches strikes. It's as if someone is directing the Comanches. They know exactly where the rangers are. Just last month when I moved the ranging unit from the Irish Colonies, the Indians struck a devious and ingenious blow. They swept well into our line of civilization to wipe out a settlement and an entire wagon train belonging to none other but Clarence Childers."

Houston's voice raised. "And don't think he hasn't used that to bring in new membership for and to give new impetus to his Imperial Movement. If Texas doesn't become a state in the Union this year, gentlemen," he declared fervently, "she never will. The Imperialists will have gained enough power to launch a candidate in the next election who will wave the flag of *empire* with Lamar and his cohorts." He wagged his index finger toward Logan. "And mark my words that candidate will win the election, and Texas' course will be set."

A seasoned politician and superb orator, Houston had the attention of his audience. His breathing almost suspended, Jim Hardee leaned forward and peered through the candlelit room at the general, who stalked back and forth in front of his desk. Although their faces displayed no expression. Thunder's and Logan's eyes glittered with interest. All three men knew they were being manipulated by Houston, but none minded. In fact, they relished this game they were playing.

"If, gentlemen, we can quiet the western front for one

year"—he lifted his forefinger and wagged it for emphasis—"if we can keep the Comanches quiet for one year, I promise you Texas shall become a state in the Union of the United States of America, and Imperialism for Texas shall be squashed for all time!"

When the booming echo of Houston's words finally died, Logan said, "That's a pretty big if, General."

"Not with you and Thunder taking the assignment," Houston declared.

"You are asking us to subdue the Comanches!" Logan didn't bother to hide his skepticism. "You expect us to do what all the ranging units together couldn't do?"

A smile of pure delight tugged Houston's lips. "'Tis the little foxes who destroy the vines, my friends. They slip in unawares to do their damage."

The chair creaked as Hardee leaned back. "I suppose Logan and Thunder will be the little foxes."

"If they take the assignment" was Houston's firm reply. He gestured them to his desk. "Come, gentlemen. I have something I wish to show you."

The four men stood around the table and stared at a map of Texas, the soft glow of the candle flickering over their faces. "Here"—Houston pointed—"to the east are our coastal plains and settlements, our major rivers and their tributaries. These hills mark the beginning of the high prairies." His forefinger moved to the west, where the map was blank, and he thumped the table. "Here, gentlemen, is Comancheria, the land where the Comanches dwell. Terrain they know like the back of their hands, terrain we can't even begin to guess about."

"Why, General," Jim exploded, "begging your pardon, sir, but how can you expect two men to subdue these Comanches? You know as well as I do that these Indians all live together. There's so many different

14

bands, we can't even give them names. They're never in one spot more than a week at a time."

Houston chuckled. He enjoyed Hardee's outburst. "True, but they seem to have one chief who is over all other chiefs."

"White-Hair," Hardee murmured. "The Comanche chief who has a streak of pure white hair running through his black hair. Let's see now. We haven't heard a word from this White-Hair in . . . about . . . twenty years, General." Hardee's voice escalated with incredulity. "You really believe he's still living?"

"Yes," Houston returned, his eyes pinned to Logan, "I think he is."

"You think he's the one responsible for all these attacks!"

"No," Houston answered, his gaze never wavering from Logan, "neither he nor his people are responsible."

Hardee snorted. "Who is, if it ain't this White-Hair and his Comanches?"

Only now did Houston move. He lowered his head and moved his hand, his finger straying to the northwest of the map. "Here in the Staked Plains, gentlemen, in the very center of the Comanches' natural fortress, is someone else whom I believe to be an even more vicious enemy than the Comanches."

Gripped by the intensity of Sam Houston's words, the three men stared at the map. The mention of Staked Plains drove fear into the hearts of Texans. Few white men had come through them alive, and those who had were unwilling to return a second time.

"The Comancheros," Houston finally said in answer to Hardee's question. "Bands of renegade white and Mexican traders, the worst of both races, who operate on the unmapped frontier between Texas and Santa Fe. They are outlaws of the worst kind, men totally

15

without consciences."

The president looked up to see three sets of eyes focused on him. He could see the disbelief in their faces. "Listen to me!" he commanded. "It is true the Comanches are the most highly trained and skilled plains warriors, but they are still primitive warriors. These latest raids—the one in Linneville last year, the one at Refugio just a few months back, the one at Dry Creek three weeks ago, and the latest one at Sommer's Settlement last week—all these have the marking of a most highly sophisticated military mind. Small bands draw the rangers away, then the main group strikes, meeting no resistance.

"I know it's hard to believe, but I have it on a reliable source, gentlemen. One of the rangers brought in a woman who recently escaped from the Comanches." Houston cast laughing eyes on Hardee. "She is the one who told me of this chief with the lock of white hair. She also told me about this group of outlaws, made up of Mexicans and white men, with whom the Comanches trade."

Houston paused and drew in a deep breath of air. "Her testimony bears witness with what others have told me since. Wanting cattle and horses to sell to the Mexicans, these Comancheros deliberately incite the Comanches to massacre our settlements. The woman said, in exchange for the plunder, the Comancheros give the Indians liquor, arms, and trinkets. The woman told me something else that is completely revolting to civilized man."

Houston paused, only waiting to let the impact of his words sink in. "The Comancheros want more than horses and livestock now. They want young, beautiful women." Again Houston paused. "Women to be sold into prostitution in Mexico!"

The huge hand balled into a fist and came down on

16

the table with a thwack that shook the candle. "We have to get rid of this scourge before it further contaminates Texas, and we must destroy the very roots of this problem; we must eliminate the source who has created such a monster." He paused for only a second before he added, "And, gentlemen, for my plan to come together, we have no time to waste. The Comancheros must be found and wiped out by July of this year."

"General," Hardee murmured, his brow furrowed in thought, "do you realize we're almost in February? Why, that gives us about—"

"About six months," Houston declared with an emphatic nod. "Logan, Thunder"—Houston's head swiveled from one man to the other, his eyes imploring—"I need you to locate the exact spot where this vermin nests. I need even more, boys." Again he paused, lifted a huge hand, and rubbed his chin contemplatively. "I need to learn who is behind this entire operation. That's the person who must be dealt with."

Logan's gaze caught and held the president's. "You think perhaps it's someone in civilization, sir?" Houston nodded. "Someone in Texas?" Again Houston moved his head affirmatively.

"You're asking a lot, General."

"I am," he said emphatically.

"Finding the hideout of the Comancheros is a pretty tough order, but I'm sure, given time, that Thunder and I can do it."

"Texas is almost out of time, gentlemen." Houston had done his best. Now he could only wait.

Logan's eyes once again strayed across the map of Texas to land on the Staked Plains area. "In order to find out who is behind this operation, sir, Thunder and I will have to infiltrate the Comancheros."

17

"That's my plan," Houston admitted. "Disguised as outlaws, you should have no difficulty in penetrating their ranks."

Logan's laughter filled the room. "If we should take this assignment, General, Thunder and I will be more than little foxes. We'll be sacrificial lambs!"

Chapter Two

Sitting astride the huge gray Arabian, Brenna Allen rode ahead of the large wagon train. Dressed in a long-sleeved shirt, trousers, and knee-high boots, she carried a revolver in a hip holster. A knife was sheathed to her belt; a whip was looped over her shoulder. Although she wore a hat to protect her face from the glaring sun, she couldn't escape the heat of the late afternoon. Perspiration glistened on her forehead.

Pride surged through her as she stared across the endless miles of flat plains that Texans had claimed for the six years since they had proclaimed their independence from Mexico in 1836 and formed the republic. The powerful surge of pride slowly ebbed to a sigh of resignation; Brenna recognized that at the present time—April 1843—this claim was more rhetoric than truth. Texas was large in area but sparse in manpower and was blocked in on two sides by deadly enemies, the Mexicans and the Comanches, each of whom also claimed the territory and was unwilling to relinquish their title of ownership to the newly formed republic. A republic that Mexico still vehemently denied. A political institution which the Comanches didn't understand—or want to understand.

Why would anyone want it? Travelers and merchants asked when they finally reached the line of settlement in Texas. Endless miles of desert! No man's land! To an extent they were right, Brenna conceded. At the moment this land belonged neither to the Texans nor to the Mexicans. Although civilization had pushed the Comanches further west, this land continued to carry their brand. Their presence was still felt and feared. When Brenna looked around, she saw unmistakable signs of its Comanche ownership: skeletons bleaching in the sun; charred remains of wagons; discarded farm implements, stripped of their metal; tattered remains of luggage scattered about.

Strangely, none of these signs frightened Brenna or caused her resolve to waver. Although this was her first trail drive as either passenger or freighter, she had promised herself that she would get these wagons from Texas to Santa Fe safely, and she would. She wouldn't be the first Texan to leave her autograph on these plains. The Santa Fe Expedition, or Lamar's Folly as it had been nicknamed because of its abysmal failure, had seen to that. But she would leave her mark. Come hell or high water! She grinned. Probably be hell coming first. Sure wasn't any sign of high water. Running her fingers around the crown of the sweat-stained hat, she wiped perspiration from her brow and nudged her horse into a trot to return to the wagon train that trundled behind her.

"Well?" The old man who rode slightly ahead of the lead wagon snarled the question as Brenna rode alongside.

Brenna looked at her longtime friend and wagon boss with concern. Strands of white hair, peeking from beneath Gabriel Langdon's hat, plastered his forehead, and perspiration streaked his gaunt face, also whitened with a day's beard growth. Tobacco stains slightly colored the wrinkles around his mouth. What caught Brenna's attention, however, were the lines of worry that creased his brow and puckered between his eyes.

"Venner"—she referred to Brady Venner, the veteran mountain trapper whom they had hired as scout because of his familiarity with the Santa Fe Trail—"says there's a river about another hour up the way. Says it's a good place to camp."

Tobacco juice splattered against the dry, hard dirt, quickly to disappear until nothing remained except a darkened circle; then came Gabby's terse words. "Good. All of us could use the rest." He raised his head to scowl into the vast, empty plains ahead. "Where's Venner now?"

"He's gone ahead to see if he can find Kirkwood. He's worried about him."

Gabby raised his brows in question.

"Venner said we were too close to Comanche territory to be riding off by ourself, and Kirkwood's been gone since early morning. Venner said to tell you that he'd meet us at the river." She reached up to wipe the grit from the back of her neck and added wistfully, "I sure hope Kirkwood keeps his promise and brings us a mess of fresh meat."

Gabby's thoughts ran to Abbott Kirkwood, the hunter he'd hired in Austin. He was thin and rawhide-tough. Spoke seldom, and when he did it was hardly more than guttural grunts. He shaved about once a month, and his hair hung below his shoulders. Always dressed in buckskins, he wore a large hat and carried a rifle, revolver, and knife. Though Kirkwood, like most trappers and mountain men, was quiet and aloof, that didn't keep him from being a good hunter. So far he'd kept the train supplied with plenty of fresh game.

For some reason Venner didn't like Kirkwood and wouldn't have much to do with him. Jealousy, Gabby thought. At twenty-five, Kirkwood was the younger of the two men, with energy to spare at the end of the day.

21

Unlike Venner, he wasn't familiar with the Santa Fe Trail, but he knew the immediate countryside better than Venner, and twice Kirkwood had saved the caravan travel time by pointing out shorter routes than those selected by Venner.

"Do you think Venner is right, Gabby?" Brenna asked, her words almost an extension of the old man's thoughts. She gazed at the western horizon, into the far reaches of the Texas frontier—land that was unknown to the white man, land that was unmapped. "Should we cut through Comancheria?"

Because he weighed his answer, Gabby was a long time replying. Eventually he said, "If it was our freight wagons alone, Brendy gal, I'd say maybe we should take the chance and head across Comanche territory. Reckon we'd save some miles and time, but we've got to think about these settlers you signed on in San Antone. Remember," he gently chided, bringing to mind the argument he and Brenna had over this, "you promised to get 'em to Bent's Fort."

"No matter which way we go," Brenna declared, a trifle impatiently, "I'm still going to get them to Bent's Fort. I'm just thinking maybe we ought to consider taking the shorter route. No need to circle all around Comancheria, going miles out of the way, to hit the Santa Fe Trail when we can head northwest and intercept it at Bent's Fort."

"Kirkwood said this was the safest route. Less likely to encounter big bands of Comanches," Gabby said, "and I agree with him. To tell the truth, Brendy, I'm downright scared of them Indians. Seen what they kin do to a body, and it ain't a pretty sight." He spat and wiped his mouth. "But you're the wagon captain. The decision is yours. I've had my say."

"I'll speak to Venner and Kirkwood about it later this evening or in the morning," Brenna mused. "Since

22

we're resting tomorrow, I don't have to make the decision tonight."

Gabby turned and looked down the line of wagons that lumbered behind. "Jest remember this, gal; these people are your responsibility."

Brenna's head turned, and her gaze also swept the length of the caravan—her twelve wagons loaded with trade goods for the market in Santa Fe, six families headed for Bent's Fort to join a larger train headed for Oregon, and Samuel Walter Roper, lately of Boston, Massachusetts, now a prospective citizen of Santa Fe. She smiled as her eyes lit briefly on the huge and elegant carriage, painted red, yellow, and blue, that seemed so incongruous with all the other sturdy, utilitarian vehicles.

Her gaze encountered the eight men who rode on either side of the caravan, the armed escort Gabby had hired in San Antonio, drifters from New Orleans come to Texas looking for excitement. Bringing up the rear was a comforting sight, the mess wagon and assistant wagon boss, Elijah Caldwell, a big, burly man with a long, bushy beard—one of the settlers who was traveling as far as Bent's Fort with the caravan. Her eyes fixed on Roger Hollis, the leader of the armed guards, who was riding beside the mess wagon.

By subtle movements of hand and knee Brenna set the gray off in a trot down one side of the caravan and up the other. As she galloped along, she called, "Another hour before we stop for the night. Mr. Kirkwood promised fresh meat aplenty, and Mr. Venner found a river large enough for us to water the animals, refill our barrels, and bathe." The cheers followed her as she drew abreast of the wagon boss.

"I'm so glad I didn't stay behind," she exclaimed after a while. "I've never been so excited and happy in all my life, Gabby."

23

Gabby simply grunted.

"We're crossing country that no one claims to know," she continued.

"Some days I wonder that anyone would want to claim to know it," Gabby grumbled. "We've hacked our way through that dense forest around the Bosque River and built an incline so's we could get the wagons up the steep embankment. And Maude Hemphill griping all the way. Bertha Caldwell always ailing."

Brenna only laughed. "With all that, we're making good time. We've been averaging twelves miles a day, and today we'll do even better." She and Gabby both gazed around them at the treeless prairie. "We should make at least fifteen."

"From the beginning, I didn't approve of your coming on this trip," Gabby grumbled, "and the further away we get from Austin, the less I like it. In fact, gal, I'm downright scared. This ain't no place for a lady. Home's where you should be." His gray eyes, bloodshot from the dust swirling about him and filled with disgust, landed on her garb. "Dressed like a man, toting hardware like a man, and riding wagon captain like a man. And sooner or later we're bound ta' run into them Comanches—and if they get the chance, they'll kill you like a man."

"Better that than be raped and tortured as a woman," Brenna returned, taking no offense at Gabby's words. "When we finish this trading trip, I'll be able to stay home and be a lady. With the money—"

"If we live to get home." Gabby wouldn't be mollified; he'd heard this argument too many times to be impressed with it anymore. "I know Clarence Childers was dead set on these goods getting to Santy Fee, but he shore didn't mean for you to travel with the train."

Not the goods so much as the letter to Peyton H.

24

Alexander, citizen of Santa Fe! Brenna thought.

"If only Childers had an inclination of what you was planning, Brendy girl," Gabby lamented. "If only he had of knowed."

"Well, Gabriel Langdon, put this in your pipe and smoke it. Politically I agree wholeheartedly with Clarence Childers, and I'm proud to be a part of the Imperial Movement. I want Texas to become an empire. But I'm my own woman. I don't need a keeper. What I do isn't any of Clarence Childers's business. The only obligation I have to the man is to deliver his goods, sell them, and return with his money," Brenna declared. "So there!"

My other obligation is Texas' future, she silently added.

Brenna frowned as she thought of Clarence Childers, a leading merchant in Houston and a longtime political cohort of her father's—now hers. Since her father's death six months ago, Childers had tried to insinuate himself into her life as a mentor and father figure. But Brenna would have nothing to do with him. Although she agreed with his political philosophy, she wasn't looking for a parent.

But he would be furious when he learned that she had accompanied the wagon train to Santa Fe! More smoke would be coming from him than the cigar which he habitually kept in the corner of his mouth. She could see him in his office at the rear of his store. Yelling obscenities, he would pace back and forth in his office, his hands behind his back, his paunch straining the buttons of his shirt and waistcoat.

And his little tirade wouldn't necessarily be out of concern for her. Since her husband was to have been the agent the Imperialists sent to Santa Fe, Childers had given him a letter of introduction to Peyton H. Alexander—an American who was now a naturalized citizen of Santa Fe and one who advocated an Empire of Texas. But Shawn's untimely death had ruined that little scheme. Clarence was biding his time and looking for another agent. He never suspected that Brenna would take it on herself to go to Santa Fe . . . to meet with Alexander.

Brenna smiled. In the throes of Shawn's death everyone had forgotten about the letter of introduction. By the time Childers remembered it, she would be well on her way.

"Sure wish you had taken Childers up on his offer to buy the company," Brenna heard Gabby say. "Right good offer it was for a company that's so far in the hole it can't be dug out."

"Clarence Childers," Brenna returned stiffly, on the defensive when one criticized her only inheritance, "wouldn't have offered to buy Garvey Mercantile and Freight Hauling if he didn't think dollars were involved, Gabriel Langdon. I may not be the lady you think I ought to be, but I'm not a fool. Childers is a businessman, a ruthless one at that. He eats the opposition for breakfast and spits his competitors out like they were persimmon seeds."

"He was your father's friend," Gabby reminded her.

"No, not a friend," Brenna corrected. "He and Papa were business and political acquaintances, friendly only because Papa knew how to handle him and never bowed to the man." At the mention of her father, Brenna's eyes filled with tears and she blinked. Spurring the horse into a gallop, she rode ahead of Gabby. Had she remained, she would have started crying, and that was an indignity she wanted to spare herself.

Brenna rode ahead of the train, the wind whipping loose tendrils of hair across her face. Except for Gabby, she was alone—all alone. The farther away from

26

Austin they traveled, the more she felt her loneliness. The vastness of the countryside reminded her of her vulnerability.

Gabby understood how Brenna felt. He ought to. He'd known her ever since she was a little tot, about five or six, he reckoned. He'd never forget the day Nolan Garvey arrived in Martin DeLeon's Colony—the tall, brawny Irishman with a brogue so thick you could ride across it on a horse, and a scrawny little girl in tow with two black braids hanging on either side of her long, narrow face and the most beautiful eyes Gabby had ever seen—green sometimes, blue sometimes.

He spat, then lifted his hand to run it across his mouth. He was sorry he had spoken to her like that. Right careless of him it was; he should have known better than to mention Nolan. Brenna was still grieving—first the death of her papa; next the death of her new husband, all within six months of each other.

Chapter Three

In mid-afternoon two riders topped a distant hill to sit on their mounts and observe the wagon train as it leisurely ambled toward the river in the valley far below. Without saying a word to one another, they watched the boss begin to guide the caravan into a double square. The men looked at each other and simultaneously nodded their heads. They moved toward the camp, a string of horses and pack mules behind them.

An hour later Brenna looked up from the fire she was tending in time to see the two strangers approaching. Because the sun was to the men's backs, she couldn't distinguish their features, but she knew they were seasoned frontiersmen. More, she knew they were seasoned Texans. The way they sat a horse; their weapons; their garb.

Gabby quietly ordered Hollis and his men to attention, something an experienced frontiersman did automatically. Even though these boys handled their guns well, they did not yet have the feel of the frontier necessary to understand the potential danger of an approaching visitor; they needed the verbal orders which the wagon boss gave. They immediately picked up their rifles and positioned themselves.

Satisfied that he was covered, Gabby walked

through the double square to greet the visitors. The settlers huddled together to peer around the wagons.

"Howdy," Gabby said, his rifle cradled in his arms. He hid his nervousness behind a quiet voice. His face screwed up and his eyes narrowed as he studied the men. About the same age he thought, but . . . *As sure as I'm standing here, one's an Indian!* The man's hair was cut short, and he wore a broad-brimmed hat, but Gabby could see Indian etched all over him: immobile countenance, chiseled features, glittering black eyes, and finely toned copper-brown skin. The other man Gabby wasn't sure about.

"Afternoon," the other man replied easily, his gray eyes never leaving Gabby's face, his hands staying well away from the revolver that rested in a holster on each hip. "Saw your camp and wondered if we could join you for the night."

"Depends." Gabby deliberately lowered his head and spat. Then he scrutinized the horses—a different brand on each one—and pack mules. "Depends on who you are and what you're doing out here."

"Logan MacDougald," the other man introduced himself. "Been a Texan for twenty years. Family came in the twenties with Austin himself. Originally from north Ireland."

Brenna eased away from the fire and the crowd so she could see better. MacDougald's voice was one of the most beautiful she had ever heard, resonant and deep. Yet it was soft and pacifying; it had a calming effect. It was reassuring. She watched as he easily swung from the saddle. He was a giant of a man, she thought . . . six feet three if an inch. At five nine she was as tall as many men, but not this one! He would tower over her. She saw him tilt his head toward the mounted rider; she heard the low, hypnotic tones again.

"This is Thunder."

"Comanche?"

"Cherokee," came Logan's soft reply. "We ride together."

"You about half-Indian yourself?" Gabby asked. He remembered Bowles, a half-Scot, half-Indian chief of the Cherokees.

"White by birth," Logan replied, taking no umbrage at Gabby's inquisitiveness. He'd lived on the frontier all his life and knew the wise man—the man who lived another day—never took anything or anyone for granted. The man who lived for another day was a wary man who questioned people and circumstances; he was cautious. Careful to make his tone and gestures friendly, Logan obviously kept his hands away from his weapons. "Indian by adoption."

Gabby nodded, his gaze shifting from one immobile countenance to the other.

The man asked the second time, "May we join you?"

"Reckon you can," the wagon boss answered. "Where you headed?"

"Doing some government work for Houston," Logan answered easily, evasively. When he saw Gabby's gaze return and linger on the string of horses behind him, he said, "They're ours. Government ration. Ole Sam had them rounded up on the day we pulled out." Logan almost laughed aloud as he recalled Houston's indignation when he had insisted on including the president's favorite Appaloosa in his herd of "stolen animals." Wasn't that the way the Wanted poster phrased it? "Anybody who had more than one horse or mule found himself volunteering his animal." He waited for a moment; then Gabby nodded his head. Logan said, "You know who we are, stranger. Mind telling us who you are?"

"Gabby Langdon, boss for Garvey Freight Hauling.

Headed for Santy Fee to do some trading with the Mexicans."

"Taking a big chance," Logan said. "Mexicans are hostile toward Texans, and Comanches range on all the land between Texas and Santa Fe."

"Way I figure it, life's a chance," Gabby parried. "You get exactly what you ask of it." He spat, wiped his mouth with the back of his hand, and said, "Come join us for supper. We have plenty of food to share with you."

"We bring food." Thunder finally spoke. For an Indian he also was tall, superbly built, and well coordinated. As he dismounted, he unhooked a large leather pouch. "We found many rabbits along the way."

"You been following us long?" Gabby held his hand out for the bag. He knew Indians never killed for the sport of it, so there could only be one reason for the rabbits. They had been planning to dine with the wagon train all along.

"All day," Logan replied.

"We weren't aware of it."

"You weren't supposed to be."

The silence lengthened as the three men measured each other. Finally Gabby said, "Well, come on in, and bring them horses and mules with you. You can let them graze with our herd."

Thunder shook his head. "Thank you, Wagon Boss, but we are accustomed to sleeping by ourselves. We will camp away from the wagons and keep the animals with us."

Gabby nodded, and Thunder turned, making his way toward the river, where he would set up camp. In two strides Logan was beside Gabby, and they were walking inside the corral formed by the wagons. As Gabby pushed his way through the onlookers, he handed the pouch of rabbits to Horace Faraday, one of the men traveling with the expedition. "Mr. Faraday, will you see that these rabbits are skinned and dressed?"

"Sure will," Horace replied, turning immediately to his wife, Barbara, who took the bundle.

Her face creased into a smile, laugh lines splintering from the corners of her eyes. The few years she'd spent on the harsh frontier had weathered her, and despite the still dark hair pulled into a tight coil on the back of her neck, she looked older than her thirty-five years.

"We sure will, Mr. Langdon," she said. "Rabbit stew will certainly taste good tonight." She cast gentle eyes on her portly husband. "Guess this calls for a celebration, don't you, Mr. Faraday? Music and dancing?"

The big man beamed and reached up to run his hand over his bald head. "Reckon it does, Mrs. Faraday. Reckon it does!" He looked at Gabby. "That is, if it's all right with you, Mr. Langdon."

"Reckon so," Gabby snorted. "Jest want you to know that we'll still be up and at 'em at five in the morning. We ain't gonna hold up the train none cause you want to fiddle and dance."

Laughter rippled through the crowd as heads nodded agreement.

"Right now," Gabby announced, his legs straddled, his hands on his hips, "figure we all have work to do before we start this shindig." Without a backward glance he tended to his horse.

Suddenly the camp was astir with activity, but Brenna was unaware of it. She stood trancelike and stared at the stranger. He removed his hat to reveal a wealth of golden-brown hair that softened the angular hardness of his gaunt face, the expressions of which she intuitively knew he kept under control at all times.

She moved closer to him to see better. She looked at the faded shirt that stretched across his broad back, the strong arms that extended from the rolled-up sleeves. Down went her gaze beyond the belt to his buttocks and legs—long, lean, muscular legs in black leather boots.

Then she felt the heat of an unfamiliar gaze. Slowly she lifted her head to encounter the most startling eyes she had ever beheld. Gray. The color wasn't unusual. Shawn had gray eyes. But these . . . these eyes were different. They were hard and unwavering, yet they were alluring. They gleamed with mystery. Like a magnet they compelled her to come nearer to discover his secrets.

Logan was as startled by Brenna's eyes as she was by his. Because she was attired in loose-fitting men's clothing and had her hair pulled back in a single plait, he hadn't immediately known she was a woman. But the moment he had looked into her eyes, he felt as if he were drowning. They reminded him of the creek that ran behind his house, the water so clear and sparkling, its color vacillating between blue and green. His father, from Ireland, always told him that it was sea-green, the color of the River Shannon, the color of his mother's eyes. This woman's eyes were that very color—sea-green.

"That's the little lady what owns Garvey Freight Hauling," Gabby said as he hoisted his saddle to the ground. "Brenna Allen, our wagon captain."

Brenna saw Logan's gray eyes easily slide down the length of her. Although she was twenty-two years old and a widow, her face flamed with color. She imagined he was thinking: *Little lady! How can anyone call a five-feet-nine-inch woman little?* How many times had she heard those words before? So many that she'd quit counting. She tensed and waited for the mock-

33

ing words.

"Glad to meet you, Miss Allen."

His greeting surprised and pleased her, but her pleasure fled when she looked into his eyes and saw the overt gleam of interest—not merely friendly interest but blatant sexual attraction. The intensity of his gaze startled her; she had never been this aware of sexuality before.

She unconsciously pulled back and said defensively, "Mrs. Allen, Mr. MacDougald."

She extended her hand to feel it clasped in a firm, callused handshake which lasted much longer than propriety called for. The warmth of Logan's hand spread through Brenna's body to awaken every fiber of her being to his touch. She watched as his gaze moved unerringly to her left hand, to the wide gold band on her fourth finger.

"Where's Mr. Allen?"

Although Logan was disinclined to let her hand go, Brenna pulled it from his clasp. "He's . . . he's dead."

They stared at each other for a long time, neither of them saying a word. A taciturn man, Logan wasted no time on unnecessary words or emotions for that matter, and if he had learned anything during his twenty-nine years on the frontier, dying was as much a part of life as living—maybe more so. "I'm sorry," he said simply, and without being callous to the living, he was glad Brenna had no husband. He was glad she was free.

Marriage to Shawn had not prepared Brenna for a man like Logan—a man who was an expert at seducing women. He knew the power of his glances, his touches, his words, and he used them without conscience. He liked women; he enjoyed them; he used them, too. But he had learned not to love them. To him heartache and grief were equated with love. The latter he had suffered

34

plenty of during his twenty-nine years; the former he could do without.

Although Brenna was mesmerized, she could have broken the spell the man was weaving about her, but she didn't want to. She couldn't understand her irrational attraction to the man, but . . . then . . . she didn't want to rationalize. She enjoyed the excitement his very proximity aroused within her. Strangely, she was exhilarated by the lust she saw stirring in his flinty gray eyes.

Logan was so well versed in women that he understood their reactions, and he could imagine what Brenna was thinking. A swift smile touched his lips. Again his eyes ran her height. The gray eyes inventoried: whip, revolvers, and knife. The thick brows lifted; now his expression gently teased. So low that none could hear but Brenna, he said, "From the looks of it, Mrs. Allen, you certainly qualify to be a wagon captain."

The tones were so intimate Brenna didn't immediately realize their meaning. She blinked her eyes and silently repeated his comment. Jarred to reality, she pulled herself straight and looked squarely into his face. "I most assuredly do! And in case you're wondering, I'm an expert in the use of each. I grew up on the frontier, and my father educated and trained me to be the son he never had."

"In case you're wondering, that wasn't what I was wondering, Mrs. Allen." Logan's laughter followed her. "But I'd be most happy to tell you . . . what I was wondering."

Brenna was embarrassed as well as excited by Logan's forwardness, but she was also adept at hiding her feelings. She smiled coolly. "No, Mr. MacDougald, I'm not wondering."

"Such a shame," he murmured.

"For whom, Mr. MacDougald?" With an air of indifference, Brenna turned and slowly walked away to busy herself with making a pot of coffee. Although her chaotic thoughts were totally absorbed with Logan MacDougald, she pretended otherwise.

While Brenna's cool reaction irritated Logan, it also intrigued him. She was a spirited woman, and he admired that trait in anyone—especially a woman. The spunky, feisty ones made the best lovers! He sat down beside Gabby, and as the two of them talked, Logan watched Brenna: The pull of her trousers across her buttocks as she squatted in front of the fire; the sun burnishing her black hair; her well-shaped hands filling the coffee pot with water.

Vaguely Logan heard Gabby as the old man talked about his and Brenna's expedition from Victoria, Texas, to Santa Fe; dimly Logan was aware of Thunder's joining them after he had set up camp and tethered their horses and mules. Later Brenna came over, three tin cups in one hand and the coffeepot in the other. Logan let her serve Gabby and Thunder first. When he took his cup from her, he deliberately closed his hand over hers. He would make her as aware of him as he was of her.

"If you don't release my hand, Mr. MacDougald, you won't get any coffee."

"Maybe it's not coffee that I'm wanting," Logan said.

"Then you'll be getting nothing," Brenna said in a steady voice that belied the erratic beat of her heart.

Logan's eyes glittered ominously. He didn't like being spurned; rejection was a condition that was rare in Logan MacDougald's life, a condition that infuriated him. But he did release her hand.

Brenna poured the coffee and returned the coffeepot to the fire; then she joined the women to help prepare supper. She didn't understand verbal sparring between a man and woman, but she knew that she had bested Logan, and she was glad. A smug smile played at the corners of her lips.

"Oh, Brenna," Priscilla Caldwell, Elijah and Bertha Caldwell's fourteen-year-old daughter, simpered, her golden locks bobbing around her heart-shaped face, her baby-blue eyes glowing, "Logan MacDougald's got to be the most handsome man I've seen."

"You said that about Roger last night," Brenna muttered, running the blade of her knife up the belly of the rabbit.

"Well"—Priscilla reluctantly withdrew her eyes from Logan—"Roger is handsome, but Mr. MacDougald is more than handsome. He's special."

"Ain't nothing special about him," Maude Hemphill announced sharply, mousy brown hair escaping her chignon to fall across her face. The frontier had taken her husband and three older sons. Now she and her only surviving son, fifteen-year-old Knox, were headed for Bent's Fort, where they were to join her brother and his family to head for Oregon.

Callie Sue Warren lifted her arm and wiped it across her forehead to brush back tendrils of auburn hair. "I think Mr. MacDougald's rather special, Mrs. Hemphill."

Maude glared at the young woman. "What would your fiancé say if he could hear you talk like this!"

Callie Sue returned the stare without blinking her eyes. "I love my Wes, Mrs. Hemphill, else I wouldn't be traveling to Oregon to marry him, but I'm not blind." She rolled her eyes suggestively. "If it weren't for Wes, I imagine I'd be giving Logan MacDougald more than a passing glance."

"Hurmph! He's trouble, if you ask me." Maude deftly cut one of the skinned rabbits into pieces and dropped them into the black cauldron swinging off the large metal spit that arched over the central campfire. "Him and that Indian spell trouble, they do! Just mark my words."

Yes, Brenna thought, Logan MacDougald's trouble all right. She could feel it in her bones. As she cleaned her knife with a dishrag, she turned to look at Logan. At the same time his eyes moved to catch hers, and again they stared wordlessly at each other. Finally that quick smile—so quick Brenna wondered if she had imagined it or not—flicked across his lips. He stood, the lazy movements deceptive, and walked to the fire. He squatted, pulling the material of his trousers tight across his buttocks and legs. Brenna couldn't draw her eyes away from his blatant masculinity. Lifting the coffeepot, he filled his cup, which he raised in salute to Brenna. His right lid lowered in a wink. When shock registered on Brenna's face, he grinned. Then he turned to rejoin Gabby and Thunder.

Brenna was irate. How dare this man take advantage of her! Wink when she couldn't retaliate! His very presence made her feel tall and gawky. She was angry with herself. Angry because she was attracted to such a forward man. Angry because she wanted to be dainty and feminine. Angry because she wanted to shed her attire and weapons. With precision and speed she cut up the rabbit, so caught up in her own thoughts, she didn't hear another word the women uttered.

So caught up in Logan MacDougald, she couldn't pull her thoughts from him. No matter what the reason, she wanted to be a woman whom Logan MacDougald would . . . *whom Logan MacDougald would what?* reason suddenly shouted, and Brenna shook her head as if the action would stop her thinking. *Have you gone daft, woman?*

Desperately she attempted to push thoughts of

Logan MacDougald aside. He would do nothing but wreak havoc in her life and in her well-laid plans, which demanded her full attention; she could share none of herself with anyone until her task was completed. Certainly not Logan MacDougald. Besides . . . she had a feeling that all Logan wanted her to share with him was her bed and body.

Once the preparation of the meal was under way, Gertrude Dawkins shooed the women to the river. "I'll cook supper," the youthful sixty-year-old woman announced, hands on hips, a large wooden spoon in each hand. "All of you go take your baths."

"What about you, Granny?" Callie Sue asked her grandmother. "When will you bathe?"

"Later, girl," Gertrude said, waving her arms. "Now, go while the going's good." She smiled fondly at the granddaughter whom she had reared as her own child. "Now go, all of you."

Brenna didn't wait to be told the third time. She walked to her wagon, which her driver, Dwight Jones, had already unharnessed. She quickly shed her weapons, then searched through her luggage for soap, washrag, and clean clothes—a white chemise and the blue cambric dress, one of three she had packed for use in Santa Fe when she set up her trading store.

She quickly reviewed her arguments against becoming too friendly with Logan. As quickly she dismissed them. He was here tonight, and she was going to enjoy him. She snatched up the dress and undergarment and spared not another thought to the wisdom of her decision not to don clean britches and shirt. That she was dressing to please . . . or to surprise . . . or to shock Logan brought a smile to her lips.

Her arms loaded, she walked to the bathing area designated for the women. Quickly setting her basket down and divesting herself of clothing, she waded into the water, gasping at the initial coldness of it. Gracefully she stretched out and began to swim, her strokes smooth and powerful. When she was through swimming, she returned to the pile of soiled clothes, which she washed, rung out, and placed in her basket; then she bathed and washed and rinsed her hair.

Taking her time, she re-dressed and luxuriated in the soft caress of her chemise as it touched her skin. She dropped the dress over her head, leaving the top button of her bodice undone and pushing the sleeves so they were three-quarter length. Thoroughly enjoying her moment of femininity, she ran her hand down her midriff. She liked the feel of the delicate fabric on her skin; she liked the snug fit of the dress. Such a contrast to the shapeless shirt and trousers she wore every day. She twirled, and the full skirt billowed around her ankles and legs. The pirouette over, she combed her long, thick hair dry and twisted it into a coil on the top of her head.

When she returned to the camp, she rolled the canvas flaps up on each side of the wagon so she could hang her wet clothes over the edge to dry. Then she tossed the blanket on the ground. She turned around and bumped headlong into someone.

"I'm sorry," she hastily apologized, her palms brushing up the masculine chest.

Two hands reached out to catch her shoulders and to steady her.

"Mr. MacDougald!" Brenna's eyes encountered Logan's. For the first time she caught him off guard and saw expression on his face. He was as surprised as she.

"Brenna!" was all he could say. The woman who at a distance could pass for a man in her bull-whacking

40

garb was now totally feminine—all woman. The afternoon sun burnished her black hair to a high sheen. The blue material of the dress molded well-developed breasts. She was soft. Desirable. He looked at her parted lips, at the tip of her tongue, which darted out to moisten them. So kissable. So very kissable.

"Mrs. Allen, do you—" Roger Hollis's voice broke the spell cast between Logan and Brenna.

Logan slowly lowered his hands and stepped back; his expression became unreadable.

Brenna stared at Logan a second longer before she turned toward Roger to give him a warm smile. Although Roger was the same age as she, Brenna thought he looked years younger. When compared to the older, more experienced Logan, Roger seemed to be a mere adolescent.

"Yes, Roger?"

"Well, uh . . ." he began, his gaze bouncing between Brenna and Logan. He jerked his hat off his head and finally said, "You look nice, Miss Brenna. Real nice. I haven't seen you in a dress since we left Austin."

"Why, thank you, Mr. Hollis." Brenna smiled and curtsied and even managed to bat her eyes coyly. "I occasionally put on feminine attire to remind me that there are certain advantages in being a woman."

For one of the few times in her life, Brenna felt utterly feminine, and she enjoyed playing the two men against one another. It wouldn't hurt to let Logan see that other men also found her attractive, and it might be prudent for her to allow him to think she was attracted to Roger. Earlier, before Logan had had time to shutter the expression in his eyes, Brenna had seen the gleam of admiration in their depths; now she encountered the same glow in Roger's eyes. Whereas she wanted no serious entanglement with the captain of

41

her armed escorts, she was enjoying the mild flirtation.

"You wanted to ask me something, Roger?" she asked.

"Yes, ma'am," Roger mumbled. "I . . . I wanted to know if you'd seen Jonesey. I need to talk to him."

"I haven't seen him since we corralled the wagons," Brenna answered. "Check with Gabby. I'm sure he'll know."

"Yes, ma'am." Roger bobbed his head. He turned, took several steps, stopped, and pivoted again to face Brenna. "Miss Brenna, may I . . . may I have the first dance tonight?"

Brenna's gaze went from Roger to Logan, and she saw Logan's jaws tighten; she saw his eyes burn with what she hoped was jealousy. She waited a moment, hoping Logan would speak up and tell Roger that the first dance belonged to him. When he didn't, she was disappointed but she didn't show it. Awaiting her answer, Roger moved until he stood directly in front of her. She laid a reassuring hand on his arm.

"Thank you for asking, Roger. You may have the first dance."

Roger's face was wreathed in a beautiful smile. He bowed low, reached for her hand, and brought her fingers to his lips. "Thank you for doing me the honor, ma'am."

Watching the exchange, Logan leaned against the wagon and crossed his arms over his chest. His eyes narrowed, but his face was void of expression. Not so his heart. He was disgusted with the gallantry of Roger Hollis; he was so angry he could hardly contain himself. He wanted to pick the pup up by the hackles of his neck and sling him aside. Why was Brenna encouraging him? Why was she deliberately flirting with him? She was years older than Hollis in experience; she was a woman—Hollis a boy. She needed a man to take care of her . . . and her needs . . . and she needed a man pretty damn quick!

"So gallant," Brenna murmured, quickly withdrawing her hand lest Roger get the wrong impression. She cut her eyes at Logan. "Always the gentleman."

She's toying with both of us, Logan thought. Just like a woman! Set one man against another! Be damned if he'd play her game! Contrary to the elation he'd felt earlier when he learned her husband was dead, he was now angry. She certainly wasn't any grieving widow! He turned and walked away.

"Shall we see you at the dance, Mr. MacDougald?" Brenna called.

"Doubt it," he answered without looking back, displaying an indifference that he was far from feeling. "I don't have time for such tomfoolery." He hadn't gone very far before he stopped without turning around and asked, "How long has your husband been dead, Mrs. Allen?"

Had he slapped Brenna across the face, he couldn't have hurt her any more.

Before she could retaliate, Logan said, "Long enough for you to be out of mourning?"

"That, Mr. MacDougald, is none of your business!" Brenna answered.

Logan's gaze swept from Brenna to Roger. "No, I don't guess it is. Enjoy yourself tonight, Mrs. Allen!"

"I shall, Mr. MacDougald," Brenna said. "Believe me, I shall."

Logan turned and walked off.

"Not very sociable, is he?" Roger remarked. He was puzzled by Logan's behavior.

Samuel Walter Roper's slight form emerged from behind Brenna's wagon. Strands of reddish-brown hair, belying his sixty-five years, escaped his hat. "Roger, Mrs. Caldwell is looking high and low for you.

Said something about your eating with them tonight."

Roger grimaced. "Damn! I forgot."

A hacking cough preceded Sam's words. "Then you'd best be on your way." He patted Roger on the back and urged him in the direction of the Caldwells' wagon. "You know how Bertha is about people being late. If she's told us once, she's told us a million times."

"Remember," Roger reminded Brenna as he scurried off, "you promised to dance with me this evening."

Brenna held a finger up. "Just one, Roger." As he disappeared, she emitted a low sigh of relief.

"I wouldn't be too hard on the young man," Samuel said soothingly. "I think he likes you."

"Me, too," Brenna admitted dully.

"Not Roger," Samuel corrected, his voice rising a little in exasperation. "Logan MacDougald."

"Logan MacDougald!" Brenna couldn't help but exclaim.

"The same," Samuel returned.

Brenna brushed Samuel's words aside with a wave of her hand.

"That's the reason why he reacted to Roger as he did," Samuel went on, not in the least ashamed of his having eavesdropped. "Logan is a man of the wilds, primitive and untamed. Roger is a gentleman, reared and educated in the East. Logan felt as if you were comparing the two of them and found him on the short end of the stick."

"I wasn't comparing the two of them," Brenna answered, "but to tell the truth, I don't think Logan's even on the stick! I've never met a ruder man in all my life, Mr. Roper!" Brenna shook her head to give emphasis to her words.

Sam simply laughed. "Well, you may be right; I don't think so, but"—he shrugged—"you never can tell. Please call me Sam. Mr. Roper sounds much too old."

His laugh ended in a spasm of coughing.

"Sit down, Mr.—Sam," Brenna said, rushing to his side. "Is there anything I can get for you?"

His chest heaving from the deep breaths he was drawing, Sam slowly slid to his knees, caught the wheel in both hands, and dropped his head. "No," he gasped, "I'll—I'll—be—all—right. Just—Just—give—me—a—few—minutes." Long, anxious minutes later, he lifted his head and leveled watery eyes on Brenna. "All this will stop once I reach Santa Fe, my dear girl. Just a few more months of this."

Brenna sat down beside Sam. "What about your family?" she asked. "Won't they mind your being so far away from them?"

"I have no family," Sam told her, quietly, his voice devoid of all emotion. "My wife and daughter died three years ago; they were all I had, and I—I had to leave them behind in Boston."

"I'm . . . I'm sorry," Brenna murmured.

"And so am I," Sam agreed. "Abigail and I had been together for forty years." He extracted a handkerchief from his coat pocket and wiped his eyes. "We thought we could have no children," he said on a chuckle. "Twenty-five years and nothing. Then one morning as I was getting ready to go to work, Abby told me that we were going to have a baby. You cannot know the joy this forty-five-year-old man felt when his forty-year-old wife told him she was with child."

Sam's eyes caught a distant glow; his voice grew dreamy. "About seven months later, Abby gave birth to the most beautiful baby girl I have ever seen. Big brown eyes like her mother; brown hair like me. Abby and I scrimped and scrimped, saving our money. We were determined to have our own place."

He paused before he said, "We rented a small house, but we were saving our money so we could go west and

45

buy our own land. I was a scrivener for a shipping firm." He smiled reminiscently. "Thought my job was secure. But nothing in this life is secure. One day the owner walked in and told me he couldn't afford to keep me."

Sam's voice quavered, and he stopped talking until he regained control. "I was disappointed, but not devastated. I had plenty of experience and was proficient in foreign languages. Why," he said, his voice rising with pride, "I can read, write, and speak fluently four different languages. I was sure I could get another job. But I couldn't. Times were hard, getting harder. I walked the streets, taking odd jobs here and there, using my savings so we could live. Finally I found a job—a clerk in an emporium—and my employer also let me rent an apartment from him. We moved into his tenement house, a cheap house infested with vermin— people, rats, and roaches. I complained to the landlord that it was a fire hazard, but he laughed in my face and told me to move if I didn't like it. But I couldn't move. I didn't have the money."

Again Sam stopped talking, and the pause lengthened considerably before he resumed his story. "One day I was across town when I saw the black smoke billowing in the air. I knew right away it was our building. I ran all the way across town, but by the time I reached our address nothing remained but ashes. Abigail and Rachael were dead."

Brenna reached out and caught Samuel's hands in hers. "I'm so sorry," she whispered fervently. "I know how you must feel. In the last six months I've buried my father and my husband."

Samuel looked compassionately into Brenna's face. "You're young, my dear. Don't let life pass you by. Don't let death cheat you out of your life." Suddenly he was his animated self again. "Look at me! I'm doing

46

what Abigail and I always dreamed of doing. I'm heading west. Gonna buy me a home of my own and make a new life for myself."

"Does that include another wife?" Brenna asked, a twinkle in her eyes.

"Could. I've been lonely these past three years without Abigail and Rachael." Sam cocked his head to the side and grinned. "I've asked Gertrude Dawkins to dance with me tonight."

"Gertrude?" Brenna looked puzzled.

"Gertrude! Gertrude Dawkins," Sam repeated in exasperation. "The beautiful woman whom all of you insist on calling Granny. If I have my way about it, no one but her granddaughter will address her as Granny."

"Granny," Brenna repeated. "But she's so much older—"

Following Brenna's train of thought, Sam chuckled. "Sure she's Callie Sue's grandmother, but she started her family when she was quite young, and I started mine when I was much older." His eyes glowed. "Really, I'm a few years older than Gertrude." Using the spokes of the wheel as a support, Sam pushed to his feet. "Now I'd best be taking me a bath and changing clothes. I'm having dinner with the dear woman, too." Sam waved and walked away to leave Brenna alone.

Not long afterward Gabby found her still sitting beside her wagon. "Worried about 'em," he announced. "Venner and Kirkwood. They've been gone a long time. Shoulda been in sooner. Neither one of them's been out this long before."

"I'm concerned, too," Brenna answered, looking up at Gabby. "Maybe I should have ridden on with Kirkwood."

"No, you shouldn't have!" Gabby declared hotly. "That's what we hired the man for, to hunt and scout.

47

It's enough I should be worried about him and Venner. Don't know what I'd be doing if you was out there with them."

Brenna smiled gently at the old man. "Gabriel Langdon, you're the dearest friend I have."

A rare smile creased the weathered face. "And you, Brendy girl, are about all I have left. That's why I'm so all-fired worried about you and this wagon train."

"Something else is on your mind."

"Comanches out here for sure." Gabby grunted as he shifted his weight and settled himself next to her. "MacDougald and that Indian said they seen signs of 'em up the ways a bit. Lots of 'em on the prowl. The plain's full of 'em. For sure, gal, we can't cut across Comancheria."

"We knew we were running the chance of encountering Comanches when we started this trip," Brenna pointed out.

"That's when me and Shawn was planning the trip. I hadn't figured on your being with us," Gabby retaliated. He watched Brenna pick a blade of grass and pull it through her fingers. "My facing them is one thing; your facing them is another."

"I'm not turning around," Brenna averred softly, as much to herself as to her wagon boss. "Everything I have is in the company." Her voice throbbed with the conviction of her words.

Not only was Brenna determined to open trade between the far reaches of Texas—and she did include Santa Fe and Taos as part of Texas—she also determined to salvage Garvey Mercantile and Freight Hauling. She had invested every cent to her name and some she had borrowed on this expedition. If this venture failed, she had no alternative but to sell the property her father had received as payment for serving in the Texas army during the war for independence.

She would lose her entire legacy—all she had left in the world . . . she felt.

"I ain't fool enough to ask you to turn around," Gabby answered. "I jest don't want you hightailing it across Comanche territory, gal. If it was necessary for you to do it, that would be one thing, but it ain't. You got me to look after your interests."

"Thank you, Gabby," Brenna said, reaching out to lay her hand over his. "There's no one in this world I love as much as I love you, but"—she pleaded with him for understanding—"seeing this wagon train through to Santa Fe is something which I must do personally." *And seeing Peyton H. Alexander to ascertain the political temperature of the Mexicans in Santa Fe is something else which I must do personally!* "That's why I insisted on coming along as wagon captain."

Gabby captured Brenna's hand between his. "Gal, Logan's been telling me about the Santy Fee expedition and what happened to those poor devils once they was captured by the Mexicans." He shook his head. "Ain't a pretty sight."

"I'm still going, Gabby."

Chapter Four

As if in time to the music that filled the air, the flames of the campfire leaped high to dissipate the blackness of night and illuminate the exuberant people who danced beside it. Off to the side Brenna leaned against a wagon and waited for Roger to claim his dance. She wondered if Logan would make an appearance. One part of her hoped he did; she wanted him to ask her to dance with him so she could turn him down. She had rehearsed her refusal until she had it down pat. But so far, he hadn't made an appearance since he'd stamped away earlier. In fact, both he and the Indian stayed at their campsite.

"My dance, Miss Brenna." Roger's announcement and gentle tap on the shoulder jostled Brenna from her ruminations.

She turned toward the young man who seemed to grow more immature the longer she was around him. When she saw his unruly golden curls greased straight and plastered to the contour of his head, her smile deepened. She almost laughed when one of the recalcitrant ringlets refused bondage and sprang across his forehead.

"Why, yes, Mr. Hollis," she said cheerfully, "I do believe it is."

Giving herself to the flow of the music, Brenna

moved away from the wagon into the center of the rectangle. She dipped and swayed and listened to Roger talk; she smiled, nodded, and murmured at the expected pauses. Then she felt a hand on her shoulder. Logan, she thought fleetingly, her heart speeding up at the idea of refusing him the dance . . . or maybe her heartbeat accelerated at the thought of his taking her in his arms and holding her. She turned.

Gabby! Although she loved the old wagon boss dearly, she was disappointed, and she was angry with herself for even thinking about Logan MacDougald.

"This dance is mine," Gabby said, laughing at Roger's groan. "You kin have her for the next one," he announced. "I'm going be heading for bed early tonight, so I need to get my celebrating done early. You young'uns can dance all night if you want to."

They spun around several times before Brenna asked, "Tired?" She had noticed that ever since supper, ever since he'd talked with Logan and that Indian, he'd been preoccupied.

"No, I'm still worried about Venner and Kirkwood."

Brenna knew without Gabby's mentioning it what else was worrying him. He was worried about the shorter route she was considering taking. "I wish Logan and that Indian hadn't shown up here," she muttered. "Their presence has brought out the worst in everyone. You included."

"I wouldn't exactly say that you are unaffected," Gabby returned, taking no exception to Brenna's grumbling. True to his nature, he burrowed to the core of the matter, not subtly but straightforward. "I wish you'd reconsider heading through Comanche territory, gal." After a slight pause, he added, "To tell the truth, I'm scared."

"I'm going to travel the route that will get me to Santa Fe the quickest." Quiet but adamant!

Brenna was more than angry; she was furious. Logan MacDougald had no right to stick his nose in her business. He may have convinced Gabby that she should take the long way around to Bent's Fort; he had yet to convince her! Brenna strained through the darkness to find Logan, but he was nowhere to be seen. Still she could feel his presence; she knew he was somewhere out there watching them. She didn't doubt but what he could hear them talking right now. She hoped he could; she hoped he heard and understood. *She wasn't going to be scared out of her trading expedition to Santa Fe! And the faster she could get there, the better the profits . . . the sooner she'd have her company out of debt! The sooner she would meet with Alexander!*

Sometimes the enormity of her task weighed heavily on her. Before her father died, she wouldn't have imagined herself the type to become involved in espionage and intrigue. She never pictured herself as the type of person who would work undercover to stage an insurrection against an institution as large and powerful as the Mexican government.

But she had chosen to do this. No coercion had been exerted. She wanted to see the people of Santa Fe and Taos liberated from Mexican tyranny; she wanted them to take their rightful place as a part of Texas; she wanted them to enjoy the freedom she and other Texans enjoyed. So she would finish the job she started.

"I wish you hadn't come, Brendy gal," the old man persisted. "Logan says—"

"Logan says," Brenna mimicked as she closed her eyes and took a deep breath, the man's image quickly materializing on the screen of her mind. "I'm tired of hearing what Logan has to say. I own Garvey Freight Hauling, and I say—"

Brenna's words were cut short. Abruptly Gabby stopped dancing and Brenna lost her footing to stumble against him. His hand dropped. Brenna's eyes flew open, and she stared beyond Gabby into Logan's immobile face.

"Logan says it's time for you to dance with him." The words were arrogant; so was the man.

"Logan should have asked earlier," Brenna said coolly. "I've already promised the rest of my dances to Roger."

"You'll just have to cancel them."

"That may be the way you operate, Mr. Mac-Dougald, but not I."

As if Brenna hadn't declined his offer, Logan brushed past Gabby and put his arm around Brenna's waist. His hand caught hers, and he twirled her easily, effortlessly to the music.

"If you refuse," he said, "you'll create quite a scene, and I'll still have my way." He smiled smugly. "As for me, I couldn't care less. I don't have to live with these people for the next seven hundred miles, but you do."

"You're despicable," Brenna breathed.

"Determined." He danced as efficiently as he sat his horse, his movements fluid and smooth.

Brenna glared her displeasure; still she couldn't help but look at him. He was so different—devastatingly different. He had been attractive before in a primitive way; now he was handsome, refined, almost sophisticated. Evidently he had bathed, she thought as she sucked into her nostrils the clean, brisk, masculine fragrance. His cheeks were smooth and shaven, his hair brushed back from his face. He wore a clean shirt and trousers. Gone were his revolvers and knife.

Even as tall as she was, Logan was taller. Brenna's eyes rested on the opened vee of his shirt, and she stared at the crisp, dark crop of chest hair. Uninvited, desire

53

began to slide down her insides to nestle in the lower part of her stomach. She felt the warmth first, then the fire as the embers burst into a flame of wanting—intense wanting. Her chest hurt, and her breathing was constricted. She had never felt this way about Shawn; why should she about Logan? The man infuriated her. He was rude, and she didn't like him. She was angry at his presumptuousness. Since he had so arrogantly demanded, or rather blackmailed, her into dancing with him, he hadn't said a word to her. Yet none of that mattered. Her body craved his nearness.

When she saw a flicker in Logan's eyes, she knew that he was as aware of her response to him as she was. This banked the fire of her anger even more. Deliberately she focused her eyes on the strange amulet, a small ball that hung around his neck on an intricately woven silver chain, and studied the delicate engravings.

"Your medallion is quite beautiful," she said, only then lifting her eyes. "I'm fascinated by it."

Logan smiled, a gesture that quickened across his face to take residence in his eyes. "A gift."

Really interested now, Brenna leaned closer and peered intently. "Indian?"

"Um-hum. It's symbolic of the spiritual eye through which all men should view the world."

Before Brenna could make further comment, Roger's hand landed on Logan's shoulder. "I'm cutting in," he announced. "This is my dance."

"I think not," Logan said smoothly, never taking his eyes from Brenna's face, his grip on her hand and waist tightening. "She belongs to me for the rest of the evening."

"I'm not property," Brenna said. "I don't belong to you or to anyone else. Now, if you'll unhand me, sir. I did promise Roger the next dance."

Logan's eyes were flames of anger, and he directed the blaze directly at Roger. The young man backed off. "That's all right, Miss Brenna. I'll . . . I'll take the next dance. Let Mr. MacDougald have this one."

Brenna jerked her hand from Logan's and smiled sweetly at Roger. "I promised you, Roger."

Although she would have preferred to dance with Logan, Brenna would not tolerate such high-handed tactics. Shawn had used her; no other man would. A brilliant smile on her face, she glided into Roger's arms and let herself be swept away to the beat of the music. All evening she danced with Roger, and Logan leaned against the wagon and brooded.

"Do you mind if we sit this one out?" Brenna asked.

"Oh, no, ma'am," Roger said.

"I think I'll get me a drink. I'm thirsty."

"I'll get it for you," Roger offered.

"No, thanks. I'm probably going to bed. I'm rather tired."

Brenna walked to her wagon and pulled the lid off the water barrel. She didn't have time to submerge the dipper before a hand banded around her wrist. She turned to see Logan.

"Do you mind?" she asked.

"You're damn right I do mind," he said. "How do you think I feel, having to stand there gawking at you and that puppy all evening?"

Brenna twisted her arm from his clasp. Turning, she plunged the dipper into the barrel. "You didn't have to gawk!"

"What do you see in him?"

"He's a gentleman," Brenna said. "That's something you're not."

"I'll tell you something else I am and he's not," Logan said. "I'm a man, and he's a boy. Why not spend your time with a man?"

"I will if I ever find one." Brenna lifted the dipper to her mouth and drank, but she was no longer thirsty.

"Come on," Logan said, grabbing one of her hands and taking the dipper out of the other. "Let's go walking."

"Roger's waiting for me," Brenna said.

"No, he's not. I heard you tell him you were going to bed."

"I don't want to go walking," Brenna said.

"Have it your way," Logan said.

Brenna thought he complied too easily. "Good night, Mr. MacDougald."

"Oh, no, Mrs. Allen, it's not good night. Far from it."

"You said I could have it my way."

"That's right," Logan said. "You'll either walk with me, or I'll sleep with you."

"I don't want to go walking with you," Brenna replied.

"Yes, you do," Logan returned. "You wanted to dance with me, too. But you were too stubborn to admit it. You want to be with me. You're as intrigued by me as I am by you." His hand clasping one of hers, he started to walk and she followed. They moved into the quiet darkness away from camp.

They lapsed into silence as they walked through the outer wagons to encounter the guard, Tommy Caldwell, who turned around quickly and took several steps in their direction. When he recognized Brenna he said good-naturedly, "Aw, shucks, Miss Brenna, I thought you was Knox Hemphill—he's my relief. Mr. Langdon said we'd be relieved every hour so's we could all enjoy the dancing, and I kinda figure my hour's up."

Brenna smiled at the young man and touched his shoulder reassuringly. "I'm sure Knox will be here in just a minute. He was dancing with your sister when

I left."

"He would be," Tommy grumbled good-naturedly; then asked, "What are you doing out here?" He peered through the darkness to see Logan better.

"It's just Mr. MacDougald and me. We're walking a ways up the river."

Even in the silvery light of the moon as she and Logan brushed past the guard, Brenna could see the sly smile that played on Tommy's face, and warmth infused her cheeks.

Logan led the way, but Brenna wasn't conscious of his doing so because he walked slowly enough that she was always a mere half step behind. They didn't talk, but they didn't have to. They simply held hands. When they reached the river, they stopped walking and stood looking at the shining surface that gently rippled.

Logan knelt and scooped up a handful of stones. He studied them until he found several that were round and flat. By the time he straightened, Brenna was sitting on a large boulder behind him. Logan hurled the stones across the river and watched as they skipped across the surface.

"I'm sorry," he said quietly.

Surprised, Brenna jerked her head up and stared at him.

"About this afternoon," he explained, still not looking at her. "When I was rude to you. When I said that about your husband and when I didn't speak up to ask you for a dance. And tonight when I demanded that you dance with me."

"It's all right," Brenna said, glad for his apology but embarrassed at the same time.

The last stone skimmed across the river. "No, it's not all right," Logan said. Abruptly he turned and walked to where she sat. Standing in front of her, with the moon to his back so that his face was shadowed, he confessed, "I was envious of the pup."

"Envious." The word, whisper-soft and tremulous, filled her with a sudden rush of happiness. The moonbeams gave her face such a delicate glow, Logan reached out to place his hands on her cheeks. "Envious of the attention you were giving him and not giving to me; envious of the smiles and kind words that you bestowed on him and didn't bestow on me."

Like a beautiful bird about to fly, joy soared into her heart, the powerful, sweeping strokes of its wings spreading a glow that totally diffused her body. For him to be envious, she thought, Logan must care. Like her, he had felt this instantaneous attraction. As surely as she was drawn to him, he was drawn to her.

"Do you like Roger?" Logan asked.

Brenna nodded, her face rubbing against his rough palms. Oddly, the abrasive touch was an infinitely gentle caress, one that sped to the lower part of her body to turn into a dull ache of desire. "Yes, I like him."

Brenna's answer didn't please Logan. Although envy was a strange emotion for Logan—jealousy a totally unknown one—he was feeling it now. It was eating his guts.

"You're so different from when I first saw you," Logan murmured, his eyes drinking their fill of her beauty. "So soft. So feminine."

Brenna's laughter floated through the air to blend with the gentle April breeze that ruffled Logan's hair. "Compared to how I looked when you first saw me."

For the first time Brenna heard Logan laugh, deep, rumbling laughter that made her feel good, that made her want to laugh with him. "From the distance Thunder and I thought you were a skinny kid. Even close up it took us—" He paused as the gentle pressure of his hands brought Brenna to her feet to stand inches in front of him. "Even close up it took me a second to realize that under all those baggy clothes was a woman." His hands dropped to encircle her waist. Not a heavy, lustful grasp but a light, tentative one. "A woman with the most startling eyes that I've ever seen in my life."

"And you've seen a lot of eyes?" The words were soft and breathless.

"Enough," he confessed, his head dropping, his lips touching Brenna's in a light introductory kiss. He felt his loins tighten when she unconsciously swayed closer to him and her breasts brushed against his chest. At that moment he wanted nothing more than to let the kiss deepen and intensify with passion, but this was not the time. Summoning all the control at his command— which was little at the moment; he had been a long time without a woman—he lifted his head and stepped back.

Brenna was disappointed that the kiss was over. It had been much too brief. At the same time, she was frightened of the emotions that his touch had unleashed. She wanted to feel Logan, to taste him, to savor him. The impact of her own sexuality hit her with such force that she inwardly recoiled.

Shawn's accusations came back to haunt her. Was she too aggressive for a woman? Was she a wanton? Shawn had accused her of being so. Suddenly the chill of aloneness—a feeling that had intensified since her father's death—swept over her. She turned from Logan, rounded her shoulders, and crossed her arms over her chest.

Logan, taught by his adopted father to know people, to look and listen to their hearts and souls as well as to their words, recognized Brenna's pose. He stood behind her and placed a hand on either shoulder. He pulled her against him in a warm, protective gesture.

"Tell me something about yourself," he suggested, gently kneading the tenseness out of her body.

Brenna took a deep breath and relaxed. Her body went limp against him as she gave herself up to the mesmerizing touch of his hands. "I'm Brenna Garvey Allen; I own Garvey Mercantile and Freight Hauling, and I'm twenty-two years old."

"So young," Logan murmured, and turned her around.

"Old enough to be a widow." She lifted her head and looked into his shadowed face. "Old enough to know that I want to make something out of my company."

"Yes," Logan mused as he studied her moon-softened features, "you're old enough for all that." A warm silence fell between them, to be broken when Logan said, "I want to know more about you, Brenna Allen. You fascinate me. Shall we find a place where we can be comfortable?"

Again the question was mere rhetoric. Without waiting for her answer, Logan caught her hand and led her to a clearing, where both of them sat down. They were so wrapped up in each other, they were oblivious to the music in the distance and the golden arc of campfire light above the corral of wagons. Logan spread his legs and patted for Brenna to sit between them. Once she was positioned, her back to him, he began to massage her again, his hands kneading up and down from shoulder to neck in gentle but firm measure.

"Now tell me all about yourself."

Oddly, Brenna found herself wanting to talk with Logan. "After the death of my mother when I was six years old," she began some time later, her voice slightly drugged from Logan's relaxing touch, "my father and I migrated to Martin DeLeon's Colony." She dropped her head, exposing her lower neck for his hands. "Do you know where that is?"

"Close to Victoria," Logan replied.

Brenna nodded. "That's where Papa opened the Garvey Mercantile Company, and as the ports opened on the coast, he expanded into a freight-hauling business. During the war for independence he fought with Houston . . ." She paused again to ask, "Did you fight in the war?"

"Um-hum."

"At San Jacinto?"

Again only: "Um-hum."

"Do you personally know Houston?"

Logan smiled. *Know* was such an ineffective word when it came to his relationship with General Sam Houston, the man who was the president of the Republic of Texas, the man whom the Cherokees called The Raven. Logan couldn't count the times that Houston had come to his village and dined in his family's lodge. He was one of the few white men who had come to give his condolences at the death of Antelope Hunter. Through the years Houston had been a true friend.

"I know Houston," Logan answered simply.

"I thought you might," Brenna returned. She paused fractionally before she said, "Guess you would have known him even if you hadn't fought in the war."

"Why's that?" Logan asked, amused by Brenna's ferreting for information.

"Heard he'd been adopted by the Cherokees."

"Yes, he's Cherokee."

"You were adopted by the Cherokees also?"

"Um-hum."

Brenna gave Logan plenty of time to continue, but when he remained silent, she finally spoke. "Papa came home from San Jacinto a proud and happy man. Texas was his country, Sam Houston his man. But the happiness didn't last long." She remembered. "His pride turned into disenchantment."

61

"How so?" Logan moved his fingers up and down her spine in therapeutic probes.

"Sam Houston is a coward."

Logan was irritated by such a rash judgment of a man whom he admired and respected, and his fingers inadvertently bit into her tender flesh.

"Ouch," she cried. "That hurts."

"What do you mean?" Logan demanded. "Houston's no coward."

Brenna squirmed around and glared into the shadowed visage. "Of course he is. Look at his policy of pacifism toward Mexico and the Indians. Look at him making a fool of himself and the people of Texas over annexation. Begging the United States to accept us as a state when they've made it clear they don't want us. Under Lamar we could hold our heads up and be proud of Texas. Under Houston we've done nothing but tuck tail and run. And," she added, her voice growing stronger with her conviction, "just think about how the damn fool treated Commodore Moore and the navy!"

"And what has the honorable Mirabeau Buonaparte Lamar done that is so commendable?" Logan asked.

"He's aggressive," Brenna defended, jumping to her feet.

"He's a fool!" Logan was vehement in his exclamation. "He drained the treasury and wiped out the Cherokees, the best buffer Texas had between them and the Comanches! Without money and men, he wants to attack Mexico and fight again in order to get them to recognize Texas independence. And the man is fool enough to think Texas ought to be an empire—and so far nobody recognizes our independence but us."

"Some foreign countries do." Her hands on her hips, Brenna glared down at Logan.

"Trade agreements that don't amount to much,"

Logan pointed out.

"For your information," Brenna returned, "I'm fool enough to think Texas ought to be an empire. I don't want us groveling at the feet of the United States, begging for statehood. I want to see the lone star flying over the western part of North America. I want the Republic of Texas to be a far greater and more powerful country than the United States." So much so, she was willing to gamble her life!

"It can't be." The blaze of argument had died from Logan's voice to be replaced with calm acceptance. "The United States needs Texas and Texas needs the United States," he pointed out as if he were a teacher talking with a student. "One nation, undivided, needs to span this great country from the Atlantic to the Pacific Ocean."

"You're an Annexationist like Houston!"

Logan nodded.

"And you're an Indian lover!" She spat the words out as if they were bitter gall.

"I don't love my enemies be they white, Mexicans, or Indians. Neither do I hate all whites or all Mexicans or all Indians."

"You're just like the rest of Houston's people," Brenna grumbled, finally sitting down close to him. "You talk in circles, never giving a straight answer."

"And I suppose Clarence Childers and his cohorts do," Logan drawled, thinking of the political movement in Houston, Texas, that was daily gaining momentum. "Napoleons of the West, they call themselves, as they envision not a Republic of Texas but the Empire of Texas," Logan mocked. "Such grandiose plans! Such flowery rhetoric!"

"I don't necessarily like Childers," Brenna qualified, drawing up her feet. She wrapped her arms around her legs and rested her chin on her knees. "But I do admire

63

his standing up for what he believes, and he believes in Texas, the Empire of Texas. And he does feel like Texas needs a man for president who is sober most of the time."

Logan's chuckle surprised Brenna. "I'd rather have Sam Houston drunk as president of Texas than any other man I know who's stone-sober."

"You would!"

"I gather your father was an Imperialist."

Brenna nodded. "He and Shawn were coming home from a political rally in Houston when his wagon overturned, and Papa was killed."

"Who's Shawn?" Logan questioned.

"Shawn Allen, my husband."

Although Logan wanted to hear more about Brenna's husband, he didn't encourage her to talk. He would listen if she did, but he wouldn't press her to unburden the intimate chambers of her soul.

Eventually she said, "When Papa died, Shawn was only a partner in the business. He was hurt badly—his face all cut up, his forehead bruised, his right arm broken—but he brought Papa's body home."

Logan could hear the tears in her voice, but now that she had started talking, he wouldn't stop her. He wanted to hear about her father; he wanted to know about Shawn Allen.

"We buried Papa, and I nursed Shawn back to health. He . . . he felt that it was in my best interest to sell Garvey Mercantile and Freight Hauling to Childers. When I told Shawn I wanted to keep the company, he agreed to help me save it." Brenna took a deep breath to still the quavering in her voice. "Before he died and under the direction of Childers and several of his friends, merchants in Houston and San Antonio, Shawn amassed this caravan of trade goods; he was going to begin trade between Texas and Santa Fe."

64

"What happened to him?"

"To make some extra money, he was hauling freight to the Irish Colonies in Refugio when he was attacked by a group of Comanches and killed."

Brenna was silent for a long time while she gathered her composure. Eventually she said, "Shawn, like Papa, wanted to see the Republic of Texas established as an empire, and he wanted to establish a trade route from Austin to Sante Fe."

"So now you're doing it for him?" Logan asked.

Brenna shook her head. "No," she replied, "I'm not doing it for Papa or for Shawn. I'm doing it for myself." She turned to look at Logan. "I have nothing but Garvey Mercantile and Freight Hauling left, Logan. Nothing. Without it I'm all alone. And unless I make it to Santa Fe before the other freighters arrive, I won't make the profits I need to survive."

"So that's why you're determined to head across Comanche country," Logan murmured. "You're trying to beat the Missouri traders."

"Yes, and I'm also doing this for Texas."

"Texas?"

"Those people in Santa Fe and Taos want to be liberated from the tyranny of the Mexican government." Brenna was so dedicated to her cause that the words came tumbling out unbidden. "We must let them know that we in Texas understand and want to help them."

Logan sighed, moved closer to her, and caught both her hands in his. "Brenna, you don't know what you're talking about. The only people who want to oppose the Mexican government are American traders who live in Santa Fe and Taos, and they're a fine minority. They're selfish and self-centered. Their only purpose is greed. The majority of the people there are gentle people who fear Texans; they don't want to break their allegiance to Mexico."

"Yes, they do," Brenna insisted. "Look at all the people who have told us about their desire to break away from Mexico."

"*All!*" Logan mimicked.

Brenna was glad it was dark enough that Logan couldn't see her discomfort. "Well . . . Henry Connelly, a Missouri merchant. Peyton H. Alexander, citizen of Santa Fe."

"All of two," Logan mocked. "One of them honest. The other an undesirable character if ever there was one. Alexander is a citizen of Santa Fe only because no other country will extend him citizenship. He's a vulture."

"How can you make such an accusation? Why, I met him in Houston last—"

"You may have met him," Logan interrupted, "but you don't know him. I do, and I know the people of Santa Fe. Alexander is totally self-serving and will sacrifice anybody or anything for his cause, which is himself. And the people of Santa Fe have no love to spare for Texans or their revolution or their independence."

"We'll see about that," Brenna said. She'd make her own judgment about Alexander.

"You're determined to get to Santa Fe, aren't you?" Logan said. He admired her spunk, but he doubted the wisdom of her venture.

"As quickly as I can."

"Don't go through Comanche territory."

"I must go the shortest route possible," she said, her eyes on his face as she studied the gaunt hardness in the glow of the campfire.

"Have you given any thought to the people who are traveling with you?"

"I have," Brenna returned. "And I've been honest

66

with them all the way. In Austin when they approached me about joining the caravan, I told them the dangers and risks of traveling through the frontier under the best of conditions. I also let them know I had to make good time by pushing hard and taking the shortest route possible. They were agreeable. I don't suppose it'll matter much to them which route I take, but if it should, I'll be happy to refund the money they paid for my services and let them go their own way or return to Austin."

"I'll have to agree, you've been honest and up-front with the people," Logan said. "And I can see your point in cutting through Comancheria. It's the shortest route, but"—he looked squarely into Brenna's face—"it's also the most dangerous."

"Comanches?"

"Comanches are out there, yes. But there's something far more dangerous than the Comanches out there."

"I don't understand."

"Thunder and I have reason to believe that the Indians are being directed by a white man."

"A white man!" Brenna said incredulously. "What makes you think this?"

"These latest attacks by the Comanches have been too precise, too calculated. The Comanches always know when and where to strike so as to meet no resistance from the rangers."

Brenna was quiet for a long time as she pondered his words, as she weighed their importance. Finally she asked, "Who and what are you, Logan MacDougald? Why are you out here?"

Chapter Five

Logan stared at Brenna's face, delicately draped in the silvery web of the moon. Finally he spoke. "Who am I?" he asked, repeating her question, then immediately answered, "I'm Logan Andrew MacDougald. What am I?" His reply was thick with laughter as he dipped his head closer to hers, his breath smelling slightly of whiskey teasing her cheek and ear. "In case you can't tell, girl, I'm a man." He caught her hand in his and guided it close to his chest. "Perhaps you'd like for me to show you."

A shiver of anticipation ran Brenna's spine, but she quelled it in the wake of curiosity. There was too much she didn't know about Logan MacDougald; he was too glib. His advances came too quick, as if they were precipitated with no thought, launched only by lust. "No, I want to know who you are and what you're doing out here."

Logan pulled back, but not before he drew in the clean scent of her. "Like I said earlier, I'm working for Houston."

"A ranger?" she asked.

"No, not really a ranger," Logan said. "Houston's worried about this new flurry of Indian attacks. He's asked me and Thunder to investigate to see if a group of white outlaws called Comancheros are behind it."

68

"I've never heard of them."

"They are men without consciences," he said, "the worst of all races. They prey on the innocent. They're most sought-after trade commodity at the moment is women, whom they are selling into prostitution."

"It's not enough that we must fight the Indians and the Mexicans," Brenna murmured. "Now we must fight this vermin." She looked at Logan. "Why do you have that string of horses, each carrying a different brand?"

"As a form of protection. So we can pass ourselves off as horse thieves when we make contact with the Comancheros or Comanches."

"You have a tough job ahead of you," she finally said, then added, "More than tough, it's life-threatening."

Logan caught her hand and turned it palm up, his thumb gently rubbing over the beginning of calluses. "The frontier itself is life-threatening, girl, and it's hard on all of us. I guess each of us makes it harder by the jobs we choose to do."

Brenna could feel the light strokes all the way to the bottom of her stomach . . . and lower.

"Are you referring to me?"

"In a way," he said casually, his attention on her hand. "You're doing a man's job."

The ache Logan created in Brenna wasn't new; Shawn had been able to do that. But it was an ache she had come to dread, for she had never had it sated. For her desire was a pain; it always ended in disappointment and frustration. She pulled her hand from Logan and drew in a deep breath.

"When I took on the job, I didn't see a label that said man." She wasn't sure how, but Logan was even closer to her, his body pressing against hers, his lips nearing.

"Then it's time someone took it upon himself to

69

teach you the difference between man and woman." He gently pressured her to the ground so that she was lying on her back and he was leaning over her.

Brenna thought about stopping him, but her body was truant; it reacted as if it were apart from the rest of her. It whisked her good intentions and conscience aside as if they were of no consequence.

Logan brushed his lips back and forth across hers in light, teasing motions. "To begin with, a man is generally hard and tough. A woman is pliable and tender. Supple and round. Sweet and delicious."

Seemingly of its own accord, Brenna's mouth opened beneath his, and she heard his low groan as his lips contoured, then moved on hers. The kiss deepened, and she welcomed the velvet texture of his tongue into her mouth. Her arms slid around his back; her fingers dug into the hard, muscular back. She arched and thrust her breasts against the steely wall of his chest.

She was so hungry for the taste of a man that tears sprang to her eyes and she sighed in contentment. When she realized what she was thinking, she was deluged with guilt—so hungry for the taste of a man that she willingly fell into the arms of the first one who came along! She pressed her hands against his chest and pushed, but Logan wouldn't budge.

"Just like I thought," he whispered, ignoring her bid for freedom, his hand threading through her hair. "Sweet and delicious." When he felt the wetness of her tears against his palm, he pulled back and looked at her in astonishment. "What's wrong? Have I offended you?" Tenderly he wiped the liquid passion from her face. "Did I make you cry?"

"No . . . yes . . ." Brenna was confused . . . ashamed . . . embarrassed . . . and downright starved for Logan's touch. She couldn't think straight; she didn't want to think straight. She simply wanted to feel and to keep on feeling—for the first time in her life, desire felt good.

"Yes or no?" he demanded softly.

"You . . . your lips felt so good on mine." The words slipped through her lips unbidden.

Logan tensed. Brenna's confession moved him like nothing else could have. He had made love to many women, but Brenna aroused something in him that had never been aroused before. She touched him deeper than any other woman had ever done. That she had the ability to do this perplexed him. Also it angered him; he didn't want to be aroused or deeply touched. He wanted to be in total control of his life because he had certain things that he must do. He had learned during his lifetime that when a man allows himself to have feelings for someone or something, he loses control. He thinks of them before he thinks of himself. Logan couldn't afford this; his mission required a selfish relentlessness.

Still, when he looked at her lying on the ground, her body begging for his love, he was compelled to feel. Angrily he lowered his head and took her mouth again, tentatively at first, then fuller, hotter. As the kiss developed, his hands began a beautiful exploration of her body. He touched her breasts, cupping the fullness in his hands, his thumb circling over and around the nipple.

"Supple and round," he murmured as he moved his mouth from her lips to the warm, pulsating hollow at the base of her neck as his hand brushed down her midriff, his fingers lightly tickling her.

Sinful! The word careened through Brenna's head. She twisted her head, but Logan wouldn't turn her lips loose. Gently he held them prisoner until all resistance had wilted. When he felt her tremble beneath his touch, he propped himself on an elbow and with the other hand opened the top three buttons of her dress. He pulled the material aside and looked at the moon-kissed breasts, and he continued to stare at them. With a reverence and adoration that Brenna thought out of keeping with the rough-tough frontiersman, Logan bent over her so that his warm breath splayed against her skin long before his lips touched the fullness.

"I'm so hungry for the taste of you," he whispered. "I can't get enough of you."

Brenna couldn't help herself. Silently the tears ran out of the corners of her eyes, down her temples. But her desire had chased guilt away for the moment. She was ablaze with passion. Shawn had not been gentle and kind with her. Never did he take the time to look at and touch her body or love her. He didn't talk to her during their lovemaking. He never took the time to taste her lips or her skin or her breasts. When she felt the moistness of Logan's mouth on her nipple, Brenna softly moaned, wave after wave of desire searing through her insides to set her on fire.

He moved his face from one breast to the other, his warm breath like a thick, rich molasses over her fevered skin. He turned his head to rest his cheek against the taut fullness. His chin burrowed the material aside, and he lowered his lips to trace a path of sheer pleasure to her waist, where his exploration was stopped by the cambric waistband.

Spurred by her own fevered desires, Brenna spread her fingers through the thickness of his hair, and she guided his head back to her face, her lips taking and molding his so that he received her tongue into his mouth. With a groan, Logan wrapped his arms around her. He rolled over on his back and positioned her on top. Frantically Brenna's fingers worked to open his shirt and to push the material aside.

Her hands moved over his shoulders, down his chest

to the small silver medallion that rested in the hollow of his throat. With a finger she traced the chain; she outlined the amulet. She leaned down and laid her cheek over the metal.

"Now you can't see," she whispered.

"Oh, but I can," he murmured in a voice thick with passion. "This is only symbolic of the spiritual eye, of the inner man. And right now, Brenna Allen, I'm looking at you with all my eyes—natural and spiritual."

"Do you like what you see?" Again she whispered, her breath fanning across his hot flesh.

"I like what I see."

Brenna felt his chest move as he spoke. She lifted her head, gently brushing her lips across his chest to pause at his nipples; she caressed them until they were pert nodules resting in a thick mat of pectoral hair. Lower her hands went until they were invading the sensitive area below the band of his trousers. Beneath her palms she felt desire as it rippled through the tight muscles.

Logan didn't want this moment to stop. Brenna was a fiery woman who stirred up a reciprocal blaze of desire inside him. He wanted to make love to her. And she wanted him to. He knew it; he could tell by the desperation of her lovemaking. And even if this was the right time for him to make love to her, it certainly was not the place to consummate the passion they were experiencing.

He and Brenna were destined to blazing moments of passion, moments he intended to prolong and enjoy. He didn't want to take her on the banks of the river this close to the wagon train and chance being interrupted or her embarrassed by someone taking a stroll. Slowly, gently, with kisses and murmured endearments, Logan brought Brenna down from the burning tower of complete abandon.

Lying on her back, she looked into his face as he straightened her chemise and buttoned her dress. As passion dissipated, guilt returned to plague her. Rejection overpowered her. She sat up, the movement defensive. "I'm sorry," she whispered. "I don't know what came over me."

"You don't have to be sorry," Logan said. "It's only natural for you to feel the way you did."

"I know what you're thinking of me," she began, but Logan laid a finger over her mouth to hush her words.

"No, you don't," he said.

"Why did you stop?" She was compelled to ask.

He caught her shoulders in his hands and guided her back down; then he stretched out beside her, propped on his elbow, his other hand resting on her waist. "This isn't the place for you and me to make love," he replied. "And if I hadn't stopped then, I wouldn't have stopped." He dropped his head and touched his lips to hers lightly, lingeringly. His mouth moved across her cheek up her neck to her ear. "You're a special woman, Brenna Allen, and I want us to discover each other in a special place at a special time."

Brenna was happy; she felt as radiant as the moon. They stayed beside the river, he half leaning over her, she lying on her back, each gently cloaked by the silvery light. Without realizing it, Brenna talked with Logan, recalling sweet, childish memories. He laughed with her; he encouraged her to talk. She didn't notice that Logan never shared any of himself with her. Neither was aware of the time until a scream pierced the night to jolt them out of their intimate little world. On their feet immediately, both ran to the compound.

"What is it?" Brenna called as she pressed through the crowd. By this time she was standing in front of Gabby and Abbott Kirkwood, who stood in the center of gaping humanity.

"This," Gabby said, jabbing a finger at the lifeless body that was draped over Kirkwood's horse.

"Oh, no!" Brenna groaned. Her hands inadvertently flew to her mouth. "It can't be!"

"It is," Kirkwood said.

"He's dead," Brenna murmured, her eyes still on Venner's body. She raised her face to Kirkwood. "Comanches?"

"Comanches," he said with a curt bob of the head. "Figure it was a small hunting party. They tortured him and stole his horse and weapons, but he was a tough man. He was still alive when I found him."

"Did he tell you anything?" Gabby asked.

Kirkwood shook his head grimly. Then he yanked his hat off and ran his hand through his hair. "I'm tired and hungry," he announced. "Let me rest some and get a bite of food, and I'll answer all your questions later."

"Come with me, young man," Gertrude Dawkins said. "I'll get you something to eat."

As Kirkwood shoved past Brenna, she moved so she could see Venner's face, but Gabby caught and held her tightly in his arms. "You don't want to look, gal."

"Yes, she does," Logan contradicted. His stomach lurched at the idea of forcing Brenna to look at the mutilated body, but he wanted her to see the ugliness of Comanche war. She was such a stubborn woman, she would only be convinced to stay out of Comancheria if she saw the horror for herself. He pulled Brenna out of Gabby's arms and walked her to the other side of the horse. Holding her arm with one hand, he cupped Venner's bloodied chin with the other and lifted his face.

So gruesome was the mutilated face that Brenna gasped and blanched. Her stomach roiled, and she swallowed bile.

"This is what a man looks like when the Comanches

get through with him," Logan said in a low voice. He raised his head and spoke to the people. "I want all of you to look," he said, slapping the horse's flanks so he would turn around. "Not a pretty sight, is it?" He lifted Venner's body into his arms and held it out for all of them to see. "This could be you."

Having seen victims of Indian wars before, Gabby backed off, but the others thronged nearer. What they saw brought gasps of horror. Not one person was unaffected by the sight. Roger's face turned ashen.

"Butchered while he was alive," Logan said.

But Brenna didn't hear another word Logan uttered. The man couldn't be Brady Venner . . . but it was. His hair gone, and the flesh around the exposed skull bloody! His eyes burned out of his head; his upper body crisscrossed with deep knife wounds. His fingers were cut from his hands. Logan didn't let the women see his lower body, but Brenna could guess. His genitals had also been burned. She was well versed in the atrocities of the Comanches.

Long after they had buried Venner and piled the grave with rocks, Logan came to where Brenna sat to the side of her wagon. He knelt in front of her and said, "Brenna, you can't take your wagon train through Comanche territory," he insisted. "Venner's fate awaits any of you, and young women who are taken alive are being sold into prostitution."

"Choosing a route is my decision," Brenna reminded Logan, with a touch of asperity, "but I assure you I wouldn't make such a decision lightly."

Logan stood, walked to the fire, and poured two cups of coffee. The one he gave her; the other he kept. As he watched her sip the coffee as if she hadn't a concern in the world, he wanted to reach out and shake some sense into her. At the same time he wanted to pull her into his arms and kiss some sense into her. He did neither.

Staring into the blackness of the night, she asked, "Where are you headed from here?"

"Why?" Logan came back sharply.

Brenna shrugged nonchalantly as if she were idly curious, but inside she was tense. "Just wondered if you'd be detouring around Comanche territory like you're telling me to." She waited for his answer.

"No," Logan answered, "I won't be detouring. I'll be headed directly into it, and you knew that without asking."

"Yet you have the audacity to ask me to go around."

Logan's eyes narrowed until they were the cutting edge of a finely honed knife. "I have to go into Comancheria, but you don't. Furthermore, it's different for me!"

"Oh, yes," Brenna exclaimed, never raising her voice a jot. "You're a man and I'm a woman!"

"Don't be ridiculous," he exclaimed. "I know this country. I've been reared by Indians; I can communicate with them. I think like them. You don't."

"You know the way to Santa Fe?" Brenna asked.

"Near enough," Logan replied.

"Would you consider signing on as my head scout?"

"Absolutely not." Logan seemed to bark the words. Even had he wanted to, Logan couldn't travel with Brenna's train. He and Thunder had given their solemn word to Houston and to Texas—and time was quickly running out. Logan reached up to lay his hand over his pocket; he felt the pendant beneath the layer of material. He had a job to finish for himself. "Thunder and I promised Houston that we'd find the Comanchero hideout."

Logan's refusal hurt Brenna; he didn't have to be so adamant. "I'm not asking you to give up your mission," she said. "Just postpone it for a little while."

"I can't and won't," Logan told her. "Time's running out for statehood."

"Texas doesn't need to become a state," Brenna exclaimed. "Let her own star shine brightly, Logan. We don't have to become one star of many."

"I believe statehood is our future," he replied. "And even if I didn't, I told Houston I'd take the job. I intend to finish it. I owe him that much."

"That's one thing we have in common," Brenna said, tossing the dregs out of the cup. "Each of us has a job to do and a certain time in which to do it."

"Is reaching Santa Fe with this damn freight train all you can think of?"

"Is running errands for Houston all you can think of?"

Silence, like the very air around them, hung heavy.

Logan finally said, "The cost of being a trailblazer is high, Brenna."

"I know."

"And you're willing to pay the price?" Before she could answer, he added, "Just remember Brady Venner is only the first payment . . . of many."

"Somebody has to be the trailblazer," Brenna pointed out, "or there can never be a second, or a third, and it might as well be me."

"If you'll return to Austin and wait for me to finish this assignment, I'll guide your caravan to Santa Fe. Promise."

"Absolutely not. I have to get to Santa Fe before the Missouri traders."

Before they could say more, Gabby's voice boomed out. "Have you talked with Kirkwood, MacDougald?"

"Sure have," Logan commented as he turned to watch Gabby's approach.

"What do you think?"

Logan shrugged. "Not much to think about," he

replied. "All signs point to the Comanches."

"Yeah," Gabby drawled, his eyes narrowing as he studied Logan's face, "and that worries me. Kinda figure it was a scouting party." Implying rather than saying the question, Gabby watched for Logan's reaction.

Logan slowly nodded his head. "I figure it was a scouting party."

"Gotta be. Otherwise they'd have attacked the wagon train. We were only a couple of hours behind Venner." Out of habit Gabby lifted his hand and rubbed his neck just below the chin. "Reckon a big party is out here somewhere."

Logan simply nodded, then said, "Brenna tells me that you were with the wagon train that was attacked outside Refugio."

"Shore was." Gabby spat. "They jest seemed to sweep out of nowhere. Seemed like hundreds of 'em. Shawn said our only chance was for one of us to get help. He sent me." Gabby stopped talking and shook his head as he recalled the gruesome sight he found when he returned. "By the time I got back, the Comanches had finished their work. Them they killed in the fracas they scalped; the two that was left they skinned alive, leaving 'em for dead."

Gabby inhaled heavily. "I could identify all of 'em but the two. Course, we didn't have no problem knowing who they was. Only other two teamsters we had. Clyde Fairfield and Shawn. Shawn . . . he . . ." A hardened veteran of the frontier, Gabby still couldn't recall the scene without his stomach knotting. "I buried him. Didn't want Brenna to see such a sight. All of them butchered by them savages." Gabby clenched his fist together and said, "I hate them savages. I wish I could kill every one of 'em with my own bare hands."

"Did they get close enough for you to identify any of

79

them?" Logan asked.

"Who?" Gabby peered at Logan in surprise. "The Indians?"

Logan nodded. "I wondered if they were the same ones who raided Rhem Sommers's place a couple of months ago. A settler who lives out of Austin. All the family was killed. Rhem was scalped and left for dead. But he managed to get to a neighbor, who doctored him, and he lived. He said the Comanches who attacked his place were led by a chief who had a white streak in his hair. He also said a white man was riding with them. Thunder and I are looking for the Comancheros who are riding with the Comanches and for the white-haired chief."

"Be hard to miss an Indian with a streak of white hair." Gabby leaned back on the heels of his boots. Deep in thought, he didn't answer for a few minutes. "Can't say," he finally answered. "Didn't get a good look at any of 'em." He shrugged, then pursed his lips and spat. As he wiped his hand across his mouth, he mumbled, "Even if they didn't have their faces smeared with paint, I can't tell one of them Indians from the other. All look alike to me. Didn't see no Indian with white hair or a white man that I can recollect."

Later, in the privacy of their own camp as they spread their blankets for the night, Logan told Thunder all he had learned.

After they lay down, Thunder asked, "Now that their scout is dead, do you think the woman will lead her train across Comancheria?"

"I wouldn't be a bit surprised."

"Did you tell her what trade good the Comancheros were most interested in?"

"Yes."

"She could not be persuaded to return to Austin?"

"No."

"Does this woman find a special place in your heart?"

"No," Logan replied curtly, irritated because Thunder could read him so accurately. He added, "I would like for her to be in my bed but definitely not in my heart."

"She is not the kind you have been sleeping with," Thunder reminded.

"No," Logan sighed, "that's why I'm sleeping alone."

"It is time you found yourself a woman," the Cherokee advised. "You cannot live the rest of your life in the shadow of love."

"I don't want to talk about it!"

Thunder was accustomed to ignoring his adopted brother when he had something he wanted to say. "You loved Dancing Dawn, and you would have married her. But she is dead. You are alive. The Great Spirit would not have you walk the road of life alone. He would give you a woman to share your joys as well as your sorrows and to work by your side. Out of your love will come sons and daughters."

Haunted by ghosts of the past, Logan bounded to his feet and moved to stand by a nearby tree. If only he had been there when the Texans attacked the village, Logan thought, his hand balling into a fist. He could have saved her.

"You can't go through the rest of your life blaming yourself for her death," Thunder said. "Someday you must cleanse yourself of this guilt you feel. Until then you will continue to race headlong into death." A while later he added, "I wonder which you will do first, cleanse yourself or find death."

Logan reached into his pocket and withdrew his watch to snap the lid open. It was too dark to see the small portrait, but in his mind's eye he saw Dancing Dawn's face clearly. The thick black hair parted in the

81

center and pulled into two braids. Big brown eyes. Warm and gentle and trusting. He remembered her low, husky voice, never once raised in anger. He remembered the way she said his name. He remembered the way she felt in his arms. She had been taken away from him before he knew the full wonder of their love.

Only one way to forget—the only way he could forget his loneliness. He had to have a woman.

Chapter Six

Logan slipped by the guard and through the compound until he was at Brenna's wagon. At the same time that he crawled under and touched her shoulder, he slipped his hand over her mouth to keep her from crying out.

His quiet "It's me" kept her from fighting the hand. Surprised, she blinked up at him.

"I want you to talk to me," he whispered, and slid his hand from her mouth to her throat.

"You just want to talk at this time of the night!" she exclaimed, careful to keep her voice low.

"I"—he inhaled deeply—"I wanted talk." He wanted to do more than talk, but Logan recognized that Brenna wasn't a whore; she wasn't even a common wench whom a man bedded and left. He would settle for a few hours of her company to rid his mind of these ghosts. "Come with me . . . please."

Sleeping in her shirt and breeches, already dressed for morning, Brenna pushed up and stared at him. She had lain awake for hours, her mind filling with stimulating, sexual thoughts of Logan that she couldn't push aside. She had argued with herself; she had reasoned, but her thoughts refused counsel. Imagination ruled. If his caresses had set her on fire, what would consummation be like with him? Would he leave her feeling as empty and incomplete as Shawn had? Somehow she didn't think so! Somehow she wanted to find out.

"Please." Logan was surprised at himself and a little irritated. He never begged women to make love to him, much less to talk with him. Why was he stooping so low with her?

Brenna knew better than to go with him. She knew what might happen if the two of them were alone together, yet she nodded . . . almost as if she were hoping something would happen.

As soon as Logan saw her head move, he pulled the covers aside to grab one of the blankets and throw it across his arms. He gave her no time to reconsider. Hand in hand they slipped through the wagons around the sleeping people, not stopping until they were safely hidden a long way from camp. Logan spread the blanket and sat down. When Brenna didn't immediately sit beside him, he patted the ground.

"I won't hurt you," he promised.

Brenna wasn't worried about his hurting her; she was concerned about hurting herself. In the few short hours since she'd met Logan, she had thrown all her principles away; she disregarded caution; she flagrantly flaunted convention and morals.

He patted again, and she sat down, but she was careful to keep her distance. She was too attracted to Logan MacDougald. Knowingly she had placed herself in a position to be gossiped about, and she didn't care. More, she had placed herself in a position to be hurt again. She knew better, but she didn't want to do better.

Drawing her knees to her chest and wrapping her arms around her legs, she asked, "What do you want to talk about?"

Logan stared at her silhouetted profile, and his loins

ached for relief. He didn't want to talk; he wanted to take her into his arms and make love to her. He wanted to sleep beside her, to hold her in his arms until the sun rose to dispel the demons that haunted his soul.

Logan stretched out, the movement so casual it betrayed none of his inner turmoil. He lifted his arms, laced his fingers together, and pillowed them under his head. "Anything," he said. "I'm interested in everything about you, and I just wanted to hear your voice again."

The hot, quiet night was fraught with tension—a tension created by their proximity.

"I've already told you about me." Brenna turned her head and looked at him. "How about telling me something about yourself?"

"Too boring," Logan said.

Brenna knew he was smiling; she saw the flash of white teeth.

When she didn't comment, he said, "So your papa's the one who taught you how to use all those weapons you wear." A softness in his tone took mockery out of his words.

Brenna laughed. "He taught me that, but he also taught me how to read, write, and cipher."

"With New Orleans so close, why didn't you go to a finishing school of some sort?"

"Papa and Gabby wanted me to, but I didn't want to leave Papa. I . . . I didn't want him to be alone." Brenna was loath to share her fears with Logan. She didn't want him to see her vulnerability because she was afraid he would think her weak. . . . She was afraid he would take advantage of her weakness. She sought love, but lust she could do without. She didn't want to be a part of sex based on intimidation ever again. She'd had plenty of that with Shawn. "Papa was all I had."

Logan rolled over on his side close to Brenna. He could understand loneliness. Twice he had gone through the grief and agony of losing his family—first his biological family, then his adopted. He reached out to comfort her, to draw her even nearer, but he quickly withdrew his hand. He couldn't touch her now. She was too vulnerable, and he was too aroused. He would be taking advantage of her, and in the morning he would hate himself. Suddenly he jerked himself to a sitting position.

Damn! She wasn't the kind of woman a man slept with! She was the kind of woman a man married! At least, she was the kind a man didn't just make love to one night and leave the next morning. Why did he have to meet someone like Brenna Allen in the hour of his greatest need? Why did he stumble across her when he was so close to finding Scar-Face and White-Hair that he couldn't give Brenna or himself the time they needed to enjoy a pleasant several weeks or maybe months together?

"I was a fool to have gotten you up," he suddenly said, his voice rough, almost angry. "You have to be up early in the morning, and I'm robbing you of your rest."

Brenna turned. "I don't mind," she breathed, inhaling the clean, masculine scent of him. "I want to stay and talk with you."

"Brenna"—his voice was hoarse—"I really brought you out here to talk, but talking isn't what I'm wanting, girl."

"I'm not a girl," she murmured, and deliberately moved even nearer to him. She was amazed at her temerity. Although she had been married to Shawn, she had never been this daring.

"No," Logan said, "you're not a girl." His eyes lowered to graze her breasts that strained against the

86

shirt material.

"I'm a woman," she whispered, her lips moving toward his.

"I know." Logan remembered her dancing with Roger; he saw the dazzling smiles she bestowed on the youth; he could still hear her trills of laughter. "That's why I couldn't imagine you preferring that boy to me."

Logan breathed deeply and caught her shoulders with his hands. He knew he should restrain himself, but he didn't want to. He was fighting against what he wanted the most, a woman. Something he'd never done before.

Ordinarily he wouldn't have resisted a woman who offered him such a delectable gift. A gentleman would have, but not Logan MacDougald, because Logan MacDougald had never professed to be a gentleman. He found gentlemen to be stuffed shirts and hypocrites. Now he had the sad misfortune to run across Brenna Allen, who was a lady.

"Let's go!" he ordered.

"No."

"Let me tell you a second time," he said, "I'm not a boy like Roger. I won't be happy only to hold a woman in my arms and dance around with her."

"I hope not," Brenna murmured.

"My God, woman, do you know what you're doing to me?"

As soon as he asked the question, he tensed. He tensed? Of course Brenna Allen knew what she was doing to him. All along she had known! She was a married woman who knew how to arouse a man. He remembered the way she had deliberately dangled Roger in front of him in an attempt to get him to ask her to dance. He could see her and Roger as they danced together. Jealousy caused Logan's imagination to run wild. He visualized Brenna and Roger hugging and kissing, and he was consumed with rage—blinded by it. Brenna was a hot little filly who'd been married before; she knew what making love was like; she probably couldn't stay away from men, and if men weren't around, she'd settle for boys.

Logan never once thought about his ulterior motive for having awakened her. He didn't even understand his anger toward her or the sudden surge of jealousy. "You're a slick one," he said. "You act like you're so innocent, but you've been married before. You know how to push a man to the breaking point, to the point of no return, and you also know how to protect your reputation. My God, no telling how you've tempted that boy. No wonder he trails behind you like a puppy dog. Have you been giving him anything or just leading him along?"

Logan's roughness startled Brenna; it broke the sensual spell between them. She could only stare at him.

"You had this all planned out, didn't you? In the morning you could soothe your conscience by saying that I took advantage of you." His laughter was bitter and scathing. "Do you make love with every man you meet like this?"

Brenna pushed away from Logan as if he had struck her a physical blow. Yet it was the truth. She had been flirting with him . . . but only because she thought he wanted her to . . . because she thought he cared about her. Her humiliation turned into anger.

"You're the one who came and woke me up! You're the one who said he was lonely and only wanted to talk. Don't you dare accuse me of your filthy thoughts and deeds." She leaped to her feet.

"You were only too willing to come along," he accused. "Flaunting your body at me. Enticing me."

"I didn't have to flaunt myself or entice you," Brenna

said. "You've been leering at me ever since you came into camp. Well, let me tell you, Mr. MacDougald, next time you want a woman to sleep with, don't come looking for me. Find yourself a squaw! Maybe you're the kind of man she wants."

Brenna regretted the words the minute they slipped from her lips, and she had no idea why she had said them. Jealousy! Embarrassment! Humiliation! Grief! No emotion was intense enough to provoke such a drastic reaction. A moment of anger wasn't worth the disgust she felt for herself.

The word *squaw* resurrected Logan's ghosts; he cast reason aside. He bounded to his feet. "You're so wrong about the squaw," he jeered. With a jerk he held Brenna against his chest. "I've never slept with one, but I sure as hell do need a woman. I haven't had a woman in a long time, and since any one will do, I might as well take you. You seem willing to share your favors with men." Anger and jealousy prodded him into saying, "What are you? The wagon train whore?" even though he knew the words were a lie as he uttered them.

Brenna drew back her hand and slapped Logan across the face. He caught her shoulders in a biting grasp and yanked her against him; his lips clamped over hers in a cruel, scorching kiss, and his arms closed around her body to mold it to his. As he slid to the ground, he pulled her down with him, the brutality of the kiss giving way to insatiable hunger.

"I don't care what you are," he said, pressing quick kisses along her cheeks and down her neck. "I'm going to enjoy you tonight, and I'm going to make you forget every other man you've ever slept with."

"If you're half as good a lover as you are a braggart, you should be magnificent," Brenna grunted as she fought against him. "But I have a feeling that you're nothing but talk."

Her arms flailed; she kicked; finally she balled her hands into fists and pummeled his chest, but she was ineffective against brute strength. By this time the heat of Logan's body was burning Brenna. When she relaxed in his arms and stopped fighting, he did, too.

"Don't fight it," he said. "It'll be good. I promise."

"I know." And she did!

He raised his head, and he looked at her. Then his lips lowered, this time taking hers more gently. The touch and the heat of his body set Brenna ablaze for Logan. The flames of passion quickly dissipated anger and resentment. Her fists slowly uncurled, and her hand slipped up his back, her fingers clutching at his shoulders. Her lips softened beneath his, and she began to return the kiss with an intensity that matched his; she was as hungry for Logan's touch as he was for a woman's.

For all his wanting, Logan was not a man to lose control. His anger had only been momentary; it was precipitate to his actions but not the impetus for his wanting to make love to Brenna. His jealousy was lingering, but it only served to whet his sensitivity; it made him determined to please her at all costs.

He was taking the beautiful body that had been tempting him all evening. He had tasted, he had sampled, but now he was going to have his fill of her delectable goodness. He conveniently forgot his promise from earlier in the day. His and Brenna's desire made the riverbank a special time and place. This night he would put his ghosts to rest; he would forget his sorrows and griefs in Brenna's arms. He promised himself that he would make her forget also— Shawn, Roger, all the other men in her life.

His kisses were long and leisurely. They demanded, but they also gave. He asked nothing without returning. The firm, hard lips coaxed hers into pouting fullness, and his tongue explored the honeyed recesses of her mouth. Finally, when she was whimpering with longing, when her body was burning with desire, Logan tenderly unwrapped her hands from his neck to pull away.

"I want to make love to you."

"Because I'm the wagon train whore?"

"I shouldn't have said that," he said, but he didn't apologize. "I want to make love to you because you're you." He stared at her a long time before he asked, "How do you feel?"

Brenna nodded her head and opened her mouth to speak, but Logan laid a gentle finger over her mouth.

"Think about it before you answer," he said. "I'm leaving early in the morning, and we probably will never see each other again. I make no promises, because I'm not prepared to keep any. I don't have time or room in my life for a permanent woman."

Through the silver shadows of night, he waited for her reply. He knew he could love her into compliance with his demands, but he didn't want Brenna that way. He wanted her to make love to him because she wanted it also.

Logan's words were stark and harsh. The truth generally was, Brenna thought. He was giving her the opportunity to leave, and she appreciated it. But Logan had promised her something she craved. He promised to make love to her, and she was heavy with unfulfilled longing. Her mind and heart recognized she was making the wrong choice, but her body needed sexual nourishment—the kind that Logan offered. She conveniently forgot propriety and morals in her desperate search for fulfillment.

"Make love to me."

"I will," he murmured. "I'll give you beautiful, golden memories."

91

With her lying flat on her back, he laid her hands to her sides and looked at her silvered in moonlight. In a low, hypnotic voice he began to talk to her, and with slow, mesmerizing movements of hands and fingers he unbuttoned the front of her shirt to push the soft material aside to expose her breasts to the pale moonshine. Again Logan wanted to do nothing but look at her, to savor the richness of her shining skin. Her breasts were beautiful. Expectancy and anticipation strutted them; they begged for his touch. Desire in pleasurable torment filtered down his body. Yet he didn't taste the wonder of her breasts.

"Who do you look like?" he asked. "Your mother or your father?" He ran a finger across Brenna's eyebrows, starting from the center of her forehead and moving to her temples.

"Papa . . . always said I looked like Mama." Her voice quavered with desire.

Logan traced the line of her nose, down to the full lips that were slightly parted. With the same gentle finger stroke, he outlined them; he brushed in their fullness, his movements stopping only when Brenna flicked the tip of her tongue against the end of his finger.

Her love strokes evoked such visions of pleasure, Logan sucked in his breath. In evocative abandonment Brenna ran her tongue around the tip, and Logan, like a fevered man, burned with desire. His eyes closed, he pressed closer to her. His hand moved from her mouth down her neck to her breasts. He trembled anew as he caught the ripe roundness in his hands and turned the nipples up for his taking. Gently he teased; then more urgently he sucked. He heard Brenna gasp for breath; he felt her quick intake of air. His head raised and moved lower, his mouth foraging a hot path down her midriff. Brenna's hand tangled in his hair, and she pulled his head up. She guided his face to hers; she wanted him to make love to her.

"Take my clothes off," he muttered in a passion-thickened voice. His head swam with delightful visions of her love ministrations.

Enthralled with his response to her touches, Brenna thoroughly reveled in her role as wanton. She sat up as he lay down on his back, and began to push the buttons through the openings of his shirt. She pushed the material aside and looked at the hair-roughened chest, her gaze skimming over the shining metal necklace. For just a fraction of a moment she hesitated. She had the eerie feeling that Logan's medallion could read her heart; the idea of Logan's knowing her most secret thoughts filled her with vulnerability.

He noticed her withdrawal. "What's wrong?" he whispered.

"The . . . the eye," Brenna replied. It made her feel guilty, as if God were looking down at her and frowning. "It . . . it . . ."

"It's only a piece of silver," he explained. "It can't hurt you."

"I know," she murmured.

He reached up and unhooked the chain to drop the medallion into his shirt pocket. Then he slipped out of the shirt. "How's that?" he asked.

The necklace forgotten, Brenna's eyes were on the flexed muscles of his back. "It's . . . it's much better."

Reared on the frontier, accustomed to seeing men work without their shirts, Brenna was familiar with bared torsos, but the sight of this one filled her with awe. When he lay back down, tentative hands reached out, exploring the muscularity, her palms discovering his nipples. She felt them crest beneath her touch; she smiled. Logan was responding to her; he enjoyed her caresses.

Following his example, she leaned over him to scatter kisses over his chest down his stomach to his navel. She felt Logan's firm body ripple with desire as she journeyed. Her hand inadvertently lit on his thigh, and Logan moved a fraction of an inch so that it slipped over his masculinity. When Brenna felt the hardness beneath her hand, her tongue began to draw tantalizing designs around Logan's navel, and she felt a burning moistness between her legs.

Logan could take no more foreplay. He pushed her aside and sat up. Quickly he unbuckled his belt, unbuttoned his pants, and peeled out of them. With wonder Brenna stared at his erectness. When she and Shawn had made love, he hadn't allowed her to touch him so intimately; she hadn't seen him naked; she hadn't seen evidence of his arousal. As if pulled to the earth by her magnetic gaze, Logan slowly bent until he was kneeling in front of her.

She reached out, and her hand gently closed around the pulsating length. Again she felt Logan's body tremble with desire. She looked at him, her face bathed in moonlight. So much about making love that she didn't understand. She would never have guessed that her touches could tame such a primitive beast as Logan MacDougald or could render him her captive.

His voice thick with desire, Logan drawled, "Much as I enjoy your touches and kisses, I've been a long time without a woman, and I can't take much more of this without—" He caught her hand, moved closer, and settled on his side. "Now, let's get the rest of these clothes off you."

Brenna nodded, and with haste she unbuttoned her britches and slipped out of them, falling on her back and opening her body to him. On his knees, Logan moved between her legs and poised for that moment, his hand running down her belly and thighs back up to the fiery inner arch of thighs. He made certain she was ready to welcome him; then he slowly lay down to fill her with his warm hardness. With a deep sigh of contentment, Brenna locked her legs about him to move with him and for him.

"How does it feel?" Logan asked. His thrusts ceased and he moved into a comfortable position.

The fullness inside her was so wonderful Brenna groaned her pleasure.

Logan stilled himself. "Am I hurting you?"

"No," Brenna breathed. "It feels wonderful." Her hands clasped his sinewy buttocks, and she pulled him even tighter against her, more fully into her.

Logan laughed joyously, his mouth descending to hers. Then his possession began in earnest as he explored every fiber of emotion in Brenna, leaving not one inch of her untouched. When he wasn't murmuring endearments to her as he guided her along passion's path, he was kissing her lips and breasts; he was moving his hands up and down her body. And when Logan placed his hands beneath her buttocks and arched her up, she received him, she welcomed him even more fully. With deep, even strokes he carried her to fulfillment—a long, breathtaking moment when her cries of ecstasy—the first such moments for her—were muted by Logan's mouth closing over hers in a sweet, warm kiss.

When her spasms of desire ceased, Logan began to move again, this time fulfilling his needs. When the release came, he groaned and buried his face in the curve of her shoulder and neck. Then he collapsed on top of her, loving the feel of her hands as they rubbed from his buttocks up both sides of his back. Finally he rolled off her, and they lay side by side, looking at the star-speckled sky.

"Thank you." He twined his fingers between hers.

"Thank you," Brenna murmured, feeling embarrassed and self-conscious.

He raised their hands and moved them so they lay flat together, palm against palm. "Look how much bigger my hand is than yours." He turned his head and looked at her face. "I dwarf you."

At five feet nine inches, Brenna had been dwarfed by few men. But she suddenly realized that height had little to do with her feeling so small. Spiritually Logan was a big, powerful man. Had he been shorter than she, still he would have dwarfed her because he exuded strength. Now she felt warm and protected as she snuggled against him.

He wrapped his arms around her and held her. And later he made love to her a second time, this time slowly and leisurely. Each of them experienced another ecstatic fulfillment—deeper and fuller this time because they were more familiar with each other.

"Thank you again," Brenna murmured as she leaned over Logan and spread tiny kisses of thanksgiving over his chest.

She had never been satisfied once in a night, much less twice. Although she was no virgin, Logan's lovemaking was a new experience for her. Shawn had acted as if he were afraid of loving her, as if he were ashamed of loving her, so he took—angrily, greedily took—without giving. Each time he made love to her, Brenna felt him stripping away her integrity and her womanhood, and always he left her yearning for satisfaction.

How quickly Shawn changed from the kind, solicitous man she married to a bestial brute. No longer did he offer her comfort and companionship as he had immediately after her father's death. She became a possession for him, a woman to keep his house and warm his bed.

When she explained to Shawn that she wanted more out of their marriage, out of their lovemaking, he was shocked. He looked at her as if she were a whore. She never forgot his reaction. *Ladies don't enjoy sex,* he said scathingly, *just men! Decent women only do it to please their husbands and to provide them with children. Something's wrong with you.* Shawn covered her with a cloak of guilt, and she in her innocence wore it.

Logan carried her beyond her hurt and pain; he lifted her above shame and degradation.

"I've never known pleasure like this before," she said.

Deep laughter, a sound of his contentment and pleasure, rumbled through Logan's chest. He caught a fist full of hair and brought her face to his, their lips meeting in a warm, open kiss. "It's always better," he said, "when both the woman and the man enjoy what they're doing."

"I've . . . I've heard that most men prefer their women . . . prefer them to be . . ."

"Not I," Logan responded, his voice laced with amusement. "I like my women experienced."

I like my women experienced! Logan's words burst Brenna's bubble of happiness. *Women* reinforced his words earlier. He wanted no permanent woman in his life. His having made love to Brenna was all he had done; he hadn't fallen in love and wanted nothing more than the night and its pleasures.

His statement brought back all the guilt Brenna had ever felt and harbored, and suddenly her dead husband's words seemed true. She was a wanton! She had known Logan less than a day, and like a whore she had allowed him to make love to her, in fact, encouraged him the second time. She rolled on her side and turned her back to Logan.

He sensed the change in Brenna; he supposed that she was thinking about Shawn. Knowing she wasn't the kind of woman who would sleep with a man outside wedlock, he could imagine her guilt. And ironically, he felt guilty, too. The conscience he had pushed aside earlier rushed forward to throw heated castigations in his face. This is why he didn't like to make love to ladies! They made him feel guilty!

"I'm sorry," he muttered, his hand closing over her shoulder. "I didn't—"

"It's all right," Brenna said.

But it wasn't all right. He'd violated one of his basic principles by making love to her. Brenna wasn't one of these women you made love to and left. "Brenna, I—"

Instinctively Brenna knew that Logan was going to apologize, and she didn't want him to. She reached for her shirt. "I enjoyed making love to you, Logan, and I did so because I wanted it as much as you did. I have no regrets." She gently moved her shoulder from his hand, scooted over and, with her back to him, slipped into her shirt.

"Brenna—"

Brenna turned to him now as she buttoned up her shirt and shook her head. "No more words, Logan, please. Don't ruin what we've shared for me."

He nodded, and the two of them quietly dressed in the darkness. The blanket slung across his shoulder, he walked her back to the wagon, and they stood for a long time, staring into each other's face.

"Will I see you in the morning?" she asked.

"No, I'll leave long before you get up." He paused and gazed down at her. Finally he said, "Be careful."

"I will."

He gave her a tender smile and bent to press a sweet, sweet kiss on her lips that lingered long after he'd gone.

Chapter Seven

Brenna didn't go back to sleep. She lay there thinking about her and Logan. Before dawn she heard him and Thunder ride away. Their making love hadn't mattered enough for him to stay with her. Of course, he had told her that from the start. No promises. To him she was just another woman . . . of many. Perhaps Shawn was correct. She was a wanton. How quickly she went to bed with Logan MacDougald! Her cheeks burned as she remembered their night together. He had made no promises, yet she had silently begged him to love her.

But he had given her memories—golden memories— but even they couldn't fill the void his departure had created. He gave her a brief moment of joy last night; his going away would give her nothing but grief. Shawn's coming and going in her life had been little more than the shadow of a fleeting cloud. Not so was Logan's. No matter how much she may wish otherwise, a part of her would always belong to Logan Mac-Dougald, the man who had touched her to the depth of her soul.

Since this was her week to cook breakfast, Brenna finally roused enough to get up and dress. In the first light of dawn, she combed and braided her hair; then she tugged on her socks and boots. By the time she leaped from the wagon, Jonesey had the fire blazing and a pot of coffee on. After her second cup, she laid the large cast-iron skillet over the fire and dropped into it slices of fatback bacon. She heard someone behind her and turned her head to see Roger.

"Good morning." She greeted the sleepy-eyed man, who yanked on his galluses as he stumbled up to the fire beside her wagon.

"Don't see much good about it." Roger plopped down on a small wooden stool nearby.

"Too much whiskey," Brenna soothed.

"Too much whiskey," Roger agreed. *And too much of that damned Logan MacDougald!*

"Perhaps a cup of coffee will help your disposition somewhat and clear your head," he heard Brenna say.

When Brenna pressed the cup into his hands, he leaned back against the wagon and gave a grateful smile. "Thanks," he murmured, his mouth already moving to the rim. After several swallows, he said, "Good, Miss Brenna. Real good. Hits the spot."

Later more of the men gathered around the fire to drink their coffee and eat their fatback bacon and corn fritters. They chatted among themselves. Brenna, caught up in thoughts of Logan, was unusually quiet.

Finally Roger's curiosity could be stayed no longer. He leaned forward and asked Brenna, "MacDougald isn't eating breakfast with us?"

"No," Brenna replied, wondering if every time someone mentioned Logan's name, her heart would sink with disappointment. Would she always feel that warmth of embarrassment when she thought of her own promiscuity? "He's already gone. He left early this morning."

"Gone!" Roger was surprised and elated.

"Morning." Gabby joined them. "Think I'll get me a cup of that coffee." He sniffed. "Sure smells good."

"Tastes right good, too," Roger said. "Miss Brenna said MacDougald and the Indian's gone."

"Yep." Gabby lifted the tin cup to his lips and blew on the hot liquid. "Works for the government, so he can't waste any time. Had to get back to his business."

While the men ate breakfast, Brenna walked to the river where she and Logan had made love last night. She draped her arms around a large, squat tree, laid her cheek against the cool, rough bark, and closed her eyes. The gentle lap of the water against the bank brought back the memories of last night—memories that had colored her dreams soft and beautiful. She could see Logan as plainly as if he were standing in front of her; she could hear his words of love; she could feel his hands on her body.

But in the light of day her deed wasn't golden; but neither was it sordid and ugly. True, she had allowed herself to become one woman of many for Logan; she had allowed herself to be used. But she had done it willingly; he hadn't coerced her. And now she did know that lovemaking was more than what she and Shawn shared.

Logan's leaving was for the best, she decided. She had a wagon train to get to Santa Fe and a letter to deliver. No telling what else may be involved with her task. She certainly didn't need her life cluttered with emotional involvements. She needed a clear head. Yes, she thought, she was glad that Logan left. Better for both of them!

"Mrs. Allen!"

Sam's raspy call jarred Brenna from her daydreams. She opened her eyes and shoved away from the tree.

"Are we—are we"—he stopped to draw in large gulps of air—"are we turning back now that Mr. Venner's dead?"

"No," she replied, a puzzled frown on her face.

"We're going to continue. Why?"

"Some of us were wondering." He wheezed more than spoke the words.

"The settlers?" Brenna questioned.

Sam nodded. "What with the Indians—and those—" Another deep breath, followed by a cough. "Your driver seemed to think it—it would be better—" Sam was so exhausted he couldn't finish his sentence.

Brenna liked Jonesey—the name Dwight Jones preferred to be called—and trusted him implicitly. He had driven for Garvey Freight Hauling for several years, and he was the only driver she trusted with her own wagon, but she was irritated with him. He knew better than to discuss his fears with other members of the wagon train. More problems to deal with, she thought.

"I can understand how all of you must feel, Sam." She gave him a reassuring smile. "Tell you what; I'll call a meeting to discuss my plans for the next leg of our trip to Bent's Fort and Santa Fe. Set everybody's mind at ease."

Deeply engrossed in conversation, Gabby and Jonesey were sitting in front of her wagon when Brenna arrived. Pouring herself a cup of coffee, she sat down beside the tall, thin man. "I'm going to have to call a meeting. Venner's death has everybody on edge."

Jonesey nodded his head and ran his hand through his scraggly beard. "Yep, it sure does for a fact. Coming up against them Comanches is a mighty frightful thing." He grinned, revealing tobacco-stained teeth. "Does this mean you're thinking about heading back, Miss Brenna?"

"No, Jonesey," Brenna replied, "I'm not turning around. These people have to get to Bent's Fort, and I have goods that need to get to Santa Fe. We have Mr. Kirkwood to take Venner's place as head scout. Since

102

the Comanches are extremely active and likely to be working with Comancheros, we'll take the long way around."

"Thank God!" Gabby breathed a sigh of relief.

"And who's to take Kirkwood's place if something happens to him?" Jonesey argued. "What if he gets us out there in the middle of nowhere and something happens to him?"

"Then we guide ourselves with the compass," Brenna replied crisply.

"What about them settlers?" Jonesey argued. "They are plenty upset about what they seen last night."

"I'm sure they are," Brenna said, "with all the talking you've been doing."

Jonesey's face turned a dull red.

"From now on," Brenna chided in a gentle but firm tone, "you let me take care of the settlers, and you keep your gossip confined to Gabby and me. Do you understand?"

"Yes, ma'am," Jonesey said meekly.

"I'm going to tell the settlers about the Comancheros," Brenna told Gabby. "I think they have a right to know."

"What's them?" Jonesey asked. "Another tribe of Indians out here?"

Brenna couldn't stay irritated at her driver for long. She grinned and shook her head. "I'll tell you later." Then she turned her attention back to Gabby. "If any of them want to pull out and return to Austin, they can. I'll refund the money they paid me to get them to Bent's Fort."

"Nary one of them's gonna want to turn back," Gabby grumbled. "They're from back East, and none of 'em knows the dangers they're facing . . . or care!"

Not daunted long, Jonesey added, "None of them understand how important it is, Miss Brenna, to have a scout who knows the way." His tone clearly implied that Kirkwood did not know the way.

"We have a scout, Mr. Jones! Maybe not the one any of us would have chosen, but one nonetheless." Brenna turned to Gabby. "Please assemble the people and I'll talk with them."

Gabby nodded his head as he finished off his coffee. Then he stood and moved through the camp to give the call that set the camp abuzz. Everyone, men, women, and children, assembled posthaste around the campfire. When Brenna had their attention, she spoke. Reiterating the speech she had made to them in Austin when she agreed to take them to Bent's Fort, she reemphasized the dangers of the trail and reminded them of the atrocities of the Comanches—a fact she didn't have to dwell upon. Vividly they recalled Venner's mutilated body. Then she repeated to them all Logan had told her about the Comancheros.

She concluded with, "As for me, I'm going to continue my journey. I'm going to ask Mr. Kirkwood to become my scout. Whether he does or not, I intend to take my wagons and go on. If you choose to travel with me, I'll take you to Bent's Fort as I promised, and from there I'll go on to Santa Fe. If you wish to return to Austin, I'll refund the money you paid me."

When she had finished speaking, Elijah Caldwell stood. He ran his hand down his long white beard. "I don't figure them Comanches to be any worse than any other kind of Indians, and I don't reckon I'm afraid of the Comancheros. I'll take my chances with you, Mrs. Allen."

"Me, too," Maude Hemphill concurred, energetically bobbing her head up and down, then added with a wave of her hand toward Roger, "We got us an armed escort." Her other hand swept to the other men traveling in the caravan. "And we got our own menfolks." Maude Hemphill was determined to reach her brother and his family at Bent's Fort. If she had her way, this caravan wouldn't be turning back to Austin.

Sam stood. "Well"—he drew a deep breath and cleared his throat—"I, for one, want to go on." He stopped for another gulp of air. "Nothing for me back in Austin but more trouble. Closer I get to Santa Fe, the better I feel."

And the safer! He was running from his past; it frightened him and caused him to have nightmares that worsened his health. His chest hurt as he struggled to breathe. Maybe . . . just maybe in Santa Fe he could find peace.

Abbott Kirkwood pushed his wiry frame from the wagon on which he leaned and walked to the center of the circle. "I hired on as a hunter in Austin cause Mr. Langdon didn't have none." He hitched his thumbs in his belt. "Told him just like I'm a'telling you. I ain't never been to Bent's Fort, but I've been to Santy Fee. Now, I plumb agree with Miss Brenna and Mr. Langdon. If we can skirt around Indian territory, I'm all for it. Don't want to tangle with any redskins if I don't have to. Reckon if anybody can get you where you want to go, I can." He turned to Brenna. "I thank you, ma'am, for having confidence in me."

In the two weeks since Logan and Thunder departed the wagon train, they traveled due west into the heart of Comanche land, the string of horses and mules behind them.

"Not a sign of Comanches," Logan complained. Exhausted and thirsty, he lifted a hand and ran it over his unshaven face. "In thirteen days we haven't seen one Indian. Now that we want them to find us, we don't see a one. Not a one!"

"Patience, my brother," Thunder admonished with quiet amusement. "We shall find the white-haired one, and perhaps at his death"—the Indian's eyes moved across the horizon—"you will lay old ghosts to rest."

"I am patient," Logan said, "but time is running out."

He lifted his arm and brushed his sleeve across his forehead. He had already put several old ghosts to rest, and in their place were memories of Brenna—memories he hadn't planned on. All during the day and night Brenna's sea-green eyes would flash through his mind to remind him of her softness. He would hear her laughter. Despite his best resolves, he found himself longing for the supple sweetness of her body; he ached for her touch.

At times like these he regretted having made love to her. He didn't want a woman to occupy any of his thoughts. It irritated him that such inconsequential things reminded him of Brenna, of something she said, something she did. At the most inopportune moments he found himself consumed with thoughts of her.

He would like to see her again—make love to her again. Perhaps after this assignment was over he'd ride into Santa Fe. If she set up a store like the other traders did, she'd be there for a while. He'd like to see Santa Fe!

That settled for the time being, he returned his attention to matters at hand.

He and Thunder climbed the crest and saw a small creek below. The horses lifted their heads and whinnied, eager for water. Quickly the men rode down the incline, but they didn't let the animals drink. As two sets of keen eyes circled the pool, they spotted the tracks. Hanging on to the reins of their thirsty horses until they could tether them on a low hanging limb, they hastened to the opposite side to kneel down and run their fingers over hoof imprints.

"Indians, all right," Logan said, a note of excitement entering his voice. He sank his cupped hand into the pool, lifted it to his mouth, and tasted the water. "Good," he muttered, and proceeded to drink his fill. Then he took off his hat and sloshed water over his face and head.

"The tracks are not old," Thunder mused. "The dirt is still damp." Straightening up, he walked to his horse and unfastened the canteens from his saddle.

"Three riders. Bound to be scouts." Logan eyed the tracks. "Could be just passing through or scouting ahead for a war party. If so, they'll be camping here, and we don't want to be here when they arrive." He looked around, then pointed to a hill close by. "We'll hide in that cluster of trees, so we can watch the water hole. Better if we join them later; it'll give us a little edge."

"We have no edge in this game we are playing," Thunder said. "If the Comanches should discover that we are not horse thieves, our punishment will be worse than death." He added, "Even if they do believe we are outlaws, I wonder if they will take us to the Comancheros."

Logan laughed shortly. "Probably kill us and take the horses." All the time his eyes were riveted to the horizon. Always he was wary and on the lookout . . . and he wondered about Brenna.

"The woman did not return to Austin," Thunder announced. "She will not stop until her mission is completed, unless . . ."

Always amazed at the uncanny ability Thunder had to read his thoughts, Logan said, "No, she won't go back to Austin. I hope she has the good sense to take the long way around."

"You have been lost in thought since we left the wagon train," Thunder replied. "She has put her mark upon your heart." The words were a statement, not a question.

"No, my brother," Logan said, his voice tinged with exasperation, "she has not touched my heart, but I am worried." Occasionally Thunder's psychic ability bothered Logan, and this was one of those times. "She's a stubborn woman—a mighty stubborn woman—and she's hell-bent on taking that wagon train to Santa Fe by the shortest route possible."

"Perhaps the man will have some influence on her."

"I hope so," Logan said.

Thunder stood and returned to his horse, draping the straps of the canteens over the saddle. As soon as the horses were watered, both men mounted.

"I'll cover our tracks and scout ahead to see if I can find any signs. I'll meet you later."

Logan nodded. Giving the roan a nudge, he moved away from the water, toward the safety of the trees. As he rode, his thoughts again shifted to Brenna.

Several hours later, Thunder moved into the shelter of the trees. After he dismounted and secured his horse, he ran to join Logan, who lay concealed at the edge of the grove, field glasses to his eyes. "The Comanches are coming," the Indian said.

"I hope White-Hair is riding with them."

"We shall soon know," Thunder returned. "At the rate they are traveling, they should be at the water in two hours or so."

"Are they that far away?" Logan asked.

"No, they're riding leisurely and making no effort to hide their trail."

"Damned arrogance!"

Thunder smiled. "Not so much arrogance as confidence, my brother. And why should they not be

108

confident? They know they are in their country."
Taking the field glasses from Logan and being
extremely careful to keep them out of the sun to avoid
reflection on the lenses, he said, "Sleep until the
Comanches come. I will keep watch."

Not waiting for a second bidding, Logan lay down,
pulled his hat over his face, and went to sleep. He didn't
awaken until he heard Thunder's quiet "They are
coming." Instantly Logan was alert. He moved to the
edge of the trees and reached for the field glasses that
Thunder held out to him. Still hidden in the shade to
avoid detection, he trained his vision on the ridge west
of the water hole. He held his breath as the Comanches
topped the rise. At least fifty of them, all excellent
horsemen and warriors. Single file, they moved toward
the pool.

"Is the white-haired one with them?" Thunder asked.

Logan studied each Indian carefully. "Not that I can
tell."

"Shall we join them?"

Logan took a deep breath and dropped the field
glasses. "Might as well. This is what we've been waiting
for."

Before either of them could move toward the horses,
Thunder said, "I think that someone else is joining
them, my brother." He pointed to the northwest.
"Look."

A lone horseman, wearing a black serape, rode into
camp. His long cape billowed behind him, and a large
hat with a drooping brim protected his face from the
sun.

"A white man!" Logan breathed, cautiously shifting
the field glasses so he could see better, but the hat hid
the man's face from view. "Houston was right."

The rider joined the Comanches, sitting with them
around the fire, his back to Logan and Thunder. For a

long time and with eloquent gestures, he silently communicated with the chief. Adept in sign language, Logan and Thunder eavesdropped on the conversation.

"You have kept your word," the chief declared. "That is good."

"In the years that we have traded and ridden together, Buffalo Horn, I have always kept my word," the man replied.

The chief nodded as he gestured.

The Comanchero asked, "Why did you bring the young chief with you?"

"Animal Talker is the son of my brother. He is riding with me because my medicine is strong, and he wishes to be blessed by it."

"I don't like this," the man said. "Animal Talker is young and impetuous; he's insolent."

"That is the way with the young," Buffalo Horn replied. "You and I are getting old, my friend." He smiled, then asked, "When do we attack?"

"As soon as my man comes." The Comanchero turned and waved toward his horse. "I bring gifts to my friends."

Talk ceased as one of the braves went to the pack mule the man had brought with him and unleashed a large trunk. Logan watched as the Comanchero passed out gifts to each of the braves. Afterward they ate with great ceremony but did no talking. When the meal was finished, the Indians played games. The white man watched.

Knowing the Comanches were preparing for battle, Logan and Thunder were reluctant to join them; they, too, watched. Hours passed until finally the sun was sinking in the west.

"What can their target be?" Logan wondered aloud.

"Who would they be attacking this far out on the plains?"

Having no answer, he raised his head to let his gaze scale the horizon. In the far distance—so far away he couldn't be sure—he thought he saw a cloud of dust. The man for whom the Comanches waited! Although the cloud, no bigger than a man's fist, was too far away for him to see, Logan focused the field glasses, trained them in that direction, and watched. Eventually he saw a speck—a speck that was moving toward the water hole. It drew nearer, its color changing from black to grey. Still it was nothing but an indistinguishable blur.

"Who is it?" Thunder asked, his eyes also trained on the rider.

"Probably the man they're expecting," Logan muttered. Long minutes passed before he murmured, "Damn . . ." His voice trailed into stunned silence. Then he exclaimed, "Damn! It's Kirkwood."

And where Kirkwood was, Brenna and her wagon train would be not far behind! Logan's blood boiled hot. That headstrong little fool was going through Comancheria after all. Logan was beyond angry; he was furious. Just when he and Thunder were finally making contact with the Comanches! Possibly with the Comancheros themselves! How dare that damned woman throw a kink in his plans because of her stupidity and foolhardiness! He knew she was trouble from the minute he laid eyes on her; he ought to let her stew in her own juice.

But he knew he couldn't do that. Gentleman he might not be, wouldn't even claim to be, but he was humane. Still, Brenna had made this choice knowing full well what awaited her. Logan had made sure he told her—explicitly, graphically. In the throes of indecision, he turned his head and looked at the

111

Comanche camp, now alive with frenzied activity in preparation for an attack. He knew he had to get word to the caravan.

"There's no way we can warn Kirkwood," Logan said, "without revealing our hiding place. No way we can reach him now."

"Do you see the wagon train?" Thunder asked.

Logan shook his head. "Not even the dust. Kirkwood must be scouting ahead." Suddenly Logan asked, "What is today?"

Thunder chuckled. "Worry for the woman is affecting your thoughts, my brother?"

"Irritation that the woman is upsetting my plans," Logan corrected gruffly. Then he answered himself, "Friday. That means the wagon train will be resting the day after tomorrow. Kirkwood is scouting ahead for a good site with water."

"He is an easy target for the Comanches," Thunder commented as Kirkwood continued to ride directly toward the creek, his pace steady. Then he said, "He calls himself a scout, MacDougald, yet he does not behave as one. Do you not think it strange that he has not noticed any signs of the Comanches? They made no effort to hide their tracks."

"I was thinking that. He rides as if he knows the country and knows what's waiting for him."

The ponderous silence was broken when Thunder said, "He is the one for whom the Comanchero waits."

"He is the one," Logan quietly agreed, his calmness hiding a fear that gnawed at his guts. This man—this traitor—was the one to whom Brenna had entrusted the safety of her life and the wagon train. Rather than listening to him, Logan thought, she had chosen to listen to Abbott Kirkwood. Logan wondered how he was going to warn her; then he wondered why he should be the one when she had flaunted his advice.

As Kirkwood neared, Logan and Thunder watched him ride into the camp. He greeted the other visitor, and the two of them talked for a long while. Then the man who dressed in black stood and addressed the Comanches in sign language. Slowly Logan learned the grim truth. Kirkwood, taking advantage of the people's ignorance of the country, had deliberately guided the caravan around water and left them corralled some thirty miles behind. Thirsty and exhausted, they were easy victims for an ambush.

Through hand language the man reminded the Indians that the women who were captured were not to be tortured or damaged in any way. If they were, they would be unsuitable for his purposes. Logan's heart lurched; his stomach tightened at the thought of the women's future—of Brenna's future—should the Comanches succeed in defeating the wagon train.

The Comanches nodded their acceptance; then their leader answered. They would pray and sing in preparation for battle until night fell to give them cover. Afterward they would move toward the wagon train. "It is our custom," the Comanche chief signed, "to attack at dawn—the time of day when the Great Spirit favors us with victory. This time we will follow your advice to attack later in the day when the train is moving." Then he asked, "What are you going to do?"

The man in black answered, "As I agreed, I shall ride with you. Kirkwood will return to our stronghold in the canyon to get your goods ready."

"You remember your promise?" the chief gestured.

"I never forget my promises, Buffalo Horn," the man's hands moved in reply. "You shall have the six-shooters."

"The same kind of weapons the rangers use?"

"The same."

Logan lowered the field glasses and turned to

Thunder. "Houston is right. The Comancheros are directing the Indians in these raids for their own purposes."

"Payment is good," Thunder said. "Horses, cattle, and women for six-shooters, which will give the Comanches the decided advantage over the rangers again."

Logan emitted a low curse. "That's my next question: Where are the Comancheros getting the six-shooters from?"

Logan and Thunder looked at each other. Without saying a word, each of them knew. Someone in civilization was supplying the Comancheros with weapons as well as information.

"I want that bastard," Logan said.

"We shall get him," Thunder promised, laying a hand on Logan's shoulder to squeeze reassuringly. "Now we have other things to do. I shall follow Kirkwood."

"I'll follow Kirkwood," Logan said.

Thunder shook his head. "If you were heart-whole, I would agree with your decision, but you are not."

Logan opened his mouth to protest, but Thunder continued to speak.

"You know as well as I that you are thinking about the woman. You must take care of the woman and the wagon train. If you leave now, you will have a few hours head start."

The two men stared at each other for a moment; then Logan nodded.

Chapter Eight

Ordinarily Logan would have taken the time to absorb the beauty of the sunrise, but not today. As if dogged by the devil himself, Logan urged his roan on. Giving thought only to the wagon train, none to himself or the beast, Logan continued to ride hard, as he had all through the night. He was exhausted and covered in dust. He lifted his arm across his face to wipe the perspiration from his forehead and gazed into the distance—nothing but endless miles of desert.

Brenna's face swam in front of him; he saw the smile that so easily touched her full lips; he saw the eyes that so quickly changed from blue to green. One minute he was angry with her because she had messed up his plans; the next he was worried sick. He would remember the cries of his mother and sister. He closed his eyes in an effort to still the voices. Instead he saw his father's mutilated body, his mother's violated one.

"Damn," he muttered.

He couldn't understand why Brenna hadn't used better judgment. Evidently where that wagon train was concerned, she didn't have any. If her stupidity affected only her, he wouldn't have given a damn. But it didn't! It affected him and Thunder and the entire caravan. Again a wave of anger rolled through him. More precious time he was wasting because of this woman.

But at the same time, he was angry because time was passing too slowly, and he felt so helpless. Darkness had obscured Kirkwood's trail, forcing Logan to stop periodically, dismount, and search until he found it again. His thoughts were in turmoil. From the beginning Kirkwood had been working with the Comancheros, so the ambush was laid with cunning and deliberation—such coldhearted premeditation. The same questions recurred to plague Logan: What was Kirkwood doing in Austin? Was he the liaison between the Comancheros and someone in Texas? Was Houston right? A Texan was a traitor!

Logan's thoughts skittered back and forth between subjects but always returned to Brenna. He knew what instructions Kirkwood left with her. Since he had told her that water was a day's journey due west and to move in that direction whether he returned or not, she would scout ahead by herself. She would have to; the people and animals needed the water.

Logan topped the crest and spotted the caravan in the far distance. *Lined up and ready to move! Only to be massacred by the Comanches at the caravan's weakest moment!* He heard the bugle sound the daily call—or did he imagine he heard it? A smile of relief briefly touched his haggard face. As if he sensed the excitement and anticipation that jolted through the man, the horse gained new wind to gallop faster. When Logan heard Gabby shout the order to move out, Brenna was bestride her horse.

Brenna took her place at the head of the caravan to ride beside the lead wagon—her personal wagon driven by Jonesey. Riding beside her, Roger tugged the brim of his hat to pull it farther over his face as a shield against the morning glare. Brenna turned to watch

Gabby move from the rear of the caravan forward as he made the final inspection prior to stretching out. She was proud of her wagon train. Under Gabby's firm hand and guidance, the men had converted from "greenhorns" into experienced teamsters and escorts. She had no doubt they would safely reach Bent's Fort. Kirkwood had promised that water was a little more than a day's travel away, and he had assured them that he had seen no signs of Indians. By pressing on, they would reach the creek tonight.

"Figured Kirkwood would be back this morning," Gabby muttered when he joined Brenna. "Don't much like starting out without him."

"I don't either," Brenna replied. She, too, was worried about the scout's lengthy absence.

"God," Roger exclaimed, "but this desert's an eerie place! I think it has eyes. I have the feeling that we're being watched." He squinted and rotated his head from side to side as he looked furtively about.

"The plains do have eyes," Gabby replied. "Only we call them Comanches."

"Comanches," Roger uttered dispassionately. "I've been promised a chance to fight the Indians ever since I arrived in Texas. So far I haven't seen a one of them." Disgust tinged his voice. "And Kirkwood assured us that no Comanches were in sight."

"Wouldn't count on that," Gabby replied. "I've been skittish ever since we've had to veer west."

"Me, too," Brenna said. "But we had to." She spoke the words as if she were convincing herself of the truth. At the oddest moments—at the times when she least expected it—she would hear Logan's words: *The price of trailblazing is high!* She shook herself mentally. "Kirkwood said that was the nearest water, and we have to have it." Again as if to reassure herself that her decision had been a wise one, she said, "And you know

117

Kirkwood wouldn't have led us this way if he hadn't felt that it was safe. All along he's advised us to steer clear of Comancheria. Besides"—optimism gave her voice added strength—"we're only on the outskirts of Comancheria. Kirkwood said the Comanches had moved even farther west since the Linneville raid, closer to Santa Fe. He said we weren't in any immediate danger." *She had to believe Kirkwood. She simply had to!* Smiling, she leaned over to lay a comforting hand on Gabby's arm. "As soon as we get water, we'll start moving to the northeast again. I promise."

Gabby's callused hand covered Brenna's, and he spared her a rare smile, but he said nothing. As she looked into the faded brown eyes, Brenna's heart lurched. Never had she seen the old man's emotions so openly revealed. That he loved her, she had never questioned. Now she saw the deep concern that she had on occasion so lightly brushed aside.

"Everything is going to be all right," she assured him.

"Yep," he said, moving his hand, "it's gonna be all right." He turned his head to spit, wiped his hand across his mouth, then lifted his arm in the air and swung it forward, giving the shout: "Stretch out!"

Wagon wheels creaked; whips cracked through the air; commands were shouted and cursed at the animals.

Everything is going to be all right! Brenna's words spun in her mind. She had said them so glibly, so matter-of-factly, but even she wasn't so sure of their truth. Gabby was a veteran of the frontier; he felt things in his bones—and generally he felt right. She knew without his telling her that he was worried about their safety—and so was she!

Brenna wasn't afraid for herself; she'd known what dangers existed when she amassed the caravan, but she was responsible for these settlers, among them women—women the Comancheros wanted for slavery in Mexico. And the deeper into Indian territory they rode, the heavier her responsibility weighed on her. She shouldn't have taken them on in Austin, but they had begged her. They had offered her a sum of money she felt she couldn't turn down. She had needed the cash.

She settled in the saddle, pushed her hat back, and gazed around, but she saw nothing disturbing—just the dust that the morning wind swirled into the air. Her eyes lighted on the distant hill. She saw the rider. Unconsciously she emitted a sigh of relief, and a smile curved her lips. She was worrying about nothing.

"Kirkwood," she shouted.

"Nope," Gabby said. "That ain't Kirkwood."

"Who is it then?" Roger asked, straining to see through the heat waves that already undulated through the air.

Brenna lifted her hand and shielded her eyes. "It . . . can't . . . be . . . Logan," she whispered in disbelief, then added emphatically, "It is," at the same time that she nudged the gray into a gallop to close the distance between her and Logan. As on the riverbank when she and Logan had made love, Brenna forgot about her wagon train; she thought only of Logan MacDougald.

Then she and Logan met; they reined their horses and stopped. For a moment they could only look at one another. Logan's anger was forgotten; Brenna's guilt and shame melted away. In that moment they knew how special each was to the other. Both were covered with dust, and their clothes were wet with perspiration—Brenna didn't have water to bathe in; Logan hadn't taken the time—but they weren't concerned with outward appearances. They were together!

Logan had never been more handsome, Brenna

thought, her eyes slowly drinking their fill of the man who had become the essence of her life and dreams. She didn't care that he had several day's beard growth; she didn't see the dust that was plastered to his skin. She saw only the man who in loving her body had touched her heart and soul.

"Logan," she murmured, and two tears of joy wended their way down her cheeks.

Logan moved closer to her and leaned over. With a crooked forefinger, he gently flicked the tears from her face and smiled. "Hello."

In an instant of fluid motion, he was off the horse on the ground, Brenna with him. Their arms went around each other, and they simply held each other tightly—so tightly it almost hurt. Tightly as if they were afraid they might lose each other again.

Brenna pulled back, and the two gazed at each other. Logan temporarily forgot the Comanches in the joy of their reunion. He was so glad to see her; he just wanted to look, but the brim of her hat kept flopping in her face. "Take this damned thing off," he commanded as he jerked the hat from her head and stared into her gritty upturned face. Once he focused on those sea-green eyes, Logan was lost. The flames of worry and anger were quickly doused, to be replaced by a fire of passion in his loins. He didn't care that Brenna was dirty, that her clothes were soaked with perspiration, that strands of hair stuck to her face. He saw her beauty; he felt her supple smoothness. He lowered his mouth to hers in a long and lingering kiss. He tasted her goodness.

"I didn't think I'd ever see you again," she confessed when Logan finally lifted his mouth from hers.

Her words brought Logan's purpose forefront. "You wouldn't have," he said, "if you hadn't made the stupid decision to travel into Comancheria."

"Stupid decision!" Brenna blazed with indignation. She had suffered enough self-recrimination; she didn't need Logan MacDougald to point his accusing finger at her. "I'll have you know," she flared at him, "I made the only choice possible. I had no other alternative. We'd been days without water." She pushed out of Logan's arms. "We are totally without water, and although he didn't want to lead us into Comancheria, Kirkwood said this was the nearest water hole."

"What happened to your wagon boss?"

Brenna looked at Logan blankly for a few minutes. "Nothing's happened to him. Why?"

"Shouldn't he be the one making a decision of this sort? Isn't that why you hired him to see your caravan through to Santa Fe?"

Brenna was abashed. Against Gabby's better judgment, she made the choice. She had listened to and been persuaded by the people. "I made the decision to come this way." She pleaded with Logan for understanding. "I had to think of the people." She saw the flicker in Logan's eyes and felt the sudden muscle spasm in his jaws. "Something's wrong, isn't it?"

"You're damned right! Kirkwood is leading you into an ambush. A couple of hours behind me are the Comanches."

"No," Brenna said, shaking her head. "That can't be true."

"I may be many things," Logan said, "but I don't make a habit of lying."

"Kirkwood isn't a Comanchero! I know he isn't!" Brenna exclaimed, trying to convince herself.

Logan caught her upper arms. "It's true. Kirkwood is working with the Comanches; they're headed toward your caravan right now. They know you're out of water and moving slow."

"How . . ." Brenna asked, unable to complete her question.

"Yesterday Thunder and I happened upon a Comanche camp close to the water where Kirkwood is leading you. A white man joined them—"

"The Comancheros?"

Logan nodded. "Later Kirkwood rode in. Since they talked in sign language, Thunder and I could understand them."

Silently Brenna listened as Logan repeated Kirkwood's conversation with the Comanches. By the time he was through, Gabby had arrived, and the wagon train was not far behind.

"Didn't expect to see you so soon," the wagon boss said, looking down at Logan.

Logan smiled grimly. "Me either."

"But I'll have to admit, I'm sure glad to see you." As Logan and Brenna remounted, Gabby asked, "Where's the Cherokee?"

"Following Kirkwood." Succinctly Logan repeated his tale for the wagon boss.

Gabby spat and watched the dry earth drink up the tobacco juice. He didn't look at Brenna or say *I told you so.* "I been feeling trouble." He wiped his mouth with his sleeve. "Felt the Comanches were out here." He looked at Logan. "How close?"

"An hour or two behind me."

Gabby turned the horse and held his arm up as he gave the order to halt. When the lead wagon drew abreast Gabby and Logan, a grin spanned Jonesey's thin face to expose his brown teeth. "Howdy, Mr. MacDougald; I'm right surprised to see you, but I'm sure glad it's you."

His words were lost in Gabby's shout. "Comanches coming! Corral these wagons!"

"Comanches!" Roger exclaimed, and a smile suddenly illuminated his exhausted features. His adrenaline started to flow heavily. "You mean we're going to get to fight the Indians after all?"

As he remounted, Logan gave Roger a squelching glare, but he said nothing to the young escort. His main thought was to save the wagon train. He and Gabby gave their attentions to the forming of the corral—only, in this instance, it was to be a fort.

The people obeyed Gabby's commands as easily as if they were making camp at the end of the day. They unharnessed the mules and oxen. Three wagons formed each side of the outward square, two the inner. Elijah Caldwell, the assistant wagon boss, drove the horses, livestock, and extra draft animals to the center of the compound. The younger women were ordered to herd the livestock to keep them from stampeding.

Logan assigned positions. The men were to go behind the wagons forming the outer square. The women he located immediately to the rear of them so they could reload the guns. Logan stationed Gabby in one corner, Roger in the other; each was to command a side of the square.

"I'll take this corner," Logan said.

"And I'll take the other one," Brenna told him.

Logan opened his mouth to protest; he didn't want Brenna endangered.

"I wouldn't have made the offer if I didn't know what I was doing," she said, her eyes never wavering from his. "And it's my fault we're in this trouble."

"Are you sure?"

"I'm sure."

Because they could see the Indians when they came, the people didn't immediately take their places. Rather, they drew together and instinctively talked in whispered tones.

"Mr. Langdon!" Sam's shout startled the men. He ran to where Gabby stood, a rifle awkwardly cradled in his arms. "Where"—he took several deep breaths—"do you want me to get?" Then he saw Logan, and his face lit up. "Mr. MacDougald"—Sam's sentence was divided into wheezing intakes of air—"we've been so busy since—you arrived that—I haven't had—the chance to greet you. Under other cir—cumstances it—would be good—to see you, but under—these, it's—absolutely reassuring."

"Nice to see you again, Mr. Roper," came Logan's curt response, the abruptness softened by a quick, fleeting smile on the otherwise impassive face. He observed the unfamiliar, careless way Sam handled a gun. "Do you know how to use that?"

Sam reached up to brush an errant strand of hair from his forehead. His eyes twinkled, and his lips parted into a smile. "Not really, but—I figure there's—no better time to begin—than now." A cough choked off his chuckle. "What do you think?"

Logan shook his head with patient amusement. "As long as you know which end to point at what."

"Oh, I think I do," Sam returned.

"Who'll be foolish enough to stand behind you and reload for you?" Horace Faraday called out, the others joining in nervous laughter.

"I will," Gertrude Dawkins replied, coming up behind Sam with another rifle and a box of ammunition.

After Logan delegated authority, he took his position next to Sam, and everyone waited, minutes turning into an hour.

"Think maybe they'll change their minds now that we've moved into the corral?" Gabby asked as he fished in his pocket for his plug of tobacco.

"No," Logan answered, "they'll attack. From Kirkwood they learned all your strengths and weaknesses, and they know you have no water." Remembering the payment the Comanches expected for their massacre of the caravan, Logan added, "Their incentive is strong enough."

Gabby bit off a large cud, settled it into the pocket of his jaw, and chewed a long time. Finally, the waiting got to him. "I hate Indians!" he muttered, his nervousness making him talk louder than he had meant to. "Ain't any of them good but the dead 'uns." As the words left his mouth, he turned his head to meet Logan's impassive stare. Wondering if he had offended Logan, the wagon boss looked embarrassed and said, "Guess it's different for you, though, being raised by 'em an' all."

"Yes," Logan replied, taking no offense at the outburst, "it's different for me. I'm not an Indian hater. I can understand how the Comanches feel; I can understand their desperation."

"You sound just like Houston!" Brenna exclaimed.

"When you've seen what ghastly things the Comanches can do—" Gabby began, only to be interrupted by Logan's quiet voice.

"I was nine years old when I watched the Comanches torture and kill my parents and take my older sister captive, Mr. Langdon." Logan's voice betrayed none of his emotions. He would never forget the chief—his image was indelibly marked on Logan's mind. Even now he could see the thick black hair with the gleaming white streak.

Dumbfounded, Brenna and Gabby could only stare at him.

"Ironically, Cherokees found, adopted, and raised me. And three years ago I saw what was left of the village I had lived in after Lamar's rangers were through with it. What they did to my Indian family

125

wasn't any different from what the Comanches had done to my white family." Logan pushed his hat back and wiped his arm across his forehead. "Should I hate all whites now?"

Having no answer, Gabby walked to his corner and resumed his watch. Talking ceased, and the sun steadily moved upward, marking the passage of time. The waiting was getting tense when suddenly Jonesey cried, "I see them. I see the Comanches! Look to the west."

The Comanches topped the ridge, their line sweeping the horizon. If their reputation weren't enough to strike fear into the hearts of the travelers, their confidence, born of years of training and surviving on the west Texas plains, was. Straight and proud they sat their horses.

"That one," Logan called for all to hear, "the one who is holding the war lance in the air, is Buffalo Horn, the chief. He's our target. If we kill him, we can win the attack." Logan hoped so, but then he remembered Buffalo Horn's nephew, Animal Talker. Being a young warrior, he might assume command of the attack at the death of his uncle.

The settlers, their eyes glued to the hill, watched the Comanches' sure descent. The silence within the wagon fort grew heavier and more oppressive.

Totally oblivious to Maude Hemphill, who stood behind to reload her rifles, Brenna raised an arm to wipe the sheen of nervous perspiration from her face. She had heard about the Comanches; she had even seen some of the friendly ones on the streets of San Antonio. She had seen the victims of Comanche raiding parties, both dead and alive. Now, for the first time in her life, she was staring directly at white settlers' most dangerous enemies.

She dropped first one hand then the other and wiped

the perspiration on the legs of her trousers. She dipped the brim of her hat lower on her forehead to shield out as much of the glare as possible. The waiting was getting to her . . . to everyone; tension built up again. Brenna felt as if her nerves were being stretched from Victoria to San Antonio.

She lifted the rifle, aimed it at one of the warriors, and teased the trigger with her finger. Too far to kill him, she knew, but she wanted to do something to end this game of nerves. Then Buffalo Horn lifted his war lance in the air; the braves stopped at the bottom of the incline.

"Why don't they come on?" the man next to Logan muttered. He was impatient for the fracas to begin. "What are they waiting for?"

"They want us to get nervous and overanxious," Logan answered. "They want us to be trigger-happy, so we'll waste our ammunition."

"Which we would if you weren't here," Sam said. "If you weren't here, I'd be shooting like crazy."

"No, you wouldn't," Logan said. "With the exception of Gabby, none of you have faced Comanches before. You'll find that you have more courage than you think."

Suddenly Jonesey's cry filled the air. "More Indians to the back of us."

Wheezing, Sam wheeled around. "More of 'em!" he exclaimed. He dropped the rifle to the ground and fumbled in his pocket for his handkerchief. "This—this sand, it's—it's getting to me." His breathing was so painful, he clutched his chest.

"What is it, Sam?" Gertrude cried. She dropped the ammunition she was holding and ran forward.

"Nothing," he gasped. "I'll—be—all—right."

Having observed that Sam's respiratory problem worsened when his emotions intensified, Logan said,

"Sam, I have some medicine which might help you to breathe better."

"What is it?" Gertrude asked as she took the handkerchief from Sam and folded it into a triangle, which she fastened over the lower part of his face.

"Medicine"—Sam wheezed—"medicine—doesn't seem—to help."

"This will," Logan promised. "Mrs. Dawkins, on my horse you'll find a small pouch—a red bandanna tied together. I keep some herbs in it. Get the small brown pieces, grind them up in some water, and give it to Sam to drink." To Sam he said, "It'll taste bitter as gall, but it'll help you. Go to bed immediately because you're going to get sleepy."

"I can't—help—you fight Indians," Sam gasped.

Logan said, "You can't help us fight Indians as ill as you are. All of us will be better off if you take care of yourself."

Sam nodded and he and Gertrude walked into the inner corral toward his carriage. The men closed the gap Sam left, and the waiting and watching continued.

"How much longer?" one of the settlers muttered.

"Not much," Logan drawled, his eyes raking the surrounding countryside to see the Indians fanning out to form a circle around the train. "They're getting ready—"

Before Logan could complete his sentence, an ululation the like of which most of the travelers had never heard before—an unearthly, bloodcurdling war whoop—rent the air to frighten them even more. Buffalo Horn's spear came down, and the Comanche warriors charged.

"Don't shoot until I give the word." Logan's voice was loud in the silence that fell inside the corral.

The Indians came closer, volleys of arrows flying through the air.

"How much longer before we shoot?" Roger hunched a shoulder to wipe the perspiration from his brow.

"Close enough that your bullet hits the mark," Logan answered.

Brenna watched as the Comanches circled with regularity and precision, coming nearer the wagons with each revolution. They were looping so fast, she could hardly distinguish one from the other. Then she saw a warrior dart from the circle and move directly toward her. She and the brave stared at each other. The paint, smeared across his cheeks, distorted his features, and his mouth was curled in contempt. His eyes, ringed in black, were deep, churning abysses of hate.

Controlling her fear, Brenna placed her cheek on the stock of the rifle and drew down on the brave at the very moment he loosed the arrow from his bow. At the same instant Logan gave the order to fire, his voice ringing clearly over the compound. Brenna squeezed the trigger, then flinched when the arrow grazed her arm; she felt the fire as it slowly spread down her arm and through her shoulder, but she also felt a grim satisfaction when the Indian tumbled from his horse.

She glanced at the blood discoloring her sleeve around a jagged hole in it, but she didn't take the time to tend her wound. She reached for the loaded gun that Maude Hemphill handed her and fired again . . . and again . . . and again.

She heard the cries of pain around her, the curses and the shouts; she heard the Indians yowling. Above all the commotion she heard Logan's orders. This had to end, she thought. The cries of the Indians were getting to her. She saw Buffalo Horn circling, moving closer. She raised her rifle, laid her cheek against the stock, and aimed. When she was sure, she pulled the trigger. She saw the spurt of blood first, then the surprised look on the warrior's face. He slumped and fell across the horse. As quickly as the attack began, it ended. The caravan was enveloped in silence.

"Is Buffalo Horn dead?" Caldwell yelled. "Did we get him?"

"I don't know if he's dead or not," Logan replied. "He's wounded." A pause followed in which Logan turned to look down the wagons at Brenna. "Yes, Mr. Caldwell," he announced with pride, "we got him. In fact, it was your wagon captain who aimed and delivered the shot."

Logan couldn't see Brenna's wound as they stared at each other, and for the moment she had forgotten it. Her entire world was Logan MacDougald. The warmth of his gaze charged the air around her with electricity. She and Logan had been one in love and purpose; now they were one in survival. She glowed with pride at the admiration she saw in his eyes.

"Is it over?" one of the escorts called.

"I think so," Logan answered. "If Buffalo Horn's not dead, he's badly wounded. His braves will probably take him back to the main camp, but," he added, "let's not get comfortable too quick. A young buck might decide to take over."

Closing her eyes, Brenna collapsed against the wagon, all energy suddenly drained away. Her arm ached so badly she thought she would scream. Then she felt Logan standing beside her. She opened her eyes and turned, and again, as if they were the only two people in the world, they stared at each other. The wound forgotten, she lifted her hand to touch his cheek. When she did, she moaned softly in pain.

"You're hurt," Logan said, gently turning her so that he could look at the arm.

"Just a surface wound."

Logan sat her down and pulled the material of the

shirt aside to inspect the cut. Fresh blood seeped out of the long, diagonal gash. "It may be," he agreed. "We've got to be careful, though. They may have dipped their arrows in poison."

"Burns pretty bad," Brenna admitted, then asked, "If it's poison . . . will the poison kill me?"

"Not on a flesh wound," he returned. "Put you off your feet for a long time with fever and delirium."

Before they could move, Jonesey's shout echoed from around the corner. "Miss Brenna! Miss Brenna, come quick. Gabby's been wounded."

"No!" Brenna screamed. Her pain forgotten, she jumped to her feet and ran to Gabby's corner position. *Not Gabby!* He was all the family she had left. The only friend. *He couldn't be part of the price she was paying to get these wagons to Santa Fe! Oh, God, no! He couldn't! Not after he insisted on her going around Comancheria!*

"I'll take care of Gabby," Logan said. "You get your arm tended to."

"I'm fine," Brenna maintained. "I want to know how bad Gabby's hurt."

"I said I'd take care of Gabby," Logan repeated firmly as he caught her good arm. "You've got to take care of your arm. I don't want both of you dead."

Brenna jerked from Logan's grasp. "I'm going to Gabby!" When she reached the corner of the square where Gabby lay, Brenna saw the arrow protruding from his chest. "No," she cried, running to kneel over him. Tears rushed down her cheeks.

"There, there, girl," the old man said gruffly, his hand coming up to cap her head. "Ain't no need to be crying." He drew in a deep gulp of air, his chest heaving with the effort. His face contorted in pain.

Logan knelt beside Brenna. "The arrow's got to come out," he said.

"Ain't no need," Gabby replied, a gurgle in his chest. "It's a war arrow, MacDougald, and it's hit me in the wrong place to do much pulling." He coughed, spitting up blood.

"Of course it's got to come out," Brenna exclaimed, slipping her arms under Gabby's shoulders. "We're going to move you and take care of you—"

Logan caught Brenna's hands. "The arrow is barbed, so the point has turned crosswise. It won't come out without tearing him up."

"What are we going to do?" Brenna asked, her voice barely above a whisper, her face drained of color.

"Ain't much you can do, gal." Another spasm of coughing stopped his words.

Brenna looked up into Logan's face. He shook his head.

"Oh, Gabby," Brenna sobbed.

"Now, gal," Gabby gasped, "don't go getting all emotional now. You've been pretty brave so far. See if you can last a little bit longer. If them Comanches come again, MacDougald's gonna need all the firepower he can get." Gabby smiled and reached out to catch and squeeze her hand. "You're the best he's got, gal, and don't—don't give up this expedition on account of—me."

"I love you, Gabby," Brenna confessed, not caring that tears flowed down her cheeks. "Really I do."

"I love you, Brendy gal." He lifted a hand, knocked her hat off, and touched her face to brush the tears away. His fingers spread into her hair. "Pretty eyes," he said. "Never quite sure what color they was." A crooked smile—filled with pain and grief—touched his lips. "I—love—" Gabby's breath came out in a long sigh; his head rolled to the side, and his eyes set.

"No," Brenna screamed, flinging herself across Gabby. "You can't leave me all alone. You can't,

Gabriel Zachariah Langdon! You can't!"

Logan caught her shoulders and pulled her back into his arms.

"I didn't mean for Gabby to die," she sobbed. "I didn't mean for him to die."

Understanding Brenna's anguish, Logan laid his hand across her cheek and pressed her face into his chest. "Cry," he murmured. "Cry all you want to, baby girl." Logan picked Brenna up. To Roger he said, "Take over while I'm gone. Keep the men at their stations and keep your eyes open. I'm going to take care of Mrs. Allen's wound. Don't want it to get infected."

Roger nodded and watched as Logan carried Brenna to her wagon. As soon as they were out of hearing distance, he said to Maude, "Cover Mr. Langdon's body with a blanket. We'll bury him as soon as we can."

Logan laid Brenna on her pallet. Then he rummaged through her things until he found some washrags and her tin basin. Setting them on the tailgate, he hopped out of the wagon. "I'll be right back."

A short time later, Logan reappeared to fill the basin with water from his canteen. "Time to clean that cut," he said, easily jumping into the wagon and kneeling beside her. He slipped his arm beneath her shoulders to raise her up. "First, this shirt has to come off."

In numbed silence Brenna followed his instructions. Her heart grieved too much for her to feel the pain as Logan cleaned and bandaged her arm. She watched as he opened the red bandanna and extracted some herbs, which he pulverized in a tin cup and mixed with Indian meal to form a paste.

"This will draw the poison out," he said, and continued to talk in low, soothing tones as he covered her wound with the salve; then he sewed a buffalo skin around it. After that he helped her into a clean shirt.

133

"Here," he said, picking up the cup before she could lie down, "drink this." He held the container out to her. "It'll help your wound to heal quicker."

"Will it heal a grieving soul?" she asked, two tears slipping down her cheeks.

"No," he replied, "but it will help you sleep, and sleep is a healing balm for your body. If your body is healthy, you can deal with your sorrow much better."

Brenna raised her head and drank the vile liquid. Then she collapsed on the pallet. "Is that what you gave Sam?" she asked.

"Yes." Logan stretched out and pulled her against him. Again he talked, and Brenna closed her eyes and listened. She heard not so much his words but the caring in his tone. "Antelope Hunter said this was a magical herb that brings healing to both the body and the soul."

"How?" Brenna mumbled, gladly letting the drowsiness settle over her to close out her pain and sorrow.

"You will go to sleep in a few minutes, and you will have dreams—wonderful dreams. The Indians believe these dreams are a manifestation of your heart's secret desires. They also say you will meet your spirit guides, who will show you things to come."

On and on he talked, telling her about the dreamlike properties of the herbs. When she was breathing evenly, Logan eased up, but the movement aroused her.

"Where are you going?" she mumbled, making an effort to sit up and grab for him.

"I have to get back to the men," he told her.

"Do you think the Indians are going to return?" Her voice was slightly slurred.

"I don't think so, but I need to be with the men in case they do. I'm going to send one of the women to sit with you."

"You're not leaving me, are you?" she asked, a tinge of desperation creeping into her voice. Because of the drug that Logan administered, she was uninhibited by conscious thought; she spoke her heart. "You're going back to your job, and I'm going to be all alone."

"No, I'm not leaving you . . . right now." He smiled and tenderly pressed her into the blankets. "Now, lie down and go to sleep." Kneeling beside her, he planted a kiss on her forehead. "I'll be back later to check on you," he whispered.

As Logan passed the multicolored carriage, he checked with Gertrude to see how Sam was doing.

"Sleeping like a baby," she told him with a smile. "Thank you so much, Mr. MacDougald, for giving him that medicine. He's breathing so much better now." Then she asked, "How's Brenna taking Mr. Langdon's death?"

"Not too good," Logan replied. "To make matters worse, she's wounded herself. The arrow was probably dipped in poison, so she's in for several days of fever. She needs to be watched closely.

Gertrude's face clouded with concern. "I'll keep an eye on her for you."

"Thank you, Mrs. Dawkins," Logan said. "I'd appreciate that."

Logan moved around the square to check on the men. He slapped some of them on the back, joked with them, and praised them for a job well done. The men intuitively respected him and his judgment. They naturally accepted his leadership now that Gabby was dead and Brenna wounded.

"Do you reckon they're going to come back?" Roger asked when Logan approached him.

"I don't think so," Logan said, "but we can only wait to be sure. If they haven't come back by nightfall, I'll ride out to check."

Roger nodded, his eyes scaling the horizon in front of him. "I put Jonesey in Mr. Langdon's position," he said. "Elijah in Miss Brenna's."

"Good," Logan murmured, moving to his corner.

The hours passed, but nothing happened. The setting sun allowed dusk to envelop the wagon train. When Logan could see the moon, he called so everyone could hear, "The Comanches aren't going to come back tonight. Go to bed and get some rest if you can. Mr. Hollis, post extra guards tonight."

"How do you know they're not coming back?" Roger rushed to Logan's side.

Logan pointed to the pale crescent moon, hardly more than an outline in the darkening sky. "Comanches don't by choice make an attack in the dark, and they never raid or attack when the moon is shaped like that with the horns pointing upward. According to them, the moon is full and running over, and there is the likelihood of rain, after which their trails can be easily traced on the moist earth."

"Are they still out there somewhere?" Roger asked.

"Yeah," Logan said, "they're still out there, and I'm going to find out what they're up to."

Chapter Nine

Logan had a difficult time tracking the Comanches, but he played a hunch and rode to the nearest canyon about ten miles from the wagon train. Coming up the southern side, he used the range of hills and darkness as cover. When he was concealed by a large boulder not far from where he figured the Indians were cloistered, he tethered his horse and cautiously made his way closer to the camp.

The braves were asleep, but guards had been posted. They were taking no chances of a surprise counter-attack by the whites. Since there was nothing he could do until morning, Logan slipped down behind the boulder for a few hours of sleep.

Movement in the camp awakened him at mid-morning. He squirmed around so that he could see better. The warriors ate their pemmican breakfast quickly and made conversation only when necessary. Yesterday he had counted over fifty of them. Now he counted only twenty or so, and he saw no sign of Buffalo Horn.

He saw no evidence of their preparing for another attack on the wagon train. Yet they made no preparation to return to their main camp either. Logan was puzzled. Periodic attacks would assure them victory, and they knew that as well as he. They had the decided advantage in this battle.

Unable to solve the riddle, Logan once again pushed his head above the boulder to see a young warrior, wearing a buffalo headdress, ride into camp and dismount. He briefly talked with warriors. Logan couldn't hear because he was too far away. Every now and then he saw the braves nod and murmur an acknowledgment or agreement. Still Logan saw none of the excitement and fervor that preceded an attack.

The warrior pointed, and Logan followed the movement of his hand to see the man in the black serape ride in. This time the stranger was facing Logan, but still Logan couldn't distinguish his features. The hat fell across the man's face. After he had dismounted and walked to the circle of Comanche braves, he whipped the hat from his head to reveal a head of graying black hair. He whisked the huge cape over his head and laid it across one of the large logs on which the braves were sitting. When he sat down, the warrior in charge resumed talking.

But Logan's interest wasn't on the Indian or what he had to say. He couldn't take his eyes off the white man. The Comanchero was tall and thin, and the black shirt and trousers he wore accented his lean gauntness. His eyes were emotionless and hollow, his nose long, his mouth slivered. Logan's stomach tied into a knot when he saw the large scar that jagged across his temple and cheek down his neck . . . into his shoulder. Logan knew the scar ran from temple to shoulder even though a bandanna was tied around the man's neck.

No longer was a twenty-nine-year-old man staring at the Comanchero; rather a ten-year-old boy was. The man without a name. The man from his past. The white man who had led the Indians in the attack against Logan's family. Memories—so vivid they seemed to be real—flooded Logan's mind. How quickly he shed nineteen years and regressed to childhood.

"Logan, run to the creek and get some fresh water," Maureen MacDougald had said to her ten-year-old son. "Tomorrow is your pa's birthday, and your sister and I are going to cook his favorite dishes."

The boy pushed a thatch of golden-brown hair out of his mischievous eyes. "And are we going to give him the brush set that you got from the drummer?" He grabbed the two wooden buckets from the peg near the door. "The one you hid and told him Mr. Basset didn't have?"

Maureen grinned at her only son. "What am I going to do with you?"

The boy gazed into his mother's bright green eyes. He loved his mama's eyes; they were so beautiful. Pa said they were the color of Erin and the River Shannon—sea-green, he called them. Her hair was a deep brown, and when she stood in the sun it flickered a deep golden red. To Logan she was one of the most beautiful women in the world; she was always smiling and humming. No matter what happened, she always saw the bright side of the situation.

"Can Flanna come with me?" Logan asked about the time the bedroom door opened and his sixteen-year-old sister walked into the large room that was both kitchen and parlor. "It's mighty hard bringing up two buckets full of water. You know, it's an uphill climb all the way."

"Not today," Flanna sang, her eyes dancing happily. "I'm helping Mama. You'll have to do the outside chores all by yourself, little brother. High time you learned to be a man."

"An' I guess you think you're a woman," came the teasing response.

"Yes," Flanna returned.

Logan watched as her eyes turned to emerald-green, and her cheeks flushed with color. "Bet you're thinking about Cyrus Basset." When Flanna's cheeks turned an even deeper red, Logan laughed. "Saw the two of you down beside the creek."

"Logan Andrew MacDougald!" Flanna screeched. "How dare you spy on me!"

Logan giggled, pure devilment sparking in his eyes. "Why, Flanna"—he mimicked Cyrus—"your hair is so pretty. Same color as a fawn."

Flanna picked up the broom and raced toward Logan. "I'll teach you to spy on me."

Grabbing the buckets and dashing out the door, Logan chanted over his shoulder, "Flanna looks like a deer."

He took his time getting the water. He set the buckets on the banks, and he jumped from rock to rock as he crossed the creek. He searched for good wood. Pa was teaching him how to whittle in the evenings when chores were done and they sat on the front porch. And naturally he couldn't stay away from the cave.

Although it was a small one, he loved to push to the very back and sit down in the coolness to daydream. Without moving from this place he had captured one of the wild mustangs that ran so freely on the plains; he loved and broke him. On other days Logan killed large buffalos or tracked Comanches across the plains, fighting the elements, to kill all of them.

Today he dug in the soft dirt at his feet and uncovered the small wooden horse that he had carved. His birthday gift to Pa! A smile touched his face as he thought about his father's surprise. He could see the expression on Pa's face, the warmth in his eyes; he could hear his exclamations; he could see the big man's exuberance. Just thinking about Pa's response filled Logan with pride.

Suddenly his daydream was shattered. He heard the war whoops of Comanches—a ferocious sound which set a frontiersman's spine to tingling. He heard rifle shots and the screams of his mother and sister.

Out of the cave the boy raced, splashing across the creek. Breathless, he arrived at the grove of trees to the side of the house. Hunkering out of sight behind the thick, prickly brush, Logan saw his father lying on the ground. He wanted to run to help him, but fear rooted him to the spot. He heard a noise and looked up to see several more Indians dragging his mother and sister from the house. Following closely behind was a tall white man, about twenty years old. He was dressed entirely in black and wore two revolvers.

The sinister man looked first into Maureen's face, then Flanna's. He laughed, the menacing sound permeating the air around them, turned to the Comanche who sat on his horse—a young brave whose war lock was a solid white—and flung Flanna to the Indian. Immediately the Comanche was off his horse, gathering Flanna in his arms. He clasped his hands over her eyes and pressed her head into his chest. The white man was ripping Maureen's clothing from her body.

Maureen screamed and fought against her captor, but he slapped her senseless. The Comanches released their hold to let her crumple to the ground. "Burn the house," he ordered. His back to the covey of trees where Logan crouched, the man hastily unfastened his pants.

Logan grabbed a nearby club and started to lurch forward to the rescue, but he felt large, strong hands band on either side of his waist to pull him back. His heart beat as loudly as a drum and instinctively his mouth opened to release a scream, but the brave, holding him, clamped a hand over Logan's mouth.

"We can do nothing," the Indian instructed in English, pressing Logan's body to the ground so both

141

of them would be concealed and Logan would not see the rape of his mother. "We are too few to battle them. We must hope they do not find us."

His attention momentarily distracted from his family, Logan gazed at his captor. Certain differences between the brave and those who were raiding his cabin were apparent to the lad. This man wore no scalp lock. Neither was he painted for war. His dark brown eyes were kind, and lurking in their depths was the same kind of expression he often saw in Pa's eyes. Slowly Logan nodded his head; he trusted this man.

"We . . . we've got to do something," he cried, unashamed of the tears that ran down his cheeks. "They've . . . they've . . ."

Logan pulled out of the man's grip, pushed up on his knees, and peered through the bushes. His mother lay on the ground, quietly sobbing, her torn clothes bunched around her waist. The white man was standing, straddle-legged over her. Then Logan saw his scalped father stir, his hand edging toward a hatchet that lay nearby.

"Pa," Logan whispered. "Oh, Pa!"

Unobserved, John MacDougald weakly pushed to his feet and wiped blood from his eyes. Both hands gripping the handle of the ax, he raised it and staggered toward the white man. Before the Indians perceived what was happening, MacDougald swung the weapon, the blade landing on the man's cheek to slice down his neck and into his shoulder. Blood gushed out of the wound. A wail of pain, followed by obscenities, filled the air, and the man pulled his revolver, shooting first John, then Maureen.

Long after the Comanches were gone, Flanna with them, taken by the chief who had the snow-white war lock in a head of raven-black hair, Logan lay in the arms of the Indian and cried. Finally, when his tears

142

were shed, the brave said, "Wait here. I will bury your dead in the white man's way."

Logan shook his head. "I will help." He lifted grief-stricken gray eyes to the warrior. "I'm Logan Mac-Dougald."

"I am He-Who-Hunts-Antelope," he replied. "A Cherokee." A smile softened the craggy face. "You may call me Antelope Hunter. Now let us bury your family. You go get the shovels and find the place where you wish them to rest, and I will take care of the bodies."

"I want to see them," Logan said.

"You will, little warrior," Antelope Hunter promised. "But first let me prepare them for burial." He didn't want Logan to remember his mother as she now lay. "We must hurry," he said. "We don't know but what the Comanches might come back."

Logan nodded and moved to the small lean-to that remained intact. Together he and Antelope Hunter dug the graves and buried them. He quoted his mother's favorite Scripture.

"Come," Antelope Hunter said. "I will take you to my village for tonight."

"Just a minute," the boy replied.

He walked through the ashes of the cabin to the far corner of what had been his parent's bedroom. Using the shovel, he lifted one of the smoldering planks—Ma's special hiding place that no one knew about except her, she thought—and retrieved a medium-size jewelry box, which he opened. He looked at Grandpa Duncan's gold watch. He looked at the indentation where Grandma's gold locket had lain.

How many times during the years had his mother taken the box out in the evening to show him and Flanna her most precious heirlooms: a gold watch that belonged to her pa and a locket that belonged to her ma. On their sixteenth birthday Logan was to get the watch, Flanna the locket. Logan had seven more years to wait; Flanna had received her locket two months before.

Logan closed the box and reached into the hole a second time to pull out the small mirrored rack on which hung the comb and brushes his mother had bought his father for his birthday. He carried them to Antelope Hunter, who waited at the edge of the clearing.

"Are you ready?" the Cherokee asked.

The boy nodded. "I have a gift for you," he said, holding the brush set out. "I want to thank you for saving my life and for helping me bury my family."

"You do not need to give me a gift," Antelope Hunter said. "I do it because you are my friend."

"I want you to have it," Logan insisted. "My ma bought it for my pa. It was his"—he blinked back the tears that threatened once again—"his birthday was tomorrow."

"Thank you, Logan son," Antelope Hunter said. "With deep gratitude I take the gift and will always strive to be a brave man like your father." The Indian set the gift aside and reached up to unfasten a chain that hung about his neck. "This," he said, holding it out to Logan, "is my totem, little warrior. I wish you to wear it from this day on."

Logan caught the delicate silver chain in his fingers and studied the intricate etchings on the medallion. "What is it?"

"It symbolizes the spiritual eye which the Great Spirit places in each man. Through this eye we see people for their true worth. We can look beyond the frailty of human flesh to see their strength of character." Antelope Hunter took the necklace and looped it over Logan's head. "When you see with this eye, my son, you will find that all men are the same;

they only wear skins of a different color."

"Thank you, Antelope Hunter," Logan said, his hand closing over the small ball. "I will wear this always."

The Cherokee smiled. "One day, my son, I shall show you the great magic of healing that goes with the totem."

Hand in hand the Cherokee and the boy walked away from the burning ruins, a bond of love developing that not even death had severed.

So many years had passed, but just seeing the man—and it was the same man who had raped his mother, killed his parents, and given Flanna to White-Hair—brought all the emotions back, all the grief and pain . . . all the bitterness and hatred. When Logan opened his eyes, he felt the warm rush of tears as they rolled down his cheeks.

A new movement in the Indian camp jarred Logan; he saw the chief sit down and the white man rise. "Buffalo Horn was slain in battle today," the Comanchero signed. "Do you, Animal Talker, take his place as chief?"

"I am a chief," the Indian answered, "but I do not take my uncle's place."

"Where are his warriors?"

"They have returned to the main camp with his body to prepare for his burial."

"What are you and your warriors going to do?"

"My braves and I shall also return so we may mourn the death of our great chief," Animal Talker answered in the silent language. "We will leave scouts to trail the wagon train, so we may follow its movement through our land."

The Comanchero spoke again, his face registering the anger he could not relay in hand gestures. "Animal Talker is not a brave warrior like his uncle; he is a coward who uses the death of Buffalo Horn as an excuse to return to camp. He does not wish to attack the wagon train again because it has brought him bad medicine." The man paused, then resumed his gesturing. "I am angry at Animal Talker. Are the Comanches cowards? Do they run from their enemies?"

"No!" Animal Talker leaped to his feet. "The Comanches are not cowards as the Scar-Faced One accuses. We do not run from our enemies, but today we saw our chief and my uncle killed. The Great Spirit has spoken. We do not fight the wagon train. We go home to bury our dead and to mourn."

The warriors nodded their heads and murmured their agreement.

Animal Talker looked at the white man. "I have spoken. So be it."

"I return to my people," the man signed. "When you have goods to trade, let me know. I have the liquor and trade goods you were asking for. If you bring me plenty of women slaves, I have the revolvers. I have a new shipment of them right now, and more are on the way. These"—he pulled a Colt six-shooter from his holster and brandished it in the air—"will be given to the first who bring me the slaves I am looking for."

"You have always traded with the Comanches," Animal Talker said. "What do you mean by the first?"

"I will trade these guns to the first Indians who come to me with the right kind of goods," the man replied. "Be they Comanche or Apache."

Animal Talker's expression did not change, but Logan knew he was beyond anger—he was furious; he could see it in the warrior's stance. "My people have always traded with you, Scar-Faced Man. Never have we let you down."

"But I've never dealt with you," Scar-Face said.

"You have dealt with my father and my uncle."

"I did. See that you bring me the goods I want, or I shall have to turn to the Apaches," Scar-Face signed, his face closed. "I have spoken. So be it. I will wait for the goods to be delivered to me. You know where to find me." He stooped to pick up his serape, slung it over a shoulder, and stalked to his horse. After he swung into the saddle, he rode northwest without a backward glance.

Immediately afterward the Indians broke camp, erased all evidence of their having ever been at the canyon, and rode in the same general direction as Scar-Face to their main camp, which was hidden in the canyons near Santa Fe. Logan scooted back to wait awhile. Although he knew the Indians would not be returning to attack the wagon train, he also knew he could not leave to follow Scar-Face.

For nineteen years he had waited for this day. He had dreamed of retribution for the scar-faced man. *Damn it!* He balled his hand into a fist. Why hadn't Brenna listened to him? If only she had chosen the route around Comancheria. For just a moment anger boiled in Logan.

He couldn't foist all the blame on Brenna. She had only been doing what she thought was right; she had been thinking about the settlers and their need for water. She couldn't know that Kirkwood had been deliberately leading them around the water holes.

Logan felt the low, dull ache of disappointment. Because of a woman he had known for the space of a few hours, because of a woman he had made love to once . . . no, twice . . . he was turning his back on his quest and was obligating himself to lead a caravan of people and trade goods to Bent's Fort. While he was playing nursemaid, the scar-faced man was slipping through his fingers.

147

But, Logan reasoned, if the Comanchero was returning to his hideout, Thunder would surely see him . . . that is, if Thunder was not— Dear God! Logan closed his eyes and began to breathe slowly and deeply like Antelope Hunter had taught him. He relaxed, letting his mind move into the Silence—the Silence who knew all the answers and who responded to the seeker. All skittering thoughts were harnessed; he concentrated on Thunder. He drew five more breaths and moved deeper into concentration. In this trancelike state Logan didn't see Thunder, but he knew his adopted brother was safe.

For the moment, Logan decided, he would have to leave Scar-Face as well as Kirkwood to his blood brother because he had to—something inside him compelled him to—take charge of Brenna's caravan. Gabby was dead, and Brenna wounded; the cut itself wasn't so bad, but the poison would debilitate her for several days. Roger Hollis was too inexperienced to be entrusted with the safety of an entire caravan. The boy had promise, but he had to be taught. The settlers were too single-minded.

As soon as he thought it was safe, Logan rode back to the wagon train—a ride that brought him into camp after dark. But the people were not asleep. Anxiously they awaited his return. Leaving the extra guards on duty, Logan called the men together to make his report.

Afterward he announced that he was taking over as wagon captain. "It's too late to be traveling tonight," he said, "so we'll be leaving for the creek in the morning. We'll be there by late evening." After the pleased murmurs died, Logan said, "In the past you've been stretching out at seven o'clock in the morning. Not anymore. From now on, we'll be stretching out at five o'clock. Our days will be long."

Logan was pleased with the nodded assents. "That means we'll be making about thirty miles a day. I don't want any of you to stray from the main body, whether it's in camp or moving."

Again his eyes swept the crowd that circled him. "I suggest that once we get to the creek, you fill your barrels and anything else that'll hold water. We have long, hard, and dry days ahead of us. The going could get a lot worse before it gets better." He paused. "Any questions?" When none were forthcoming, he said, "That's all then."

Logan turned to Roger. "Post extra guards and make sure they understand the Comanches left scouts out there to follow and demoralize us. Change guards every three hours, so they don't get tired or lazy. I want them to be extremely alert to every sound and sight. If we're not careful, the scouts will steal our animals."

"Yes, sir," Roger replied. "Anything else you want me to do, Mr. MacDougald?"

Logan shook his head. "I'm going to rest. If you need me, I'll be at Mrs. Allen's wagon." Before Roger could nod, Logan was gone. When he passed Sam's wagon, Gertrude said, "She awoke once, Mr. MacDougald, and I gave her another dose of the herbs, like you instructed. She's been sleeping ever since."

"Good," Logan murmured. "Thank you for watching after her, Mrs. Dawkins. I'll repay you for the favor one of these days."

When Logan reached Brenna, he found her sound asleep. The sheet was tucked under her chin, and she was curled into a ball on her side. He rolled the sailcloth up on both sides of the wagon to allow a breeze to blow through and cool them off. Then he climbed in to take off his hat and belt. He laid his revolvers nearby, where they could be easily located if needed. Then he pulled off his boots and unbuttoned his shirt, letting it fall open and loose. Before he settled down, he lit the lantern and suspended it from the top of the wagon.

Because the wagon was stacked full of boxes, he had no place to lie down except beside Brenna. Careful not to disturb her, he stretched out on his back and stared out the back of the wagon. In the quietness that fell over the wagon train, he heard her soft, even breathing, and he turned his head to look at her.

She was lying on her side, her knees drawn up, her hands under her chin. Tendrils of hair had loosened themselves from the confines of the braid to curl around her face. Long, dark eyelashes rested against her soft, smooth cheeks. He lifted a hand to brush the hair from her forehead and temples.

Brenna stirred, but she wasn't fully cognizant; she floated in a beautiful world in which she had no cares or worries. She heard the scraping and grating sounds as Logan rolled the canvas curtain up around the wagon. She saw the light of the lantern when it glowed against her closed lids. When she felt the wagon shake with Logan's movement, she smiled and stretched, kicking out from under the sheet and bringing the chemise above her buttocks. A strap slipped off her shoulder to expose one of her breasts.

Unable to help himself, Logan looked at her smooth body, glowing in the muted light of the lantern which swung from the rafter. Her braid lay over one shoulder and across one breast, the dark color contrasting with the satiny swell of creamy flesh.

Brenna opened her eyes and looked at the emotion that flickered in Logan's eyes. Still under the influence of the Indian herbs, unable to tell where the dream-world ended and reality began, she lifted her arm and caught the nape of his neck with her hand. "You're a handsome man, Logan MacDougald."

"You're a handsome woman."

"Your woman?" Brenna unclasped her hand to let it slide slowly down his chest, her fingers inadvertently grazing his nipple.

Logan smiled. "Yes." He lowered his head to press a sweet, gentle kiss on her lips. "Now go back to sleep."

Brenna squirmed close to him and immediately went back to her dreamworld. The sheet slid down, and the material of her chemise pulled tight against her breasts. But tonight Logan's primitive instincts were not aroused; he wanted only to protect her, to cosset and nurse her.

At five o'clock the next morning, Logan yelled the command and the journey resumed. By the time the wagons corralled by the creek, the effects of the herbs had worn off, and Brenna's arm and shoulder ached so badly she could hardly endure the pain. Her heart was heavy because she was thinking of Gabby—left alone out there with nothing to mark his grave but a pile of stones. Soon it wouldn't even be marked.

Logan was at the wagon almost as soon as the wheels had stopped rolling. "How're you feeling?" he asked, lowering the tailgate and gently leaping in, the red bandanna in hand.

"All right," she returned.

When he reached out and brushed a tear off her cheek, he asked, "Is your arm hurting?"

She nodded and murmured, "If only I had listened to Gabby, he would still be . . . he would . . ."

"You can't spend the rest of your life grieving over your decision," he told her gently. "You did what you thought was best. No one can ask any more of you. It will take time for your heart and body to heal, but they will." He smiled. "Does your arm still burn?" When she nodded, he said, "That's the poison. That's the reason why you're feeling so bad." He opened the pouch and extracted some herbs, which he was soon cutting up into a small bowl. "This poultice that I'm making burns like hell, but it'll draw the poison out."

"Thank you . . . for taking care of me."

"The pleasure's all mine," he returned.

"Hardly a pleasure taking care of a wounded person."

"Depends on how you look at it," he reasoned, concentrating on doctoring her wound. "I get to dress and undress you." A quicksilver smile traced his lips.

"Logan!" Brenna whispered.

Her arm bandaged, he leaped out of the wagon and rolled the flaps up. Afterward he leaned over the tailgate and said, "Now get some sleep. I'm going to check to see that everything is all right."

By the time Logan returned to Brenna, she, like the majority of the camp, was fast asleep. He took his hat off and shed his revolvers. Then he undressed and pushed back into the wagon to stare at the heavens. He wondered where Thunder was and what he was doing. He had expected the Cherokee to join the wagon train before now. He hoped nothing had gone amiss. Then Logan's thoughts shifted to the scar-faced man—the man without a name—the man who had ridden with the elusive Chief White-Hair.

Excitement gripped Logan. For twenty years he had dreamed of the day when he could find these two men and kill them. He had questioned men who traveled the plains and deserts of the frontier; he had questioned captives who managed to escape or who were ransomed from the Indians; he questioned every Indian whom he met. Trappers, frontiersmen, and captives had heard about the invincible Chief White-Hair, but they had never seen him. If the Indians had seen him or did know about him, they would not speak of him!

Logan reached up to feel the locket in his pocket. This was his first clue to Flanna's whereabouts. A sense of hopelessness assailed him. He was afraid that he was going to lose Scar-Face; he needed to be pursuing him. But he couldn't. It would be days before Brenna would be strong enough to take over as wagon captain, and the caravan had to roll. The people couldn't sit out here in the wilderness, easy prey for Indians and Comancheros. He'd have to stay with her. He only prayed that Thunder hadn't lost sight of Kirkwood and that he had located the hideout of the Comancheros.

Brenna snuggled against Logan and mumbled something unintelligible. He pulled her into his arms and held her. In her dreams she frequently begged him to stay with her, and the pitiful cry tugged at his heart. He wanted to stay with her. He had wanted to promise her that he wouldn't leave, but he was a man who kept his promises. He knew the day would come when he must leave . . . and he would.

Chapter Ten

Brenna awoke and lay still for a moment; she closed her eyes against the morning glare as she eased into a more comfortable position and oriented herself. For the first time since the attack she was lucid; she was in the real world; she could feel the hard, unyielding wood of the wagon bed against her aching body, but she wasn't jostling. The air around her was still and oppressive.

She realized the caravan wasn't moving; evidently they were in camp. She listened to the noises around her. Men repairing wagons and harnesses, the lowing of the cattle in the corral, the women talking. She smelled the fire and the cooking food. Yes, they were stopped for the midday camp.

She wiggled some more and winced; her back ached; her shoulder and arm throbbed. She was miserable. Her nightgown and pallet were drenched with perspiration. So was her hair. Wearily she reached up to run her hands through the wet hair at the base of her neck and flipped her braid from beneath her. She needed a bath. She lifted the corner of her sheet and wiped the perspiration from her face.

Brenna's stomach growled to remind her that she hadn't eaten much during the past four days. She would get dressed, she thought, careful as she moved around to find her luggage. Then she saw a pile of clean clothes, folded and sitting on top of a box. Her trousers and shirt. She reached for the trousers first. She hadn't realized how weak she was until she exerted the effort to pull the pants up her legs. Dressing was slow and tiring. When she had them fastened around her waist, she grabbed for the shirt.

When she lifted it, another piece of clothing fell to the wagon bed; Brenna leaned over and picked it up—Logan's shirt, the faded cotton shirt that he had worn the day he returned to warn them of the Comanche attack. She looked at the stack of clothes again. His were folded with hers. She felt that same oneness with him that she had shared when they made love and when they fought the Comanches.

She looked at the second pillow on the pallet, at the indentation where Logan's head had lain, and memories began to return. He had been sleeping with her. Although she had been in a euphoric dream world, she remembered his body curved to hers at night. The drinks of water. The basin baths. The kisses on her forehead. She looked at her arm, wrapped in a clean white cloth. He had been taking care of her . . . since the . . . since Gabby's . . .

She drew Logan's shirt to her chest and buried her face in it. Now in broad daylight, reality with all its harshness returned to her. The safety and beauty of her dreams were gone. Gabby was dead—dead because she had listened to Kirkwood and had traveled into Comanche territory. Jonesey was the remaining original employee of the Garvey Mercantile and Freight Hauling. Just she and Jonesey were left!

She thought of Jonesey's misgivings, and in his simpleminded way, he had been right, as had Venner. Kirkwood wasn't a scout at all; his only purpose had been to guide them into an ambush, and she had willingly fallen into his plans. For a few minutes she sat there, her mind growing heavy with depression. As quickly she pushed the guilt away.

That was the past, she thought. She had today, and she must make it the very best she could. She couldn't look over her shoulders at past mistakes and weaknesses. She couldn't let them become a weight to drag her down. She had a wagon train to get to Santa Fe, and the people needed her. She had to see Peyton H. Alexander. Like her father, who had fought in the war for Texas independence, she would be instrumental in helping the people of Santa Fe and Taos throw off the oppressive yoke of Mexican tyranny. She was a strong woman; she could take care of herself. She didn't need anyone to look after her.

Then she remembered one of her drug-induced dreams and her mother's words. She smiled. *Mama was right! I'm a grown woman. I don't need anyone; I have everything within myself I need to get this job done and to have self-worth.* Brenna was elated at the peace that flooded her soul; she was filled with a calm acceptance. Too weak to sit up any longer, she lay back down and emitted a sigh of relief. Everything was going to be all right. She closed her eyes and felt the wash of tears behind her lids. Yes, everything would be all right.

"You're awake," Gertrude called out as she peeked into the wagon. "How're you feeling?"

Brenna's eyes opened, and she blinked up as the older woman lowered the tailgate. "Much better, Granny—I mean, Mrs. Dawkins."

"I don't mind you calling me Granny," Gertrude said as she laid her hand over Brenna's brow. "Of course, it is nice to hear my name now and again."

Brenna managed a weak grin. "I'm trying to remember."

"Your fever's broken," Gertrude announced. "That's

a good sign." Then she heard Brenna's tummy growl. "That's not such a good sign. We need to get you some supper. Are you hungry?"

"I'm hungry enough to eat a bear," Brenna retorted.

"Bear we don't have," Gertrude replied, "and it wouldn't be too good for you if we did. I think you'll get some bland cornmeal mush tonight."

Brenna laughed. "Even that sounds like a meal for royalty." She wiped the perspiration from the back of her neck. "Are we close to water?" After Gertrude nodded, she asked, "Could I take a bath and wash my hair?"

"I think that can be arranged," Gertrude replied. "I'll let Callie Sue go with you to the creek while I fix the mush. Now let me see your arm." Brenna extended her arm, and Gertrude quickly untied the bandage and looked at the cut. "It's healing beautifully," she said. "You're not going to have much of a scar." She shook her head. "That Logan sure knows what he's doing."

"Speaking of Logan," Brenna said, "where is he?"

"He and some of the men have gone hunting," Gertrude answered. "Said he might not be back until close to time to leave." Without a pause she added, "I'm going to leave the bandage off now and let this air out. Looks like it's scabbed over now."

Shortly after Gertrude left, her granddaughter appeared at the wagon, a large smile dimpling her face. "Granny said you wanted to take a bath."

"I'd like to," Brenna said. "I'm sorry to be such a bother."

"No bother," Callie Sue replied. "You've done a lot for us. This is the least we can do for you."

"Thank you," Brenna said, genuinely touched by the girl's comment.

Callie Sue hopped into the wagon and searched through the trunks. "You'll need your soap, washrags, and clean clothes." She looked over her shoulder. "A dress or your trousers?"

For just a moment Brenna toyed with the idea of wearing her blue dress, but she didn't give in to the urge. Soon they would be on the move again, and she needed to dress functionally. "I'll wear these trousers that I have on," she replied, pointing. "Get me that shirt, a pair of socks, and my boots."

Brenna didn't realize how weak she was until she reached the creek. She was so winded she sat down on the bank for a few minutes to catch her breath. With Callie Sue's help she undressed and moved into the water, sitting down in the shallows to bathe.

"Do you need me to help you bathe and wash your hair?" Callie Sue called from the bank.

"No," Brenna answered, "I'll be all right. I'm just going to sit here for a while and enjoy the water."

"I forgot the brush and comb," Callie Sue said. "I'll run back and get it while you're bathing." She ran a short way, stopped, and called over her shoulder, "If you're sure you'll be all right, I'm going to change your pallet."

"Go ahead," Brenna answered. "I'll be fine." She bathed and then she just sat in the water, leaning back in order to submerge the back of her head. She closed her eyes and allowed her body to bob in the gently lapping water.

When she heard the rustling on the bank later, she called, "If you don't mind, I think I'll let you wash my hair. My arm hurts too much for me to be lifting it." She heard the splashing in the water.

"I don't mind at all." Logan's strong hands were on her head and he was massaging her scalp.

"Lo—gan," Brenna sputtered, jerking her head from his clasp. "I thought"—she turned her head to look at him—"you were out hunting."

158

"Just got back," he replied, gently turning her around again. He took the bar of soap and rubbed it through her hair. "And just in time, I see." He worked the lather.

"Callie Sue will be coming back," Brenna reminded him. "What will she be thinking?"

Logan laughed. "What a fine time to be thinking of that. I've been caring for you for the last four days and nights, sleeping with you, feeding you, and bathing you. And now you're wondering what Callie Sue will think!"

The impact of his words hit Brenna, and she spun around, oblivious to her nudity. "What are they thinking, Logan?"

He rinsed his hands before he cupped her face. "I don't know. I've never been bothered in my life with what other folks think." When she was quiet for a long time, he asked, "Are you worried about what they're thinking?"

"No," she eventually answered, "I'm not."

"Good!" He lightly kissed her, a tantalizing promise of what could be if his lips would just settle down over hers. "You're my kind of woman." His lips covered hers in a warm, slow kiss. Finally he raised his head. "You tempt me to do other things," he told her, his eyes blatantly wandering over her nude body, "but as you said, we must get you bathed."

"That's right," Brenna gasped, "before Callie Sue returns."

Again Logan laughed, the sound rich and warm, touching and thrilling Brenna's heart. "She won't be coming back," he finally said, "but Miss Gertrude will be plenty mad if I don't have you back in time for some warm cornmeal mush." He shoved Brenna's head under the water and rinsed her hair.

She came up sputtering. "If I'm not drowned first."

"Never," he said on a soft chuckle. "I have plans for you, lady, as soon as you rest up a bit and get your strength back."

When he was through washing Brenna's hair, Logan carried her ashore. He picked up the towel and turned to dry her off, but he didn't touch her. He stood for a moment looking at her. As if he'd never seen her naked before, his eyes moved over Brenna's body. He drew in his breath as his gaze lingered on her beautifully shaped breasts, then slid down to her smooth, rounded hips and her long, shapely legs.

Logan knew at this moment the most beautiful and perfect woman he had ever seen was standing in front of him. Every woman he had ever known before paled into insignificance. Oddly, he didn't look at her as a man who wanted to possess her, but as a man who was in love—deeply in love. Yet he had never admitted this to her . . . or to himself. When Logan raised his face, his eyes encountered Brenna's solemn gaze. For endless seconds they stared at each other.

Brenna saw eyes that were such a gentle gray it took her breath away. She had loved her parents; she had loved Gabby; but she had never known the bonding love of a man and a woman. In her grief after her father's death, she had turned to Shawn, who had comforted her, and she had mistaken this comfort for love. She had married him for security. Now she knew: She had never loved Shawn Allan. She loved Logan MacDougald. No matter what the future held for her and Logan, no matter what tomorrow might bring, she loved Logan.

Logan encircled her body with the towel, and she became pliable in his arms. "Lord, give me strength," he murmured.

His husky words caused Brenna to tremble with anticipation.

"You're so beautiful, I can't keep my hands off you."

"Then don't," she whispered.

Logan pulled back and smiled. "I've made love to you for the last time on a riverbank, woman. The next time we're going to have privacy of some kind."

"On a wagon train?" Brenna laughed, the sound light and bubbly.

"At least, I feel like we have privacy when we're shut up in your wagon."

Logan dried her off and helped her dress; then the two of them, Brenna leaning against Logan for support, walked to Sam's carriage. Brenna ate a small bowl of the cornmeal mush and for a little while visited with Gertrude, Sam, and Callie Sue. But soon her exertion caught up with her. She was so exhausted she could hardly sit up.

"Come on, Miss Brenna," Logan finally said, swooping her into his arms. "Time for you to rest. You look like you're tuckered out."

"Absolutely," Gertrude clucked like a mother hen. "And you just stay in bed until you're much stronger, dear. Before we stretch out, I'll bring you another bowl of porridge."

Brenna smiled at the kindly woman and waved goodby to all of them. She nestled her face against Logan's chest, breathing deeply of his clean, masculine odor. She closed her eyes and relaxed. She measured distance with the even cadence of his heartbeat.

Logan set her in the wagon, then climbed in himself. After he situated her on the clean pallet, he leaned over and kissed her on the forehead. His lips moved down her nose to the indentation of her upper lip. He played with her mouth, then his lips closed over hers in a warm, tender kiss. His hand gently cupped one of her breasts and he kneaded it as his tongue entered her mouth.

When he pulled back, both of them were breathing heavily. "Sweet dreams," he murmured.

Brenna was disappointed. "You're not going to take a nap with me."

Logan shook his head as he stripped her boots off. "Can't, sweetheart." He threw them to the back of the wagon. "I have work to do. A wagon boss can't laze around like the wagon captain."

Brenna smiled at his teasing. She lifted a hand to run her fingers through his hair. "Tonight."

"Tonight," he promised.

The caravan slowly moved, following the route Logan had mapped out the day he took command of the wagon train. Brenna's strength returned quickly, and two days after they crossed the Red River she was riding beside Jonesey and Roger. Logan scouted ahead.

Sitting forward in the saddle, Brenna shielded her eyes with her hand as she gazed across the flat plains upward to the western sky, nothing but a red-orange blaze of fire that baked the earth. As far as the eye could see the ground was barren—dry and cracked— and all vegetation was dead. She lifted an end of her bandanna and wiped the perspiration from her face and neck; at the same time she turned her face from west to east and sought respite from the blinding glare. Although devoid of the sun, the eastern sky promised no rain either; it wasn't graced with a solitary cloud.

When she saw Logan returning to meet the train, she nudged her horse forward. "No water in the last two creeks," she said as she rode abreast of him, "and no rain in sight."

"No rain," he agreed, his gray eyes scaling the far horizon. The Comanche scouts were out there. At times he saw them, trailing from afar; then they would swoop close to the caravan, whooping and hollering; other times, when they dipped behind the crest of the prairie, he just felt them. Then quite casually he commented, "I'd say we're only about four hours away from water. Could reach it by sundown, but—"

"Water!" she exclaimed, interrupting Logan. "Only four hours away! Oh, Lord, Logan, this will be the best news the wagon train could have. Morale will jump a mile." She pulled the reins of the gray. "Who's going to tell them? You or me?"

Logan's gray eyes sparkled at Brenna's enthusiasm, and he reached over to grab her reins. "We'll both tell them, but first I have something else I want to show you. Something that may keep us from reaching the water until tomorrow."

"Nothing could make us stop short of water!" Brenna looked down at her dusty clothes, then wiped a hand across her gritty face and ran her fingers around the sweat-moistened hatband. "Absolutely nothing."

"We'll see," was all he said. "Come with me. I want you to see one of the most beautiful sights in the world."

Together they rode, soon to top a small ridge. As they stopped, Brenna stared at the sight below. Against the clear May sky, she saw in the valley beyond about sixty buffalo, separated from the main herd, lying down for the midday rest. Sixty shaggy beasts, covered with dark brown curls.

"They're magnificent!" Brenna seemed to breathe the words.

For a long time the two of them sat there, she watching the buffalo, Logan watching her.

"Look!" she exclaimed, and leaned forward to point. Reluctantly Logan turned his head. The buffalo began to rise slowly and move away. As they stood up,

163

four yellow-red calves that had been hidden by their mother's bodies appeared.

"These are the animals of the plains," Logan said. "They provide the Indians with every necessity of life—food, clothing, and fuel."

"Something to eat tonight besides fatback and beans," Brenna said. "What a welcome treat."

"Now," Logan said, "we ride back and tell the others. This will not only give us a change of menu for tonight, but will provide us with enough food and fuel for the rest of the journey to Bent's Fort."

They raced across the prairie to the caravan, their cry of "Buffalo" sending everyone into a fever of excitement.

"Lead me to 'em!" Roger shouted.

"I came back to get you so you could get your share of the kill," Logan told the men as they scrambled for their rifles and horses, "but I don't want you to scare off the herd before any of us have a chance to get an animal."

"How big is the herd?" Jonesey shouted.

"About sixty," Logan replied. "A splinter from the main group."

"Enough to feed us all the way to Bent's Fort," the driver added. "If we take them right."

"More than enough," Logan agreed. "Now I want you to listen to me," he addressed the hunters. "It's not necessary for us to kill the entire herd in order to have enough food to last us until we reach Bent's Fort."

"Aren't you afraid that while we stand here yakking," one of the armed guards said impatiently, shuffling his feet, "the buffalo are going to get away?"

"They're not going anywhere," Logan promised. "I was downwind, so they didn't get my scent." He looked over the crowd of men who circled him. "How many of you have ever hunted buffalo before?" Not a hand rose.

164

"Just as I thought," Logan murmured, the quicksilver smile racing across his face. "Before we go, I'm going to tell you how to stand this herd."

Though eager to be off, the man quieted and sat down. They listened as Logan talked. When he finished outlining his plan, he said, "Not all of us can go. Some of the men have to stay here with the wagons to protect our women and goods. Now we'll draw lots to see who's going with Brenna and me—"

"Miss Brenna and you!" one of Roger's men howled indignantly. "She's a woman. How come she's going? She should stay here with the women and give a man an opportunity to go."

"Brenna is the owner of the trading expedition," Logan returned in a soft, pleasant voice, "and she's the wagon captain. Both positions give her the right to go. Besides that, she's a veteran Indian fighter."

Deceived by Logan's tone, the man opened his mouth to protest, but then he saw Logan's eyes; hard, unyielding, they reminded the man of the cold metal of a gun barrel. He immediately bit back his complaint and nodded his head in compliance.

In the minutes that followed, lots were drawn. Part of the men accompanied Logan and Brenna; the remainder stayed with the caravan. When they reached the crest of the knoll, everyone dismounted. The hunters slowly fanned to circle the buffalo. Logan and Brenna moved so they were directly in front of the herd. They lay on their bellies.

Time hung still as the two of them watched the herd slowly move forward. When the huge brutes were within three hundred yards, Brenna was perspiring profusely. The bulls seemed to be as big as her freight wagons. She was shaking so badly, she wondered if she could hit a mile-long barn broadside.

Logan laid his eye along the barrel of his rifle. The

bulls came closer—so close Brenna could hear the grinding of their teeth as they chewed. Dear Lord, but she was frightened. She didn't know if she was this scared when the Comanches attacked or not! Logan's gun went off.

The buffalo snorted and fell in his tracks. The rest of the herd ran about a hundred yards from where their leader had fallen. Logan waited until another bull had assumed leadership and led the herd in the same general direction as the first leader. The second took care to avoid the dangerous place where the first had fallen.

Logan aimed his rifle and shot the second time, bringing the leader down. The herd ran back a few yards, gathered into a compact mass, grunting and moving about in as small a range as possible.

"They'll choose their third leader now," he told Brenna, "and if we get him, the herd is ours. If not, they go on their way rejoicing, excepting what few can be brought down by the shots sent after them as they run." He waited a moment before he said, "This one is yours."

"Yes," she whispered, excitement quivering in her voice, her hands clammy with perspiration, "this one is mine."

Brenna wiped her hands down the sides of her britches, laid her eye along the barrel of her rifle, and took careful aim. She watched the new leader run. Her finger curled around the trigger and she squeezed. Long after the echo of the shot died, the bull continued to run.

"Damn!" she cried, her heart sinking. "I missed." She had lost the herd.

"No," Logan corrected, pointing his finger. "Look." The bull ran about two hundred yards more, then dropped. "Good shot," he whispered, his hand closing over hers.

Their eyes met, and again they shared that oneness of soul. Words weren't important to either one of them. Silently they communicated.

The hunt was soon over, and although they were still hours from the water hole, they camped for night.

"How are we going to keep all this meat?" Maude Hemphill called as she came running toward Logan. "Got nothing to cure it with."

"We'll keep it Indian-style," he replied. "Let me show you." He moved to Brenna's wagon, unfastened her trunks from the tailgate, shoved them farther into the wagon, and took the ropes, which he strung along the side of her wagon. The people crowded around him and watched, fascinated. When that was finished, he knelt beside the butchered animal. "Now we cut the beef into thin strips and hang it in the sun to dry. As we march, it cures."

A general feeling of well-being permeated the camp. The buffalo were butchered, and the women gathered the buffalo chips in gunnysacks for future fires.

Logan knelt down beside Brenna. "Well, Miss Brenna, I guess I'll help you butcher your buffalo." With several deft strokes of the large knife he carried, he held the buffalo tongue up. "This," he said, "is a much-prized delicacy, and the hump ribs make an unsurpassed soup."

Time passed quickly, and soon the buffalo was simmering over several fires, the odor permeating the camp.

"Mm," Brenna sniffed hungrily, kneeling to stir the pot, "I just hope this tastes half as good as it smells."

Moving away from the fire, she leaned against the wagon wheel, forgetting about her injured shoulder and putting too much weight on it. She winced and quickly repositioned herself.

"Still bothering you?" Logan asked.

Gently rubbing her upper arm, Brenna replied, "A little."

"Didn't stop you from picking off that bull," he said admiringly. The face lifted from his task, a slice of fresh meat dangling from his hands, and his gray eyes fastened on hers. "You're a good shot."

"Thank you."

His voice lowered. "You're good at everything you do, Brenna."

They stared at each other for a long time, and everything around them disappeared. Once again they were aware of each other as a man and a woman. Logan didn't see her in the dusty britches and baggy shirt; instead he saw her swinging and swaying in the blue cambric dress to the sound of the fiddle. He felt her sweetness in his arms, her lips beneath his, her breasts pressed against his chest.

"Why don't you go bathe and change clothes," he softly suggested.

"What about the water?" she asked.

"When we reach the river tomorrow, we'll have plenty," he answered. "Now, scoot. Supper will be ready by the time you return."

"What about you?"

"I'll bathe after supper."

She nodded.

"Would you wear a dress for me tonight?" he asked.

Brenna looked down at her garb. "You don't like what I'm wearing?"

"I like you in whatever you're wearing," Logan replied, "but tonight I would like to see my woman in a dress."

Brenna saw the embers of desire flicker in Logan's eyes, then flare into a blazing flame. "Then you shall." The same desire smoldered in her eyes.

Brenna climbed over the boxes and trunks to find the one she sought. Then she dropped the canvas curtain at each end of the wagon and stripped out of her clothes. Filling a basin with water, she washed away all the dirt and grime. When she was through, she took her time in combing her hair and re-dressing. She smiled her satisfaction as she dropped the soft yellow dress over her head. Through dressing, Brenna raised the curtains and hopped off the wagon. She saw Logan standing beside the wagon, wiping his hands with a cloth. When he saw her, his movements stopped. His eyes slowly, appreciatively moved down her body, from the shining coil of hair on the crown of her head to the tips of her shoes barely showing beneath the hem of her gown.

"Very pretty," he said. "Very pretty indeed."

"Thank you," Brenna returned, catching the skirt in both hands and twirling around. "It's new. I bought it in San Antonio."

"Saving it for a special occasion?" Logan asked, the gray eyes a sultry charcoal color.

"Uh-huh." She enjoyed flirting with him.

"And tonight's to be a special occasion?"

Brenna was beautiful, Logan thought. Her eyes were dark and secretive; they glittered, vacillating between promise and mystery. Delicate rose color blushed her cheeks and lips, and strands of black hair shimmered around her temples.

"Very special," she agreed, and watched as Logan moved closer to her. When he was directly in front of her, she felt the heat of his virility. His hat was off, and the wind had naturally whipped his hair so that it roughly framed his face—the gaunt face and cool gray eyes that hid his thoughts and emotions from the world—the face Brenna didn't think she would ever forget, the face she would love the rest of her life.

She reached up and ran her hands down the cheeks,

shadowed with beard stubble. She cupped his chin and brought his firm, hard lips to hers. Unconsciously she swayed toward him; her face lifted, and her lips parted for the kiss. She didn't realize she had closed her eyes until she felt his warm breath against her skin.

"If I weren't so filthy"—Brenna heard Logan's deep murmur—"I'd take you in my arms and make love to you this very minute. But we'll wait for a better time. As I promised, more privacy and more time."

"Strangers." Tommy Caldwell's cry echoed through the camp.

Logan and Brenna turned at the same time and ran to where Tommy stood. Brushing past Brenna, Logan raced through the corral and leaped over the tongue of the lead wagon. Roger and several men stood behind him.

"Howdy!" one of the newcomers called, leaping off his horse and holding his hands in the sky so the people would know that he meant them no harm. "Willard Ellington, hide hunter. Headed for Bent's Fort, then back to Missoury."

Logan looked behind Ellington to see four other riders and several pack mules.

"My boys. Rowdy, Charlie. My brother, Benson, and his boy, Jonas William Ellington. We call him Billy."

"Logan MacDougald."

"Wagon boss?"

Logan nodded.

"Could we join you for the night?"

"Be glad for you to join us," Logan said, "if you don't mind handing your guns over to us for safekeeping."

Ellington was displeased with this mandate. "Ain't this just a mite too much, friend?"

"If we were friends, it would be a mite too much," Logan agreed coolly. "But we're not acquaintances,

170

much less friends, and I have a passel of people to protect."

Ellington eyed him warily.

"Sorry. That's the way it's going to be," Logan said.

"Come on, Paw," one of the men said. "That food shore does smell good. Better than what we been eating for the past two months."

"Buffalo." Willard sniffed and smiled. "See you had a good hunt."

"Just enough to supply us with food until we reach Bent's Fort. Well?" Logan asked. "What's it going to be?"

Ellington smiled and held out his guns. The rest of the hide hunters followed his example. As they walked into the compound, Logan said, "Since we're also headed toward Bent's Fort, you're welcome to travel with us."

"Shore appreciate the offer," Willard said, "but me and the boys are wanting to get there as fast as we can. Benson's wife and our younger brother are supposed to be waiting for us. While me and the boys head for Missoury, Benson and Lilly are gonna take Little Billy here"—the grizzled hunter pointed to the towheaded ten-year-old boy—"and go on to Santy Fee to set up a store for trading. Jest like to sleep with you for the night. Be heading out long 'fore the rest of you are up and going."

Although supper was relished by every member of the wagon train, it was eaten quickly, and soon everyone crowded around the hide hunters, eager for news of any kind—most of which centered on the Mexicans and Indians.

"Everything looks pretty good back where we come from," Willard said. "Couldn't see no signs of Indians on the warpath. Not even any random hunting bands. Saw some pretty deep wagon ruts. Figured the

171

Comanches got them a train somewhere that was full of goods. Real full! Reckon they'll be contented for a while with that."

The settlers' spirits were uplifted with this news. Days and nights of being dogged by the Comanche scouts were taking their toll. And Logan was pushing them at such a breakneck speed, they fell to bed exhausted at night, barely able to get up the next morning.

"How about a little music before we call it a day?" Horace Faraday asked, pulling out his fiddle and bow. Without waiting for an answer, he tucked the instrument under his chin and drew the bow across the strings, filling the air with stomping-good hoedown music.

With characteristic optimism, the people pushed their worries aside and celebrated life. They sang and danced; then they gathered around the fire and listened as one by one the old-timers spun tall tales.

Hand in hand Logan and Brenna walked to the wagon. He lowered the tailgate and helped her in. Then he watched as she lit the lantern and hung it from the top of the wagon. "Go ahead and get ready for bed, honey," he said. "I asked Willard to sit up a little longer. I want to talk to him."

"All right," she answered, swallowing her disappointment. She waited for an explanation, but he gave none.

"I'll be back as soon as I can," he promised.

"I'll wait up for you."

He shook his head. "Don't. I'm not sure how long I'll be."

Brenna wasn't far from tears as she spread her pallet. Logan had been warm and loving; they had shared so much of themselves with one another. Now with these strangers coming, he had changed. She could feel him

172

withdrawing. She wondered how soon before he would be leaving . . . and she knew he would be leaving. He had been so careful not to speak words of love to her; he had made no promises.

She uncoiled her hair, combed and braided it. Then she blew out the lantern and undressed, wearing nothing but her chemise. Because the night was extremely dry and hot, she didn't don her britches and shirt. Rather, she ran the canvas curtains up on both sides and lay down, enjoying the breeze.

She awakened. For a minute she lay still, blinking her eyes to get accustomed to the dark. The camp was quiet. Nothing to be heard but the noise of the cattle. The fires were out; no light to be seen but the pale illumination of the moon. But something had awakened her! Then she felt the wagon shake, and she saw Logan ease over the tailgate. She sat up.

"Sorry," he whispered. "I didn't mean to wake you."

In the moonlight she could see his smile.

"But I'm glad I did." He crawled closer to her, and in the silvery light she could tell that he wore nothing but his britches.

He took his boots off and stretched out beside her, his chest coming into contact with her hands. He bent his head, touching his lips lightly to hers. Her head tilted back, her eyes closed, and her lips parted on a little sigh.

Logan needed no more incentive. He caught fire immediately, goaded by Brenna's half sigh and her instinctive acquiescence. His hand moved from her cheek to the nape of her neck, sliding around the curve of her long, elegant throat. He held his palm to the base of her skull, threading his fingers through her black hair, and tilted her head to one side, angling his own so that he could take full possession of her willing mouth.

Logan broke the kiss to lift his head slightly. With difficulty he tore his mouth from hers and pulled back to look down into her face. "Brenna. Brenna," he murmured. His lips still hovered a mere sigh away from hers. His breathing was rapid, his heartbeat accelerated. His face lowered and his lips moved over her face as his hands moved over her flat stomach and lower. He felt her tremble in his arms. Then his mouth closed over hers in a passionate kiss.

Chapter Eleven

Clad in britches and shirt, Brenna sat around the campfire with the teamsters who were drinking their first cup of coffee for the day. Like them, she quickly downed her share and ate some of the warmed-over buffalo stew. Then all were busy at their tasks, getting ready to pull out and head for the water.

In the fifteen or twenty minutes it took the men to harness and yoke their animals, Brenna, as did the other women, cleaned and stacked the three camp kettles, the frying and baking pans, and the Dutch oven. She checked to see that the water kegs were securely attached on all her wagons.

When she heard Logan's shout, "Stretch out," she was bestride her horse. As she joined him at the head of the caravan, she pushed up on the saddle and gazed behind her. Proud of the sight of her wagon train, she smiled. Now that Logan was their scout and wagon boss, she had no doubt they would safely reach Bent's Fort. Yet always present to nag her was the thought that one day she would awaken and Logan would be gone.

"We'll be at water by noon," Logan told her, tilting his head back to look at the sky. "We'll probably halt longer than usual today to let the cattle drink their fill of water, graze, and rest."

Brenna turned her head and looked around. "I have an eerie feeling that we're being watched," she commented.

Logan had been aware that they were being watched for some time, but he wasn't overly concerned about it. He figured it was more Comanche scouts. His thoughts were on the conversation he and Ellington had last night. He kept wondering about the deep wagon ruts—depth caused by the heaviness of the load. Willard had made another observation that troubled Logan. The horses traveling with the wagons were shoed, and Indians did not shoe their horses.

"Reckon it's those Comanche scouts?" Brenna asked.

"Figure so," Logan said to keep Brenna from worrying unduly. "Every once in a while I'll see a smoke signal in the sky, so I figure they're reporting on our progress."

That satisfied Brenna, and she relaxed, ready to enjoy the journey to water. Jonesey, in his usual place on Brenna's wagon, set a fast pace, and the hours passed quickly. Before the caravan reached the river, Logan slowed them down, and he and Brenna rode ahead and scouted out the campsite. Along the way both looked for Indian markers but found none. This made Logan uneasy.

Attuned to Logan's feelings now, Brenna knew he was concerned. "What's wrong?" she asked.

Logan didn't push the subject aside. "I'm not sure."

"Indians?" Brenna asked, but even as she uttered the question, she knew better.

"No," he answered quickly and emphatically. "I'd have seen some signs." He dismounted and tethered his horse behind a large boulder, indicating for Brenna to do the same. "Cover me," he ordered. "I'm moving in for a better look."

Brenna watched as he scooted through the rocks to the narrow stream of water, her eyes darting about to catch any unusual movement. She strained her eyes to catch any unfamiliar sounds. The minutes dragged by.

"Brenna!"

Logan's cry caused her to start. She wiggled through the rocks and was soon racing toward him. "What's wrong?" she asked when she saw his kneeling form. The words hadn't echoed into silence before she saw the dead bodies. The buffalo hunters. Willard Ellington. His boys. She saw the lifeless form of the brother, Benson, the front of his shirt saturated with blood. She looked for the towheaded boy, but he wasn't to be found.

"Where's Billy?" she asked. "Where is he? I don't see his body."

"I don't know." Logan walked around the area, his eyes reading all the signs as he moved.

"Comanches," Brenna said, looking at the scalped men. "It's got to be Comanches. They did this, didn't they?"

Logan was kneeling by now, his hand lightly running the heel mark of a set of small prints that pointed toward the rocks, prints that an Indian wouldn't have missed. "I don't think it's Indians who did this work," he returned, his eyes scaling the huge boulders to the right.

"Who then?" Brenna asked.

"Whites."

"No!" Brenna exclaimed. "Not whites. These men have been scalped, Logan."

"To make it look like Indians."

The words frightened Brenna, and she looked around. "Do you think *they're* still around here?"

"No, *they've* been gone quite some time." Never taking his eyes from the huge boulder, Logan said in an

177

undertone, "I think someone is in the rocks over there. Maybe Billy. A set of prints head in that direction." Logan rose slow and easy and followed the tracks.

Brenna followed behind until the trail disappeared on the hard surface.

Hands on his hips, Logan stood and squinted against the glare of the midday sun. He called, "Billy, can you hear me?"

"They took him with them," Brenna said, a note of desperation creeping into her voice. "They took Billy, Logan."

"Maybe," he said, "maybe not." He pointed in the opposite direction. "You search over there. I'll search over here."

Brenna and Logan separated and looked behind every bush they could find and around every rock. In every crevice. In any nook, small or large. Finally Brenna gave up hope of finding him. She returned to find Logan kneeling beside a large clump of bushes.

"Billy!" She ran to Logan. "You've found Billy." When she reached the spot, however, Logan held up a shredded bag. She looked at the ground. Marbles—the marbles he had played with last night—were scattered all around.

"He was here." Logan's hand went to the scuff marks and beyond to some boulders at a distance. "He's over there." He rose and started walking, his stride so long Brenna could hardly keep up with it.

Her heart was beating in her throat. She wanted to find Billy. At the same time, she was afraid of what they were going to find. Logan moved through the rocks until he found a small cave, too small for an adult, large enough for a child. He knelt and peered into the opening.

"Billy, can you hear me?"

There was no response, but Logan's keen ears

detected movement.

"It's Logan MacDougald, Billy." Quietly Logan spoke. "You know, the boss on the wagon train, and Miss Brenna." He waited but still received no answer. "Billy, we're your friends. We won't hurt you. Please come out."

The seconds crept by as Logan and Brenna waited.

Brenna knelt beside Logan and called, "Billy, please come out. If you don't, I'm going to crawl in the cave to get you, and I'm—I'm afraid of small places."

They heard the whimpering first, then a scraping noise; soon Billy's blond head appeared. "Mr. Mac-Dougald," he cried, his small face swollen from his tears. "Miss Brenna."

Logan scooped the child into his arms and held him tightly. He closed his eyes to hide his own tears. "It's all right, Billy," he murmured. "It's all right."

"No, it ain't." Heartrending sobs filled the air. "I hid. Like a yellow-bellied coward, I hid behind them bushes. I saw 'em killing Uncle Will and Pa and the boys, but I didn't do nothing." Billy turned his face to Logan's chest and cried.

"Cry, little man," Logan said in a low, soothing tone. *Get it out of your soul now, so that it doesn't haunt you the rest of your life.* Logan turned and carried Billy back to the creek. He laid him beneath the shade of the tree.

Brenna knelt beside him and gazed at the pale little face, streaked with dirt. The blue eyes were faraway and blank. "Hello, Billy."

"Hello, Miss Brenna." His voice no longer held any emotion.

"I'm . . . glad we found you."

"I should be dead like them," Billy said. "I should be dead."

"No, Billy!" Brenna exclaimed. "You shouldn't be

179

dead. Mr. MacDougald and I are here to take care of you."

Dispassionately the child said, "I let them kill Pa."

Brenna looked at Logan. She didn't know how to talk with Billy; she didn't know what to say to him.

But Logan did. "No, Billy," he said, "you didn't let anyone kill your pa."

"How do you know?" The child turned on him in anger. "You wasn't here. You didn't see none of this."

Logan pulled the struggling boy into his arms and held him tightly. As Antelope Hunter had done many years ago for him, Logan gave love and courage. "I know how you feel."

"No, you don't," Billy screamed, his fists pounding against Logan's chest. "You don't know how I feel."

Logan loosened his hold on the child, but he didn't turn him loose. "When I was ten years old, I saw the Comanches kill both my parents," Logan said.

Billy quieted, and Brenna sat down, both of them listening to Logan as he talked, describing the death of his parents and the kidnapping of his older sister. He left none of the lurid details out; he spared himself no grief. For the first time in the nineteen years since his parents' death, he talked openly and candidly. His main concern now was to see that Billy didn't carry self-recrimination with him throughout his life, that he grew to manhood without all this bitterness and hatred festering in his soul.

"Now," Logan said some time later, "let's have a drink of water and something to eat, and you can tell me what happened to you."

Brenna was on her feet, moving to the horses. She returned with her canteen and food. While Billy drank thirstily, she rolled a piece of buffalo meat in a corn fritter and handed it to him. She fixed one for her and Logan also, the three of them eating quietly.

Finally Billy said, "It wasn't Indians who killed my pa and Uncle Willard, Mr. MacDougald. It was white men. About twenty of them. I heard them tell Pa they was rangers working for the government of Texas." Billy's eyes fell to the revolver in Logan's holster. "One of them had guns like yours. I heard them talking to Uncle Willard about the new six-shooter."

Brenna's head jerked up, and she looked at Logan. "Texas Rangers? Surely they wouldn't do this."

Billy nodded his head. "They did, Miss Brenna. I heard them tell Uncle Willard they was going to get plenty of the revolvers. They're expecting a whole shipment of them."

Perhaps the men who had killed the hide hunters wore six-shooters—and only rangers wore the new Colt six-shooting revolver—but Logan couldn't believe these men were affiliated with the ranging units out of Texas. He remembered that Scar-Face had promised the Comanches new Colt six-shooting revolvers. This was the shipment of guns he was waiting for.

"Billy"—Logan caught the child's eyes—"let's don't tell anybody about what these men told your uncle."

Brenna looked at Logan and wondered why he would make such a request of the child.

Billy asked, "Why?"

"I don't want the people any more frightened than necessary." He waited for a second, then asked, "All right?"

Billy nodded.

"How did you happen to be in the bushes?" Logan asked.

"I was out playing when they come," Billy answered, "and didn't get back to camp until they was here. Had their guns pulled on pa and the others by the time I got back." Tears ran down Billy's cheek. "That's when I ducked behind that clump of bushes. They killed them, Mr. MacDougald, and took all our hides. Now me and Ma ain't gonna have nothing to sell in Santa Fe. That was all our money." He added passionately, "I hate them Texas Rangers. When I grow up, I'm gonna kill all of them."

"No, Billy," Brenna quickly said. "You can't grow up hating all people because of what a few did. Hate will ruin your life. If you're not careful, you'll be obsessed by it. When your heart is filled with hate, you have no room for love."

"Brenna's right," Logan said. "You can't live your life hating these men."

"I'm going to kill them," Billy sobbed, his face pressed into Logan's chest. "I should of got me a club and beat them to death," he ranted. "I should of died fighting with Pa."

Logan's heart went out to the boy. He understood his despair and humiliation. He understood his desire for revenge. He had lived with the same ghosts, shame, and desires for the past twenty years. Nothing Antelope Hunter ever said to him had dissipated that hatred and burning passion for revenge.

Logan looked at Brenna. She had been speaking directly to him and didn't know it. All she had said was true. His heart was filled with hatred: He hated the scar-faced man who had raped his mother and killed his parents; he hated the white-haired chief who had taken Flanna. He didn't have room for love—not the kind of love Brenna deserved, and Brenna did deserve love.

"I'll get the men who murdered your family for you, Billy," Logan promised. "You don't have to worry about them anymore. Now let's get up. We've got some living to do." He picked the boy up in his arms and turned to Brenna. "Let's get back to the caravan.

They'll be worried about us."

Logan settled Billy in front of him on the horse, and the three of them rode to meet the wagon train. The people crowded around as Logan recounted the scene he and Brenna had found, and Gertrude Dawkins quickly took Billy under wing, shuffling him off to her and Callie Sue's wagon. As soon as the train was corralled, Brenna went to check on the child to find him helping Gertrude with her chores.

Logan saw to the burying of the hide hunters. When the task was completed, he asked Roger and Elijah to meet with him at Brenna's wagon. The three of them were in deep conversation when Bertha Caldwell came running.

"Elijah! Mr. MacDougald!" she called. "You need to come quick. Henry Gibson has called the men together so they can vote to see what we're going to do now."

The three men spun around and ran to the campfire. Brenna followed. Because he was the wagon boss and directly over the train, Logan asked, "What kind of meeting are you having, gentlemen?" His voice was deceptively soft. He looked at Dwight Jones. "Did none of you think to inform the wagon boss or captain?"

"Not one called by me, no sir-ee," Jonesey grumbled. "Been in a dither, they have, ever since we found them hunters dead and scalpt and the boy told us the rangers had done it."

"As soon as we get our water, we're moving on," Henry Gibson announced. "We think it's dangerous to sit in one spot too long. And you did, too, until now."

"I still agree with you, Mr. Gibson; we need to make as many miles a day as we possibly can," Logan replied. "That's why I've been pushing you so hard. And I can understand your worry. I'm not too comfortable myself, but the animals need rest. As wagon boss, I'm

183

responsible for your welfare and safety, and I must take into consideration that we're in a part of the country that has little water. When we do find it, we must let the animals drink and rest; they need to eat the grass."

Gibson opened his mouth to protest, but Logan held up his hand. "If you'll allow me, I'll get you out of Comanche territory as soon as I can, but we have to do it my way. If we don't, you won't have enough draft animals left to pull your wagons to Bent's Fort."

"I don't like this," Gibson mumbled. "The Comanches and Comancheros are chasing us. Now we've got these Texas Rangers out here, killing innocent folks and stealing their goods. We just can't take a chance by sitting here."

"Comanches are not chasing us," Logan declared emphatically, "and Texas Rangers did not kill the hunters."

"That's what the boy said," Henry pointed out.

"The men may have passed themselves off as rangers," Logan said, "but they were not rangers."

"Passed themselves off as rangers," Sam mused. "Are you saying—"

As Sam spoke, Maude Hemphill came from behind one of the wagons with a rifle. Brenna, who had been watching the people closely from Sam's carriage, observed the movement. She walked to stand immediately behind Maude.

"I'm saying I don't know who did it."

"And we don't care," Horace Faraday said. "We've voted to leave as soon as we've eaten and refilled our water barrels, and we are going to leave. Thank you for your concern over our livestock, Mr. MacDougald, but with or without you, we're leaving. You and Mrs. Allen can come along later if you wish to remain here."

Logan's hands easily moved to rest on the butt of his revolvers. "You may have voted," he informed them,

184

"but you won't be leaving until I give the word. You have been a part of this caravan up to this point, and you will remain a part of it until we reach Bent's Fort." His voice was as flinty as his eyes.

"And what if we don't listen to you?" Faraday blustered.

"Out here, Mr. Faraday, the voice of the real law is the revolver, not the vote, and the law of the wagon train is in the hands of the wagon boss." Faraday's eyes darted from Logan's immobile face to the weapons at his waist. "Now, gentlemen, I suggest you calm down and listen to me. Because of the excessive heat and the exhausted condition of our draft animals, we're going to spend the night here."

"No, Mr. MacDougald"—Maude Hemphill pointed a rifle at him and cocked it—"we've listened to you all we're going to. We're taking matters into our own hands." Henry Gibson and several of the other settlers moved behind Maude, murmuring their agreement.

"Mrs. Hemphill," Logan said, "do not point a gun at me unless you fully intend to use it, and remember that's my own practice. If I point a gun, I shoot it."

"I would advise you to put the gun down, Mrs. Hemphill," Brenna said, and pressed the barrel of her revolver into Maude's back to give emphasis to her words.

Maude didn't obey. She watched Roger move to stand behind Logan on one side, Elijah and Sam on the other. The majority of the wagon train was soon standing with him. Maude lowered the gun, and her supporters slowly melted back.

"Now that this matter is settled"—Logan addressed the entire assembly—"I suggest you get to work. Fill every container you can find with water, and take as many baths as you wish. No telling when we'll hit water again. Then get some rest, because once the train starts moving, you'll be pushing hard."

Roger joined Logan and Brenna as they walked a ways down the river. "Not that I agree with the settlers," he said, "but you can't really blame them for their reaction. This thing with the hide hunters has left the people jumpy."

Logan nodded. "They have a right to be, Hollis. I don't hold any hard feelings, and I hope they don't. But I'm not going to have them think they can pull away from the wagon train every time they disagree with what the wagon boss orders. You can't do that out here and survive."

"No, I reckon not," Roger replied.

"You've done a lot of growing up since you've been out here," Logan said. "You're a good man."

Roger's eyes glistened with pride. "Thank you, Mr. MacDougald. Coming from you, that's praise indeed."

"No"—Logan shook his head—"just a fact. From now on you're going to be assuming more responsibility, and with responsibility comes authority. You'll have to make decisions that won't please the crowd; then you'll have to stick by them and make sure everybody else does."

Roger laughed. "As long as you're wagon boss, Mr. MacDougald, I don't reckon I have too much cause to be concerned."

Logan lightly slapped Roger on the back. "You never can tell."

Roger soon left Brenna and Logan alone. The two of them walked even farther from the corral. They stopped when they stood beneath the cluster of trees lining the riverbank.

Brenna asked, "Why do I have the feeling that you're going to leave?"

"Because I am." Logan didn't look at her when he said the words because he didn't want to see the hurt in her eyes, and he knew it would be there. He felt guilty enough about his decision without her adding to it. "It's high time I was moving on. You've got some good men now who can take over and work with you to get this train to Bent's Fort and on to Santa Fe."

Brenna said nothing.

"Besides, you knew when I joined the wagon train that I couldn't remain with you."

"Yes, I knew." *But deep down, I hoped. I hoped that what we shared was enough to keep you by my side. I hoped that in time you might come to love me as I love you.*

"Hollis has matured since he's been on this expedition," Logan said. "He's a strong man now, well acquainted with trail life. Caldwell is another strong one. Both of them will help you with the train."

"Logan"—Brenna cast pride aside—"don't go."

"I have to," he answered, still avoiding her eyes. "I have to find out who and what these men are. I must find out where they're getting the guns from. This is serious. Only the government of Texas is ordering those guns, and they're for the rangers."

"Let someone else have this assignment, Logan."

"Time's running out, Brenna. I've got to stop these people now."

"So Texas can become a state in the union." Brenna knew her accusation was unjust, but in her despair she had to lash out. "So Houston can take credit for putting an end to the Comanche wars! So Houston can get the glory for ridding Texas of the Comancheros."

"Not because of Houston," Logan answered. "So honest and decent people can be safe."

"Oh, God, Logan," Brenna cried, "I can't stand the thought of your going out there by yourself. You're one man, not an army. You don't stand a chance against those men."

187

"I have to go. I haven't heard from Thunder since he left that night to follow Kirkwood. I don't know if he's dead or alive. I don't know who these men are or why they're posing as rangers. I have a strong hunch that they're Comancheros, but I must know for sure. I have to find out who's supplying them with guns and information." He took a step and caught her shoulders. "I saw enough today to know that we're up against butchers who kill for the sheer pleasure of it, be they Indian, Comanchero, or white."

Brenna studied the masculine face that was near to hers. She could see clearly the lines of fatigue that winged from the corners of his eyes, hours of strain that came from endless looking and searching. She looked at the grayness around his mouth, the shadow of beard stubble—which she wanted to touch with her fingertips—the rivulets of perspiration that glistened on his temples.

And as surely as she was standing here, she was losing him! The thought terrified Brenna. When she lost her papa, she had both Shawn and Gabby; when she lost Shawn, she had Gabby. Now she was losing Logan, and she had no one. Absolutely no one!

Logan stared at her. As if he were an artist, she the subject, he studied her face; he committed every feature to memory. The eyes that could vacillate easily and quickly from blue to green. The vibrant hair that crowned her head and framed her face. He lifted his hand and ran his fingers over her lips, the dainty curve of the upper one, the sensuous fullness of the lower one.

"Logan"—Brenna sighed, wanting him to take her into his arms and comfort her—"I'm scared."

She moved her face beneath his callused hands, loving the friction on her cheeks. But she wanted more—much more. Logan caught her in his arms, pulled her against him in a warm, engulfing hug, and buried his face in her hair.

"Sweetheart—"

The endearment came so easily and sounded so wonderful to her ears.

"—I'm a little frightened myself," he confessed. He tenderly brushed the soft strands of hair back from her temples as he struggled to find the words to express what he wanted to say. "You've aroused emotions in me that no other woman ever touched. You've stirred me up so, woman, I don't know if I'm going or coming."

Brenna laughed shakily. "What are you going to do about it?"

"Right now," he admitted sadly, "there's nothing I can do about it."

Brenna stiffened and pulled out of his arms. "If you wanted to, Logan, nothing could stop you."

He stared deeply into her eyes and implored, "Brenna, please understand."

"Well, I don't understand," Brenna blazed. "Finding your sister, yes, that I can understand, but chasing after the Comancheros and Indians by yourself because you think you owe it to Sam Houston—a drunk who won the war of independence because he couldn't retreat any farther! No, I don't understand."

"I . . . you're different from any other woman I've ever known."

"I most certainly am," Brenna answered. "I expect more from you than your splendid body. I'm not content with your merely sleeping with me. Now I'm going to tell you something else, Logan MacDougald, and it'll probably scare you to death. I more than desire you. I love you. I'm not asking you to make the same declaration to me, but I am asking you not to run off and leave me. I need you, and I want you. I'm not afraid of love and its responsibilities like you are; I'm not

189

afraid of what we feel for each other," Brenna continued, completely ignoring the tightness around Logan's mouth. "But I am afraid of losing you to the Indians or to the Comancheros."

"I don't like being tied to someone," Logan said, lashing out at her because he felt guilty and it irritated him, lashing out because everything she accused him of was true. "That's why I never became involved with one woman. Women become possessive and use love to tie a man to their side. Just like you're doing now. If you love me, you'll stay with me," he mimicked in a hard, cold voice. "It's a trap I'd rather avoid."

"I'm sorry you feel that way," Brenna returned. "I thought when two people felt the way we do about one another that they also felt a certain obligation to them. Whether you do or not, I do. Within nine months I've lost my father, my husband, and my dearest friend—two of them to Comanches. I won't lose another man out of my life, Logan."

"You're not going to lose me, baby." Logan laughed as he again reached for Brenna, but she dodged him. "I'll probably be in Santa Fe before you get there."

"If you leave me now, Logan, don't expect me to look you up in Santa Fe."

A devilish grin spanned Logan's face. "How about my looking you up?"

"No, Logan. When you leave, you're leaving for good. I don't ever want to see you again. We're through."

Logan was generally the one issuing ultimatums. Now that the shoe was on the other foot, he found that he didn't like wearing it at all. In fact, he was downright infuriated with Brenna. "You're giving me an ultimatum?"

"If that's what you want to call it," she told him. "I won't be left to the mercy of my emotions again."

"Evidently what we shared wasn't special enough, was it?" Logan said.

"Evidently not." Brenna's heart was breaking within, but she refused to show it. She would never give Logan the satisfaction of knowing how much he affected her or how lonely she was going to be when he rode off.

Half an hour later Brenna stood and watched Logan ride away. Before he was out of sight, he turned and waved, but Brenna didn't move a muscle. She stood and watched until he had disappeared over the horizon.

Chapter Twelve

After Logan left, the days dragged by for Brenna. Long hours of hard travel were taking its toll on everyone. Ill feelings multiplied rapidly; tempers flared easily and fights erupted continuously, though little harm was done. Water was so scarce that thirst was not slaked. Water holes were far apart, and many of them were dry, or alkali and unfit for drinking. Without enough water the beasts were beginning to die of dehydration and fatigue.

Roger and his men, now experienced frontiersmen, were doing an excellent job of maintaining order, but they were few in number compared to the teamsters and the settlers, the latter joining together to grumble and complain. The slower pace irritated the settlers; they feared missing the Oregon-bound wagon train they were to connect with at Bent's Fort; the teamsters were eager to reach Santa Fe so they could receive their wages.

At midday camp on Saturday, the sixth day after Logan departed, Horace Faraday, leading a delegation of settlers and teamsters, approached Roger. "Mr. Hollis," he said, mopping his face with his handkerchief, "I want to talk with you."

Brenna sighed. She had been expecting this all day.

She had seen them gathering in small groups, talking quietly and looking at her. She moved away from her wagon and joined Roger.

"We're running out of water," Horace said. "Last two water holes were dried up, the one before that was alkali, and our cattle are dying. Soon we'll be doing the same."

"What do you suggest we do, Mr. Faraday?" Roger asked.

"You need to find us another route," Horace blurted. "This here is the quickest route to hell, I figure. We'll all be baked to death in a few more days."

"MacDougald said this was the best route to take," Roger said.

Horace shuffled his feet nervously and carelessly tucked the handkerchief into his back pocket, the corner trailing out like a flag. Instead of looking at Roger, he looked at Brenna. "Well, that's one of the things we're a little worried about. MacDougald's more an Indian than a white."

"That's right," one of the teamsters called out to give Faraday moral support. "Been raised by them, he has. Makes him more Indian than white."

"The one he rides with is sure Indian," Horace pointed out. "And, well, we're just downright worried. Right after the murder of them hide hunters, he decides to leave us on our own."

Although Brenna shared Horace Faraday's sentiments, she wouldn't give voice to them. "The wagon train wasn't Mr. MacDougald's obligation," she said. "He wasn't part of the deal when you asked to join me."

Horace saw that he wasn't going to gain any ground by moving in that direction. His eyes darted furtively about until they settled on the distant ridge. "In full view, them two Comanches have been following us every since Mr. MacDougald rode out of camp."

"The Comanches have been trailing us ever since they attacked the wagon train, Mr. Faraday. Mr. MacDougald explained that they would keep a watch on us, but he said we were in no danger of another attack. He also warned us not to let them taunt us into straying from the caravan. One on one, not any of us is a match for a Comanche."

Brenna was tired and frightened. The people were restless, and in their anxiety they were developing mob tendencies. Emotion—intense emotion—seemed to be ruling the day. She only hoped she and the armed guards were enough to keep order. At the moment she could easily hate Logan MacDougald for having left her to face this alone.

"But look at them," Faraday said. "They come close enough that we can see them dangle those water pouches in front of us. They're drinking water. When they get close enough that we can see real good, so's we can almost taste and smell it, they pour it on the ground and laugh at us."

"They've never gotten that close," Roger said. "They're just trying to lure us away from the wagon train. They want us to think they have water."

"Well, I happen to believe they do have it," Faraday maintained. "And I think it's bound to be close around here. We'll probably die from thirst, and water only a few miles away."

"I don't want to die, period," Brenna declared, "nor do I want you to die, but just as sure as we deviate from the way Mr. MacDougald pointed out, we're walking straight into death. We're letting them lure us deeper into their territory."

Sam moved to stand behind Brenna and Roger. He was calm, his breathing more controlled than usual. "Way I see it . . . Faraday, MacDougald . . . he saved us from the Comanches . . . and left his job with the govern . . . ment . . . so he could lead us safely part of the way to Bent's Fort. Didn't see . . . you griping none . . . when he was fighting them savages."

Elijah Caldwell heaved himself to the front of the crowd, running his hand down his flowing beard. "I don't rightly know who MacDougald is that we should trust him," he announced. "Said he was working for the government of Texas, but there's no way we can prove that. And I agree with Faraday. MacDougald sure chose an odd time to leave."

"He just ain't what he appears to be," Maude added.

"Your argument is valid, Eli . . . jah," Sam said. "But I don't . . . reckon any of . . . us are what we appear to be." Stepping behind Brenna, he adjusted the wire frames of his glasses around his ear and took several deep swallows of air. "But then . . . that's one of . . . the reasons why . . . all of us are headed west. We didn't . . . want to be what . . . we were back East." Sam's chest swelled as he drew in needed oxygen. "We—we want . . . to be somebody else—somebody better . . . or somebody richer. You ought . . . to know better than to make a super . . . ficial judgment of a man."

"Wife's pretty upset," Elijah continued. He blamed no one for the predicament they were in. He was only looking for a solution to the problem. "Got to admit, I'm worried, too. Plenty worried, and," he added, "we got the youngun to think about now."

"Yeah," the murmur went up through the crowd.

"Billy is my responsibility," Gertrude said, drawing the boy closer to her, "and although I'm like you, I don't understand why Mr. MacDougald chose this time to leave us, I also agree with Brenna: We must follow MacDougald's instructions if we plan to survive."

"We done agreed on what we're going to do," Horace

replied. The anger had died out of his voice, but he was still determined to have his own way. "Tomorrow's the Lord's Day, and we're going to rest as usual, but we're also going to send the men out two by two in all four directions so's they can search for water. When they find it and report back, we're heading in that direction."

"No, Mr. Faraday," Brenna said, "you're not going to do that. When you joined this caravan, you agreed to abide by wagon train law, and that's exactly what you'll do. Unless I or Mr. Hollis dispatch a scout to search for water, no one will leave this corral." She cast contemptuous eyes on the settlers.

"How foolish can you be!" Roger exclaimed, also glowering at the people. "Those two Comanches could take our entire wagon train in a few days of such nonsense. You're leaving the women and possessions with no protection, and you're laying yourselves open for attack."

"And," Jonesey added to the argument, "What about them so-called rangers? They could be out there hiding. Don't look like they intend to take prisoners or let anyone live to tell about the robbery."

"We're going to do it whether you like it or not," Faraday announced.

"I don't like it," Brenna said. Her tone was a cutting edge. But she also realized that nothing would be gained if chaos broke out in camp. Shooting at one another wouldn't solve any problems; it would only create more. She had to pacify them; she had to convince them that safety was in number. "If you'll just be patient, Mr. Hollis and I will get you to water and to Bent's Fort. If we use the water sparingly, we'll have enough until we find more."

"We've tried it Mr. MacDougald's way, Mrs. Allen," Barbara Faraday said. "Now we're going to try it ours."

"If we find water and decide to go another route, Mrs. Allen, we'll just pull our wagons out." Elijah didn't want to hurt or anger Brenna. Even though he disagreed with the woman, he respected her. "And since we'll be breaking the contract, you won't be responsible for our well-being anymore."

"My God," Brenna exclaimed, "what do you take me for! It's not the money that worries me. It's your safety. I'm responsible for your well-being." She turned from one settler to the other. When she saw their minds were made up, she ceased her arguments. She, Jonesey, and Roger walked off.

"Don't worry about it, Miss Brenna," Roger told her. "The boys and I will take care of it. We won't let them go half-cocked out there."

"No, I'm sure you won't," Brenna said. "But I don't want them dead either. Post your men, but warn them I want no shooting until you or I give the word."

"We have today," Jonesey assured her, "and tomorrow to rest, and, well, Miss Brenna, Mr. Logan might just happen to show up before we stretch out again. He might tell us that water's just over the next rise."

"Mr. Logan just better not show up here," Brenna said through clenched teeth. "I'd kill him with my own bare hands."

"Aw, Miss Brenna," Jonesey said. "You can't blame Mr. Logan cause the water holes have been dry. He couldn't have knowed about that."

I blame Logan MacDougald for leaving me in this mess! Brenna seethed silently. *And he'd better not come back if he knows what's good for him.* However, through the afternoon Brenna turned anxious eyes from the Indians who remained on the ridge to the empty horizon that surrounded them.

Since the settlers had made the decision to search for

water by twos, the heaviness had risen. The quarreling had ceased; people were actually laughing and talking again, eager to be off.

Once more Brenna turned her face to the northwest. She saw a small black dot that seemed to be moving toward her and was growing larger by the minutes. Although she didn't want it to, her heart fluttered erratically. Something akin to joy surged through her veins. *Logan! Logan was coming!*

"Somebody's coming," she yelled.

Soon the people thronged around her, hands over eyes, as they peered into the afternoon sky.

"Reckon it's MacDougald?" Gertrude asked.

"Don't think so," Jonesey answered, squinting at the approaching figure. "Don't sit his horse like Mac-Dougald does." He dropped his hand, turned, and spat. "It's a stranger," he announced.

By the time the man rode up, the men were armed and in position, Roger's men up front, the settlers to the back. Brenna and Roger walked through the wagon fort. She was frightened, but she didn't show it. She waited for the stranger to identify himself.

He was an older man, Brenna judged, about fifty. He was definitely a frontiersman. His thin gray hair was shoulder-length, and both it and his beard were straggly and unkempt. His clothes testified to many days and nights of wear without benefit of soap and water. He carried a rifle, and tucked into his belt were two of those repeating revolvers like Logan and Thunder used and a large knife.

But she wasn't going to be fooled a second time. Abbott Kirkwood had fooled her once: this man wouldn't!

"Sandy Thomas," the man introduced himself, extremely narrow eyes assessing the crowd as he spoke.

198

"Roger Hollis, wagon boss. This here's the wagon captain, Mrs. Brenna Allen."

The man's eyes swept from Roger to Brenna, then beyond to the men stationed beind the wagons. The narrowed eyes swiveled back to her. "Kinda dangerous for a woman to be leading a wagon train, ain't it?" He didn't hide his contempt.

"Kinda dangerous for you to be traveling alone out here, ain't it?" Brenna parried.

"Reckon it is, but I know what I'm doing," he said.

"I know what I'm doing, too," was Brenna's cool reply.

"Been traveling with a wagon train that's recently arrived in Bent's Fort," the man said. "Headed toward Oregon, they are. Been waiting for another train to join them, one from Texas."

"That's us," Elijah exclaimed. "That's us."

"The people been worried about you," the man said. "Ask me if I'd come looking for you, so's I agreed to."

"Dudley Rawlins," Maude Hemphill called out. "Was there a Dudley Rawlins on the train?"

"Yep," the man muttered. "Sure was. Short man. About five foot seven, kinda heavy. Brown hair and beard. Wife named Clementine. Two girls and a boy."

"That's them," Maude sobbed. She lifted her apron to her face to wipe her tears. "That's my brother and his wife Clemmy."

"Get down and join us," Elijah invited, flagrantly disregarding caution. "We have some food cooked."

"Believe I will," the man said. "Put in some long hours on this saddle since I left the fort."

"Just a minute," Roger commanded, his hands hovering over his revolvers. He knew his men were backing him up. "We only have your word about who you are, Mr. Thomas, and about where you come from."

199

The two stared at each other for long, tense minutes. Finally Thomas nodded his head. "Reckon that's right. You just have my word."

"That's not good enough," Brenna said.

"It's good enough for me," Maude Hemphill yelled. Then she turned to the people. "We can't let this woman ruin our chances of getting to Bent's Fort."

With grudging respect Thomas said, "I reckon you need to be leery out here." He handed his rifle to Brenna, then the revolvers, then his knife. "I'll ride without these. Just want to reach Bent's Fort alive and in one piece."

The settlers swarmed around Thomas before Brenna or Roger could utter another word and ushered him to their campfire. Brenna was irritated, but all she could do at the moment was keep a close watch on the man.

"Did you see any Indians between here and the fort?" Elijah asked, following the men into the center of the compound.

"Nary a one till I got in sight of you," Thomas responded. "Saw two of them sitting on that hill like they was statues."

"Been following us for days," Horace lamented.

"Ain't going to do anything," Thomas assured them as one who knew. "Just want to make sure you don't do nothing."

"Just waiting to pick up our remains after we die of thirst," Maude grumbled.

Thomas laughed. "Ain't no need to die of thirst when water's so close. Just need to veer a little to the west."

"See," Faraday exclaimed, shaking his hand in Brenna's face. "See! What did we tell you! We're this close to water and would have missed it. MacDougald didn't know what he was talking about."

"Whoever MacDougald was," Thomas said, "he probably knew what he was talking about. Just hadn't

200

reckoned on a dry year like this one." Clearly ignoring Brenna, Thomas looked at Jonesey. "Who's MacDougald?"

"Was our wagon boss," Maude answered. She quickly told Thomas about the massacre of the hide hunters. "Large group of men posing as Texas Rangers."

"Didn't see nobody on the trail I took," Thomas offered.

"Probably wouldn't have." Maude Hemphill seemed to snort the words rather than speak them. "He's Indian, so he'd know how to hide himself."

Thomas's head snapped in Maude's direction, and his eyes suddenly burned with interest. "Indian?" He, like most people, always equated Indians with Comanches.

"He's white," Brenna explained. "His friend is a Cherokee. They work for Sam Houston."

The fire died in the eyes of the scout and he relaxed again. With a chuckle he said, "Wonder what ole Sam's got men out here for."

Not really interested in the answer to that question, Horace Faraday spoke. "You said there was water close by?"

"Sure did," the man said, nodding his thanks to Bertha Caldwell when she set a plate of food in his hands. He immediately crammed his mouth full and mumbled as he ate, "There's a river not too far from here. About two days' travel."

The members of the wagon train turned to Brenna, and she knew what they wanted her to do. Yet she couldn't. She had listened to Kirkwood; she had trusted him. But could she refuse Thomas's offer? Without water the people couldn't go much farther . . . nor the animals.

"I think, Mrs. Allen," Elijah said, "we really don't

have much choice. We've got to have that water."

When the others nodded and murmured their agreement, Brenna moved away from the circle of people and stood by herself thinking. Soon Roger joined her.

"What do you think?" he asked with a jerk of his head in Thomas's direction.

"I don't know what to think," she replied. "He seems to be all right. Knew about the caravan that's waiting for them in Bent's Fort. From the way he's talking to them about the people, I'd say he knew them."

"I think we ought to go with him," Roger said.

Jonesey walked up, his hands thrust into his pockets, in time to overhear the conversation and answer the question. "I don't rightly reckon we have much choice, Miss Brenna."

Brenna nodded her head. "That's what I've been thinking, too," she admitted. "And one or two days won't make that much of a difference. Among the three of us we can keep an eye on Thomas to make sure he doesn't stir up trouble."

"I kinda figured Mr. Logan would come back." Jonesey scanned the horizon. "Just wish if he was, he'd get here soon."

Deep down Brenna hoped that Logan would come back, too. He'd know how to deal with the people; he could handle Thomas. Throughout the afternoon and evening, Brenna found herself pacing from one end of the corral to the other, straining through the glare first, then the dusk. Finally she lay down. She slept fitfully and was up before anyone else, again her eyes racing the distance.

Sunday passed. Monday morning, at the break of day, without breakfast, the wagon trail pulled out. Brenna rode scout with Thomas. Trailing them from the rear were the two Comanche warriors; ahead of

202

them stretched those endless miles of barren plains. Morning turned into afternoon and night.

On the second afternoon as they were eating their meal, Thomas said to Brenna, "Need to cut due west. Believe it'll be easier traveling," he explained. "Traveled it on the way down. A little out of the way, but we'll make better time."

The second day turned into the third, and the farther west the caravan traveled, the more Brenna's concern grew. Deeper into Comanche territory they went, and she hadn't seen a sign of water; they had precious little left. She took her hat off and ran her fingers through the damp hair that stuck to her head. She wiped the dust and perspiration from her face with her sleeve.

Nudging the gray up beside Thomas, she said, "You told us water was only two days away. This is the second day. Where's the water?"

The scout turned his weather-beaten face toward her. "We're traveling slower than I first thought." He jerked his thumb over his shoulder in the direction of the wagons. "Animals don't have as much energy." His hand swept the desolate countryside. "No water and not much food."

"When do you think we'll find water?"

The man stared at Brenna with a slight degree of resentment. "Just a few more miles, I reckon." He pulled a plug of chewing tobacco out of his shirt pocket and stuffed it into the corner of his mouth. He wiped the back of his hand across his beard.

"Just a few more miles is all you'll have, Mr. Thomas." Brenna's voice was calm and assured. She left the man with no doubt to her intentions. She spurred her horse and moved away from Thomas. As she contemplated the future of the wagon train, she looked up and saw the sprinkle of gray clouds. They were small but they were there. The first promise—

although small, it was still a promise—of rain they had had since they entered the plains.

They camped at midday. The women busied themselves with the meal, and the men did the maintenance and repair work. Because of the unbearable heat, no one stayed out in the open too long. Thomas assured them they were quite safe from attacks of any kind, so as soon as they could they sought shade in or under the wagons or under makeshift tents. They posted a guard, and since they would be traveling well into the night, they rested as much as they could.

Brenna lay beneath her wagon on a blanket and stared at the sky—stared at the small, dark clouds. So many times the rain clouds tempted them—forming, then dissipating without so much as a drop of moisture; other times they would feel a few drops, then nothing. The draft animals were restless; they were hungry and thirsty. They couldn't go much farther without water. Neither could the people, for that matter.

Brenna closed her eyes and soon was asleep, but she was only lightly dozing. She heard voices; one of the guards was talking; she was instantly awake and alert. *Logan!* He had found them. He had come back. Somehow she had known he would. She rolled over to greet him, but her movements were stopped.

"Howdy—" She heard Thomas speaking to Knox Hemphill.

Disappointment knotted so big in Brenna's throat, she could hardly swallow.

"Howdy, Mr. Thomas. How far do you think we are from the water?"

"Should camp beside the river tonight, boy," the scout replied. "Not far from here at all." Brenna heard the scout slap Knox on the shoulder. "Well, think I'll get me a bite to eat. Then I'm going to take myself a nap. Got to get some rest. Be late tonight before we stop traveling."

Brenna watched the old man as he crossed the corral to the campfire. He leisurely ate, then sought the shade of a nearby wagon, where he lay down and went to sleep.

Brenna wished she could find sleep that easily. The minutes seemed to stretch into hours. The heat was unbearable. Perspiration dripped off her forehead and rolled down her cheeks; her clothes were plastered to her body. She'd give anything to get in a nice cool river. At the thought she lifted her head and gazed at the clouds. Closer, she thought, and darker. A good sign.

Then she felt the whisper-soft touch of a summer breeze. Closing her eyes, she breathed deeply, the air thick with the smell and taste of rain. She drifted off to sleep.

"Riders coming!"

Knox's shout awakened the entire camp. Brenna and Roger reached the young guard at the same time. As they watched the cloud of dust materialize into riders, Roger shouted orders, posting the men at their battle stations. Jonesey ran to stand next to her.

"It's not Logan." Brenna leaned against the wagon for support.

"Don't think so," Roger said, spitting dust out of his mouth. "Too many."

"Who is it then?" Jonesey murmured.

"Not sure," Brenna replied absently, capping her eyes with her hand in order to see through the early-afternoon glare.

"Ain't nobody I've seen before," Thomas drawled.

Jonesey watched the careful approach of the riders. "Dressed like whites," he said. "About a hundred in all. Ride like soldiers."

Brenna watched the leader of the men raise his left hand, signaling the others to halt. With his right hand he beckoned, and a young man broke out of the military formation to move forward.

"Who are they?" Elijah Caldwell whispered.

"Looks kinda like soldiers," Gibson murmured.

"Yep, but . . . whose soldiers . . . would be out here? Certainly . . . aren't those . . . of the United States," Sam said.

"Ain't Mexicans neither," Jonesey supplied.

The men who are posing as rangers! The thought careened through Brenna's brain.

The man neared the wagon train, his hands well away from his weapons. His hat shaded his face but didn't hide his features. His eyes were wary as he studied the group who stood behind the fortified wagons. His smile and expression were friendly.

"Howdy," he called, waving a hand to brush the sand from his mustache. "I'm James Steeple, private in the Texas army."

"Didn't know the republic had any men this far north," Brenna said, making no effort to leave the safety of the corral.

Steeple grinned. He was right surprised to see a woman dressed in such attire. "Yes, ma'am, we sure do. Now, if you'll just move your wagons so we can enter, we'll inspect your bills of lading and your loads. If your papers carry the official seal of Texas, you have nothing to fear from us."

"To have rangers inspect freight wagons is highly unusual and illegal," Brenna said, her eyes narrowing. "Texas is not in a state of martial law."

"Well, now, ma'am," Steeple said, "times are pretty tough in Texas, so's the president hired us." Steeple flashed Brenna a quick smile. "You might call us one of Houston's special ranging companies. Carry out special tasks for him, you know. Now, ma'am, by the

206

authority invested in me by the Republic of Texas, I'm ordering you to move these wagons and let us enter this corral."

"That's an order you'll have to be prepared to carry out by force," Brenna replied.

"We are, ma'am."

Chapter Thirteen

The man's words struck fear into the hearts of the people. For Brenna this seemed to be an affirmation of her earlier suspicions about Sandy Thomas. Like Kirkwood, he was an outlaw, and he was leading them into another ambush. A heavy silence hung like a funeral shroud over the caravan travelers. Brenna's unwavering gaze remained on the man who called himself Private Steeple.

"If you're a ranging unit duly authorized by the Republic of Texas," she finally said, "you can understand our wanting to see your commission before we allow you inside our corral."

"Of course," Steeple said, his smile widening. Garbed as she was and covered in dust, the woman was quite handsome. "Colonel Warfield assumed you would." Careful to keep his hands away from his revolver, the messenger slowly insinuated his hand under his vest to withdraw a small leather portfolio. As he opened it, his gaze swept over the wagon fort in a quick evaluation: the number of armed men; their positions; their strengths. "Here you are." He held out the document.

"Move the wagon," Brenna instructed the two guards.

She walked through the narrow opening to take the

paper from the man's hand. After she unfolded it, she read, "On this day"—she recited the day and year—"Charles A. Warfield, formerly of Missouri, is commissioned a colonel in the Texas army, authorized to raise five hundred volunteers, and empowered to prey upon Mexican commerce in the name of the republic, to levy contributions, and to capture Mexican property." When she finished reading the commission, she turned to Jonesey. Her voice was filled with incredulity. "It's authentic, all right. Signed by George W. Hockley."

Jonesey nodded. "Best I can recollect, Hockley was secretary of war at the time this here went into effect." His murmur ended with a splat of tobacco juice. "Now the question is, Miss Brenna, are these men indeed the ones who Mr. Hockley commissioned?"

Brenna nodded, her gaze riveting to Steeple's face.

"Colonel Warfield has his identification on him, ma'am, and a roster with all the names of his recruits," Steeple returned.

"Please get your identification papers, so I can review them."

Steeple looked at her narrowly for a few minutes before he nodded his head curtly and returned to the group of rangers. Coupled with the midday heat, the tension was more than Brenna could stand. She felt as if she were being drawn in two different directions, as if she would break any moment. When Steeple returned, Brenna took the documents. All seemed in order, but she had no way of positively identifying the men.

She refolded the papers and looked up at Steeple. "What can we do for you?"

"Colonel Warfield needs to see your bills of lading," Steeple replied. "If you're indeed citizens of Texas doing trade that will benefit the republic, you have no need to fear us. If not, ma'am, we'll be relieving you of your cargo."

"Nobody will be relieving me of anything," Brenna informed the young officer. "These goods don't belong to the republic or to anybody else. All this rightly belongs to me, and that's the way it's going to remain."

"What message would you have me give Colonel Warfield?" Steeple asked.

"Tell the colonel that I'd like to talk with him. Just the two of us. No weapons. Middle of the field."

Steeple nodded, turned the horse, and galloped toward the waiting men. Brenna, Jonesey, and Roger returned to the corral, the wagons being tightly drawn together after their entrance.

"Miss Brenna," Roger said, "I can't let you go out there alone."

"No, ma'am," Jonesey agreed. "You can't go out there, Miss Brenna. What if something happens to you? This here's yore wagon train. You need to stay with it. Let me go."

"I'll go," Roger said. "I'm the wagon boss, and that's one of my duties."

Brenna started to protest, but Roger was right. She had given him the title of wagon boss. Now she must delegate him the authority. She nodded and said, "Both of us will go." Then she turned to Gertrude. "Get Billy and bring him up here. While you're doing that I'll get my copies of the bills of lading."

When Brenna returned from her wagon, she had a small leather pouch in hand.

Roger turned to his men. "Make sure you stay in your positions, and be ready to fire at the least sign of trouble."

"Miss Brenna!" Billy came running. "Miss Gertrude said you wanted to see me."

"I do," Brenna replied, catching Billy's hand in hers and leading him to where Roger and Jonesey stood.

"You're sure reacting strongly to these here men," Thomas said as he walked up to join them. "What do you have to fear from them?" His gaze moved from Roger to Jonesey to Brenna. "Can't see they'll do us any harm if they be part of the army from Texas."

"Texas don't have no army," Jonesey exclaimed.

"We're not sure who they are, Mr. Thomas," Brenna said. "There's a bunch of thieving murderers loose in these parts, posing as ranging units of the republic. They massacred a wagon train and killed four buffalo hunters."

"Them's the ones your wagon boss took after?" Thomas asked.

"They're the ones Logan took out after," Brenna said. "You're not one of them?"

Thomas met and returned the gaze with equal measure. "Nope! Just what I said I was. Scout and guide for the wagon train from Missoury to Bent's Fort. Promised the people that I'd guide them on to Ory-gon. But they refused to get started without these wagons. That's why I volunteered to come get them." He waited until Brenna nodded. "If you'll give me my weapons, I don't mind standing with you and Mr. Hollis out there."

"Thank you, Mr. Thomas—" Brenna began, only to be cut off by Roger.

"Don't reckon we'll be giving you your guns," Roger informed the scout. "If anyone stands with us, it'll be Jonesey."

Brenna turned to Billy and handed him her field glasses. Pointing to the group of men who surrounded the wagon train, she instructed, "Look at them and see if you recognize any of them as the men who killed your uncle and cousins."

In order for Billy to see better, Roger lifted him in his arms.

Slowly Billy turned his head, looking from one of the men to the next. When he had studied all of them, he shook his head. "No, ma'am, I don't recognize one of them."

"Good," Brenna muttered as Roger set the boy on the ground. "That's what we needed to know."

"That don't mean anything," Jonesey protested. "The boy was rightly scared out of his wits, Miss Brenna. He don't know what or who he seen. Just because—"

"I know it doesn't," Brenna said, her face crinkling into a smile, "but it makes me feel a little safer to think it does." She unloosened the knot of her bandanna and slipped it from her neck. "I just have a feeling that maybe this colonel is legitimate, that he's really working for the government. Now, let's go do what we have to do." Over her shoulder, she said to the armed men, "Watch my right hand. If I wave this rag through the air, start firing."

"What about you?"

"I'll take care of myself," she returned. "Your duty is to protect the wagon train."

As she, Roger, and Jonesey walked through the opening in the wagon fortification, she looked over her shoulder. The men were positioned at the most strategic points along the walls of the fort. Some of the women were herding the cattle in the corral; others were behind the men, ready to load guns. All eyes were on Brenna and the bundled-up red and black cloth she held in her right fist.

Colonel Warfield dismounted and handed his weapons to his second in command, Lieutenant Arnold. He walked toward Brenna. When he was standing in front of the wagon captain, he bowed. "I'm Colonel Charles A. Warfield, ma'am."

Brenna studied the face, in particular the eyes, of the

212

man standing in front of her for a full minute before she said, "Brenna Allen, wagon captain for Garvey Mercantile and Freight Hauling. This is Roger Hollis, my wagon boss, and Dwight Jones, my lead driver."

Warfield acknowledged the introductions. Then he repeated his commission and instructions to Brenna. "If you're duly authorized by the Texas government, you and your members are free to keep your goods and to continue on your journey. If not"—he shrugged—"I shall have to relieve you of your cargo."

"Whether we're duly authorized by the government of the republic or not, Colonel, I don't think you'll be relieving me of my cargo without a fight on your hands," Brenna replied.

Warfield raised his head and looked at the caravan, sunlight reflecting off the barrels of the rifles pointed toward him and his men. When he returned his gaze to Brenna, his eyes glinted, and his voice hardened. "You read my commission?"

"I read it!"

"Then, ma'am, you understand my position."

"It's not your position I'm concerned about, sir," Brenna replied. "I'm concerned about ours. I'm concerned about the safety of the people in my caravan."

Jonesey spat, the tobacco juice barely missing the toe of Warfield's boot to splatter dust against the black leather.

Not a flicker of the eye or a twitch of a facial muscle revealed Warfield's thoughts. "I am a representative of the Texas government, Mrs. Allan, not some outlaw on the loose."

"I find it hard to believe that you're a ranger," Brenna said. "I've never heard of them riding this far west in Comanche territory. I find it quite suspicious that so many of you *representatives of the Texas*

213

government are operating out here on the plains!"

"I'm not sure I follow your meaning."

"Five buffalo hunters were robbed and killed, and a ten-year-old boy left for dead. When we found him, the boy said the men who did it—a group of about twenty, Colonel Warfield—identified themselves as rangers."

Warfield lifted his hand to rub the corners of his mouth. He nodded. "I can understand your concerns, Mrs. Allen, and I assure you my men and I are not killing and butchering innocent people." He shrugged his shoulder and waved his hands.

Brenna reached into her belt and pulled out the bundle of documents. "Here are our papers."

As soon as Warfield had gone through the freight bills and was satisfied, he said, "Sorry to have bothered you, Mrs. Allen. You and your people are free to go without any further delay from me and my men." He stepped back. "May I speak with the boy?"

"We'd invite you and your men in to have some food," Brenna said, "but first you'll have to let us keep your weapons until you decide to leave."

"We'd be your prisoners?"

Brenna nodded.

Warfield stared long and hard at the wagon captain. Finally he gave a curt nod. "Guess I can't blame you for being suspicious. We'll turn our weapons over to you."

Two hours later the settlers were getting along quite well with Colonel Warfield and his volunteers. They were cheering him as he told them of his mission.

Sitting on a small folding chair by Brenna's wagon, he waved his hands as he spoke. His eyes were bright, his voice loud with enthusiasm. "I plan to lead an expedition to Santa Fe and then to Chihuahua, so the people can overthrow the governments there," he announced proudly. "The people are eager to shed the oppressive yoke of Mexican bondage."

"That's what Lamar and Childers think," Brenna said. "They feel that Texas will be a nation mightier than the United States."

Warfield nodded his head vigorously. "There are a few farsighted people in Santa Fe who envision the same thing."

"Have you been to Santa Fe, Colonel?" Brenna asked, interest sparking in her eyes.

"Why, yes, ma'am," he drawled. "I sure have. Right nice little city it is. Wonderful hospitality." He continued to talk, regaling them with story after story of Santa Fe.

When he had concluded, Brenna asked, careful to keep her voice casual, "Did you happen to meet Mr. Peyton H. Alexander while you were there, Colonel?"

Warfield's eyes caught and held Brenna's for a second, an enigmatic flicker in their depths. "Well, Mrs. Allen, I did just happen to meet Mr. Alexander when I was in Santa Fe. Why? Do you know him?"

"Not really," Brenna said. "He made a trip through Texas recently, and I met him. My father and I were in Houston on business at the time. We all had dinner with Mr. Clarence Childers."

Warfield's head bobbed again. "Don't know Childers, but I've heard about him. Real big in politics in Texas right now."

Brenna smiled. "I'm not sure how much of a power he really is, but he would like to run for president."

"You don't sound like you're for the man or his idea." Warfield studied the woman who sat cross-legged on the ground in front of him.

"I'm all for his ideas," she admitted. "And yes, I'd vote for Clarence Childers as president."

"Miss Brenna," Roger said, interrupting the conversation, "I hate to interrupt your visit with the colonel, but we need to be moving out. We have a lot of

215

miles to cover."

"Of course," Warfield said. "My men and I need to be leaving, too."

With Roger's announcement the crowd began to disperse, leaving Warfield and Brenna alone.

"Mrs. Allen," Warfield said, "I am delighted to have had the opportunity to meet you. You are indeed a courageous woman. I wish you God's blessings on your trading venture with the people of Santa Fe. But I must warn you, be careful of Manuel Armijo, the governor. He's a bad lot, mean to the very core. He does not welcome Texans into his territory, especially not Texans who dream of an empire. If you ever need a friend, look up Peyton Alexander. He'll help you."

"Thank you, Colonel, for your kind words."

Warfield looked around, making sure no one was close enough to overhear his words. Even then he was cautious. He ducked his head closer to Brenna's and lowered his voice. "Peyton is expecting a valuable shipment from Texas. Is it on this train?"

Brenna shook her head and said, "Not to my knowledge." But Warfield's question set the cogs of her mind working. "The majority of my goods came from Childers, but I'm sure if any of this were being shipped directly to Alexander, Childers would have told me."

"Of course! Of course!" Warfield brushed his words aside with a laugh. "Now me and my men will be on our way. Again, Mrs. Allen, I must thank you for your hospitality and your company. I hope someday that I can be of service to you."

Colonel Warfield promised that he would be on the lookout for the outlaws who robbed and killed the hide hunters, and he concurred with Thomas that good water was only about twenty miles away.

"But either way," Warfield announced, his face lifting to the sky that was roiling with black clouds, "looks like you'll get water."

With a light heart and great anticipation, the wagons stretched out far earlier than usual for the evening journey. The animals, smelling the water, were eager to reach their destination, so their gait was faster than it had been.

As the caravan moved, the blue sky was replaced by a thick blanket of black storm clouds that seemed to reach to the very earth. Huge gusts of wind began to blow, the dust almost blinding everyone. As many as could took refuge in the wagons and pulled the drawstrings to close off the front and back.

Her bandanna tied over her face, Brenna raced to the rear of the line to the assistant wagon boss. "Herd the cattle closely," she yelled. "One clap of thunder and they'll stampede."

Then she was galloping off again. "Take the lid off your barrels," she ordered, her hand on the crown of her hat to keep it on her head. "Get as many containers ready as you can, so you can catch some water."

The wind was howling with fury now, straining the canvas against the hickory frames of the wagons and whipping the drawstrings loose so that the coverings on others flapped and popped. The sun was completely hidden, and day became as night. Jagged streaks of lightning flashed through the sky, causing the mules and horses to bolt.

The long-awaited rain started to fall, coming down in sheets so heavy no one could see through it. Jonesey, on his mule, moved up and down one side of the columns, yelling orders that were whipped into oblivion by the wind. Brenna, her head down to protect her face from the pelting force of the rain, rode the other side. She saw one of her teamsters knocked to the ground by a bolt of lightning. Closer to the man than she, Roger dismounted and bent over him. Brenna leaped off her horse, tied it to the back of the wagon, and ran to the terrified oxen. She grabbed the bullwhip—an eighteen-foot whip that cracked out like a rifle shot—and goaded the oxen to keep a steady pace.

Despite the attention the herders were giving the cattle, a tremendous thunderclap sent the livestock into terrified stampede, but no one had time to round them up. Human lives were at stake. Everyone was needed to keep the wagons upright. Jonesey kept riding the line, shouting encouragement and instructions to the people; Roger carried the unconscious man to Sam's carriage; and Brenna continued driving the wagon.

The wind blew with renewed force, successful in turning several more wagons over, spilling people and goods over the muddied plains. In the midst of the screaming and yelling, Brenna fought with the oxen. Then she was struck so viciously with hailstones that her eyes filled with tears. Finally another teamster came and took over her wagon. Her hat gone, she reached up to push wet strands of hair from her face. She sloshed through the mire to the Faradays' overturned wagon.

"Anybody hurt?" she yelled.

Kneeling, Barbara picked up her precious possessions that were scattered here and yonder. Unable to speak for the tears and the heartache, she merely shook her head. Her young fruit trees were crushed; her grandmother's mirror shattered; her sack of flour soaked with rain and covered in mud; her seeds scattered over the lonely west Texas desert.

Through the noise of the storm, Brenna heard Maude Hemphill's scream. "Somebody come help me!"

Brenna turned to look at the distraught woman who ran down the line of wagons, stumbling and falling, only to push to her feet and move forward again. Her hair had come loose from the coil to tangle at the nape of her neck, and long strands whipped across her face. Water ran down her face and her mud-slicked garments.

"Knox!" she cried, her hands digging into Brenna's shoulders. "My boy's caught under the wagon."

Food and possessions forgotten, Brenna and Barbara leaped to their feet and hastened to the Hemphill wagon. The number of rescuers grew as the women ran, as did the congestion and disorder. One would scream an order; two more would countermand it. They would get the wagon part of the way up; it would slip and fall again. Maude was having hysterics. Brenna couldn't get a word in edgewise.

Then over the storm, over the commotion, Brenna heard Logan's familiar shout—a shout that oddly seemed so quiet and calm and reassuring. "Brenna, you and Mrs. Faraday get that woman out of here and take care of her. She's probably worse off than the boy."

Logan was back! Brenna took one moment to look into his face—a swift moment to reacquaint herself with all its angular beauty. But she couldn't be happy with his return for being so bitter and angry. Had he been here when she needed him, then most of this wouldn't be happening to her! She didn't smile or speak to him; she simply stared.

"I'll take care of Maude." Gertrude sloshed through the rain to put her arm around the woman's shoulder and lead her to a wagon.

Shielding her face with her hand, Brenna looked at her caravan, wagons overturned, goods spilled all across the plains, people injured. She saw the men carrying Knox Hemphill to his mother's wagon. She smiled her relief. He wasn't injured severely. Mostly he was frightened and bruised.

For the next hour everyone relentlessly worked, setting wagons on their wheels, pushing them against the huge boulders that jutted out of the ground, and bracing them so they wouldn't overturn again. Once the injured were rescued and nursed, people turned their efforts to reloading their wagons.

Exhausted, Brenna sat on the gray, her gaze wandering to the end of the caravan. Logan's return was forgotten as she stared at the storm damage. She saw perishable goods—her precious commodities for trade in Santa Fe—strung across the now muddy plains; wagons were damaged beyond repair. And the cattle . . . they were gone.

"The cattle," she yelled. "We've got to round them up."

Logan was at her side before she could spur the horse on. "Where do you think you're going?"

"Going to get my cattle," she screamed above the elements.

"It's too dangerous for you out here. Get in the wagon out of the storm," he ordered. "I'll take care of the cattle."

She jerked away from him, the rain dripping in sheets around her. "That's what you should have thought about a long time ago. Now just leave me alone. I'll take care of my business. You take care of yours." She urged her horse off to a gallop, leaving Logan sitting there.

Logan was angry beyond words. Now that he had found her, now that he had returned to her when he should have been hunting Thunder, when he should have been following White-Hair and Scar-Face, when he should have been tracing those guns, she was hurling accusations into his face. A savage, cruel war raged inside Logan. For the first time in his life, he was shirking duty because he cared for a woman, because

220

he wanted to be with her, and now she didn't care. She was too caught up in her damned cows and horses.

By nightfall the square was formed, and what remained of the livestock were grazing in the corral. Thankful for the rain, people sought shelter anywhere they could. Looking around and not seeing Brenna, Logan moved toward her wagon. He was tired and exhausted and worried. He was ready for a dry place to rest, and he was ready for Brenna's company.

He still hadn't heard from Thunder; he had followed the trail left by the outlaws who had killed the hide hunters until it disappeared into nowhere—as if the men whom he sought had been caught into the secret bowels of the earth. For days he had been searching for Brenna and the wagon train, the trail clearly marked, deep wagon ruts, dried water holes, bloated carcasses, and circling buzzards. His worry increased as time passed: the drought had forced her deeper into Comancheria.

When Logan reached the wagon, he lifted the flap and peered inside, but Brenna wasn't there. He dropped the canvas covering and stood there in the downpour, looking around, straining to see through the heavy curtain of rain. He pivoted and moved through the compound as he searched for her. He went from wagon to wagon and finally found Jonesey.

"Last time I saw her, she was headed off in that direction." The driver pointed.

"Walking?" Logan asked.

"Nope, on her horse."

Logan's thanks was lost as he ran and mounted the roan. Soon he was riding across the storm-ridden plains after Brenna. The gray was galloping full speed when Brenna thought she heard her name. She turned and saw Logan coming after her at breakneck speed, but she was too angry to stop. She didn't want to talk to him now. She needed time to think, time to be by herself.

"Stop, before you kill yourself," he yelled, but Brenna lowered her head and continued to ride.

She heard Logan's horse snort; out of the corner of her eye she saw him pull even with her.

"Stop," he called the second time. When she didn't slow down, he grabbed the reins and jerked her horse to a quick stop. "What the hell are you doing?" he demanded.

She grabbed at the reins, but he didn't turn them loose. "What do you care?" she yelled, brushing hair out of her face.

"A whole damn lot."

"You weren't concerned about me two weeks ago, Logan," she accused. "Nothing's changed but the weather, so I can't see why you should be so worried now."

"How do you think I felt when I returned and expected to find you on the route I had marked? How do you think I felt when I saw that you were venturing right into the Comancheros' nest?"

"I don't know what you were feeling, and I still don't," Brenna yelled, hurt at the anger he was unleashing on her. Taking advantage of his distraction with her tirade, she jerked the reins from him and spurred her horse. Over her shoulder her words rode the wind, "You didn't care about my feelings, so why should I give a damn about yours!"

These words were the short fuse that set off the powder keg in Logan. He was after her with no thought. For days he had been tormented by memories of her. During the nights he had been gone from her, restless flames of passion licked at him, burning and searing him with remembered desire but never consuming him, never sating that deep-seated hunger in his loins—a hunger that only Brenna Allen could fulfill.

Brenna looked over her shoulder to see Logan bearing down on her again. Even through the rain she could see the anger on his face. She pushed the gray faster, but she knew he was catching up with her. A strange exhilaration pumped through her body. As if she were running from Logan herself, the blood rushed through her body, her heart pounded, she gasped for breath.

The same primitive feelings surged through Logan. When he caught up with her, his arm, like a band of iron, circled her waist, and he pulled her from the gray to situate her precariously in front of himself. "Now, Mrs. Allen, I'm going to show you exactly how I feel about you."

"It's too late," Brenna said, twisting her head as she dodged his hand. "I told you when you rode off and left me that I didn't want to see you again, and I don't."

"I find that hard to believe."

He dropped the reins, finally caught her face with his other hand, and lifted it to his hard, hot kiss. Brenna clenched her mouth shut, refusing his angry, possessive touch. His hand moved and his fingers bit into her cheek, not really hurting her but applying enough pressure that she opened her mouth. Before his tongue could seek entrance, Brenna bit his lips and crammed her fists between their bodies and pried herself loose. Surprised at her reaction, Logan loosened his hold and Brenna slipped out of his arms to fall to the ground.

She leaped to her feet and ran into a shelf formation of rocks that offered shelter. Grateful for the respite from the rain and hoping that Logan was gone, she breathed deeply and looked around for the gray. Then she saw Logan as he moved through the curtain of rain, slowly, deliberately riding toward her, the gray in tow.

"Get away, and leave me alone."

"I tried to, but I can't." His voice was soft against the howl of the wind, but Brenna had no difficulty hearing him.

For a moment she stood defiantly and stared at him. The wind had long since whipped his hat from his head, and wet brown hair, sun-bleached so that it was streaked golden, framed his face. Rivulets of water ran down his face and neck through the thick mat of brown hair revealed in the opening of his shirt.

He dismounted and tethered the horses; then he turned toward her, his hands on his hips. Brenna watched him, the hypnotic rise and fall of his chest beneath the shirt that the rain had molded to him like a second skin. Without her being aware of it, Brenna breathed in rhythm with him. Slower and deeper. It seemed as if the spring storm were washing away her anger and grief, but the rain was doing nothing to dissipate the flames of yearning within her body. She felt desire settling through her, a slow fire building in her lower body.

"Memories of you, Brenna Allen, kept me alive."

She looked at Logan, the water-drenched clothes sticking to his muscular physique. Then she lifted her head slowly, her wide eyes settling on his face. She couldn't decide which was blacker, the sky or his countenance. His eyes were filled with the fury of unleashed passion in its most primitive state. His mouth was set, his eyes pure flint.

She pulled her gun from the holster and pointed it at Logan. "Don't come a step nearer to me, or you'll just be a memory."

"If you pull the trigger," Logan said, "make sure you kill me, because you're not going to stop me any other way."

"Damn you, Logan MacDougald."

Logan stared at Brenna. She was beautiful in her

anger. Totally enthralling in her wildness. Her eyes were large and round, their color deep and vibrant. Anticipation? Anger? Her mouth was parted as if she waited the entrance of his tongue and the pressure of his lips.

His eyes lowered to her breasts, the strutted nipple straining against the wet material that molded their fullness. Logan lifted a hand and wiped his wrist over his mouth. He could feel the creamy texture of her skin; he could taste the honeyed sweetness. His nostrils were filled with her scent. Down his gaze wandered to linger at the juncture of thighs and hips where the material of her soaked britches clung enticingly.

Logan's gaze was hot and lustful; it banked the already raging fire within Brenna. She could hardly stay where she was or keep her hands to her side; she wanted to run to Logan and to press herself against his chest.

He took the step that jarred the mesmeric bonding, and Brenna bolted. She tripped and fell and dropped her revolver. She was crawling away from him when Logan landed beside her.

"No," he gasped, his hand clutching her hair to drag her face to his, "you're not getting way from me this time, Brenna Allen."

The rain pounded around them in torrential fury. The lightning clawed through the blackened sky, and thunder reverberated across the plains. He pressed her into the ground and covered her mouth with his in a hard, hot kiss—a demanding kiss.

His eyes lowered, and Brenna, looking into his face, saw the blaze of passion rekindle in his eyes. When she dropped her head, she saw that he was looking at her breast, exposed by a tear in her shirt. Logan lowered his head, his lips reverently taking the tip into his mouth. He laved it with his tongue and gently nipped.

225

Brenna moaned softly; then he opened his mouth to take more of her. She was desperately hungry for his touch.

She pressed her hands between them and tore at his shirt, wanting to strip away anything that stood between them. Her fingers wrestled with the buttons until finally Logan pulled away, and dragging in deep gulps of air, he unfastened and discarded both his belt and his shirt.

"I've dreamed of this for days," he murmured.

Brenna scooted down and caught a booted foot. When his boots and socks were off, his legs spread out in front of himself, he put his arms behind him and braced his weight on his palms. Brenna balanced on her knees, her eyes moving down his chest, down lower to the beckoning swell. Then she scooted between his legs and reached out to unfasten his trousers.

Her breath was labored as one by one the buttons slipped through the openings and the material separated to reveal a wealth of golden-brown curls. Logan lifted his buttocks, and Brenna pulled his trousers down ... below his hips and thighs. He kicked out of them. Mesmerized, she stared at his erectness.

Slowly she brought her face up to his and looked at him. A smile gently curved her lips. When Logan mouthed "Come here" and beckoned to her, she shook her head. At his surprised look, her smile became more brazen and enticing.

She stood, the movement setting her outside the confines of the shelter, but Brenna didn't mind. At the moment she was one with the elements—a mere extension of the raw energy flashing around them. She unbuttoned her shirt, drew the material aside, and posed for a moment, the rain sluicing down her breasts, drops forming on the nipple, clinging for a second before they dropped, to be replaced by another. The shirt slid off her arms to fall on a large rock nearby.

"Did you dream of this?" she asked.

Her hands easily unfastened her trousers, and they, too, slid from her body. Her cotton undergarment clung to her hips and legs, but Brenna made no effort to take it off. She smiled at Logan, never moving from the spot. She felt his hot gaze as it traveled from her breasts to her stomach. At the same time that the thunder clapped and lightning streaked the firmament, Brenna lifted her face and her arms to the heaven. Her silvered body looked as if it were a streak of electricity itself.

"Did you dream about this, Logan?"

Logan stood, august and majestic as a god, Brenna thought. A bronzed god.

"Come and take it if you want it." She lifted a hand and beckoned Logan to join her. She wanted the primeval mating this promised, for both of them were like the storm. Dominant. They were flashing and furious. An element of danger interwoven into their lives, both craved excitement and adventure.

Logan didn't move. Rather he stood that moment longer, surprised—but not really surprised—that Brenna had taken the initiative away from him. He looked at her slender beauty, the cotton pantalets that clung tenaciously to her hips. Enticing him through the soaked material was the hint of pink flesh and the dark mound of femininity. As if Brenna knew what he was thinking, she pulled the undergarment down.

"Come and make love to me," she said, her voice drowned out with another boom of thunder.

But Logan didn't need to hear her words to know what she wanted. He walked to her and, standing in the rain, pulled her into his arms. Their lips clung together in physical prelude to their spiritual joining. The rain washed their bodies, and the fire of their desire burned

227

out the dross in their spirits.

Brenna looked deeply into the gray eyes. She wished Logan would let down that invisible curtain that hid him from others. She wanted more than his body; she wanted to share his thoughts and feelings. But until he was willing to give her more, she had to have this. She was glad that he had returned to her, but she wondered when he would leave again.

Brenna moved a breath, and her lips gently settled on his. They were light and tentative at first, but then when Logan's arms tightened around her waist and he pulled her against his chest, her lips fastened on his in earnest. Her tongue moved into the musky warmth of his, and she explored all the delightful contours.

He lowered her so that she was lying on the water-softened earth, their bodies washed anew in the downpour. He drew his fingers from her shoulder over her breasts, lingering to knead her nipples with his fingers, then down her stomach to her femininity.

Again and again he teased her, heightening her anticipation, loving her, preparing her for the moment of consummation. His lips traveled down her belly, and he lapped the water from around her navel. He felt her convulsive shiver beneath his tongue.

"Logan, please take me."

"I am," he promised.

Opening her legs even wider for his entry, he gently inserted his manhood into the warm, velvety sheath at the same moment that the renewed fury of the storm exploded through the heaven. The slashes of lightning across the heavens and the threatening claps of thunder exhilarated them, adding to the intensity of their coming together. Logan's thrusts were deep and powerful, but they were careful and loving.

Brenna's hands traveled down his back, and she caught his flexed buttocks in both hands. She ran her finger down the indentation, smiling when she felt the tremble that racked his massive frame.

He carried her to the very heavens, where each of them at almost the same moment exploded. Their cries of fulfillment and ecstasy mingled with the roar of the heavens, and as they gently drifted down to earth, their energy spent, the strength of the storm—within and without—dissipated.

Chapter Fourteen

During the following weeks Brenna and Logan moved the caravan northward to cross the Canadian and the North Canadian rivers. Amidst great hurrahs, the weary travelers exited Comanche territory and turned due west to lumber down the Santa Fe Trail that ran adjacent to the mighty Arkansas River.

The afternoon sun to their backs, their horses, tethered behind them, munching on tender blades of spring grass, Brenna and Logan stood on a hill overlooking their immediate destination.

"Bent's Fort," Brenna breathed as she stared at the huge, imposing adobe building in the middle of the plain—the walls of which Thomas had said were more than fourteen feet high and three or more feet thick.

Behind the main establishment, adjoining its western wall, was the corral just as Thomas had described to her. Its walls were only six or eight feet high, and to prevent raiders from scaling them, the Bent brothers, so Thomas said, had thickly planted their broad tops with cacti, which now in the spring produced profuse, brilliant red and white blooms. This mud fortress west of Purgatory Creek was the center of a primitive empire that spread across the entire watershed of the upper Arkansas.

Elation swelled through Brenna's bloodstream. She

looked up at Logan. "We made it. We really made it."

Logan caught her in a warm embrace that knocked her hat off. "I never doubted for a minute that you'd make it," he murmured, rubbing his cheek on the crown of her head. "I have faith in you, Brenna Garvey Allen."

"And I have faith in you, Logan Andrew Mac-Dougald."

Brenna's confession touched Logan. It hurt him as well as brought to the front of his mind his inner torment—his continual battle between duty and his feelings for Brenna. Now that he'd gotten the wagon train safely to Bent's Fort, he was leaving; he had to . . . for himself as well as her.

Concern for Thunder had turned into gnawing anxiety; Logan hadn't heard from his adopted brother since that night so long ago when they had parted, he to warn the caravan of the imminent Indian attack and Thunder to follow Kirkwood. Time was running out for Texas. Time was running out for Logan. He had to find the guns. And the Comancheros. Maybe through them he could find Chief White-Hair. Maybe—just maybe—he could find Flanna. At least, he could learn what had happened to her.

As Logan held Brenna close to him, he finally admitted to himself that he loved her. He wanted to marry her, to remain with her forever. But he knew this could not be. Not now. This was his newest torment. Until he had cleansed his soul of this burning hatred, of this burning desire for revenge, Logan knew he could not marry Brenna.

He couldn't even give her a declaration of love. He had nothing to offer her: He was nothing but a shell of a man. With this admission came the heavy weight of guilt. He had taken everything from her and had given nothing in return but a few nights of pleasure—what

231

any man who cared anything at all about a woman could do.

Brenna drew her head back and peered into Logan's face. "What is it?" she asked, pressing her palm against his chest to feel the solid, steady beat of his heart.

Logan's hand caught hers, and his fingers gently massaged her fourth finger—the finger now void of the wide gold band that declared her allegiance to Shawn Allen. The pale indentation that announced her availability to him. Logan felt a rush of feeling he couldn't explain. He had to bite back the tears; he had to swallow the knot that threatened to choke him. Never had he been caught by the horns of dilemma; now he was, and he was being gored to death. He didn't want to leave Brenna; he wanted to marry her; he wanted to see that she reached Santa Fe safely . . . but he had a responsibility to Thunder, to Sam Houston, to the people of Texas, and to himself.

Brenna saw the shadows lengthen in Logan's eyes; they turned from a soft dove color to a stormy gray. She felt his body tense; she saw the lines of his face grow sharper and more pronounced with despair.

"What's wrong, Logan?" She repeated her question.

"Brenna, you know . . . you know that I care about you," he said with an urgency that both pleased and concerned Brenna. "What we've shared has been special. You know that?"

"I know."

She pressed herself closer to him and burrowed her head against his chest as if to reassure him of her total love and trust in him. Even without his telling her, she wondered about the demons he had been fighting; she had been aware of his slipping out of the wagon late at night when he thought she was asleep. She had heard his restless stirring. On one occasion she had joined him and had invited him to share his troublesome

232

thoughts—his past—with her, but he hadn't. Several times she had made overtures; each time he turned them down. Although it broke her heart that Logan wouldn't allow her to help him, she allowed him the right to fight his own battles. He was a powerful man; he must cross his deep streams and dark currents himself.

Logan gently gripped her shoulders in both hands and set her back, so that he could look into her face. The face that had replaced Dancing Dawn's in his dreams. The face he knew better than his own. Her sea-green eyes were washed in love. The love that compelled him to take Dancing Dawn's portrait out of his watch and to put it in a safe place. He would do that tonight, and someday soon he would tell Brenna about Dancing Dawn. The portrait now belonged to Thunder; Logan knew his friend would like that.

"I love you." Logan finally said the words. "And I wish we could get married. I want to travel all the way to Santa Fe and back to Texas with you."

"But you can't," Brenna murmured.

Logan's face grew even more gaunt. His voice was a mere rasp as he said, "I can, but I won't." He saw the hurt in Brenna's eyes. "My decision has nothing to do with my loving and wanting to marry you."

Brenna lifted her hand to cup his face. "Is it Thunder?" she asked.

"Partly"—he reached up to his pocket—"but more this." He extracted his sister's necklace.

Brenna caught the locket in the palm of her hand, and she looked at it. Glad that he was finally going to tell her about his past, she turned it over and read the inscription.

"Flanna," he said when Brenna looked at him. "My sister was named after my Grandmother Duncan. The locket belonged to her. She was wearing it when the

233

Comanches kidnapped her."

"How did you get it?" Brenna asked.

"From Rhem Sommers. He jerked it off the neck of a Comanche."

The explanation dulled Brenna's disappointment over his impending departure. "You must find her."

"I'm working for Houston," Logan said, "but I'm really working for myself. I want to find out what happened to Flanna if I can. She may still be alive. If I don't, I will hate myself for the rest of my life. I wouldn't be any good for or to you."

Brenna pressed the locket into Logan's hand. "I understand."

"I want to marry you, but I can't stand the thought of marrying you and leaving you immediately. You've been through the heartache and grief of marriage and widowhood once. I don't propose to do the same thing to you again so soon."

Brenna waited a moment and composed herself before she asked, "When . . . are you leaving?"

"In the morning."

"So soon?" she whispered, despair mirrored in her face.

"I must," he told her.

For the longest time they clung together, Brenna's joy in having safely reached Bent's Fort giving way to sadness that Logan would be gone on the morrow. But she really could understand his decision. She had let and would let no one stand in her way of reaching Santa Fe to deliver her letter to Peyton H. Alexander. She must allow Logan the same freedom. Perhaps her freely letting him go was the invisible tie that would bind him to her and bring him back.

She raised her face to his. His pearl-gray eyes, fixed on hers, seemed to darken. He raised a hand to her chin and tilted her face even higher. A sweet second of anticipation passed before Logan's mouth covered hers. Flesh met flesh. His mouth widened over hers. His kiss was an extension of his own personality—bold and sure and firm.

Brenna's mouth willingly opened beneath the insistent pressure of his, and their lips clung wetly, warmly. With all the sensuousness of silk rippling across naked skin, the fingers at her chin slid up her face. His palm cradled her cheek in gentle possession, while his fingertips foraged in the hair at her temple. He tipped her head upward and deepened the kiss, tasting, savoring. Slowly he raised his lips from hers, and she felt bereft at their absence.

"I love you," he confessed.

"I love you."

"I didn't want to love you," he admitted.

"I wanted to love you."

He dropped his hand from her cheek and possessively slipped his arm around her waist and hauled her to him. His mouth took hers again, his lips rubbing back and forth against hers before locking them together. His other hand found the middle of her back and further molded her to him.

Brenna felt both his hands exerting their sensual pressure on her. His touch was filled with a gentle, smothering fierceness, and she gloried in the sensation. She couldn't ever remember feeling this raw sense of urgency before, this need to find some way to dissolve into another human being.

Logan's tongue entered her mouth, claiming and possessing yet another part of her. Brenna moaned and boldly welcomed the invader. Logan gave her more of his tongue's velvet caress. Inhaling the faint smell of leather and man, Brenna spread her hands across the front of his buckskin shirt. She felt Logan's knife pinned between their bodies, and that excited her.

Logan felt the heat of her body and tugged her still closer, until her breasts flattened against his chest, until his hardness nestled against her soft belly, until no one in the world existed but the two of them.

Brenna's heart rate increased. Her breathing was shallow and ragged. Her skin was flushed and hot. A heaviness had blossomed in a secret place deep within her.

Logan finally wrenched his mouth from hers, took a long steadying breath, and rested his chin against her forehead. They just held each other, saying nothing, savoring for as long as they could all the moments they could. Finally Logan drew away, and holding hands, they stared into each other's eyes.

"We need to guide the wagon train into the fort," he said, and Brenna nodded.

Silently they walked to their horses, mounted, and joined the caravan, Jonesey's wagon in the lead, Roger and Sandy Thomas riding beside him. The five of them topped the rise together.

"So this is Bent's Fort," Roger murmured as he looked at the massive building. "We've finally arrived at Bent's Fort." He yanked his hat off his head and threw it in the air. "Yippee," he yelled. "We've reached civilization."

Down the small incline the wagons rumbled, the pace of the oxen and mules picking up at their drivers' insistence. Brenna couldn't take her eyes off the imposing rectangular building. Constructed of thick adobe blocks, its front wall, facing the east, the direction from which approaching caravans came, was at least one hundred thirty-five feet long and fourteen feet high. Over the main gate on the east side was a watchtower—a single room that had windows on all four sides—on top of which was a belfry and a flagpole that flew the American flag. At the southeast and northwest corners rose round towers eighteen feet tall.

Pointing at the bastions, Thomas said, "Them towers are filled with sabers, heavy lances with long, sharp blades, pistols, and flintlock muskets. They're to be used if anyone should be so stupid as to take the fort by means of ladders on the outside walls. From inside you can sweep all four walls with fire."

"A fortress for sure," Brenna murmured. "The only way someone could defeat those within would be to starve them out."

Thomas nodded. "And considering the nature of the Indians, the Bent brothers decided to take their chance. Figured the Indians wouldn't stay in one spot that long." He pointed to the watchtower. "Have a high-powered telescope on a pivot in there. Been watching our approach."

Armed guards stood on either side of the gate, and a loaded brass cannon was aimed directly at the caravan.

"Who are you and where are you headed?" the guard called out.

"Logan MacDougald, wagon master for Garvey Mercantile and Freight Hauling," Logan answered, slowly moving the roan closer to the guard. "We're on our way to Santa Fe with eight wagons of trade goods. Have seven families with us. Six are headed for Oregon, one for Santa Fe."

"One carriage and fourteen wagons," the man said matter-of-factly.

Thomas rode forward. "Sandy Thomas," he identified himself. "Came in with the settlers bound for Ory-gon. Went to find these here ones." His hand swept the wagon train.

The guard nodded and motioned them through the gate, six and a half feet wide and seven feet tall, made of heavy planks sheathed with iron. Two huge warerooms stretched along most of the front, or eastern, side of the fort, and the entry itself was a tunnel between the walls of the warerooms. Wickets in these walls allowed the distribution of goods without the necessity of admitting suspect Indians into the inner part of the fort. Through a second gate Brenna rode.

"Call this the *placeta*," Thomas said as they entered the gravel-covered inner court. He fanned his hand in a semicircle. Along the other three walls a square of rooms—about twenty-five of them in all—were built, their doorways facing the placeta. Also within this inner court was a well of water and a huge press for packing buffalo robes. "And over there," Thomas pointed, "are the food storerooms, the kitchen, and the dining hall. There"—his hand moved—"are the shops for blacksmithing, tailoring, and carpentering."

"Come with me," the guard called. "I'll take you to the corral and the wagon sheds."

Brenna and Logan, still leading the caravan, followed the man to the back of the fort to an alleyway that was about twelve feet wide which ran north and south behind the main wall. Bordering this alleyway, its rear abutting the great western wall, was another row of buildings.

"These here," the guard said, "are the storerooms and wagon sheds. Back yonder"—he motioned to a gate in the western wall—"is the corral. Make an inventory of your goods, livestock, and horses, and give 'em to Mr. Dapier. He's our head clerk." The guard's hand waved to the southwest corner of the square to a second-story blockhouse. "His office is in that building. He'll assign you vacant storerooms and wagon sheds. He'll also keep up with your accounts, which are payable on leaving Fort William."

"I'll take care of storing the wagons," Logan told Brenna. "You go see about getting an apartment. I'll join you later."

238

Leaving her gray with Logan and bringing only a small valise with her, Brenna returned to the placeta. She stood in awe, her eyes sweeping the huge complex. Moving to the western wall of the inner court, she mounted the stairs and walked to the blockhouse, where the clerk's office was housed. She opened the door and entered the large room. A tall, wiry man behind a counter greeted her.

"May I help you?"

"I'm Mrs. Brenna Allen," she said, moving in the man's direction to set her valise on the counter, "wagon captain for Garvey Mercantile and Freight Hauling. My wagon boss, Logan MacDougald, will be here shortly with an inventory of our goods, livestock, and horses. He'll rent the wagon sheds and take care of the feed for our animals. I'd like to rent an apartment and have my valuables locked in your safe."

"Of course, Mrs. Allen," he agreed. "Let me make you a receipt." As he inventoried Brenna's possessions, he talked to her, extolling the beauty and efficiency of Fort William—the true name, he explained.

As soon as she had her receipt, Brenna exited the office, only to be followed by Clyde Dapier himself. "I'll show you to your quarters," he said, leading her around the walkway to the second-story apartments.

"What's that?" Brenna tipped her head at the large rectangular room directly north of the office.

"That is the second-floor aerie of the owners," Clyde informed her. "Along one wall runs a bar, and a large billiard table has been transported from Missouri with the other necessary game supplies." Dapier led Brenna to the edge of the wall. "Climb the ladder," he instructed, taking Brenna's valise from her, "and look to the southwest." When she had done as he requested, he asked, "What do you see?"

"Another adobe building near the river," she replied.

239

"That's our icehouse," he bragged. "In the winter when the river is frozen we fill the building with large squares of ice chopped from the stream. When summer arrives, fresh meat is kept cool in the icehouse, and it also provides an ample supply of ice for cold drinks. You'll be served one tonight," he promised.

After Brenna climbed down, he led her to the small apartment, opened the door, and walked into the room. As Brenna moved to the foot of the bed to set her luggage down, Dapier threw open the shutters on both windows and allowed afternoon sunshine to pour in.

"Can I do anything else for you, Mrs. Allen?"

"I'd like to take a bath."

Dapier nodded. "I'll send the servants up with a tub and water. Give me about thirty minutes."

As soon as he was gone, Brenna's gaze swept around the sparsely furnished room. One straight-backed chair, a double bed, a table, and candle. But she was grateful. At least the bed had a mattress on it, and the linen was guaranteed to be clean—that's what Clyde Dapier had promised when he was making her receipt.

While she waited for her bath, she walked out of the apartment and leaned over the railing to look at the activity in the patio below. Under a pole shelter in the corral, men were working on the score or more hard-used wagons and carts, making them ready for their next trip. The carpenter and blacksmith shops clanged continually. In another room—opened to allow ventilation—Brenna saw a tailor at work: With a three-sided needle and sinew thread, he sewed buckskin into stacks of hunting shirts and leggings. Several Indians trudged into the fort with huge sacks of buffalo chips over their backs. They moved to large containers on the side of the courtyard and emptied the fuel. An old man lifted several barrels of trash onto his wagon and hauled it to the rubbish pile outside the walls.

Brenna was so caught up in everyday life at Bent's Fort, she failed to observe the arrival of her tub and water. Only when she heard a soft call did she turn around. A beautiful young Cheyenne maiden stood in the opened door of her apartment. A smile curved her lips, and her eyes glowed with friendliness.

"You wanted a bath?" she asked in faltering English.

"Yes," Brenna replied, also returning the smile.

"I bathe you?" the girl asked.

"No, thank you." Brenna moved to her valise. She unfastened it and pulled out the yellow calico dress she had purchased in San Antonio. "Would you iron this for me?" As the girl nodded, Brenna picked up a beautiful multicolored scarf. "Here. You may have this for yourself." The girl was hesitant to take such a lovely gift, but Brenna insisted. "Please take the scarf. I want you to have it."

"Singing Wind thanks you," the girl said as her fingers closed over the soft, silky material. "Now she will be one of the most beautiful women in the fort." A smile twitched at the corners of her mouth. "All the other women shall be jealous."

As sunset faded behind the mocking coolness of the surrounding peaks, Brenna closed herself in her apartment and luxuriated in a bath. After she had dried off and slipped into her chemise, she heard a knock. A smile lit her face; Logan was here at last. She ran to open the door.

Singing Wind smiled and held out the yellow calico. "Here is your dress. Mr. William also tells me to invite you to dine with them in the big apartment." The girl pointed to William Bent's quarters. Her eyes sparkled with excitement. "Tonight we have much company. We will have feasting and songs and dance."

Later, dressed in the yellow calico Singing Wind had ironed for her, her clean, shining tresses coiled atop her head, Brenna left her room. Candlelight flickered through opened windows, and flaming torches lit the courtyard.

Smiling at the passing couples who were promenading behind the parapet of the walls on the flat roofs of the ground structures, Brenna made her way to the Bents' apartment. She wondered where Logan was; she had expected him to be up sooner. When she entered the apartment, brightly lit with candles, she saw a stately Indian woman sitting on the colorful cushions at the far end of the room.

"Come sit with me," the woman invited in a soft, husky voice. "I am Owl Woman, wife to William Bent."

"Thank you," Brenna replied, sitting next to Owl Woman. "I am Brenna Allen."

"I know. You have come a long distance with your wagons. You are planning to carry your goods into Santa Fe?"

Other women arrived, wives of the fort employees and the settlers, and they sat along the wall on cushions with Owl Woman and Brenna. As they talked, Brenna kept looking around. She couldn't imagine what was keeping Logan. When she felt a gentle touch on her shoulder, she turned to look into Owl Woman's face.

"You are looking for your man?"

Brenna nodded.

"He will be here soon. He is visiting with my people, the Cheyenne."

By the time dinner was served, the room was full of people, everyone laughing and talking at once. Brenna smiled, glad to see the settlers jovial once again. When she started the next leg of her journey, she would miss them; she had become attached to them.

Her gaze strayed to Sam and Gertrude and Billy. The older couple had taken the child to their bosom. Then Brenna saw Callie Sue and wondered what Gertrude would do. Brenna knew the older woman was in love with Sam, but she didn't know if Gertrude would give up her granddaughter in order to marry Sam and remain in Santa Fe. The decision couldn't be put off much longer. The train for Oregon would be pulling out day after tomorrow.

Brenna heard the low rumbling of men's voices, and she turned to face the door. William Bent entered first, a small smile erasing some of his facial gauntness. Several other men followed, but Brenna recognized none of them. Grace was said, the meal begun. Still Logan made no appearance. Brenna paid lip service to talk around her, but her thoughts were on Logan. She wondered if he had so soon deserted her for an Indian woman; she wondered if he found the Indian way of life preferable to that of the white man. Perhaps Horace Faraday had been right: Logan was more Indian than white.

She had no more than formulated the thought than she looked across the room. The doorway framed Logan's body; his arms were spread wide, his hands resting on each side of the jamb. The magnificent proportions of his physique were clearly revealed by the tight buckskin trousers and shirt he wore. The strong line of his jaw was set, self-assured, even arrogant. But she knew that he was also warm and gentle and loving.

His pearl-gray eyes never left Brenna's face. His lips didn't move, but his eyes smiled at her. They touched her intimately, stirring up her desires.

Logan pushed away from the door and trod through the crowd to sit by Brenna. As he moved, Brenna watched, drinking in everything about him: his legs, lean and muscular; the tapered waist and hips; the muscular arms and shoulders. He was altogether a vital, powerful-looking man. Aware of her scrutiny,

Logan returned her stare. His lips parted, and his rough-soft tongue—Brenna could feel the rough tenderness of it now—came out to glaze his firm mouth wiht a fiery nectar. Unconscious of her reaction, Brenna opened her mouth to tip her lips with her tongue.

Disappointed that he had waited this long to come to her, Brenna said nothing when he sat down beside her. Fork in hand, she picked at her food.

Leaning close to her, his mouth at her ear, Logan whispered, "Are you upset?"

She turned, and the clean scent of his soap filled her nostrils. His chest was in front of her face; he exuded masculinity. Again Brenna's eyes hungrily moved over him, visually tasting his virility, glutting on the handsomeness of his broad shoulders. Her eyes lowered to the opening in his shirt, and she looked at the wiry crispness of the hair. She remembered the feel of his hardness; in her mind she felt the soft tips of her fingers as they ran over his chest, his stomach, his abdomen . . .

When Brenna's eyes hit the familiar belt buckle, she lifted her face and stared boldly into his, no thought given to the people sitting around them. In Logan's eyes she saw undisguised hunger. The wanting haunted his eyes, exposing his fevered desire.

"I like your dress," he said, "and your hair."

Brenna smiled her thanks. "I like your clothes also."

"Big Timber, a Cheyenne chief, gave them to me."

Brenna gave in to jealousy. "I thought perhaps a Cheyenne maiden had given them to you."

Logan laughed quietly. "Do I detect a note of jealousy?"

"More than a note, Mr. MacDougald."

"You have no need to be. There's only one woman in my life."

They stared into one another's eyes, Brenna's a deep green and stark with anguish over his leaving.

"Damn it," he muttered, his hand clasping hers, "let's get out of here. I can't say or do what I want to do with all these people around." He rose, pulling Brenna with him, and they slipped out of the room into the welcome coolness of the spring evening. "Where's your room?" he asked, and Brenna pointed. Hurriedly he guided her around the promenade, not stopping until they were inside her apartment, the door closed behind them.

Logan's hands closed around her body, and he pulled Brenna to him. Willingly she moved, letting the fullness of her breasts press against his chest. Her hands traveled the familiar route, closing around his neck, her fingers playing in the thick golden-brown hair.

Higher her fingers moved in frenzied pitch to spread through his hair, the tips kneading the scalp, mussing the thickness as they inched to his face and cupped the sun-bronzed perfection. Her mouth, hungry for the taste of him, moved over his lips, his chin, sampling first, then thoroughly reacquainting herself with his lips.

"So good," he murmured as she nipped on the fullness of his bottom lip. "So very good."

Her hands tightened on the base of his neck, and she urged his mouth to hers, her lips parting for the touch. His mouth, passionate and tender, caught hers hungrily, and his hand moved over her back, arching her, pressing her breasts into even closer contact with his body. His tongue's sweet probing poignantly reminded her of that deeper invasion.

His hand moved around her back, under her arm, cupping one of her breasts, and with great urgency his mouth bore down on hers. His tongue moved inside her mouth, exploring all the sweetness, all the nooks and niches of delight. Remembering all the wonder of his hard body, Brenna squirmed against him, her hand stroking his shoulders.

"I love you," he whispered, lifting his lips slightly. "I love you so very much." His warm breath was honey spilling against her creamy flesh, slowly oozing like fan tracery; wider and wider the circle grew.

He's leaving in the morning! The thought tumbled hazily about in that region called her mind, but Brenna couldn't worry about it now. She had this moment with him, and she must make it count. Her heart pounded, and her entire body was aflame with only those feelings that Logan could generate. She arched her neck, and Logan's lips began to caress the silken curve. Against the smoothness of her shoulder, Logan's mouth moved, savoring her sweet warmth, sending renewed shivers of ecstasy through her body.

"I love you," she confessed when he lifted her in his arms and carried her to the bed. "I'll love you always."

The first rays of dawn were slipping into the room when Brenna and Logan heard the commotion at the gate. Both of them were out of the bed and dressed in minutes. They ran across the promenade and down the stairs, arriving in the placeta just as the second gate was thrown open, and a group of men on horseback galloped into the fort.

"Where's Bent?" the leader of the men called. "Tell him to get down here right now! We have trouble on our hands."

Recognizing the voice, Brenna cried, "Colonel Warfield, is that you?"

"Mrs. Allen!" Charles Warfield dismounted and rounded the horse; a smile radiated his face. "I am so glad to see that you and your caravan arrived here

246

safely. Others were not so fortunate."

A scowl on his face, Logan was standing beside Brenna now.

"Colonel Warfield," she said, "this is my . . . my wagon boss, Logan MacDougald."

Warfield extended his hand and clasped Logan's in a firm grip. "Glad to meet you, MacDougald. Heard about you when I first met Mrs. Allen." Warfield's gaze slid to Brenna. His voice warmed with admiration. "Right fine and courageous woman, she is." His gaze riveted back to Logan. "Any man would be proud to claim her for his own."

Logan's lips thinned. For a moment his body was tense with jealousy. But he controlled his emotions; he wouldn't let them get the best of him. "Glad to meet you, Colonel Warfield." He turned his head and gazed at Brenna. He slid his arm around her shoulder. "And I must agree with you. She is a fine courageous woman, and I'm right proud to claim her for my own."

Brenna's smile widened, and she swelled with joy. She didn't mind Logan's possessive hug; in fact, she relished it. Equally she relished his proclamation of love.

Fastening his trousers around his waist, Bent hurried down the stairs. "What's all this commotion about?" he shouted. "Waking up the entire fort?"

"A group of freebooters, posing as Texas Rangers, are on the trail to raid Mexican caravans," Warfield answered.

"To hell with you Texas freebooters," Bent swore, doubling up a fist and pawing through the air. "Why don't you get in your territory and stay there and leave us alone!"

"This isn't any of my doing, Mr. Bent," Warfield denied. "I admit I'll raid any Mexican or American wagon train that steps a foot into Texas territory, but I

247

draw a line at murder." His voice raised. *"At mass murder!"* With each word he spoke, he walked to a litter attached to Private Steeple's horse. "We arrived on the scene right after the butchers destroyed Don Felipe Andesoto's caravan. We managed to rescue one of the women. She's in shock right now."

Bent's eyes were flashing, and he pushed through the gathering crowd to follow Warfield. "Andesoto's train?" he blustered. "The one on which Doña Francisca Sandoval was traveling?"

The men knelt at the litter. They stared at the prostrate young woman. Her lacerated face was covered with blood and dirt; her dress was filthy, her hair torn from her chignon. "Señor Bent," Francisca Sandoval whispered, large tears rolling down her cheeks, "the Texas Rangers massacred the train on which I was riding. They killed my fiancé and his parents; they took all the women captive, my future sister-in-law among them. Only I escaped. Had it not been for these kind gentlemen, I, too, would have shared the same fate as the others." She reached up and brushed strands of blue-black hair out of her face.

"Come with me, child." Bent scooped and held his hands out to her. "I'll let Owl Woman look after you." He caught the girl's hands in his and helped her to stand.

Francisca took a step, faltered, and slowly crumpled.

Before she reached the ground, Logan was through the crowd, his strong arms banding around her small body. Effortlessly he lifted her. In long strides he was across the courtyard, up the stairs, and at Brenna's apartment. Gently he deposited Francisca on the bed. When Brenna followed him into the room, he said, "Get some fresh water in the basin. These lacerations on her face need trending to."

Brenna soon returned to her room with a basin of

fresh water; she also brought soap, a clean washrag, and medicine which Bent gave to her. She stood and watched as Logan cleaned Francisca's face and anointed it with salve.

"She needs something to eat," Brenna said. "I'll go get her a bowl of broth."

Shortly Brenna returned with a tray, which she set on the table. Francisca was sitting on the bed, her back braced with the pillows. Logan sat beside her, talking in a low voice. Brenna sat in the straight-backed chair.

"I know it's painful to talk about it," he told Francisca, "but it's better if you can. You don't want to keep such grief bottled up inside you."

"It was horrible, señor," Francisca whispered, her dark eyes filling with tears. Quietly she told Logan about the massacre; she described the men who rode up and identified themselves as Texas Rangers; the massacre that followed; the killing of innocent men, women, and children. All the while the tears rolled down her cheeks. "They rode off with all the women," she said. She covered her ears with her hands. "I can still hear the screaming."

Logan grabbed her hands and held them tightly. He knew about the screams; to this day he could hear his mother and sister screaming. "I can understand how you feel."

"No, you can't," Francisca lashed out. "I saw my fiancé and his parents killed, señor. Butchered as if they were animals!" She jerked her hands from his and curled into a protective ball. "No one can know how I feel!"

Logan reached into his pocket and withdrew his grandfather's watch. He clicked open the lid and looked at the small portrait. He held his hand out to the girl. "This is Dancing Dawn," he told her. "She was my fiancée; her family was my adopted family. I arrived at

249

her village in time to see her butchered by Texas soldiers."

Brenna was so surprised, she stood. She caught her breath and looked down at her naked left hand. She had taken Shawn's ring off, but Logan still carried Dancing Dawn's portrait in his watch. She had discarded her past; Logan hadn't. Until he did, Brenna knew that she could never completely fill his heart; he couldn't fill hers. He didn't have enough to give to her; he didn't want to share all of himself with her. Feeling like an outsider, at most an interloper, Brenna turned and walked onto the promenade.

"My parents live on an hacienda out of Santa Fe," she heard Francisca say. "I have been to school in the East and am returning home for my wedding." She hesitated, her eyes filling with tears. "I mean, I was returning for my wedding."

Logan picked up the corner of the sheet and wiped the tears from Francisca's face. When she began to tremble and her body convulse with sobs, he dragged her into his arms and held her tightly, rubbing her head with his hand. "Cry," he said. "You'll feel much better. Everything is going to be all right. I promise."

Brenna listened as Logan quietly reassured Francisca; then from her post at the railing she watched him feed her. She didn't dislike the girl; she didn't resent Logan's kindly ministrations, but she was envious. Out of the kindness of his heart, Logan shared things with strangers that he'd never shared with her. That hurt! Brenna wanted him to share them with her, too. Her feelings for Logan were too new for her to be exposed to this.

After Francisca had finished eating the soup, she looked at Logan and smiled. "You are an Indian, no?" she asked in her low, musical voice.

Logan chuckled. "No, I'm not an Indian."

Francisca laughed with him. "You are dressed as one."

"I was reared by the Cherokees," he told her.

Francisca ran her hand over the fringed yoke on Logan's chest, and Brenna's heart turned somersaults. No matter how much compassion she may share with the younger woman, no matter how much she might like the señorita, Brenna did not want Francisca touching Logan.

"I like these clothes on you, Señor MacDougald."

"Not Señor MacDougald," Logan told her. "Call me Logan."

Shyly Francisca said, "Logan MacDougald. That is a pretty name. I like it."

"What shall I call you, child?" Logan asked.

With quiet dignity Francisca said, "I am not a child, Logan. I am a woman."

For the moment Logan said nothing; he stared into the dark eyes, so velvety and warm.

No, Brenna thought, *Francisca Sandoval is no child!*

"'Tis a fact, you're not a child," Logan eventually admitted.

The gentleness of Logan's voice washed Brenna with acute disappointment, but she didn't have time to ponder her feelings. Roger hastened up the stairs to her apartment. However, when he saw Logan and Francisca sitting on the bed talking, he didn't go into the room. He approached Brenna.

"Mr. Bent and Colonel Warfield would like to see Logan in his office as soon as possible."

Brenna managed a smile. "I'll tell him."

Roger hovered at the door, his gaze fixed on Francisca Sandoval. "She's the most beautiful woman I've ever seen," he breathed, his voice full of awe and reverence. "Such a lady."

Such a lady! Brenna thought long after Roger left.

The phrase summed up the difference between her and Francisca. She was a woman; Francisca was a lady. And men wanted to bed women and marry ladies!

So deep in her thoughts, she was surprised when she heard the door to the apartment close. She turned to watch Logan as he moved toward her.

"Francisca is sleeping now," he said.

"Mr. Bent and Colonel Warfield want to meet with you as soon as possible," said Brenna.

He nodded, angling his head so that he could see the activity in the office. "She's young." He raked his fingers through his hair.

"Yes," Brenna murmured. So he couldn't see the emotion in her eyes, she turned so that she faced the railing, her back to him. "But it's good that she is young; she'll get over the grief and sorrow quicker."

"No one gets over this kind of grief and sorrow!" Logan exclaimed, his hand banding Brenna's wrist. He pulled her around so that he could look at her. "She'll bear the scars of this the rest of her life. She'll never be the same again. That boy's face will forever swim in front of her eyes. She'll hear his cries; she'll see his mutilated body."

"I didn't mean to imply that she would forget it," Brenna returned, managing to keep her voice quiet. Her disappointment was quickly turning to despair. "I simply meant that she has the resilience of youth. The unhappy images will diminish with age to be replaced with better ones."

Brenna's words of wisdom touched Logan, and his anger, his frustration at being unable to do anything about the atrocities, dissipated. "I'm sorry, baby," he said as he pulled Brenna into his arms. "I didn't mean to speak so harshly. I'm worried."

Brenna rubbed her cheek up and down the soft doeskin shirt. She smelled the fragrance of the outdoor air in his clothes, mixed with his own warm scent.

"I'm worried about Thunder. I'm worried about you." Logan's arms left her waist; his hands tenderly cupped her face. Her cheeks burned against his palms.

"Logan," she whispered. She wanted to dispel his ghosts and fears; she wanted to assure him that she would be all right; Thunder was all right. Most of all, she wanted to assure him that he was all right. But no other words came. She simply repeated his name, which was like a kiss to Logan.

His mouth touched hers to seal his name there. Brenna's eyelids closed, and her entire body was aglow with a fiery light within. Logan's hands that held her face so gently now traced her jaw, her neck; they caressed her shoulders. Where he touched her, a tingling warmth spread, as if his very touch were creating her, shaping her, bringing her to life beneath his hands.

"I love you," he whispered.

Brenna could only nod. Logan began to kiss and caress her tenderly, slowly, almost without passion, as if he wanted only to cherish her face, as if he wanted to put them to memory.

Then he said, "I'm going to replace my ugly memories with images of you. You're my woman."

"Yes," she murmured, "I'm your woman."

Chapter Fifteen

Since he was the last one to walk into Bent's office, Logan sat in one of the vacant chairs near the door. He looked at the other six men in the room. Three he knew: Charles Warfield, Sandy Thomas, and Roger Hollis. The other three were strangers.

Still dressed in his long-sleeved undershirt and trousers, Bent stood at the front of the room, his thumbs hooked under his suspenders. "Mr. Mac-Dougald, this is Fester Hinkelrod." He nodded his head toward the man who sat beside Thomas. "He's wagon master for the Oregon-bound train, the one your settlers are joining up with. These"—now he indicated the two heavily armed men who sat to themselves—"are officers in my personal army, Nolbert Greerson and Elton Verde."

Logan looked at each of the men and nodded. Once the amenities of introductions were made, attention returned to Bent, who paced back and forth in front of his desk.

"You are now guests of William Bent at Fort William." His dark eyes studiously moved from one man to the next. "My friends and my brothers helped me to build this fort, but by far and large, this is my creation." He doubled his fist and pounded his desk. "This is my empire, and I won't have the United States,

Mexico, or that upstart Republic of Texas dictate to me what I can or cannot do." His face reddened. "I *will not* have my freighters frightened off the trails my people have forged with their lives and blood. And you, sir"—Bent pointed his finger at Warfield—"I will not tolerate your tampering with trade goods moving back and forth on the Santa Fe Trail. I'll see that you and all freebooters get their just reward. You can be sure the United States will hear about the actions of Sam Houston."

The chair creaked as Warfield shifted his weight and straightened his legs, crossing them at the ankles. His gaze rested on Bent's face. His voice was low but forceful. "According to the government that employs me, Mr. Bent, a great portion of the Santa Fe Trail, including the city of Santa Fe itself, is located in the domain of the newly formed Republic of Texas. I am empowered by this self-same government to confiscate any of these trade goods and to transport them to the capital of Texas."

"Then, Mr. Warfield"—Bent jabbed his finger through the air in Warfield's direction—"I have no alternative but to believe you have instigated all these massacres. And in this fort, I am the law. In case you're not aware of it, we believe in quick justice. In one day we provide judge, jury, judgment, and hanging. And make a note of this, sir: The people of Santa Fe and Taos don't consider themselves part of Texas!"

Warfield leaned forward. "I told you, Mr. Bent—"

Anger permeated through the room.

"—I confiscate goods belonging to the hostile governments around the republic, but I do not murder innocent people." Warfield's voice lowered as he warned, "And I would advise you, sir, not to attempt to pass judgment on me and my men."

"I remember you coming here last winter, Mr.

Warfield. You promised the trappers who were sitting out the snowy winter here at Bent's Fort rich plunder." Bent raised his arms in the air theatrically. "You waved that bullet-torn flag which had been carried in the early days of the Texas revolution. When you couldn't get enough men to enlist as your recruits, you headed toward the forts along the South Platte." Bent laughed harshly. "If rumor is correct, sir, you finally mustered about twenty-four ragged, whiskery, ill-equipped, buckskin-clad mountain men."

Bent measured the man. "If you and your band of misfits aren't the ones plaguing these wagon trains, then somebody from that bloodthirsty nation is." Bent lifted his arm and wiped his forehead. "And they call themselves Texas Rangers." Again his eyes fixed accusingly on Warfield. "The same name which you and your unit of volunteers are going under, Mr. Warfield."

Logan stood and pulled a folded sheet of paper from his pocket. "Gentlemen," he said as he moved to Bent's desk, "I believe I can shed some light on the subject and take the pressure off Colonel Warfield." He smoothed the document. "If you'll gather around, I'll tell you who and what we're facing." When eight faces were peering down at the map, Logan said, "Do any of you know anything about the Comancheros?"

Logan's eyes—gun-barrel gray, as cold and lethal— moved around the circle. Thomas scratched his beard. Warfield shook his head.

"Comancheros," Warfield repeated. "Can't say that I've ever heard of them."

Bent's face suddenly lit up; he snapped his fingers. "Traders," he exclaimed. "People who trade with the Comanches."

"Bandits and outlaws," Logan said. "The worst of all races congregated in one spot for one purpose: to prey on the innocent." Quietly he told them all he had learned about the Comancheros from Houston; he described the Comanche attack on Brenna's caravan and the white men who rode with the Indians. "This is something bigger than any of us can handle alone," Logan concluded. "These men respect no government and no people."

Bent's eyes narrowed and his brow furrowed with consternation. "You think these rangers are Comancheros?"

"If they're not Comancheros," Logan qualified, "they're working with them."

"Pretty good story," Thomas said as he moved to the opened window and spat. "Have you ever figured that maybe Sam Houston is in cahoots with these here rangers?" He retraced his steps until he was once again part of the circle around the desk. "Think of all the wealth these men could be bringing to your bankrupted nation!"

As far as Logan was concerned, Thomas's exclamation deserved no answer. As if the man had never spoken, Logan continued, "I followed the tracks of the men who murdered the hide hunters. They traveled this way." He moved his hand westward across the panhandle. "The same as the Comancheros. And all of them disappeared as if the earth opened up and sawllowed them. Gauging by the depth of the ruts, the wagons were heavily loaded, gentlemen.

"If these groups are operating together," Logan continued, "all of them are interested in taking women prisoners. They have a lucrative prostitution business in Mexico, willing to pay top dollar for women. Guess you could label this as slavery, gentlemen."

"Damn," Warfield muttered. He raised his head to Logan. "What are we going to do about this? How can we catch them? My men and I have been riding this area for weeks and we haven't spotted another living soul except some Indians and your train."

"None of my wagons venture that far south," Bent murmured, rubbing his palm against his whisker stubble. "And this is the first I've heard about freebooters other than Warfield." He walked to the window and peered into the courtyard that was already teeming with morning activity. "I can't afford this scare. I depend on freighters for my livelihood."

"You have a high-powered telescope," Logan said. "Do you announce the arrival of coming traffic?"

Not immediately following Logan's train of thought, Bent continued to look out the window. "The watchman keeps Dapier informed, and he posts all arrivals and departures. Scouts generally come in several days before the trains." The impact of his words hit him, and he jerked around. "Do you think someone working with these outlaws is operating out of my fort?"

"Yes, sir, I do," Logan answered. "I agree with President Houston. This is a highly sophisticated group of outlaws. He believes they have spies working out of our settlements. Now, I believe they have a network of spies in key places: in major towns in Texas; here at Fort William; in Santa Fe; in St. Louis." Logan waited a moment before he added softly, "If these men have their way, sir, your empire will soon become theirs."

The meeting dragged on, finally to break up, questions still unanswered, fear paramount. As Logan and Hollis walked out of the office, Thomas lingered behind.

"Mr. Hinkelrod," the old scout said, "does any of this change our plans? Are we still planning on leaving in the morning?"

Hinkelrod nodded and said, "That we are, Mr.

Thomas." The wagon master turned to Bent. "If you'll have your clerk prepare our bills, sir, we'll be settling up tonight. Plan to leave at five in the morning. I'll see that all the settlers get word of the plans."

Warfield joined Logan and Hollis at the top of the stairs that led to the placeta. "Since you're more familiar with this country and the Comanches than I and my men are, MacDougald, what do you think we should do?"

"Colonel Warfield"—the steely gray eyes sliced through the Missourian—"I have to agree with Mr. Bent: Although you're commissioned by the Republic of Texas as a ranging unit, you and your men are nothing more than freebooters. As such, you're a disgrace to me and my nation."

"I am a soldier, sir!" Warfield bristled. "I am helping your government."

"Not like this!" Logan declared. "Houston wants the United States to annex Texas, not declare war on us. If my advice means anything to you, you'll plunder no more trains in the name of Texas. Whether you heed my words or not, you'd best be careful. The Comanches and Comancheros won't be any more fond of you than Bent, the Mexicans, and the Americans are."

After Warfield strode off angrily, Roger asked, "What are we going to do? Head on to Santa Fe?"

"Expect so," Logan said absently. "Brenna's wanting to beat the Missouri freighters."

"When do you think we'll be pulling out?"

As Roger asked the question, both of the men looked across the compound to see Brenna and Francisca walking out of Brenna's apartment.

"You'll have to ask Brenna," Logan said.

His eyes fastened on the señorita, Hollis said, "I believe I will."

He was gone, and Bent's two men brushed past,

leaving Logan alone at the railing. Bent joined him. "What's your stake in this, Mr. MacDougald?"

"I'm a scout for Garvey Freighters," Logan returned.

"That's not all you are," Bent said. He paused and waited for Logan to speak. Finally he broke the silence himself. "Told the men to be extra careful. Always have a band of armed patrols pacing the battlements, but I'll be doubling that. Also sent word about the freebooters to my brother Charles in Taos. Double up on the patrols that I send with the wagon trains, too."

Out of the corner of his eye, Logan watched Roger greet Brenna and Francisca. He heard Brenna's soft trill of laughter; Francisca's was low and husky. Bent heard the laughter also and turned his head in the direction of the two women.

"I'm willing to make a deal with Mrs. Allen," Bent said. "I'd like to buy her merchandise."

Logan turned to look at the man who stood beside him. "Have you talked with her?"

"Not yet," Bent answered. "I wanted to talk to you about it first. See what you thought."

"What's your deal?" Logan asked.

Bent said, "I've checked over her inventory lists, and I'm prepared to give her a fair market price." He talked longer, itemizing some of Brenna's goods; then he quoted a price. "Now, mind you"—he wagged his finger in the air—"I know this isn't what she expects to get in Santa Fe, but it's a good price, and she's free to return to Austin to her business. Getting the goods to Santa Fe then becomes my problem. And," Bent added, "trading in Santa Fe isn't going to be easy for a Texan. Right now there's open hostility between Texans and Mexicans. Governor Manuel Armijo is going to make it plenty tough for Mrs. Allen. He levies a flat five-hundred-dollars tariff on every incoming wagon."

For a long time Bent grumbled about the adverse trading conditions in Santa Fe and Taos under the present government. As he talked, Logan leaned over the railing and surveyed the patio below. He watched the Cheyennes entering the fort with their trade goods. The blacksmith was shoeing a horse, the carpenter repairing a wagon wheel. Women were bustling to and from the general store. An old man drove a cart filled with water barrels into the placeta.

When he reached the center of the court, he called out, "Come and get it. Nickel a tub! Water for washing your clothes."

"Well," Bent finally drawled, "guess I'd better be getting dressed."

A group of wild-looking men, wearing full beards and hair that hung below their shoulders, sauntered into the fort. Although they were small, wiry men, Logan could tell they were tough. Before Bent could leave, Logan pointed and asked, "Who are they?"

Bent gave them a quick glance. "Mexican traders. Uneducated, simpleminded vagabonds who live about four or five miles upstream. They bring us some meal and dried vegetables at odd times. They prefer to trade Taos whiskey to the trappers for valuable pelts." Bent grudgingly added, "They're as good with bows and arrows as the Indians. Some say they're better. When they take the notion to hunt, they become hell-for-leather riders."

Bent paused and leaned over the railing. "I don't recognize that Indian with them," he said, peering at the tall, blanket-covered figure who walked with the Mexicans, "but we have so many Indians coming and going, I can't be expected to know all of them. That's why we put all of them out of the fort come sunset."

Logan tensed, but his expression never changed. His stance never betrayed his tension. The Indian looked up, and ebony eyes bonded with the gray ones—for a split second, no longer. Yet the two men greeted one another; silently they spoke; inwardly they smiled. The Indian lowered his head and moved with the traders.

Unaware of the silent communication between the two men, Bent scurried to his apartment to dress for the day after he extended Logan a cordial invitation to join him and his wife for breakfast in their apartment. Logan remained on the rooftop, his gaze following Thunder and the Mexican vagabonds.

Finally Logan joined the Bents for breakfast. Sitting at the table were Brenna, Francisca, and Roger. Roger and Francisca were entertaining each other; Brenna and Bent were in deep conversation. When Brenna looked up at Logan, his lips curved into a smile.

"Logan," Francisca called, her face radiating her happiness, "I am so glad you are joining us. Here"—she patted the chair next to her—"come sit beside me."

Logan's eyes flitted from Roger's crestfallen face to Brenna's expectant one. "I'll tell you what," he suggested. "If you'll move over, I'll sit between two lovely women."

Francisca looked at Brenna, winked, and affected a beautiful pout. "Oh, all right." Then she laughed and scooted to sit next to Roger.

Brenna chuckled with Francisca. She couldn't help but like the girl. Brenna's heart went out to Roger: Truly he was the love-struck swain.

"I have just posted a letter to my father," Francisca told Logan. "One of Mr. Bent's men took it for me." For a moment sadness flickered in her eyes. "I wanted Papa to know that I was safe." She paused, took a deep breath, and blinked back the tears. "I wanted to tell him about the death of Don Felipe and Doña Isabella." Now she smiled. "And I wanted to tell him about Brenna and you, Logan. You've been so kind to me.

And about Mr. Roper, who speaks so many languages."

Out of the corner of her eye, Brenna saw Logan lower his head so that he could hear Francisca better. When he turned back to her, Brenna saw the gaunt features relax; she saw warmth in his gray eyes—a gentleness and a warmth brought on by something Francisca said. Brenna felt a tinge of jealousy.

After the meal, Brenna said, "Logan, may I see you in my room for a moment?"

"And what about me?" Francisca teased.

"What about me, señorita?" Roger asked, his eyes twinkling. "I would be most happy to keep you company."

"Thank you, Señor Roger." Francisca smiled warmly.

Brenna smiled. "You're both welcome to join us, but I guarantee this is for business only."

"Then Señor Roger and I shall stroll around the fort," Francisca announced gaily. "When you get through," she said to Brenna, "come join us."

Later, when Logan and Brenna were in her room, she said, "I wanted you to know that I'm pulling out come Monday morning. That gives nearly a week of rest to the teamsters and the animals and plenty of time to repair the wagons. We can restock our food and get all our clothes washed and mended." She looked at Logan, who lounged in the door. "I thought you were leaving this morning." Her statement implied more than it specified. She wondered if Francisca's coming had anything to do with Logan's change of mind.

"No, I've decided to stay longer." But he offered no explanation for his change of plans. "Did Bent talk to you about buying your goods?"

Brenna nodded.

"You're not going to take him up on the offer?"

"I can't," Brenna answered. When she saw the irritation that skittered across Logan's face, she said, "I really can't."

"And why can't you?"

"I promised myself that I'd get this wagon train to Santa Fe, and that's what I intend to do," Brenna returned. As always, she hid her other reason for going on.

"At times, Brenna, I hate this damn caravan," Logan said. "Where it's concerned, you have no common sense. You have the opportunity to sell all your goods, to have all the cash you need to salvage your company and your property. Why must you push your luck and go on to Santa Fe?"

Brenna thought about the letter, tucked into the lining of her valise. She almost confessed, but she held herself back. Delivering that letter and meeting with Peyton H. Alexander was something she had to do personally. Furthermore, Logan would be furious. He was allied with Houston. She wasn't in the mood for one of his lectures . . . or for his anger.

"Bent won't give me what I can get in Santa Fe, Logan," Brenna pointed out. "You can wager that whatever he's willing to pay me, he'll more than double in Santa Fe."

"I agree," Logan pointed out, "but he'll also be taking the chances of smuggling it into Taos and Santa Fe. He'll be the one dealing with Governor Armijo."

"I'm going to take my chances, Logan."

"My God, Brenna!" Logan felt as if he would explode at any moment. "You evidently weren't listening to Bent. Armijo made his wealth through the Santa Fe/American trade. He's not going to let anyone supplant him. Bent told me he imposes an arbitrary duty of five hundred dollars flat on each wagon that is brought to the customhouse, regardless of content. The entire time you are in Santa Fe, Armijo will keep you under guard." He pleaded with Brenna. "Let Bent take the responsibility for the goods from here on. He'll give you enough to make the trip worthwhile."

"I don't want him to give me enough to make the trip worthwhile," Brenna said. "I've already told you I want to help establish trade routes throughout all the settlements in Texas. And Santa Fe is a part of Texas. If I allow Bent to buy my goods, I won't have accomplished my goal."

Logan asked, "Have I ever given you bad advice?"

"No."

"Armijo has incited the Mexicans; they fear and hate all Texans," Logan told her. "Ever since Lamar's Santa Fe Expedition, they have become even more suspicious. You'll be no exception."

"I'm not leading an army into Mexican territory," Brenna argued. *But what you're doing isn't too far from that,* reason stated. "The . . . the Mexicans have nothing to fear from me."

"I know that," Logan said. "But you have something to fear from them."

After prolonged argument, all Brenna could promise was, "I'll have to think about it," which was more than Logan was doing for her. She had been thinking about Logan's leaving her, and she had promised herself she wouldn't beg him to stay. She knew he had to find the Comanchero hideout and report back to Houston by July; she knew he was determined to find out about the contraband guns. She understood his desire to learn about his sister, to find out if she was alive or dead, but Brenna was so much in love with him that she was selfish. She wanted him; she wanted him with her.

"Come to Santa Fe with me," she said.

"No." The answer was soft but emphatic, and Logan was looking directly at her. "I've already told you that I

can't come to Santa Fe with you. I promised Houston."
He turned his face, and his eyes once more located the
Indian who moved with the Mexican traders.

"Are you planning on staying here at Bent's Fort?"

Doubts began to resurrect; they nagged her conscience. She loved Logan, but she didn't know who he
was or what he did. He had shared so little of himself
with her . . . and never really with her or because of
her. Always when she learned something personal
about him, she was the eavesdropper. She had heard
about the massacre of his parents when he was
consoling Billy; she had learned about Dancing Dawn
when he was consoling Francisca. So little of himself he
had shared directly with her. Yet he said he loved her.
He didn't love her enough to push the past behind him;
he didn't love her enough to postpone his searching for
his sister and accompany her to Santa Fe. He didn't
love her enough to marry her.

"I'm not sure what I'm going to do," he finally
answered.

His refusal to accompany her hadn't surprised
Brenna. Disappointed her, yes, but surprise, no. She
had known the answer before she asked the question.
Yet she was compelled to ask him. His refusal to
discuss his future did hurt her. She honestly wanted
him to share that with her.

She stood and looked out the window, her gaze
following Logan's. Because a great number of Indians
freely wandered the fort, she didn't pay much attention
to the tall, blanket-clad one who stood close to
Francisca Sandoval, the one on whom Logan focused
his attention. Rather she saw the woman and assumed
Logan was looking at her.

"If you're hell-bent on going to Santa Fe," Logan
finally said, "I suggest you hire one of Bent's men as a
scout since they're familiar with the trail from here to

266

Santa Fe. Also hire some of his armed guards. You may need them."

Logan was at war with himself. He wanted to go with Brenna; he couldn't stand the thought of her being alone in Santa Fe, but he couldn't go with her. He had an obligation to Thunder; he had dragged his Cherokee brother into this personal vendetta with Chief White-Hair and Scar-Face. Thunder hadn't identified himself, so Logan could only surmise that he hadn't revealed his true identity to the Mexican traders. Logan had to find a way to meet with Thunder, to find out what had happened since the two of them parted.

"Of course I'll ask Mr. Bent for a scout and more armed guards," Brenna answered absently, her mind clearly on other matters. Logan had told her that he must find his sister or information about her. Yet she wondered if this was all the truth. Part of her—the emotional part—argued that his interest in remaining at the fort was Francisca Sandoval, but reason quickly denied the assertion. *Logan loved her! He did!*

"I'm sure he'll let me have them for a price," Brenna said. She moved to the foot of her bed and picked up a gunnysack with her soiled clothing. She managed a weak smile. "I need to wash my clothes. I've already paid O'Hara for the water and tubs."

"Brenna—" Logan turned to her, supplication in his tone.

Brenna managed a weak smile. "From the beginning, we knew what we were facing," she said. "You've made no promises. I knew you couldn't go all the way to Santa Fe with me." Her voice grew husky with tears. "I just hoped, that's all."

Logan took the sack from her unresisting fingers. "I'll walk down with you," he said. "I want to take a walk around the fort."

He accompanied Brenna to the washing area, a

267

square composed of rows of benches on which rested tubs of water. In the center of the square was a large fire, the wood stack nearby. One Indian woman was chipping lye soap into the boiling water in the large wash pot. Another was periodically stirring and jabbing the clothes with a large stick. An empty tub for clean clothes sat in a small wagon.

"Come," the woman who stirred the clothes called, "you will be next. Put your sack here."

Using the pole as a pick, she began to lever the clothes out of the water, holding them above the wash pot and letting as much hot water drip from them as possible before she slung them into the waiting tub. As soon as all the clothes were taken from the wash pot, a child pulled the wagon to the rinse bench.

Logan watched Brenna sort her clothes and drop them into the black cauldron of soapy water. For the first time since the death of his parents, he was ready to abandon his search for White-Hair and Scar-Face. In his heart he felt that Flanna was dead; he'd felt that for a long time now. But he had to think about Thunder. Perhaps after he talked with him he would see a way out of this situation. Even so, he had to get word to Houston. He was tightly ensnared in a trap of his own making.

"I'll see you later," he called. "I'm going to talk with Bent."

As his boots crunched over the gravel, he moved back to the placeta. As he walked past one of the rooms, a tenant staggered out, a whiskey bottle in hand.

"Howdy, stranger," the man drawled, the smell of liquor mingling with the stench of body odor. "Like to have a little drink?" He held the bottle out.

"No, thanks," Logan answered.

"Taos whiskey," the man called after Logan's

retreating form. "Can get it for a few hides from Mexican traders."

Logan stopped walking and slowly turned to look at the grizzled man. "Which Mexican traders?" he asked.

The man waved his hand toward the river. "Up the river four or five miles," he said. "Have a village. They just call it The Town." He staggered through the doorway. "Have plenty of liquor, they do."

"Come on, Busby," a masculine voice called from inside the room. "It's your bet."

Later in the afternoon, after he visited with Bent and talked with several of his scouts who were familiar with the countryside, Logan decided to pay a visit to the Mexican village up the river. When he arrived, the sun was sinking in the western sky. Around a large oblong clearing he saw thirty or so small houses, wall to wall, some with second stories. Goats, donkeys, dogs, buffalo calves, and children swarmed in the dust. The men whom he'd seen at the fort now lounged in the shade, smoking clay pipes and filing iron arrow points. Slowly he guided the roan across the small plaza and pulled it to a stop directly in front of the men. He pushed back his hat.

"Heard at the fort that I could pick up some Taos whiskey here."

The men turned bland faces to Logan, and no one spoke. The filing never stopped. Curious women and children soon surrounded him.

"I have valuable pelts," he said as he reached for his bedroll. He untied them and threw them on the ground in front of the men.

One of the men, younger than the others, laid his file and arrowhead aside. He flattened the skin on the ground and rubbed his hand over the fur.

"This is good," he said in English, his accent heavy. He rose, the pelts in hand, and motioned with his head to Logan. "Come with me. You can have your whiskey."

Logan dismounted and tied his horse to a low hanging limb on the nearby tree. He followed the diminutive man into one of the buildings. The whitewashed room was about twelve feet square, a fireplace in one corner. Sparsely furnished, it contained a large, rough-hewn table, a bench on either side. The man unfastened the wooden shutters on the opposite wall to reveal a cupboard that was built into the thick adobe walls. He waved his hand, and Logan looked at the cache of liquor.

"For these pelts, señor"—the man walked to the table, lifted a booted foot, and propped it on the edge of a bench—"you may have four bottles of my finest whiskey."

Logan's eyes never moved from the liquor cabinet, but he knew he was surrounded by suspicious, if not hostile, men. As if nothing were amiss, Logan walked to the wall and selected his whiskey. When he set the bottles on the table, he saw the Mexican holding a revolver—a Colt six-shooter—on him.

"Do not think because we live here, señor," the man said, a sneer creasing his face, "that we are stupid."

"I never thought you were stupid," Logan returned quietly. Certainly not now! Logan eyed the gun and wondered from whom the man had gotten it.

"Why did you bring us pelts that bear Bent's mark?"

Logan knew he'd slipped. He hadn't given a thought to the hides' having been marked already. He'd put too much confidence in Bent's description of these vagabonds. These men might be uneducated, as Bent had said, but they were far from stupid and certainly not simpleminded. From now on he'd have to be more careful.

"I heard at the fort that you sold whiskey for pelts. I had none, so I bought these from Bent's commissary."

"We've been known to do business for gold and silver, señor," the man mocked. He figured Logan's explanation was a weak one.

The wild-looking bunch closed in on Logan. Two or three propped themselves in the opened windows; the others crowded into the room.

"You are not a trapper, señor," the man continued in his maddening monotone. "You are not a man who drinks Taos whiskey—whiskey with more water than alcohol." He waved the barrel of the gun at Logan. "So tell me, why have you come to our town?"

"Bent tells me that you are traders."

"*Sí*. We raise produce and livestock for the fort."

Logan had to smile. From what he'd seen of their gardens when he rode into the town, he imagined they used the water in their alcohol rather than on the gardens.

"Sometimes we hunt the buffalo and supply Bent with fresh meat."

"Do you trade with anyone except Bent?" Logan asked, pretending interest in the crude bottles of whiskey.

"Mostly Bent." The man's eyes glittered with undisguised interest.

"I understand there are more profitable trade outlets around here than William Bent."

The man shrugged.

"How about the Indians?"

The Mexican laughed. "Around here, señor, the Indians trade only with the Bents."

"What about the Comanches?" Logan asked, his eyes never leaving the man's face. He watched the black eyes for a telltale sign, but they never wavered.

271

"Ah, señor," he drawled, "only a fool would trade with the Comanches." He paused, then said, "And I, señor, am not a fool."

They were playing a game. Logan knew it; so did the Mexican. At this point Logan wasn't sure which one of them would win. He hadn't been dealt a good hand, but he had to play it. He had to make the best of it.

"I've heard of those who do trade with the Comanches," Logan ventured. "In your language they are called the Comancheros."

"Comancheros." The man rolled the word with his tongue as if savoring it. "Sí, señor, I have heard of them. Through the ages there have been those who dealt with the fierce Comanches."

"Surely trading with the Comanches would be more profitable than trading with Bent," Logan suggested, his eyes blatantly leveled on the revolver. "I never saw a weapon of that kind in his commissary."

The Mexican laughed. "Ah, señor, I think I'm going to have to kill you. You know too much or have guessed too much."

"If you kill me, you'll ruin your chances of breaking into the Comanche trade market in a big way," Logan said. "If you could do that, you'd no longer be a pawn. Rather you'd be the big chief. You'd control trade between the Comanches and the Comancheros. You'd be a big man, señor."

The Mexican weighed Logan's words carefully. Finally he moved his foot and dropped his revolver into his holster. He was interested in commanding trade between the Comanches and the Comancheros.

"Tell me how I, Mario Laguna Jamarillo, can become a big man in this Indian trade."

Mario sat down on one side of the table and clapped his hands. A young woman darted through the crowd that congregated outside the door of the house. In

272

Spanish Mario said, "Fix us some food, woman. We have a guest."

Mario's words sent the villagers scurrying. A guest meant fiesta.

"And now, señor," Mario said, "please tell me more."

"I saw several of you in the fort earlier today," Logan said.

Mario nodded.

"A tall Indian was with you."

Mario furrowed his brow. "No, señor, I think you are mistaken."

"I am not mistaken. A tall Indian came in with you. To blend in with all the other Indians on the fort, he had a Mexican blanket wrapped around his shoulders and head."

"I do not know this Indian," Mario maintained. "Now speak before I change my mind and kill you."

"Bent and his brothers and St. Verain, his partner, have a monopoly on trade along this route," Logan iterated. "And Comancheros monopolize it throughout Comanche territory." His gaze was pinned to Mario. "I have reason to suspect that you are the ones who have been giving information to the Comancheros about the going and coming at Bent's Fort."

Mario slipped from the bench and walked to shuttered doors on another wall. He slid the bar through the bolt and took out a bottle of whiskey. He laughed as he brandished the label through the air. "This señor, is fine whiskey. That which I keep for Mario Laguna Jamarillo. We will drink, no?" He also brought two glasses with him, which he set on the table. After he had poured the liquor, he picked up his glass. "Even if I were the man who was providing the Comancheros with this information, señor, what makes you think I would admit it to you? And what do

273

you think is in it for me?"

"Not enough when you consider what's in it for them," Logan needled. "You get a small load of whiskey and trade goods, a few of these six-shooters. They get the horses and livestock; they get the American trade goods; and they get the women." Logan rose and walked to the window. He saw the rude corral to the right of the plaza. When his eyes landed on the Appaloosa, he didn't bother to contain his smile. "And it's the women who bring the good price in Mexico, is it not, Mario?"

"Who are you, señor?" Mario asked. "And why should I trust you? You could be setting me up, no?"

"I'm Logan MacDougald," Logan answered. "I'm an outlaw on the run because I've been branded a horse thief by the newly organized Republic of Texas. Sam Houston has sworn himself to get me and bring me in." He laughed. "You see, one of the horses I stole happened to belong to the president of Texas himself."

Mario smiled. "That's an interesting story, but I have only you word for it, señor."

"You have the horse in your corral," Logan replied. "The Appaloosa with the huge SH brand." A grin crossed Logan's face as he remembered Houston's vociferous explosion when he had demanded the Appaloosa as part of his outlawed herd. "And, señor, the Indian of whom you have no recollection can identify me. He and I stole the horses together in broad-open daylight from the corral next door to Bullock's House. Thunder and I left the good senators and representatives of the Republic of Texas afoot."

Mario laughed loud and heartily; he swallowed his whiskey in one gulp. Setting the glass down with a thud, he said, "We shall see if you're telling the truth, señor." He clapped his hands, and the young woman poked her head through the window. Mario moved to where she stood and conversed with her in Spanish. When she left, Mario linked his hands behind his back and smiled. "Yes, señor, we shall soon know if you're telling the truth."

Logan gulped his whiskey and poured a second glass. His hand went to the medallion around his neck, and he played with the slick metal. He could only hope that Thunder would corroborate his story. Not having talked with the Cherokee since they had parted the night before the attack by the Comanches, Logan couldn't begin to guess how Thunder had managed to become a part of the Mexican community. Or the question presented itself: Was Thunder a part of the community?

The Mexican señorita returned, Thunder walking behind her. When the Indian entered the room, he looked from Mario to Logan, absolutely no expression on his face at all.

"You wanted to see me," Thunder said.

"This man," Mario said. "Who and what is he?"

Thunder slowly moved his head, his eyes fastening on his adopted brother's. He saw Logan's hand close over the medallion. Thunder moved his arms, smoothly swinging the blanket from his shoulders. He dropped it on the bench closest to him. He, like Logan, could only hope his brother and friend had told the story they agreed upon.

"This is Logan MacDougald, the man I told you about. He and I stole the horses from the corral at Bullock's House in Austin."

"Why did the two of you separate, and how did you end up with the horses?" Mario questioned, his eyes slitting.

"My friend went a little soft in the head and heart over one of the women on the wagon train," Thunder replied. "He wanted us to return so we could travel with

275

them. I didn't wish to, so we argued. That night while he was sleeping, I disappeared with the horses. I figured he was going to get us into trouble."

Mario lifted his hand and scratched his face. "No," he finally shouted, his hand coming down in a thud on the table, "I cannot believe you."

"Sounds like the truth to me," came a familiar voice from behind Logan.

He spun around and found himself face-to-face with Abbott Kirkwood. The man grinned, exposing tobacco-stained teeth. He moved farther into the room, picked up a glass, and filled it with whiskey.

After he quaffed it down, he said, "I never did reckon you and this here Indian was working for Houston." He laughed. "Don't reckon you had anybody fooled on that train but the woman what owned it."

By exerting all the control he had, Logan kept from betraying his revulsion of the man. Remembering all that Antelope Hunter had taught him, Logan kept his face and eyes void of expression.

"Right comely woman she was," Kirkwood added with a snicker.

"You know this man?" Mario demanded.

Kirkwood filled his glass the second time and threw the liquor down his throat in one swallow. "Yep, I met him on the wagon train. Him and that Indian was posing as honest men. Said they was working for Houston. Knew when I saw them horses strung out behind them, each one carrying a different brand, that they was one of us." He dropped his hands to his hips, threw back his head, and guffawed.

Playing a hunch, Logan said, "You're the one who runs messages back and forth between civilization and the Comancheros."

"Reckon I was till that woman upset things. Now I can't show my face in the fort. They'll be stretching my hide in that press. But now you, Mr. MacDougald, can come and go as you please with no one the wiser." Kirkwood moved closer to Logan, so close Logan could smell the stench of his sweaty body. "How would you like to throw in with us, MacDougald?"

Logan pulled the cork out of the bottle and poured whiskey into the two empty glasses. He lifted his head; an easy grin spanned his face. "How would you like to throw in with me, Kirkwood?"

Chapter Sixteen

The afternoon sun smashed off the walls of the adobe fort as Brenna gathered her laundered clothes from the line and put them in a large basket. She carried them to a room that was furnished with ironing boards, flatirons, and a gaping fireplace, the fire always burning. Dipping her hands in a large basin of water, she sprinkled her clothes and rolled them up.

As she let them sit for a moment in the basket so the moisture was uniformly distributed, she walked to the door and gazed into the placeta. Logan had ridden off earlier in the afternoon, and she was curious about where he had gone. She also wondered why he hadn't told her that he was leaving.

"Here you are!" Gertrude Dawkins's exclamation jarred Brenna from her thoughts. "I've been hunting everywhere for you and Logan."

Brenna smiled. "Well, you've found me. Hiding behind the washtub and rub board."

"Where's Logan?"

"I don't know," Brenna replied, her gaze straying to the fort gate. "I saw him ride off earlier this afternoon."

"He'll just miss out on the good news then," Gertrude said, her face radiant with happiness. "Sam and I are going to be married this evening."

"How wonderful!" Brenna exclaimed.

"Afterwards we're going to have a celebration supper, and we'd like to invite both of you to the ceremony and the supper. You'll tell Logan, won't you?"

"If I see him," Brenna replied, her gaze straying to the main gate of the fort. "He rode off earlier, and I don't know where he went or when he'll be back. But," she added, "I promise I'll be there. I wouldn't miss it for anything."

"I'm so excited," Gertrude confided. "I feel like I'm a young girl again. I hope I don't disappoint Sam."

"You won't," Brenna assured her. "The two of you seem to have been made for each other. Where have you and Sam decided to live?"

"That's the hard decision," Gertrude admitted. "I want to marry Sam and live with him in Santa Fe, and I also want to be with Callie Sue. I've been more like a mother to her than a grandmother. I've had her ever since her mama and papa died when she was a baby. I can hardly think about letting her go on to Oregon without me, and I sure can't have her ruin her life by staying with me in Santa Fe."

"How does Sam feel about this?" Brenna asked.

"Sam's agreed to go on to Oregon with me and Callie Sue, but I can't do that to him. He's going to Santa Fe because of the climate. The doctors back East told him that would help his breathing. Either way I go, I'm going to be hurting someone, and I'll lose either Callie Su or Sam."

"No, Granny," Callie Sue said from the opened doorway. She had been standing there long enough to overhear the conversation. "You won't lose me." The young woman moved so that she was in front of her grandmother. "If you feel the same way about Sam that I feel about my Wes, I understand. I love him, too, and I think you should stay here with him. Your entire life

279

had been dedicated to raising me. I think it's time you thought of yourself for a while."

The two women embraced each other. Later, after saying goodby to Brenna, they slipped out of the room so they could be by themselves.

Evening shadows had darkened the room when Brenna finished her ironing. She replaced the flatirons on the hearth and picked up her basket. As she walked through the courtyard, she saw the guards close the inner gate. She heard the grating sound as the bar slid into the bolt. Her gaze swept around the small square, filled with men wearing buckskin shirts, but none of them were Logan. She ascended the stairs and walked to her apartment. As she passed the clerk's office, she stopped and poked her head through the opened door.

"Mr. Dapier," she said, "I want to take a bath. Please have a tub and water delivered to my room."

The clerk smiled and nodded his head. "Give me about thirty minutes, Mrs. Allen."

By the time Brenna repacked her valise, her bath was prepared. She removed her clothes, stepped into the copper tub, and sank below the hot water. As she relaxed and the tensions of the day ebbed from her body, she heard the cries and shouts of the milling crowd in the courtyard. She heard the traffic passing in front of her apartment. But she didn't hear that sound for which she longed the most: Logan's return.

Dusk had settled over the fort when she finally emerged from her room, wearing her blue gingham dress. She was moving toward Bent's apartment when she saw Dapier rushing in her direction. He was so intent on reaching his destination, he didn't see her until they collided.

"Oh, Mrs. Allen," he blustered, his thin face creased in worry, "I'm so sorry."

"That's quite all right," Brenna assured him. "I'm

none the worse. Are you?"

"If it's not one thing," the man murmured, "it's ten more, and all of them worse than the first." He waved a worn document through the air. "Have you seen Mr. Bent? Or Mr. Hinkelrod?"

"No, I haven't seen either one of them since early this morning."

"I must find Mr. Bent," Dapier fussed. "I really must." He took his spectacles out of his pocket. "Mr. Bent is going to be so upset. First the freebooters. Now this." He adjusted the wire frames behind his ears.

"Can I be of any assistance?" Brenna asked, curious about the cause of Dapier's concern.

"A fellow just rode in." Dapier leaned closer and lowered his voice as he confided in her. "An Ingus McCallaghan. He's an officer of the law, duly authorized by the state of Massachusetts."

"How ominous-sounding that is," Brenna murmured. "We have our share of the outcasts and outlaws, but seldom do we attract law enforcers."

"Well, let me tell you something," Dapier said, careful to keep his voice low. "This man is looking for someone."

"Here at Bent's Fort?"

"Fort William," Dapier automatically corrected her, then went on to say, "Here at the fort." He handed Brenna the sheet of paper. "Read this, will you?"

Brenna took the document and unfolded it. She skimmed the faded print. "Why," she gasped, her head jerking up after she had read only a few words, "this is a Wanted poster!"

"Yes, ma'am. McCallaghan thinks the man came in from Missouri on a wagon train. I told him we have trains coming in regularly from Missouri, but he wants the keys to the sheds, so he can inspect all the wagons. Says the man has lots of money stashed somewhere.

Claims he shot and robbed a man in Boston before he headed west." Dapier grabbed the paper from Brenna. "I must go, Mrs. Allen. I need to find Mr. Bent. McCallaghan is causing a ruckus in the office."

After the clerk disappeared, Brenna stood a moment longer in the golden-brown shadows of soon-coming night. Boston, Massachusetts. That's where Sam came from. But the name on the poster was different. Samford Waltham Roberts. Samuel Walter Roper. The same initials. Both names would carry the same diminutive: Sam. But Brenna could not believe Sam was a murderer or a thief. She had always suspected there was a lot Sam kept to himself, but didn't most people who migrated to the frontier! Before she was aware of having moved, she was knocking on Sam's door.

"What a pleasant surprise," he said, his breathing normal tonight. "I was just about to leave for dinner. I understand you and Logan will be joining us."

"I will," Brenna answered. "I don't know about Logan. He rode out of the fort this afternoon and hasn't returned."

For a brief moment Brenna was envious of the love Gertrude and Sam shared. To join Sam in Santa Fe, Gertrude was giving up everything: her granddaughter, who was like a daughter to her; her plans to settle in Oregon; her independence. Because of Gertrude's love for Sam, she was making these sacrifices.

Sacrifice! What neither Brenna nor Logan was willing to do at the moment. Give up their independence! Give up their mission! Something neither one of them was prepared to do.

Then Brenna was aware of Sam's talking to her. She heard him say, "Well, I must hurry now. I want to talk to Mr. Bent about the wedding ceremony. I'll see you later, my dear."

"Sam . . ." Brenna began a little clumsily; she didn't really know where or how to begin. She didn't really know if it were her place to say something to him about his past. But she kept thinking of Gertrude and their coming marriage. She cleared her throat. "Sam, I would like to talk with you in private for a few minutes, please."

Sam sensed the urgency in her request. "Come in." He backed out of the doorway and made room for Brenna to enter. He waved to a chair. "Won't you sit down?" He sat on the edge of the bed and waited for her to speak.

"I just ran into one of Mr. Bent's clerks. He said . . ." She paused. "He said a man named Ingus McCallaghan just rode into the fort."

Sam's expression never changed.

"He's a law officer from Massachusetts."

Still Brenna saw no change in Sam's demeanor.

"He's chasing a murderer by the name of Samford Waltham Roberts—a man who answers to the name Sam."

Sam laughed, the raspy sound filling the room. "Sam is such a common name, my dear. How many of us are named that! I doubt we could begin to count."

"This Sam that we are talking about," Brenna continued, "is traveling from Missouri."

Again Sam laughed and brushed her worries aside. "How many Sams have left Missouri for Oregon? No need to be concerned on account of me, Brenna."

"What about Gertrude?" Brenna asked. She saw a muscle twitch at the corner of Sam's mouth, and she knew she had struck a tender cord.

"Does Gertrude Dawkins strike you as a woman who would fall in love with a murderer?"

"Not deliberately. But sometimes with matters of the heart, Sam, we have no control."

"Let's just pretend for a moment," Sam said in a soft voice. "Let's pretend that this Samford Waltham Roberts—and rather than call him Sam, let's say he calls himself Ford. Well, Ford went into an office to confront a man about some money this man owes Ford—back salary and a return on the unused part of his lease, money this Ford needs desperately to bury his dead wife and daughter."

Sam stood and moved to the window, his eyes on the glowing orb that was settling into the ribbon of myriad colors. He breathed deeply for a few minutes. Then he spoke. "Say the man got angry with Ford, pulled out a gun, and ordered Ford out of his home. Now, remember, Ford no longer cares about himself. His whole reason for living has been taken from him. But he promises himself that the woman who loved him and who bore him a child will not be buried in a pauper's grave. Because Ford couldn't do better, he had subjected her to live in poverty for the last few years of her life, but he didn't intend for her to rest in poverty throughout eternity."

Sam's voice wavered; he was a little wheezy. "Can you understand? All this other fellow wanted was money that rightfully belonged to him. So he charged the man, and the gun went off. Left were a corpse and a victim. Having nothing else to lose, Ford probably took enough money to bury his family and to stake him to a new life."

Long after he stopped talking, the two of them sat there in silence.

Finally Sam spoke. "What are you going to do?"

"Since I don't know this Samford Waltham Roberts, better known as Ford Roberts," Brenna replied, "I have nothing to say to McCallaghan. I think Samuel Walter Roper and Gertrude Dawkins should be married and live happily ever after in Santa Fe." She stood and moved to the door. "Nor do I think you have anything to add to the story, Sam. I have a feeling that the man who McCallaghan is hunting has already left for Oregon, don't you?"

"Yes, ma'am, I do," Sam replied, donning his hat and ushering Brenna out of the room. "Now I must be on my way to talk with Mr. Bent. I'll see you tonight."

As Sam and Brenna walked onto the promenade, they met a harried heavyset man. His three-piece suit clearly marked him an easterner.

"Evening, ma'am," he said, doffing his hat.

Before Brenna and Sam murmured a greeting to the stranger, he was hurrying down the stairs. Brenna heard steps and turned to see Dapier moving toward his office.

"Mr. McCallaghan?" She pointed to the retreating easterner.

Dapier nodded. "That was Mr. McCallaghan," he said. "He talked with Mr. Bent and Mr. Hinkelrod. Since Mr. Hinkelrod didn't have anyone on his train meeting Mr. McCallaghan's description of the fugitive, we figured the man he's after must be on the train that pulled out for Oregon three days ago."

"Speaking of trains from Missouri," Sam said, "do you have any idea when another one is coming?"

"No," Dapier replied, "can't say that I do. Why?"

Sam was concerned. "Lilly Ellington," he said. "Billy's mother was supposed to have been here by the time her husband arrived, and that was several weeks ago."

"Oh, yes," the clerk exclaimed, "the little boy who was with the hide hunters who were murdered. I'm sorry, sir, I have no idea when the next train is coming."

"I guess Gertrude and I will take the boy on to Santa Fe with us," Sam mused as he and Brenna walked toward the candlelit apartment that was decorated in preparation of the wedding. "I'll leave word here at the fort that Mrs. Ellington can find Billy in Santa Fe with us."

Brenna enjoyed dinner, but she didn't stay for the celebration afterward. She slipped out and stood at the railing in front of her room. Roger and Francisca invited her to join them as they promenaded in the cool of the evening, but Brenna declined. She was worried about Logan; she couldn't understand why he hadn't returned to the fort or why he hadn't sent word to her. Brenna walked the battlement, her eyes peering through the darkness for sight of Logan, her ears trained to every sound.

At eight she finally decided to go to bed herself, but she glanced at the blockhouse and saw candlelight flickering through an opened window. She smiled. Clyde Dapier was still working. For reasons unknown to herself, she hastened toward the clerk's office. When she turned the knob and walked into the room, Dapier laid his quill down and smiled.

"Mrs. Allen, what can I do for you?"

"Couldn't sleep, so I was walking," Brenna returned.

Dapier nodded. "I enjoy the spring evenings when the cool breeze blows in from the mountains. Hate to be shut up in a room myself."

"I . . ." Brenna paused. She had nothing to discuss with Dapier; she didn't know why she had hurried to his office. "I guess Mr. Bent told you that we'll be pulling out Monday morning."

The clerk nodded.

"I'm going to need a scout and some more armed guards."

Dapier moved the candle holder and shuffled through some papers that were scattered over his desk.

"My desk is such a mess," he grumbled. "Ah, yes! Here it is!" He lifted a ledger. "Mr. Bent left me with a list of names. Pretty good men. All of them trustworthy. Been with us a long time." He shoved the book toward her. "Would you like to see?"

"Not right now," Brenna said. "I'll look at it in the morning and talk it over with Mr. Bent." She smiled and backed out the door. "By the way, Mr. Dapier, you haven't seen Mr. MacDougald, have you?"

"Not since later afternoon," he replied, peering over the top of his spectacles. "He was asking directions to the Mexican village up the ways a bit."

"What Mexican village?" Brenna asked, an acute pain of disappointment shooting through her. Something else Logan hadn't shared with her.

"Small village," Dapier said. "Made up mostly of Mexicans and a few stray Indians. Mexicans came from Santa Fe and Taos. They're traders of a sort—trade just enough to eke out a living."

Brenna listened as Dapier gave her a description of the town and its occupants, neither of which was favorable.

"But it's the best place to get cheap liquor. That is, if you like Taos whiskey—more water than alcohol, and the reason why most trappers like that kind of whiskey is because it's served by pretty little señoritas." Dapier laughed. "Guess that's what MacDougald had a hankering for."

Brenna was alternately worried and angry when she reached her room. She knew Logan was no saint, but he wouldn't travel to a Mexican village five miles upriver to buy watered-down whiskey. If he wanted a drink, he would have bought his here on post. *And he'd better not have a hankering for a pretty little señorita!*

Too caught up in her thoughts to go to bed, she returned to the walkway and leaned on the railing. She glanced at the moon-coated placeta. Clearly outlined were the well, the hide presses, and several empty wagons. She glanced at the shops which were hidden in the shadows: the blacksmith, the tailor, the commissary. With a smile she remembered the vendors. She remembered the group of Mexicans who came in with the brightly colored blankets. The tall Indian wrapped up in one.

Brenna clicked her fingers. That's what she had thought so odd when she looked at him today. The weather was too hot for him to have been wearing a blanket . . . unless he needed it for concealment rather than for warmth. *Thunder!* The Indian was Thunder. He had to be, and Logan had gone to meet him.

Logan could be in trouble! That could be the reason why he hadn't returned yet. Maybe he needed her help.

Brenna spun around and hurried into the apartment. Without lighting the candle she quickly shed her dress and donned her trousers, shirt, and boots. With deft movements she strapped her guns around her waist and grabbed her knife and whip. As she walked out of the darkened room, she swished her hat on her head and eased around the promenade undetected. With no trouble she slipped into the corral and saddled the gray. A word to the guard and she was out of the fort, riding upriver toward The Town.

She heard the sounds of the fiesta long before she saw the community. Lusty music and the odor of spicy food filled the air. Soon she saw the arch of light—a large bonfire in the center of the plaza—that illuminated the entire area. Men and women were dancing; children were running to and fro. Brenna pulled the horse to a stop, tied the reins to a low-hanging limb, and crept through the brush until she was close enough to see.

For a long time she lay hidden in the cover of the

bushes. The children were finally rounded up by scolding mothers and put to bed; the dancing stopped; the bonfire died out. Still Brenna did not see Logan. She saw no sign of the tall Indian. Perhaps she had been mistaken earlier! Perhaps she had allowed her imagination to run away with her.

Then she saw the door to one of the houses open; a wedge of light filtered into the street. Out walked Logan, a bottle of whiskey in hand. Standing behind him was a beautiful, young señorita. From her vantage point Brenna could see the woman clearly. The petite figure was clad in a white scooped-neck blouse, tucked into a bright, colorful skirt that gently swirled from her tiny waist. Black hair was parted in the center and hung in long, thick braids over each shoulder. A lovely smile curved full lips; a smiling face tilted up at the man who stood in the door.

"Please come back and see us again, señor," Brenna heard the woman say. She pressed herself against Logan and laid her lips on his cheek.

Logan chuckled softly as he gently pushed her away. "With an invitation like this, señorita, I don't see how a man could keep away. What more could he ask for than a beautiful señorita and good whiskey?" he asked dryly.

"No!" Brenna cried. She had never suffered such acute pain in all her life. Her chest was tight; it hurt. Her head spun, but she couldn't draw in the needed breath of air. At first she wanted to cry; then she grew angry; finally she was wrapped in numbness. Still she couldn't take her eyes off Logan; she watched him march down the street to enter another house . . . to meet another señorita.

Brenna had no reason to stay any longer. Logan wasn't in trouble and certainly didn't need her help. Evidently Dapier was right: Men who came to Taos for whiskey were really hankering for the women. Brenna let her imagination fly freely to fan the flames of anger. The idea that Logan had come to this village for whiskey and women infuriated her. She had no doubt that she was woman enough for Logan, but one woman evidently wasn't enough for him. Like Shawn, Logan's proclamation of love was nothing more than words. Something he said to pacify her.

Although she liked Francisca Sandoval, Brenna couldn't help but think about her. She remembered how Logan had insinuated himself into the señorita's life and how tenderly he had administered aid to her. How quickly Logan had come to Francisca's rescue and offered her a shoulder to cry upon! Again Brenna felt the sharp stab of jealousy.

Was Logan merely being friendly, or was he attracted to Francisca? Brenna compared herself to the Mexican and in all points found herself lacking. Francisca was beautiful. She was young, and she was a lady. Brenna strongly suspected that Francisca was one of the reasons why Logan hadn't already left Bent's Fort—and he had said that he was leaving this morning!

When Logan had returned to Brenna during the storm, she had welcomed him back into her life and her bed on his conditions with no questions asked. His purpose in life hadn't changed; his quest was not complete. Again she had hoped that her love for him was strong enough that he would change, but it hadn't been. She had hoped that his love for her was strong enough, but it wasn't.

Logan was a man driven by his past, and until he laid all his ghosts to rest, he could never rest or make a commitment of love. Logan hadn't even let her know that he was leaving the fort or told her where he was going. That could only mean he had not yet learned to trust her fully. Trust was the cornerstone of love.

Eventually Brenna returned to her horse and mounted. Before she struck out for the fort, however, she turned her head for that last look. She watched as the woman closed the door, the only light on the dirt street that which came from the window. A shutter banged. Before the other shutter closed out the room entirely, Brenna saw a man. Logan was forgotten as she leaned forward.

The man in the room was Abbott Kirkwood! Logan had been with Abbott Kirkwood! He had made contact with the Comancheros.

Just seeing the man who had schemed to lead her and her caravan into an Indian ambush filled her with hate. The rush of hatred was so great, she turned her horse and headed into the village. She wanted to kill Kirkwood herself. He was the man responsible for Gabby's death. But Kirkwood spoke, and she pulled the horse up short.

"Now, MacDougald," Kirkwood drawled, "I think it's time I introduced you to some more of the people we're going to be working and living with." She watched Kirkwood slap Logan on the back as if they were old friends. She heard him say, "Bonita there is a mighty fine little woman, but later I'll provide you with a señorita who'll wipe all memories of that wagon captain out of your mind."

"We'll meet the señoritas later," Logan said. "Right now I'd like for us to have a talk."

Kirkwood laughed. "Nothing I'd like better, but I have some unfinished business I need to take care of. I'll just leave you with Dolores. I'll see you first thing in the morning."

Then Brenna could hear no more; they moved away from her into a darkened end of the village. She turned her head and nudged the gray toward the fort.

Evidently Logan would spend his night with his new *associates*. Brenna was upset . . . angry . . . betrayed. She remembered the nights she had spent in Logan's arms. His words of love. His touches. His declaration of love. Now she felt him drifting away from her, and it wasn't necessarily the woman whom she feared. She feared his single-minded purpose in life. His entire world centered on revenge. She was losing him, but she wasn't sure that it was to a woman.

Loneliness, like the darkness of night, soon enveloped her. As the gray ambled through the trees that lined the river, Brenna was preoccupied with her thoughts almost to the exclusion of everything else. Then suddenly she was alert to the environment around her. Her keen sense of survival instinctively took over. She felt a presence behind her. She couldn't hear anything unusual, but she knew she was being followed. It couldn't be Logan. He was visiting with the señorita. Who was it then? Kirkwood? He said he had some business to attend. Perhaps his business was at the fort?

Brenna flexed her hand over the braided leather handle of the long, coiled bullwhip looped over her shoulder. The gray she guided with her knees. Her revolvers she didn't want to use; they were too noisy and would attract too much attention, most of which she could do without.

She eased off the horse as soon as she passed a large tree and crouched behind the trunk. The coils of the whip slid down her arm, and her hand closed over the handle. She heard the soft thud of the horse's hooves, the scratch of the brush as someone moved through them. She waited patiently. The rider moved out of the cluster of trees just enough that his hand was exposed by the moonlight. His hat hid his face, the billowing serape his body. Brenna saw the revolver in his hand.

She had wondered if friend or foe followed her. Now she knew it was foe.

As soon as the rider neared her, Brenna lifted her arm, every movement fluid and flowing. The whip seemed to move out like a long, big snake, back, back, then it looped up into the air and traveled swiftly. The long leather lash flicked past the horse's head, never touching the animal, then licked down and tore the weapon from the man's hand. The bullwhip came sailing back over Brenna's shoulder. The revolver fell and slid across the ground near her feet.

As quickly the whip was licking through the air again, this time to coil its deadly fang around the rider. Surprise was her best weapon, and she used it. She dragged him from his horse, but the minute she heard the thwack of his body as it landed on the ground, she knew she was in for a fight.

She had to even the odds; she wasn't strong enough to take a man. Before he could uncoil the whip, Brenna pulled her revolver from the holster, ran to the flailing man, and rested the barrel against his head. But the man was not frightened of the gun. He freed himself of the whip and rose to his feet.

Brenna felt the impact of his body as he hurled himself at her. They rolled and tumbled to the ground, each grunting and swearing, their sounds primitive and guttural. Brenna reached for her knife, but Logan was atop her. She was on her back. His hand caught her flailing arms and he pulled them above her head; her body he imprisoned with his.

"My God," he whispered, "it's a woman."

"Logan!"

"Brenna! What are you doing out here?"

"I think that's my question," she said.

Logan slowly turned her hands loose and sat back. "I was taking care of some business."

"I saw your business," Brenna snapped as she pushed into a sitting position. "Ebony eyes, black hair, and voluptuous." Her anger quickly resurfaced. "I saw you kiss her, Logan."

Logan laughed quietly. "By chance, love, are you jealous?"

"Yes, I'm jealous," Brenna admitted, "and I'm angry. How dare you stand there pawing over that . . . that woman!"

Logan's laughter was deeper and louder. "Evidently you weren't looking, or you would have seen that it was the other way around, love. She was kissing me."

"I didn't see you trying to stop her."

"I wasn't encouraging her either," Logan defended. "I had to be careful. The room was full of hostile men who were waiting for an excuse to end my life."

"I'll bet it was."

His voice softened as he added, "I was on my way home to you, sweetheart."

"I know where you were headed. You left one señorita to go to another. Dolores was her name, wasn't it?" Brenna wouldn't be placated. "Maybe you were planning on coming back to the fort, but only after you had your fill of the señorita."

She picked up her hat and crammed it on her head, unmindful of the strands of hair that escaped her chignon. She stood and raked her hands down her trousers in an effort to knock off the twigs and dirt. Then she bent over and looked for her whip and revolver.

"Is this what you're looking for?" Logan asked as he stooped over to pick up the bullwhip.

Brenna reached for it.

Logan didn't hand it to her. Instead he coiled it around his shoulder. "What are you doing out here by yourself?"

"Neither of us owes the other an explanation," Brenna said. "Each of us is a free agent. We can come and go as we please, no questions asked."

"I told you what I was doing in the village." Logan dropped the whip, strode to where Brenna stood, and caught her shoulders. "Now I want to know what the hell you're doing riding around the countryside this time of the night unescorted."

"I needed some fresh air," Brenna retorted.

"We're going to get this misunderstanding straightened out right now," Logan said. "I don't intend to spend tonight with a nagging woman."

"I didn't think you intended to spend the night with me at all."

"Let me show you my intentions."

Logan's hands dug into her shoulders as he hauled her into his arms. His head lowered and his lips settled on hers in a warm kiss. He pressured her mouth open, and his tongue slipped inside. His hands moved down her arms to the sweet curve of her buttocks, clearly exposed in the ever-shrinking trousers she wore. He urged her nearer to the hardness of his body.

"This," he murmured, "is what I intend to do. This is what I was returning for."

He lifted his mouth and spread quick kisses over her face, down her cheeks, to the cradle of sensitivity between shoulder and neck. He burrowed there under her shirt, his whiskey-scented breath splaying warmly against her skin. His hands pushed beneath the waistband of her trousers and his fingers gripped the supple flesh of her buttocks. He pressured her closer; he arched against her.

"Oh, baby!" He lifted his mouth just enough to speak. "Why would I want that woman when I have you? You're all the woman I ever want."

Brenna clung to Logan. Her anger, hurt, and

disappointment dissipated in the face of his admission. She knew that she was strong enough to stand on her own two feet; she could fight her own battles, but she didn't want to be alone. She didn't want to spend her life without Logan. She loved him and wanted him to be with her always. She only wished he felt the same way toward her.

She lifted her face to meet his. Again their lips touched. So easily he lit the flame of love within her, so easily he set her desires on fire anew. His lips moved on hers, the touch firm but gentle. Wanting more, needing more, Brenna moaned, winding her arms tightly around him, her hand savoring the feel of the hard muscles of his back.

Their movements in harmony with their passions, they quickly divested each other of clothes and sank to the ground. Kneeling beside her, Logan's lips traced the outline of her collarbone while his hands explored her body leisurely, delighting her with their wondrous discoveries and thrilling her with fevered search. He found that secret place, so warm, so moist. His pleasure heightened with her inarticulate moans and cries, her heady breathing, her whimpering of joy.

His fingers traced paths of fire up her inner thighs; they trod lightly back and forth over her femininity, causing her body to shudder with raw desire. Brenna's blood raged through her veins, pounded through her head, each pulse station beating. She grasped the hair at the nape of his neck, and she guided his face up to hers. Her lips captured his, and she pulled his warm body over hers.

The hardness of his lower body demanded entrance to the musky sweetness of her body. Brenna was ready; he knew. She wanted him; she needed him as much as he wanted and needed her.

"My darling," he sighed, his hand moving with that

reverential tenderness, "you're so sweet, so very sweet."

His lips closed on hers, parting them wider and wider, his tongue probing, filling her mouth with its velvety thickness as his manhood slipped into the warm haven of her intimacy, stroking, constantly building the flame of desire.

Her lips tugged gently, sipping the goodness of him. Instinctively her body responded: Her hands caressed; they stroked; they gave joy. Her hips swayed with his motion, heightening his anticipation. Their cries were thick and inaudible. They were totally consumed with their passion.

They lay in the peaceful afterglow, hardly moving, barely breathing, not daring to break the spell that bound them together. They gloried in their moment of togetherness, that moment that no one, nothing could take from them.

Brenna tucked her face against Logan's chest and breathed deeply, filling her lungs with the smell of him. Her heartbeat slowly returned to normal.

Logan pushed her hair out of her face. "I'm glad you're here," he whispered, "but why? What were you doing?"

"I was worried about you. It dawned on me tonight that the Indian we saw in the fort today with the Mexican traders was Thunder." She paused a second before she added, "I saw you with Kirkwood."

The only sounds to be heard were those of the forest and its creatures and the steady thump of Logan's heart beneath her ear.

"I recognized Thunder earlier today when he came into the fort," Logan said. "I knew there was a reason why he didn't speak to me or identify himself, so I came out here to meet him. I had no idea that I'd also find Kirkwood."

"What are you going to do now that you've found

him? Infiltrate the Comancheros?"

"Yes."

"My God, Logan, that's suicide," Brenna exclaimed, bolting up. She reached for her clothes. "How can you and Thunder hope to expose these . . . bloodthirsty savages? Two men against so many! What can you hope to gain?"

"I'm sorry you had to find out." Logan reached for her, but Brenna dodged his hands.

With agitated movement she jerked her trousers on. "You wouldn't have told me." She leaped to her feet and walked away, turning her back to Logan. She buttoned up her shirt, but she didn't tuck it into her pants. "You would have just disappeared in the morning?"

"I wouldn't have told you," he admitted, "and yes, I would have just left in the morning."

"Why, Logan?" Brenna asked. "Tell me why."

Logan didn't immediately answer; rather he dressed. Eventually he said, "I wanted to spare you the anguish." He moved to stand behind her, his hands on her shoulder. "I love you."

"You've spared me no anguish," she said. "My entire association with you has been one pain after the other. I live from day to day waiting for you to tell me that you're leaving again." She waited a long time before she said, "And I don't think you love me. You desire me, but I don't think you really love me."

"After what we've shared, you can think it's nothing more than desire?" His fingers gripped into the tender flesh.

"Love means more than making love." She whirled around. "It means sharing and trusting. The only thing you've shared willingly with me is your body. What I've learned about your past life, I've learned as an eavesdropper. First I overheard you telling Gabby that

298

both sets of your parents had been murdered. Second I overheard you telling Billy about the specifics of their deaths. Then I listened as you confided in Francisca about your fiancée. I, the woman you profess to love, the woman you've been sleeping with for the past seven or eight weeks, didn't know you carried a portrait of Dancing Dawn in your watch." Silver tears trailed down her cheeks. "How do you think I felt when you showed that watch to Francisca? When you shared something so precious and sweet with her and not me?"

"I'm sorry," Logan murmured. "I didn't mean to hurt you. Dancing Dawn is no longer a part of my life. She's a wonderful memory, but that's all." He caught Brenna's face in his hands and lifted it, but in the darkened shadows of night, he couldn't read her expressions. He couldn't see her eyes. But he could feel her slipping away from him. "Honestly, yesterday morning when we first spotted Bent's Fort and I told you I loved you, I promised myself that I would tell you all about Dancing Dawn. I was planning on removing the portrait and putting it in a safe place so I could give it to Thunder. She's his sister, you know."

"Logan, when you first left me, you accused me of being possessive and selfish. You said that was the reason you don't like to become involved with one woman. I thought about it, and I promised myself that if you returned, I wouldn't issue ultimatums or make any demands. I've tried it your way, but I want more than what you're offering me. Where you and I are concerned, I'm extremely selfish. I want all of you."

"You have more of me than any other woman ever has."

"That's not enough," Brenna whispered.

"I want to marry you."

"When?"

"After I complete my mission. I'd like us to marry,

settle down, and raise a passel of children."

"Never now; always later," Brenna said, then asked, "When are you leaving?"

Logan waited a long while before he said, "Tonight. I was coming to tell you goodby."

"Do you have any idea where you're going?"

"No. Thunder and I are going with Kirkwood to meet some of his contacts." He added, "I'll see you again as soon as I can. I'll come see you when you're in Santa Fe. I promise."

After a moment Brenna said, "No, Logan, I don't want you to come to see me."

"You don't mean that."

"I've never meant anything more," she replied. "I can't take any more of this parting, Logan. My heart has been torn to pieces so many times that it's threadbare. I want more out of life than a man dropping in and out between missions. Please leave me alone."

Chapter Seventeen

Uriah Weldon, the scout Brenna had hired at Bent's Fort, eased his horse over the rise and pulled it to a stop. Riding immediately behind him were Brenna and Francisca. Uriah pointed to the sleepy town that lay at the foot of the Sangre de Cristo mountains.

"Well, ma'am," he said as Brenna and Francisca drew abreast to him, "we're at the trail's end."

"Sí," Francisca murmured lovingly, "this is the trail's end." Looking at the Mexican outpost, she smiled, her cinnamon skin a beautiful foil for her even white teeth. "We are home."

Trail's end. Home. How wonderful the words sounded to Brenna. Her only disappointment was that neither Gabby nor Logan was here to share in her moment of glory. She gazed at Santa Fe with its low adobe huts and unpaved streets—the city she had come so far to see. A city that was separated by more than fifteen hundred desolate miles from Mexico City and was isolated from the nearest American settlements by prairie, mountains, and desert—all of which Brenna had traveled and conquered. For this moment she had slaved over eight hundred miles of hardship.

Her spirit lifted immeasurably, and the tribulations of the trail seemed small in consequence to her having achieved her goal. She, Francisca, and Uriah turned their mounts and headed back to the caravan, the number of wagons having diminished after the storm from twelve to eight—six freight haulers, Brenna's personal wagon, and the mess wagon.

"Santa Fe over the rise!"

Brenna's call echoed down the line of wagons. Shouts of delight rang out and gunshots echoed through the clearing. Roger, now the wagon boss in Logan's stead, halted the train. Sam and Billy jumped off the carriage, the child running to open the door for Gertrude.

"We're here, Granny," Billy shouted, throwing his arms around Gertrude. "We finally got here. Now Grampa's breathing will get better."

Gertrude looked at the child whom she and Sam had brought with them. Following Bent's suggestion, they agreed to introduce the boy as their grandson to avoid legal red tape in getting their permit to live in Santa Fe. "Yes, son, we're home," she said, clasping the child to her breast, but her eyes were on Sam as he moved toward both of them.

Callused, hardened teamsters hugged one another and danced around, so great was their joy at reaching the trail's end.

"Gentlemen," Roger called as he urged his horse down the line of wagons, "I appreciate your excitement, but we still have work to do before we can proceed to the customhouse."

Following Bent's instructions, goods were piled up on as few wagons as possible since a flat tax was levied on each wagon, regardless of content or weight. In turn extra teams were harnessed to the wagons to make up for the heavier loads. Bent's dragoons and teamsters were taking the empty vehicles and returning to Bent's Fort with them, where they would be stored until Brenna came back through and picked them up, at which time she would reload them with goods she bartered for and bought in Santa Fe.

Once the loads were shuffled and shifted around, everyone cleaned up. The wagoners polished the harnesses on the horses and tied new crackers to their whips. As they worked they bragged and lay wagers with one another, each claiming he could outdo his comrade in the dexterity with which he flourished his favorite brand of authority as they drove through the streets and the *plaza publica*. They bathed and cleaned themselves up. Now they were prepared to meet the dark-eyed señoritas who were sure to stare at them as they passed: Their faces were clean, and their hair sleek-combed. They wore their choicest Sunday suits and fired their guns in the air in a continuous roar.

First Warfield and his men, then Bent's men had regaled the Texans with stories of the Spanish city. This outpost on the outer reaches of the Mexican frontier was a totally new world where Latin frankness combined with a natural gaiety to produce the appearance of licentiousness. All classes met at the faro tables: dice and cockfighting were equally popular.

Excitement ruled the day as Roger, Francisca riding beside him, lifted his arm in the air, waved, and called, "Stretch out." Immediately behind him was Sam's faded carriage. Sitting on the seat beside him were Gertrude and Billy. Next came Jonesey, driving Brenna's wagon, then the freight haulers. The caravan slowly rumbled into the dusty town to be cheered on by a growing crowd of citizens.

Los americanos! Los carros! La entrada de la caravana!"

The teamsters, cracking their long whips in the air, shouted greetings and waved their hats above their heads. They drove the wagons into the plaza, where they formed a moving circle, stirring clouds of dust into the air. Brakes screeched as the wagons stopped. Colorfully dressed Mexicans and Indians rushed up to greet them. So glad were the citizens of Santa Fe to see Francisca Sandoval alive—word had reached Santa Fe of the horrible massacre of the wagon train—they touched her and signed the crucifix in silent thanks for her safety.

Brenna could hardly believe that she was in Santa Fe at last. She glanced around the crowded plaza—the treeless, flowerless, and shadeless plaza—that was bordered on two sides by an irrigation ditch. She saw Mexican soldiers by the numbers and Indians wrapped in blankets. She saw the women. They wore short, full, brightly colored skirts topped off with loose, low-cut blouses and large scarves they wound around their head and shoulders. She heard a babble of Spanish and English as the Mexicans chattered with the Americans. The whole town seemed to be made of adobe. Dusty in the summer, Brenna figured. Muddy in the wet season. She noticed that many smaller streets radiated and straggled from the square. With the exception of the uniformed soldiers, Santa Fe was not much different from San Antonio, she decided.

Shrill vendors clustered at the western extremity of the plaza. Here dark-complexioned women in their brilliant colored skirts sat behind pyramids of soap, pats of goat cheese, eggs, onions, and sweet rolls, or they dipped up fiery chile and tamales from simmering braziers. They sold firewood, sacks of beans, bundles of hay, even live animals. Cuts of buffalo and pork, limp-looking chicken carcasses, and bits of liver and tripe stood under the protective netting of pink cloth.

"Come on, ma'am," Uriah said. "We need to head toward the Governor's Palace to pay our custom duties. You, too, sir," he said to Sam. "You'll need to get your permit to live in Santa Fe."

By the time Brenna was off her horse and tying the reins to the hitching post, solemn, hostile-looking soldiers were marching toward her caravan. She straightened up and stared at them.

"Nothing to be scared of," Uriah said in an undertone. "They're going to inspect the wagons and make a list of all your goods." He turned. "Hollis, give the men orders to unfasten the covers so the soldiers can see what's inside. Don't give the soldiers any lip, but watch them closely."

"I think it will be in your best interest, Brenna," Sam said, "if I stay here to oversee the inventory. Since I read, write, and speak Castilian Spanish proficiently, I'll make sure the lists are kept honest." After several deep breaths, Sam turned to Gertrude. "You and Billy go with Mr. Weldon and Brenna. Find out what we must do to get our permits."

Uriah cupped Brenna's elbow with his hand, Francisca's with the other, and guided them to the north side of the square. Gertrude and Billy followed. "Now we'll go see the governor." Uriah lowered his kindly face and smiled at Francisca. "Then where shall we go to await your parents?"

"If our townhouse were unlocked," Francisca said, "we could go directly there, Señor Weldon, but I have no keys. So we'll wait for Mama and Papa at the La Fonda." Francisca was so happy she laughed. "Oh, señor, I can hardly wait. It has been six months since I've seen my family." Francisca cut her eyes at Brenna and grinned. "Joaquin is a *caballero*—a fine gentleman. You will like him. He is very handsome."

Brenna smiled. Logan couldn't be classified as a fine gentleman, she thought, but no man could be as handsome as Logan MacDougald. And even if a man were better-looking, no one could replace Logan in her heart. Not for the first time since she and Logan had parted at Bent's Fort, a twinge of fear twisted Brenna's heart. She wondered where her love was and what he was doing. She wondered when she would see him again . . . *if* she would see him again.

"This," Brenna heard Francisca say, "is the *Palacio,* the seat of Mexican government on the frontier."

Brenna looked at the long, squat building with a portico or arcade running along the whole front.

"And that is the *Presidio,* originally planned as a place of defense." Francisca's hand waved to an enclosure of thick adobe wall of which the Palace was architecturally a part; it ran about four hundred feet east and west and about twice as far north and south. Brenna found the fortlike structure reminiscent of Bent's Fort.

As they continued to walk, Francisca described the buildings. "Within this enclosure and forming parts of the wall are not only the Palace," she explained, "but garrison quarters, the prison, a chapel, a small cemetery, and the *plaza de armas,* or drill ground."

The three of them walked under the portico, their boots snapping against the adobe-tiled floor. When they entered the Palace, their footfalls echoed through the large, cool room. At one end they saw massive, imposing doors—the doors that led to the governor's office. On either side stood armed guards. Uriah stopped the group at the entrance desk, and the young Mexican officer, resplendent in his blue uniform, looked up from his writing.

"What may we do for you, sir?" he asked coolly in stilted English, his gaze directed at Uriah.

Brenna stepped in front of the scout and said, "I'm Brenna Allen, owner of Garvey Mercantile and Freight Hauling out of Victoria, Texas. I've brought in five wagons of trade goods. I would like to pay the custom fees and obtain a license so I might sell them."

"Have you applied in advance for this license?" the officer asked, knowing full well that she hadn't.

Francisca moved to Brenna's side. She smiled at the young officer and addressed him in Castilian Spanish, "Hello, Roberto."

Roberto Onega stood so quickly, he knocked his chair over. "Francisca," he exclaimed, his face wreathing with a smile. "How wonderful to see you again." As quickly his joy at seeing her was replaced with sadness. In a gesture of genuine bereavement, he caught Francisca's hands in his. "I am so sorry to hear about what happened."

"Thank you," Francisca murmured, and for a moment they clung together, friend to friend. Eventually Francisca smiled through her tears and swallowed the knot in her throat. "I would like you to welcome my friend from Texas and to extend her hospitality." Francisca's words broke the delicate moment.

"Texans!" Roberto spat the word as if it were poison. So great was his vehemence, he yanked his hands from Francisca's and jerked to military stance.

"Texans," Francisca softly repeated, "but they are not the enemy. They have only armed guards for protection from hostile Indians. As I'm sure you already know, this is a trading expedition only." She laid her dainty gloved hand on the sleeve of Roberto's light blue uniform and smiled beguilingly. "Please see that Brenna gets a permit to sell her wares."

For a long moment Roberto looked into Francisca's lovely eyes. Again he was docile, tamed by the gentleness he saw in the dark depths. He laid his hand over hers and sighed. "I'll see what I can do. I'm making no promises. You know how the governor feels about

Texans." His eyes rolled toward Brenna.

"But their coming is no surprise," Francisca gently accused.

Roberto shook his head. "Texans are so stupid," he said. "They record their every move in their newspapers."

"And we receive the newspapers with relish," Francisca added, a twinkle in her eyes, "because we can keep up with their movements. How else did we know about the Santa Fe Expedition!"

"*Verdad,*" Roberto admitted, a sheepish smile playing his lips. "It is true."

"We'll be at the La Fonda Inn," Francisca told him. "I sent word to Mama and Papa through one of Señor Bent's trappers that I was traveling with Brenna, so they are coming to meet me." Her smile widened, and she batted her lashes coyly—an art she had learned early in life and had practiced until she was quite proficient. "Why don't you join us for supper tonight? You could bring the permit with you, no?" When she saw that Roberto was acquiescing, she added as she turned to Gertrude Roper, "I would also like for you to meet Señora Gertrude Roper and her grandson, Billy."

Roberto's eyes grew chilly. "More Texans?"

"No," Francisca gently chided, "they are not Texans. They have traveled from America, and they wish to live here and become citizens of Santa Fe."

"We do not need any more *Americanos* or Texans," Roberto declared. "Already we have too many. They are causing us nothing but trouble."

"But I think perhaps the governor would be interested in meeting Señora Gertrude's husband and in giving him Mexican citizenship. My father is," Francisca informed the young officer. Although she spoke softly, her tone was firm, her meaning clear. When Roberto arched raven-black brows, she said,

"At my father's request, I am bringing Señor Roper to our hacienda. If Señor Roper is interested, my father plans to hire him as his secretary." She opened her reticule and withdrew a crinkled letter she'd received from her father while she was at Bent's Fort. "Señor Roper writes and speaks several foreign languages, *mi amigo,* and he's a scrivener. He will be much help to us in dealing with the growing number of *Americanos* coming to our country."

Roberto looked at Gertrude and asked in English, "Why do you come in your husband's place?"

"My husband is overseeing the inventory lists which your soldiers are making of the goods in Mrs. Allen's wagons."

Roberto's eyes narrowed, and he spoke more sharply than before. "You understand that citizenship comes to some at a high price?"

"My husband and I came prepared, sir."

"That is good. I will schedule Señor Roper an appointment with the governor. When I come to supper tonight, I shall give you the time and date."

"Thank you," Gertrude replied.

Roberto dismissed her with a click of his heels and returned his attention to Francisca. "I will see you tonight at the La Fonda."

"What about my wagons?" Brenna interrupted.

With a disdainful glare Roberto turned to her.

"I'm not about to leave them in the middle of the plaza through the night," Brenna declared.

"The host of La Fonda will have wagon sheds you may rent for the night."

His words were curt and dismissive, but Brenna was satisfied. At least she hadn't been sent packing. Pleased with the turn of events, Uriah returned to the wagons to help Roger and Sam oversee the inventory; Brenna and the others trudged across the dusty plaza toward the inn. They walked along a continuous and forbidding wall with an arcade to keep off sun and rain. The wooden shutters, flung open, exposed windows barred with wrought iron; the massive doors were securely closed.

Francisca observed the disappointment so visible in Brenna's expression. "Do not be deceived," she said. "Santa Fe is not all that it appears. Behind the walls and within the doors, life is going on. Truly this is a city of enchantment."

The words were no sooner out of Francisca's mouth when a portly man swept out of one of the buildings and bowed low in front of the women. "Welcome to La Fonda," he called in Spanish, gesturing for them to enter the large door. "Come. I have rooms for you. Also food and wine." Following the man, the three women and boy entered the enclosed courtyard, upon which opened the various rooms of the inn. Francisca, speaking in Spanish, ordered accommodations for the evening; then she introduced the group to the owner. Carmela, a shy young servant, led each to a separate apartment—the Ropers at one end, Brenna and Francisca at the other.

Accustomed to the bare adobe walls at Bent's Fort, Brenna was surprised when she walked into the room. A thick, coarse domestic fabric carpeted the floor, and calico cloth covered the wall. The ceiling beams were painted. The fireplace was in a corner and so constructed that the wood had to be placed upright against the back. The room was simply furnished: a low dresser over which a mirror hung and on which an earthen pitcher and bowl rested; an armless straight chair; a carved chest on removable stand; a *trastero,* a tall cupboard with four shelves and doors; and a long settee. The walls were hung with tin candle holders and

310

portraits of the Virgin Mary and other saints and crosses.

Brenna set her valise down and watched as the servant hastened to the several windows. She threw open the shutters to let the morning sun flood the room with warmth and light, then turned to Francisca and spoke.

Francisca interpreted for Brenna. "Carmela would like to have your clothes. She'll wash the soiled ones and iron you a dress for tonight."

Brenna opened her valise and extracted the only dress she hadn't worn on the trip—the one she had kept for Santa Fe. It was made of aqua silk and ecru lace, delicate fabric and color. As soon as Brenna handed the dress and undergarments to Carmela, the girl darted across the room and grabbed the pitcher from the dresser. Chattering in Spanish, she exited the door and disappeared.

Francisca laughed. "Carmela has gone to get you some water and clean sheets for your bed. She will be back shortly."

"Sheets," Brenna breathed. Bed linen was a luxury she had rarely enjoyed since leaving her home in Victoria. But her surprise turned into question. "Where's the bed?"

Francisca walked to the reclining couch and unfolded it. Now it was as wide as a double bed and boasted a mattress. "Your settee by day," she said, a smile dimpling her cheeks. "Your bed by night." She moved to the door. "Now I will leave you, so you can rest. I'll have your bath ordered. You may come into the patio any time you wish; otherwise, a servant will come get you when it's time to eat."

Brenna nodded. "Did you get rooms for Roger and the men?"

"For Señor Roger only," she replied. "He said he would take care of the men's accommodations." Francisca smiled, her cheeks turning a rosy hue. "I like Señor Roger," she admitted. "I think he would make a fine *caballero*."

This was the second time that Francisca referred to a *caballero*. Brenna's interest was piqued. "What is a *caballero?*"

Francisca's eyes twinkled with a secret. "You will see later, mi amiga. Now rest, for tonight we have a *fandango,* and wear your prettiest dress." Her deep, husky laughter warmed the room. "We will have a fiesta."

Long after Francisca departed, her laughter echoed through the room. Brenna moved to the window and gazed at the courtyard, full of activity as the teamsters began to pour in. She looked up to see Jonesey swagger through the entrance door, and for that fraction of a second she expected to see Gabby.

Tears burning her eyes, she whispered, "We made it, Gabby. We made it all the way to Santa Fe with our goods. I made it with the letter."

No, she as quickly corrected herself, *we* didn't make it! Gabby wasn't here. He was part of the price—the high price—she paid to mark a trail from Texas to Santa Fe. She reached up and wiped the tears from her cheeks.

She wished she had someone to share her elation with, to share her sorrow with. She wished Logan were here. In her mind's eye she saw the admiration shining in the depth of those beautiful eyes; she heard the words of praise. She felt his arms around her as he swung her through the air and said, "You made it, baby, all the way from Texas to Santa Fe!"

Her eyes still closed, the warm tears caressing her face, Brenna felt Logan's arms tighten around her as he gently pressed her face against his chest. "Don't cry, love," he whispered. "Gabby wouldn't have it any other way. He loves you and doesn't blame you for his death. Neither should you."

A gentle breeze wafted through the opened window and touched her caressingly. She opened her eyes and Logan was gone.

Never had Brenna felt more alone!

Chapter Eighteen

After several trips Carmela had brought clean bed linen, laid out Brenna's dress, and prepared a bath in an oblong copper tub. Perfume from the bath oil gently permeated the room. Speaking in Spanish, Carmela helped Brenna undress and motioned her into the water. After Brenna bathed and dried off, Carmela pulled out the settee and made the bed; then she gestured for Brenna to lie down. With strong but gentle hands, coated with lotion, Carmela massaged Brenna's shoulders and back, her thighs, lower legs, and her feet.

Totally surrendering to the blissful touch, Brenna relaxed into a peaceful near sleep. She remembered Carmela covering her body with a sheet. She heard the door creak as the servant opened it. Without stirring, Brenna murmured a lazy *"Adiós,* Carmela"; then she heard the door close and the lock click securely into place.

When Brenna awakened, the room was shadowed by dusk. She stretched and rolled over. She lay there a moment before she got up, listening to the noises in the courtyard. The loud, boisterous sounds of the teamsters. Chattering in broken English and Spanish. Laughter! Brenna smiled. Laughter filled the air. And excitement! And anticipation!

Without her knowing exactly when and where,

Brenna was caught up in the enchantment of the Mexican outpost. She was lost in the beauty of Santa Fe. Using the sulfur matches Carmela had left on the table, Brenna quickly lit the candles, their flames sputtering to life quickly to discard the shadows. She combed her hair and swirled it atop her head, letting recalcitrant strands curl around her face and neck. She donned her stockings and shoes and undergarments.

Then came the knock and Carmela's soft voice. "Señora Allen."

Brenna hastened across the room and opened the door. Amidst laughter and chattering—the laughter being the common language for both of them—Carmela buttoned Brenna's dress and stepped back to admire the Texan.

"Muy bonita," she declared, clapping her hands together.

Another knock.

"Brenna, may I come in?" Francisca called. "It is time for us to eat. My parents will be here soon, and I want—" Carmela opened the door, and Francisca walked into the room. Her words forgotten, she stared at Brenna. "You are beautiful," she breathed in awe. "Simply beautiful."

"Thank you," Brenna murmured, a little embarrassed.

"That dress is so . . . so . . ." Francisca couldn't think of a description worthy of the silk and lace creation.

Suddenly a young boy's cry echoed through the inn patio. "A message from the governor for Doña Francisca Marina Sandoval."

Francisca hurried out of Brenna's room. "Here," she called to the messenger. "I am Doña Francisca Marina Sandoval." She took the folded paper and gave the lad a small coin. *"Gracias, hijo,"* she said, and rushed back into the room. She broke the seal with her thumbnail as she neared the table. Holding the letter close to the candle, she read the message. "Brenna," she squealed her delight, "we are to dine with the governor tonight. He will send his carriage to fetch us, and we will meet Mama and Papa over there." Francisca dropped the paper on the table and turned to Carmela. Speaking in Spanish, she said, "Go to my room and get two *rebozos*. One for me and the other for Brenna."

The servant girl bobbed her head and disappeared through the door. "Come," Francisca called, catching Brenna's hand in hers. "We will wait in the courtyard for the carriage. I am so excited," she added. "I want you to meet Mama and Papa." She cast her head over her shoulder as they left the room, a sweet smile turning her lips. "And Joaquin."

By the time Carmela emerged from Francisca's room with the shawls, an officer was walking through the courtyard door. He spoke to the host, who in turn pointed toward Francisca and Brenna. The man moved to them and bowed stiffly and formally.

When he spoke, his Spanish was also stiff and formal. "I am Private Huberto Morales, personal aide to Governor Armijo. You are expecting me, yes?" His face was cold and unfriendly; he waited for no answer. "Governor Armijo sent me to escort Doña Francisca Sandoval and Señora Brenna Allen to his home for dinner."

"Sí, señor," Francisca answered. "I am Doña Francisca Sandoval, and this is my friend, Señora Brenna Allen. We were expecting you."

Morales bowed low, but his expression never changed. With a sharp click of his heels, he led the women out of the door under the portico to the awaiting carriage. Morales helped the women into the grotesquely carved and gilded gubernatorial coach and

316

shut the door. He climbed on top with the driver.

Giggling, Francisca leaned over to whisper to Brenna, "We call this the wheeled tarantula." Her voice lowered even more. "We also call the governor a tarantula. He is unprincipled, greedy, and brutal. you must be careful of him, Brenna, extremely careful."

This was the first time Francisca had been critical of her government, and Brenna took the opportunity to say, "I suppose you and your people would like to be freed from this kind of political authority."

"Oh, yes," Francisca said. "Papa is working for just that. He is planning a trip to Mexico soon."

"We Texans sympathize with you," said Brenna. "Having gained our freedom from Mexico, we can understand your wanting to."

"Oh, no," Francisca exclaimed, her eyes wide, "you misunderstand me. We do not wish to be free from Mexico, *mi amiga*. We wish only to be rid of Manuel Armijo. Our loyalty is to our government." She laid her hand on Brenna's arm. "I like you, Brenna, and I am grateful that you have brought me home, but you will find that we in Santa Fe have no sympathy for what the Texans have done. You will also learn that we still consider Texas to be a part of Mexico."

Brenna had no time to reply. The coach pulled up and stopped in front of the Governor's Palace. She and Francisca disembarked, and Morales led them inside the large reception room. Whereas the building had been austere and unfriendly earlier in the day, Brenna now found it warm and gracious. Hundreds of candles filled the room with light and spilled into the dining room. Brenna could see the long table was resplendent with fine china and expensive silverware. Servants, in new, crisp uniforms, silently moved in and out of the rooms, unobtrusively seeing to the guests' needs. Francisca took her friend in hand and made the

317

introductions. Given no time to ponder Francisca's earlier political statement, Brenna concentrated on matching the names and faces of Santa Fe's elite society.

About an hour had passed before she was aware of a sudden quiet descending on the room. She turned, as did those around her, to see a uniformed man enter the door. Governor Manuel Armijo. She knew without anyone's telling her. He cut an imposing figure. He was a large, florid man, running to paunch, and he affected a brilliant blue uniform with gold epaulets.

Immediatey his ebony eyes fastened on Brenna, and he made his way toward her. He was six feet tall if an inch, Brenna decided, and he had once been extremely handsome. Even now, she could feel a certain charisma exude from the man. His nose and eyes were strikingly arrogant, his lips full and sensuous.

"Doña Francisca," he said, addressing the young woman in Spanish, "I am so happy to see that you survived the wagon train massacre. My condolences on the death of your fiancé and his parents."

"Thank you, sir," Francisca curtsied. "I would like to introduce you to my friend, Señora Brenna Allen."

"Yes," Armijo said, his eyes already on Brenna, "I would love to meet her." After the introduction, he bowed low and spoke, still in Spanish. "Señora Allen, I am so happy to make your acquaintance. We are happy to have you in Santa Fe."

Brenna extended her hand, which he took in his and squeezed. He raised it to his mouth, and Brenna cringed when his moist lips crawled over her skin. Not a greeting, she thought, but a caress. She listened to Francisca's interpretation of the governor's words.

"I understand you desire a license to sell your goods in our fair city."

When the translation was made, Brenna withdrew

318

. her hand and nodded.

His eyes, black and shiny like ebony, searching like the black bird of Hades, fastened to hers. "Is this all you desire, señora?"

After Francisca's words died, Brenna stared at him for a full second. Could he possibly know about the letter? she wondered. For a moment panic seized her, but she quickly squelched such emotion. No one—not even Clarence Childers—knew she carried the letter. She straightened her shoulders a little more, if that was possible, and tilted her chin confidently.

"Tell him I don't know what he's talking about," she replied. "What else would I desire but to sell my goods?"

"Texans seem to have a great desire for spreading unrest and rebellion." Manuel Armijo laughed, the sound rather sinister. He bent his arm and extended it to Brenna. "Doña Francisca," he said, "I would like for the two of you to come to my office with me for a moment." He didn't wait for the young woman to interpret the words before he swept Brenna through the room into the quietness of his office.

The door had barely closed behind them when he said, "You Texans have already attempted to send military forces into Santa Fe." He left Brenna in the middle of the room as he moved to a tall trastero standing against the opposite wall.

Iberian in design, the cupboard bore gracious touches of carving and was decorated with bold mineral paints used by the Indians. He opened the doors and extracted three small glasses and a bottle of fine wine, which he set on his desk. He poured the drinks, handing one to each of the women. The one he kept.

"I would hate to think that Señora Allen and those dragoons who accompanied her into Santa Fe would attempt to lead my people into an uprising against our legitimate government." While Francisca translated his words, Armijo sipped his wine, his eyes never leaving Brenna's face.

"Repeat to your illustrious governor that I am here to trade," Brenna maintained.

And that was the truth. She didn't, however, tell Manuel Armijo *all* the truth . . . Why should she? He was the kind of tyrant she wished to deliver the Santa Feans from. But she herself was not a liberator. She was simply a go-between. She was here to deliver a letter to Peyton H. Alexander and to learn as much about the political climate of the area as she could. She would make her report to Childers when she returned to Houston, Texas. If Alexander was to reply to the letter, she would carry the answer back. The Imperialist platform would be based on what she learned while she was out here—an aggressive policy calling for the liberation of Santa Fe and Taos, the first step in publicly proclaiming Imperialism for Texas. Brenna Allen was much too intelligent and cautious to admit this to the man.

She smiled. "Surely your governor can't believe that I'm here for any other reason."

"I would hate to be in the señora's place if I were to think that!" Armijo said when he heard Francisca's interpretation. "Come, Señora"—he beckoned to Brenna—"I would like for you to see a souvenir which I have kept of your ill-fated Santa Fe Expedition."

Hardly had Francisca's words died out than Brenna was moving to the wall where Manuel Armijo stood.

He pointed. "See these, Señora Allen."

Brenna looked at the dried and crinkled semicircles of flesh, secured to the wall with a long nail.

"Five sets of Texans' ears," he announced proudly.

Brenna blanched and could hardly get the words out

of her mouth. Brenna was sick to her stomach. Such a macabre reminder of the Santa Fe Expedition filled her with revulsion for Manuel Armijo. Now she fully understood all the warnings she had received about Manuel Armijo. This man was not to be trusted. He was deadly.

"Doña Francisca, tell the señora that, much to my regret, the custom duties have recently been raised. A little," he said with a wave of his hand. "One thousand American dollars for each wagon."

Brenna was shocked by his declaration. She had expected five hundred dollars, but not this. She schooled her expression and was glad when she looked up to see Armijo's ebony eyes riveted to hers.

The governor gave an expressive shrug and smiled. "Of course, we can always talk. Perhaps the price is negotiable."

As his hooded eyes slid over her body and Francisca repeated his words in English, Brenna shivered. She knew where he planned to carry on the negotiations. She knew the full price he planned to extract from her.

"Francisca!" The masculine call came from the door to the governor's office. Three heads turned.

"Papa," Francisca cried, rushing across the room to throw herself in her father's arms. "Oh, Papa, I'm so glad to see you."

"Don Sebastian," Armijo said coolly, definitely displeased, "you couldn't have chosen a more inopportune time to interrupt. I was talking with Señora Allen about her permit to sell Texan goods in Santa Fe."

"I am most apologetic, Governor," he said, his voice belying his words, "but I could not wait to see my little one." Sebastian Sandoval, also a tall Mexican, turned kindly brown eyes on Brenna. "And I wanted to meet the woman who had befriended her in time of such grief." Francisca stepped out of her father's arms, and he moved to where Brenna stood. He swept his hat from a head of thick black hair, smiled, and bowed. "Señora Allen," he said in heavily accented English, "my wife and I wish to extend our gratitude to you for escorting our daughter home."

"I enjoyed her company," Brenna replied. "I feel as if I've known Francisca all my life."

"From the letter which we received from our daughter while she was at Bent's Fort, we feel as if we know you," he said. "Francisca mentioned Señor Roper and his wife, but mostly she talked about you, Señor MacDougald, and Señor Hollis." He saw the telltale color that stained his daughter's cheeks. "Come." He caught Brenna's hand and led her to the door. He laughed as he slid a fatherly arm around each woman's shoulder. "Let us go greet Mama. She can hardly wait to see her little girl."

Armijo was more than displeased. He was angry. His dinner invitation had not been issued so the Sandovals could be reunited. He was interested in the beautiful Texan. His sources had informed him of her coming, long before she arrived. Today he had seen her as she drove her wagons into town, and the thought of taking her to bed had warmed his loins. Her vendor's permit would come at a high price!

But neither would Armijo cross Sebastian Sandoval. The *hacendado* commanded a loyal following in the surrounding area. He owned the largest hacienda and maintained the largest army of *vaqueros* on the entire frontier. But, Manuel smiled to himself, the pleasure spilling onto his full lips, soon that would end. Don Sebastian Sandoval would be nothing but a memory in Santa Fe. Francisca would marry Roberto Onega, and Joaquin would marry Felecita Chavez, Armijo's niece. And at Joaquin's death—the last Sandoval would die an early death, Armijo prophesied—the vast holdings of the Sandovals would then come under the personal jurisdiction of Manuel Armijo, who was Felecita's guardian. Patience, Manuel admonished himself. While patience was not at the top of the list of his virtues, Manuel admitted, it was on the list nevertheless.

Glad to escape the vile man who ruled over the Mexican frontier, Brenna surrendered to the gentle warmth of the Sandoval family. She watched as mother and daughter greeted each other, both crying, laughing, and talking at once. Finally, however, Doña Anna, a small, rotund woman with a warm smile and glowing eyes, turned to Brenna and immediately took her to heart.

"Where is Joaquin?" Francisca asked. "I did so want to introduce him to Brenna."

Doña Anna hid a knowing smile behind her ornate fan. "He will be coming later, *querida*. He had work to do."

"You mean"—Francisca lowered her voice to a whisper—"he didn't want to have dinner with The Tarantula."

Doña Anna whisked the fan shut and tapped her daughter's hand. "Shhh," she warned. "We do not want any more trouble with the man than we already have, child."

After dinner, a meal with many varied courses, the guests were led into the large ballroom. A small orchestra sat in one corner, and music filtered through the room. Roberto soon claimed Francisca as his partner, and the two of them mixed with the crowd to perform a slow, decorous dance with candles.

Armijo stood across the room, smoked his cigarette, drank his whiskey, and stared at Brenna. To avoid his gaze, she concentrated on the dancers, but she felt as if the governor were stripping her garments off her piece by piece.

Aware of Armijo's intentions toward Brenna and correctly reading the vulgar proposal in the stare, Don Sebastian suggested they leave. "We would like to show you more of Santa Fe," he said. Then he led her to the tall man who still stood across the room. To Manuel Armijo, Don Sebastian said, "I'm sure you'll understand our leaving early."

The governor played the game with Sebastian, but he was angry. He didn't like to be thwarted in any way by anyone. And Sebastian Sandoval had kept him from obtaining many of his goals. Armijo's longtime hatred of Sebastian Sandoval was growing to such proportions, Armijo could hardly endure the festering emotion any longer.

"Of course," Armijo said with deceptive pleasantness, "I can understand your wanting to show the señora our beautiful city," but the black eyes glittered dangerously, ominously. He turned to Brenna. "Tomorrow, Señora Brenna"—he took liberty in using her first name without permission—"I shall call on you at the La Fonda, and we will further discuss the granting of a license."

"I'm so sorry," Don Sebastian interjected smoothly, without bothering to translate Armijo's words, "but Señora Allen is going to be our guest while she's in Santa Fe. You may call on her at our townhouse." He smiled. "We'll be more than happy to have you for supper tomorrow evening. Also, we'll be entertaining Señor Samuel Roper and his lovely wife, Señora Gertrude. If all goes well, Señor Roper will be joining my staff as the secretary in charge of all my finances. I will no longer need Roberto's services. Señor Roper is fluent in many foreign languages."

Armijo didn't bother to conceal his hatred. He bowed low. "Until tomorrow, Don Sebastian."

Glad to leave the governor's presence, Brenna welcomed the warmth of the scarf which she wrapped around her head and shoulders as she walked into the evening chill. She stood for a moment, looking about the plaza—so different from earlier in the day. By night the dusty square flickered with the red light of bonfires. In front of the Palace and all around the plaza, torches flared smokily on long poles, and through the deep, narrow window embrasures leaked the glow of rare, expensive candles. As they walked down the arcade, Brenna saw gambling tables around the square, surrounded by men and women.

"We Mexicans enjoy gambling," Don Sebastian murmured. "You will find the men and women of rank making their wagers alongside the commoners and the criminals."

As they walked farther, Brenna observed that those who were not gambling were dancing to the lively music of fiddles, guitars, and violins.

Then they arrived at the gates of a fortlike house. Don Sebastian knocked, and the door was soon opened. The Sandovals and Brenna entered into the crowded but elegant monte room. They threaded their way to a table in the corner. The dealer, an older woman, looked up at Don Sebastian and smiled. With a deft flick of her wrist, she motioned someone to take her place and she slid from behind the table. She led the Sandovals into another room, large and comfortably furnished. The walls of the building were so thick, the minute the door clicked into place, all noise was blocked out of the room.

"Hello, Anna and Sebastian," the woman said, reaching up to tuck a curl of her wig back in place. "What are yo doing in Santa Fe tonight?"

Sebastian smiled and spoke in Spanish. "I have brought a friend for you to meet."

"Ah," the woman murmured, her aged but beautiful eyes moving from the top of Brenna's head to the bottom of her feet. "The woman wagon master from Texas."

"The same," Sebastian said, watching his old friend closely.

"Please sit down." Doña Tula waved to an adobe bench covered with bright blankets that circled the wall. As Doña Anna, Francisca, and Brenna sat down, Doña Tula walked to a table that sat against the wall. She opened a small box and rolled herself a cigarette, which she situated in a golden pincer and lit with a flint-struck twist of cotton carried in a little metal tube. She inhaled the smoke deeply, held it in her lungs for a moment, then exhaled. She poured whiskey into two of the glasses. One she quaffed in a swallow; the other she gave to Sebastian. "Has she met Manuel yet?"

"Tonight."

Doña Tula laughed. "The price of her vendor's permit will come high."

"Can you help us?"

Unable to understand the conversation between the man and woman and disinclined to ask either Doña Anna or Francisca, Brenna sat on the couch, looking about the richly furnished room.

"I am a prominent figure in Santa Fe's social life," Doña Tula admitted without conceit, refilling her glass, "and I have been Manuel's mistress, but I do not know if I have any influence over him anymore. He was always determined to get what he wanted and didn't care how he had to get it, but as he gets older he becomes worse; no longer is he careful in his dealings." Down went the whiskey in one swallow. She turned and smiled at Sebastian. "I will do what I can, but it will be in the señora's best interest if she does not stay in town by herself."

"She will be staying with us," Sebastian said.

Doña Tula smiled, crossed the room, and laid her hand on Sebastian's arm. "I will help you all I can, my friend. Now introduce me to the young woman."

After the introductions were made and they had talked awhile, Doña Tula led the Sandovals and Brenna back into the gaming room. With a smile and a wave, she took her place at the round table in the corner. Brenna watched as the people thronged to her to make their wagers. She couldn't believe the ease with which the cards fell from Doña Tula's hands.

Afterward the Sandovals and Brenna exited the gaming room and returned to the plaza, walking toward their residence. "We will have your luggage moved to the townhouse tonight," Doña Anna told Brenna. "You will stay there with us. We do not think you will be safe by yourself at the La Fonda." Only now did Francisca's mother repeat Don Sebastian's conversation with Doña Tula. "She will see that you get the permit you need."

"Thank you," Brenna murmured.

When they reached the house, candlelight filtered through the opened windows, and torches gleamed brightly along the front of the portico. Don Sebastian flung open the door and gave a call. A young male servant came running. Don Sebastian dispatched him to La Fonda with instructions to return with Francisca's and Brenna's luggage. On saying good night to the women, he went to his study.

"Show Brenna to her room," Doña Anna instructed. "I must speak to the servants now. I have to prepare the menu for tomorrow."

Francisca led Brenna to a large bedroom at the front of the house. "Tonight you will sleep with me. Tomorrow we will have your room ready. That way you can have your privacy."

The servants had already opened the shutters, and a cool breeze wafted through the opened window, gently riffling the crimson worsted curtains.

"I will be to bed later," Francisca said. "I would like to visit with Mama and Papa for a while."

Without taking the scarf from her head, Brenna walked out of the room and stood in the small walled garden while she waited for her trunks. Finally she heard the approaching horses. Supposing it to be her luggage, she returned to the house. Minutes later the door opened, and a man raced into the room and swept Brenna into his arms.

"Hello, little sister," he said affectionately in Spanish, swinging Brenna through the air. "It's about time you came home to your family."

Brenna instinctively lifted her arms and clasped her hands around his neck. Her eyes were wide and questioning. When she tilted her head back, the scarf fell.

"*Madre de Dios!*" the man murmured, his ebony eyes taking in every detail of the lovely face. His dancing stopped, but he did not put Brenna down.

"I think you've made a mistake," Brenna said, breaking the silence.

Beautiful ebony eyes—the same color as the riotous curls on his head—glittered in a face that was totally handsome. A roguish smile twitched firm lips. "I would like to think not," he said in perfect English.

Chapter Nineteen

"Joaquin!" Francisca bounded into the room. "You are here!"

"No!" Joaquin laughed as he reluctantly set Brenna on her feet and turned to the doorway to greet his sister. He opened his arms and enfolded her in a huge bear hug.

"I didn't think you would ever get here," Francisca said. "I was so afraid you wouldn't make it. I know how you feel about having to meet the governor, but I did so want you to meet Brenna." Without giving Joaquin time to get a word into the conversation, Francisca chattered on.

Although Brenna couldn't understand what they were saying, she didn't feel excluded. Rather she felt herself wrapped in the magnitude and warmth of their love as she watched them together. She also took the time to study the man she had heard so much about. His black jacket, ornately embroidered with braid and fancy barrel buttons, called attention to massive chest and shoulders. His trousers were form-fitting across the buttocks, but the legs flared out from hip to ankle. The outseam was decorated with filigree buttons and expensive braid and lace. A long red sash was wound around his waist, the long ties contrasting against the black of his trousers. Brenna had to admit that Don

Joaquin Sandoval cut a dashing figure and was altogether male.

Joaquin pulled back and looked into his sister's lovely features. "For you, my little sister," he said, "I would turn the world upside down. But surely you knew I was getting all the work done. So we could have a fiesta for your lovely friend." Joaquin chided Francisca with a gentle smile. "And speaking of your friend, are you going to introduce me?"

"Oh," Francisca gasped in English, her hand covering her mouth. She spun around to Brenna. "I have been so rude. Please forgive me, Brenna."

Brenna laughed. "There is nothing to forgive."

Francisca ran across the room and slipped her arm around Brenna. She led her to where Joaquin now stood, his arms folded across his chest. "Brenna Allen, I want you to meet my only brother and one of my favorite people in the entire world," she said, her eyes darkening with the intensity of her love. "Joaquin Roman Sandoval."

Joaquin flourished a low bow. When he raised up, he reached for Brenna's hand. "Señora Brenna Allen, I am honored to make your acquaintance." He brought her hand to his lips and kissed her—the barest, the fleetest of touches. "Through Francisca's letter I feel as if I already know you."

A beautiful smile captured Brenna's lips as she withdrew her hand. She could understand how this man had charmed many young maidens. If she weren't already in love with Logan MacDougald, she could have so easily swooned at his feet.

"I am also honored to meet you, Señor Sandoval. I, too, have heard much about you."

"Joaquin Roman Sandoval!" Doña Anna's scandalized cry echoed through the house. "What are you doing in Señora Allen's bedroom?" The diminutive

330

woman stood in the door, her hands planted firmly on her hips, her face furrowed into a scowl.

Joaquin slowly pulled his gaze from the captivating beauty of Brenna's eyes. So pretty, he thought. So vivid. The same color as her dress. They sparkled with life. He turned to see his mother hovering in the doorway. He held his arms out.

"Mamacita, I would not be here if I had known it was Señora Allen's bedroom. Until tonight this has been Francisca's bedroom." As he had done with his sister only moments before, he caught his mother in a bear hug and danced around the room with her. He charmed her scowl into infectious laughter.

"Put me down!" Her cheeks heightened with color, Doña Anna playfully fought her way out of Joaquin's clutches. Still speaking in English so that Brenna would not feel excluded, she said, "You're a naughty boy, Joaquin, and if I did not love you so much, I would punish you."

Joaquin chuckled at the absurdity of his mother's words. "You would punish me," he teased, "when I have been working so diligently to plan a wonderful fiesta for Señora Allen," he said. "Will we be returning to the hacienda on the morrow?"

A shadow crossed Doña Anna's face as she shook her head. "The day after." When Joaquin lifted arrogant brows, she explained. "The governor is coming here for lunch tomorrow, at which time he will visit with Señora Allen. He hasn't agreed to give her a vendor's permit yet."

Joaquin's face set in uncompromising lines; his eyes hardened until they looked like black marble. "That lecherous old man. I hate him, Mamacita, and someday I will kill him with my own bare hands."

Doña Anna reached out and laid a hand on her son's upper arm. "He is a dangerous man, mi hijo. You must be careful. We do not want to do anything that will turn his anger and vindictiveness against us. Your papa is going to make a full report to the government when we journey to Mexico City this fall. Please be patient until then."

"Texas Rangers may carry the blame for killing Juno Andesoto," Joaquin said tightly, "but Manual Armijo is responsible for my best friend's death. I will repay Armijo in kind one day. I will kill The Tarantula myself." As he uttered the promise, he clenched his hands into fists.

Francisca stepped closer to Joaquin and laid her hand on his shoulder. "I grieve the death of our friends," she said quietly, her eyes warm with compassion and understanding, "but we cannot dwell on the past, my brother. We must live today and plan for tomorrow."

The hard lines of Joaquin's face suddenly eased and he smiled down at Francisca. "Sí, little one, that is true." He looked at his mother. "I shall remain in town with you, and I shall dine with our illustrious governor tomorrow. And I promise, Mama, that I shall be on my best behavior." He looked beyond Francisca to Brenna and said, "And then we shall go to the hacienda and celebrate."

"And now," Doña Anna said, "we all go to bed." When she saw the way her son was looking at Brenna, she said quietly in Spanish, "In our own beds in our own rooms, my son." Doña Anna walked out of the room but waited in the hall for Joaquin.

"*Buenas noches,* Mama. *Buenas noches,* Joaquin," Francisca called over her shoulder as she walked to the trastero to get her nightgown.

As the good nights were called back and forth, Joaquin kept his gaze on Brenna. She had the most fascinating eyes he had ever seen.

"I will see you in the morning, señora?"

"Until tomorrow," Brenna said in Spanish.

A quick smile fluttered Joaquin's lips. "Until tomorrow." Still he made no effort to leave.

Brenna walked across the room and caught the door. As she swung it to, she said softly, "It is time you were leaving, and high time I was in bed, Señor Sandoval. Buenas noches."

Joaquin raised a hand and planted a palm on the door to stop the gentle movement. "Please call me Joaquin."

"Don Joaquin."

"No"—he gave a slight shake of his head, and curls tumbled over his forehead—"just Joaquin . . . and may I call you Brenna?" When she nodded, Joaquin said, "Buenas noches, Brenna."

"Buenas noches."

Manuel Armijo wiped the smile from his face as he said good night to his last guest. He slammed the door, slid the bolt in place, and twisted the key in the lock. Then he walked through the silent house to a small, private office at the rear of the building. He sat down at his desk and shuffled through a stack of papers. Finally he located Roberto Onega's report on Garvey Mercantile and Freight Hauling. Señora Allen had left Austin, Texas, with twelve wagons. Only five had arrived in Santa Fe.

The governor was pleased to see that the señora had brought many luxuries to Santa Fe: cast-iron stoves, rolls of bright cloth, tools, candles, hunting knives, ink, tobacco, pots and pans. Plenty of items on the banned list, which he could either confiscate in the name of the government or impose ridiculously high taxes on.

The governor leaned back in the chair and smiled—

333

really smiled this time; the light from the candelabra played across his features. This Texan promised to be a delightful diversion. He certainly hoped she didn't have too much currency with which to bargain.

Above the noise of the plaza Armijo heard several short raps at the door, and he looked up in surprise. Thinking perhaps he was mistaken, he sat longer. He strained to hear. He was expecting no one, especially at this hour of the night. He heard the knocks again; they were louder. The chair grated against the floor as he stood and pushed it back. Wondering who would be calling so late, he slowly walked across the room, opened the small shutter in the middle of the door, and peered through the barred window. When he saw the man, Armijo gasped and drew back in shock.

"Open up, Manuel." Amusement underlay the hoarse command that was issued in Spanish, albeit the accent was more Mexican than Castilian.

Metal grated against metal as Armijo slid the bar and unlocked the door. A tall man swept into the room, an immense brown serape billowing around his body so that nothing was exposed except his face and feet—feet covered in black boots that shined even in the dim glow of the candlelight; spurs that jingled as he moved across the room to the trastero. His face was hidden in the shadows of a large flat-crowned hat.

"What are you doing here?" the governor demanded, his voice quavering with indignation.

The visitor ignored the question. Totally familiar with the room and its furnishings, he made himself at home. He reached for a bottle of whiskey and a glass. Walking to a table, he set both down. He took his hat off and hung it on a nearby clothes rack. Smoothly he swept the serape over his head, folded it, and laid it across the back of the chair.

"What are you doing here?" Armijo repeated his

334

question. He watched as the man poured whiskey into the glass; he watched him take a sip.

"Mm," the visitor murmured, holding the glass up so that the light filtered through the amber liquid, "I'm envious of your liquor cabinet, Manny. When so many have so little, you always have so much of the very best."

"Don't call me Manny," Armijo shouted, his hands balling into fists. "No one, absolutely no one, calls me Manny!"

"But then"—the man moved to Manuel's desk, where he lifted the lid on a small wooden tobacco box—"no one knows you quite as intimately as I do, my friend. And I have always called you Manny. I don't see why I should stop now."

Manuel's face twisted in contempt. "You and I are not friends, Oswald Lattimer."

Lattimer chuckled quietly. He picked up a cigarette paper from a nearby container and filled it with fresh, aromatic tobacco. Deftly he caught the small square with both hands, his forefingers and thumbs forcing the tobacco into a neat, tight cylinder. He licked the flap to seal it, then inserted the cigarette in the corner of his mouth. He picked up a tin candle holder, tilted the flame toward his face, and inhaled deeply, the end of the cigarette glowing. Before he set the candle down, he turned, and light flickered across his face—a hard, sinister face, made harder and more sinister by the long, puffy scar that jagged down his face and throat.

"You can't deny that we are business partners." Lattimer held his cigarette in one hand and reached for his whiskey with the other. "And it is about business that I have come tonight, Manny. Only business would bring me from my haven in the canyon to your barbaric city."

"What if someone saw you?" Manuel ranted. "What

335

if they can identify you?"

Lattimer's loud, coarse laughter sent shivers over Manuel Armijo.

"Traveling at night and wearing my serape and hat," he said, "I blend into the crowd, and you, Manuel Armijo, should know that the streets of Santa Fe are still teeming with people, and everyone is too involved with their gambling and sporting to notice me."

"I still don't like it," Armijo hissed.

"The quicker you sit down," Lattimer ordered, "the quicker we can talk." His lips smiled, but no emotion touched the dull, dark brown eyes—eyes that were muddy brown. "The quicker you'll find out what I'm doing here." He pitched the whiskey into his mouth, savored it for the merest moment, then swallowed.

Armijo moved to his desk and sat down. With shaking hands he rolled himself a cigarette, spilling more tobacco than he put in the small square of paper. He licked the edge of the thin sheet and sealed the cylinder. Putting it in his mouth, he leaned toward the nearest candle.

"Getting rid of Felipe Andesoto came at a price higher than that which we agreed upon, my old friend."

Armijo jerked air into his lungs; his chest heaved; his hand trembled even more. He didn't mind committing the crimes, but he didn't like being reminded of them. He didn't like discussing them as the ordinary order of the day in his office, where there were too many eyes and ears—all of which were ready to report to the government in Mexico City.

Yet Armijo was adept at playing deceitful games. He may be afraid, but he had learned not to show it. "We agreed upon the price," he returned, "and I have kept my part of the bargain."

"Yes," Lattimer murmured, "you did provide me with some beautiful young women. They brought a nice price." He was so proud of himself, he almost purred with satisfaction. He crossed one leg over the other. "You see, Manny, I didn't keep them for my bordello in Mexico City. I sold them. The young señoritas are on their way to Europe now."

Manuel Armijo wasn't squeamish, but Oswald Lattimer frightened him. The man was totally without a conscience; he was evil. Armijo was forced to admit he had made a mistake in dealing with the man; he had underestimated Lattimer. Now the man was blackmailing him.

"I came here tonight, Manny, to tell you the price for getting rid of the Sandovals has gone up."

Armijo jerked his head up and glared at the man who sat across from him. "No!"

"I think so," Lattimer answered.

"What do you want more of, Lattimer?" Armijo asked, perspiration popping out on his face. "More money or more women for your bordellos?" Before Lattimer answered, the Mexican was on his feet. Bracing his weight on his hands, he leaned across his desk. "Well, I can't give you any more women. I'll have the authorities in Mexico City on my head."

"And if the Sandovals make it to Mexico City this fall," Lattimer reminded Manuel, "they will make a full report of their suspicions of your activities since you've been governor of Santa Fe." He spread his hands expressively. "The way I see it, Manny old boy, you really don't have a choice."

"What do you want?" Manuel exhaled the words.

"I want Francisca Sandoval."

"Francisca Sandoval! What do you want her for?"

"What do you think I want her for?" Lattimer mocked. "I want her for myself. I want to take her to bed and to enjoy every inch of her luscious virginal body. She's a beautiful woman." He leaned his head

337

against the back of the chair and closed his eyes. "Too beautiful and too much of a woman for Juno Andesoto. Thank God we got rid of him. Had he and the girl been married, the scene would be a lot messier than it is."

"But my nephew—" the governor began.

"I don't care this much"—Lattimer snapped his fingers—"about you, your nephew, or the land. You can have that without her marrying your nephew. I'm sure you can figure a way to steal it. You have everything else you've wanted." Oswald laughed. "Started with sheep stealing, didn't you?" As quickly as he laughed, he sobered. His eyes narrowed and he leaned forward. "But I want Francisca Sandoval, and I intend to get her one way or the other."

"What if I say no?"

"The way I see it, Governor Manuel Armijo, you are in absolutely no position to say no. To phrase it another way, you have no say in the matter." Lattimer laughed. "I'm sure you wouldn't want to start dealing directly with the Comanches, would you?"

Armijo picked up the crystal decanter, but his hand was shaking so badly he poured whiskey all over his desk as he filled his glass to the brim. He drank it so quickly his eyes watered and his throat burned. He coughed. He wasn't comfortable with Oswald Lattimer, and he was frightened by the man's threats. He certainly didn't want a Comanche war at this time.

"Why . . . why have you decided that you want Francisca for yourself?"

"I didn't know until I saw her the other day what a lovely woman she had grown into. Somehow in my mind's eye I always saw her as Joaquin's little sister. I thought of her as a little girl."

"What about the Andesoto girl?"

Oswald shrugged. "Weak woman with absolutely no

338

constitution. After only a few of my men had taken her, she died. I didn't even get her to Mexico."

"You were with your men when they attacked Andesoto's wagon train?"

Lattimer hesitated only a second before he admitted, "Yes, I was riding with them."

"The girl reported they were set upon by a group of Texas Rangers."

"That's the way we planned it, Manny." Again Lattimer's laughter—controlled and sinister—filled the room. "Little did Sam Houston know when he authorized these freebooting ranging units that he was signing a death warrant for his lovely little nation!"

"Why didn't you take Francisca then?"

A scowl crossed Lattimer's visage. "I would have," he said, "but that damned Warfield and his soldiers interfered." Lattimer trained those cloudy eyes on Armijo. "I won't lose her a second time."

"Do you have a plan?"

Lattimer shook his head. "No, Manny, I'm leaving this task up to you. My mind is too occupied with the demise of the Sandovals." He pushed to his feet, walked to the window, the jingle of his spurs loud, and flung open the shutters. As he stood there, looking at the moon-dappled garden, the evening breeze ruffled his white hair. "I understand a wagon train arrived here today."

Armijo took great pleasure in saying, "Yes, it did. You can imagine my surprise. The señora and her men managed to fight off a large Comanche attack—an attack that was led by white men."

Lattimer evinced no emotion whatsoever. "You will send word when she prepares to return to Texas?"

After a lengthy pause, Manuel asked, "What is your greatest interest? The trade goods or the señora?"

Lattimer turned his back to the window and stared

through the smoke-hazed room at the paunchy governor, who stood in front of his desk. "Ever since I learned of Brenna Allen's expedition, I have been interested in both her and the goods." Out of habit born through the years, Lattimer reached up and lightly stroked his fingers down the scar.

"Your Comanches were unable to stop her?" Again pleasure washed through Manuel as he watched Lattimer drop his hand and clench it into a fist.

"The journey is not over yet, Manny. I promise you neither the señora nor her trade goods will ever reach Texas." As quickly he dismissed the subject. "But that is not my concern this visit. I have told you what I wish. See that I get Francisca Sandoval. By the way, are you still watching Alexander?"

"I am," Armijo answered, "and I've searched his premises. If he has the guns, he has hidden them elsewhere. My men report that he never leaves town."

"I must have those guns; otherwise, I'm going to lose control of the Indians." Lattimer breathed deeply and reached into the inner pocket of his shirt. He pulled out a tattered sheet of paper and unfolded it as he walked to Armijo's desk. "Be watching for these men. They will probably show up here sooner or later." He unfolded the paper and laid it down. Armijo stood on the other side of the desk, looking down at the newspaper clipping—a sketched drawing of two men. "Who are they?"

"Logan MacDougald and Andrew Thunder," Lattimer read. "A Cherokee and a white man. Wanted in the Republic of Texas for horse thieving. They've been snooping around and asking a lot of questions about the Comancheros. I suspect they're trying to undermine my trade agreement with the Comanches."

The idea pleased Armijo, but he was prudent enough to keep his counsel. "Perhaps they wish to join your operation?" he suggested.

"Or ruin it," Lattimer said.

"What do you wish me to do if they should come to Santa Fe?"

"Send word to me promptly. I want to see and talk with these men." Lattimer raised his head and stared at Armijo; then he picked up the newspaper clipping, refolded it, and inserted it in his pocket. "Also keep an eye on anyone Alexander has any dealings with." He walked across the room to pick up his serape and hat. "Everyone, Manny." He flashed a quick, cold smile. "Now, Manny, I must be on my way."

A troubled man sat in the governor's office through the long, dark hours of the night. The candles had burned until they were little more than globes of distorted wax at the bottom of the candle holders. The flickering wick afforded little light. But the man was not concerned with such mundane things as re-dressing the candelabra. He had other problems to address. Big problems.

He was still sitting behind his desk when the first rays of dawn eased through the window Lattimer had opened during his visit. Manuel watched as the light steadily crawled through the embrasure, weak at first but soon overcoming all the black shadows until morning flooded the room.

Chapter Twenty

Brenna roused when the sun touched her face through the netting around the bed, but she only stretched. She made no effort to get up and dress with Francisca.

"Would you like to go riding this morning?" Francisca asked.

"I've ridden enough these past two months to last me for a while," Brenna murmured, snuggling her head in the soft pillow. "Right now I want to sleep."

"Joaquin is going with me."

"The two of you need some time together," Brenna said. "I think I'll just stay here and laze around." She watched as Francisca donned her riding habit. "You really are dressing up just to go riding with your brother."

Francisca's cheeks colored beautifully. "I have asked Joaquin to go with me to La Fonda so he can meet Señor Hollis." When Brenna laughed, Francisca said, "I have told Joaquin what a wonderful *vaquero* Señor Hollis is. The three of us are going for a ride."

Long after Francisca had gone, Brenna lay on the bed, but she didn't sleep. She was consumed with thoughts of Logan. She remembered the days when the two of them had ridden together across the wild, open country. She remembered the day they had fought the

Indians together; the day they had hunted buffalo; the day each had admitted the importance of his goal and they had parted.

Although her head repeatedly told her heart that it was for the better that she would never see Logan again, she couldn't forget him. She heard his laughter; she saw his gray eyes—warm when he was compassionate, steely when he was angry, stormy when he was in the throes of passion. She yearned to have him by her side throughout the day and the night.

But as she had told him the last time she saw him, she didn't want to share him with the ghosts of his past; nor did she want to be destroyed by the fire of revenge that burned deep in his soul. Each time he left her he would take a piece of her heart until she had none left to give. . . . She feared these restless flames would destroy both of them.

Somewhere in the milieu of such thoughts, Brenna went to sleep, not to awaken until she heard the door quietly open and close. Francisca, she thought as she inhaled deeply and stretched.

"Are you back already?" she mumbled as she rolled over and peeped through barely opened eyes. A tall man, his body and features hidden in a billowing serape and big hat, stood at the side of her bed, gazing down at her through the gauzy netting. "Joaquin, what are you doing here in broad-open daylight? Last night I told you—"

Brenna's words died when she saw a hand whip out of the folds of the serape to catch the gauze, pull it, and fasten it to the bedpost. The movements were angry.

She was frightened. "Joaquin, is that you?" She pushed up on the bed, and her heart seemed to beat in her throat as she watched the man sit down, the mattress sagging with his weight.

"Who are you?" she asked. As if it afforded

protection, she clutched the sheet beneath her chin. "What are you doing here in my room?"

The man lifted his hand and swept the hat from his head and sailed it across the room to land on the floor.

"Logan!" Brenna cried, disbelief escalating into joy. "I didn't expect to see you again. I told you not to—"

Smug was his smile when he interrupted her to say, "I remember what you said the last time I saw you, but I knew you didn't mean it. You were angry and weren't speaking from your heart." He reached out to touch the tip of her nose. "And I was right to come. I see the welcome in your eyes."

Using her elbows, Brenna crawled up the bed. "Yes," she admitted, "I'm glad to see you, but I'm also disappointed that you could be so selfish."

Logan's eyes narrowed and he looked at her a long time before he said, "I had to see you."

Brenna heard the desperation, the pleading in his voice, and it touched her deeply . . . as only Logan could. His words were a weight Brenna's heart could hardly bear. She understood how he felt; she understood his compulsion to be near her. She loved him and could hardly stand to be parted. Even now, she wanted to run to him, throw herself into his arms and tell him it was all right. But she must stand her ground. If she didn't protect herself, no one would, and protect herself she must!

"Logan, I meant what I said," she stated quietly. "I only have so much heart, and each time you leave me you take a part of it with you. You're hurting me so much I can hardly stand it."

Brenna thought Shawn had hurt her, but it was nothing compared to the anguish she was going through now—yet another heartrending departure. Albeit, this time she was issuing the command for Logan to leave.

After a long period of silence in which Logan walked around the room and Brenna stared at him, he asked, "Who is Joaquin, and what about last night?"

Quietly Brenna answered. "Joaquin is Francisca's older brother, and since I'm staying in her bedroom, he mistook me for her."

Logan's face was solemn. "What happened?"

"I told him buenas noches, señor."

Logan was across the room in an instant, both her shoulders grasped tightly in his fingers. His countenance was dark, his eyes stormy. The deeper, darker side of Logan strangely exhilarated and excited Brenna.

"You'd better not—" he began.

Brenna leaned forward, the sheet slipping down a little to expose the upper part of her breasts, and placed her finger over Logan's lips to stop the spill of words.

"I haven't, but it doesn't mean that I won't," she said when the frown deepened on Logan's brow. "Please leave," she whispered, the cry from the deepest part of her soul. "Please leave now, Logan."

He removed his hands from her shoulders and stared at her for endless seconds before he finally said, "I can't." He reached out and brushed the errant curls from Brenna's face. Then he leaned down to press his mouth gently over hers, their breath becoming one, their kiss soft, sweet. His hand captured one of her breasts. As he kneaded the nipple through the material of Brenna's nightgown, she emitted a low moan and pressed herself closer to him.

"Brenna," Logan whispered, "please don't send me away."

"You must go," Brenna insisted, although her heart contradicted her words.

"We'll go somewhere else," Logan said. "Just the two of us."

"I can't leave," Brenna told him. "I'm a guest, and—"

"Yes, you can." Logan stood, his hands catching hers as he pulled her out of bed. "If your hostess is the older woman whose room is on the other side of the house, she's not up." His hands clasped her waist, and he pulled her into the warm circle of his embrace. "So just put on one of Francisca's riding habits, so you'll look like a respectable matron of this fair city—"

"In Francisca's riding habit, I wouldn't look like a respectable anything," Brenna said. "I'd attract more attention. Remember, she's much shorter and tinier than I am."

"I never really noticed." His hands thoroughly enjoyed their exploration of Brenna's body. "I've had another woman on my mind too much."

Talking stopped as he captured her mouth in another long, leisurely kiss. Desire pushed reason aside and Brenna felt her resolve dissolving as she gladly welcomed the fiery passion of Logan's touch.

"In order to find you," Logan confessed, "I peeped into several bedrooms before I found the right one. The woman whom I presume to be your hostess, God bless her soul, snores and wears a sleeping mask."

He caught the material of Brenna's gown and pulled it up, his hands brushing against warm, silken flesh. Brenna was lost in his caresses. She readily forgot that soon he would be riding out of her life again, thinking only of the moment.

Logan's mouth captured Brenna's again; his lips guided hers open, and she moaned as she accepted, as she welcomed the ardent yet gentle thrust of his tongue that deepened their kiss. At the same time, she accepted and welcomed the gentle thrust of his knee between her thighs. She felt a delicious tremor wind through her to settle in the center of her femininity. He was

346

wonderfully warm, and Brenna inhaled deeply his distinctively male scent interlaced with the faintest hint of buckskin and soap. Then his lips moved across her cheek to her temple.

"Brenna," Logan breathed, his voice husky, "we've got to get out of here." His hands moved down her back to cup her buttocks and pull her against his hardness.

"I can't," she said, struggling against the magic of his passion. "I must meet with the governor today at lunch to discuss my vendor's permit."

Logan tensed, then pulled away. Brenna felt the materal of her nightgown slowly slide down her body. She saw the immediate change in his expression. His eyes, the color of cold, tempered metal, glittered.

"So the caravan comes before me?"

The words were so soft Brenna could hardly hear them, but their impact was like a slap across her cheek, and more hurtful.

"How conveniently you forget all the things you have allowed to come before me," she returned with cold sweetness as she watched Logan walk across the room to stand in front of the opened window. "For instance, your thirst for revenge."

Without answering, Logan pulled the curtain aside and looked in the garden.

"The caravan isn't my first thought, but it is my responsibility. I've come too far to fail now," Brenna acknowledged without apology. She stared at him, his brown hair shining like polished gold in the morning sunlight, and willed him to say something, but he didn't. Finally she asked, "Have you made contact with the Comancheros yet?"

"I can't until I prove myself," he answered. "That's what I came to see you about."

So now we get to the real reason for the visit!

Brenna hurt so deeply she felt as if someone had run

a dagger into her heart and was twisting the blade. He accused her of always placing her expedition first but was unable to see that he was guilty of the same crime. Always his quest was of foremost importance. She was something to be used. She had been right that night at Bent's Fort to tell Logan she didn't want to see him again. How weak she had just proven herself to be, but no more. When he left this time, it was for good!

Logan turned. "I need one of your freight haulers with all the contents intact."

Brenna stared at him across the room, and inwardly she cried, but she had no tears left. Her eyes were wide and dry; they burned as if they were full of grit. Logan had never loved her for herself; always there was an ulterior motive behind everything he did. She felt exactly like she had when Shawn finished having sex with her: naked and used. With dignity she turned her back on Logan and walked to the chair, where she picked up her dressing gown.

"Don't ever point an accusing finger at me again, Logan MacDougald," she said, her voice so quiet Logan had to strain to hear her. "I'm a novice when it comes to using people. You're an expert. You've played with me ever since you first met me. What were you going to do today? Love me into giving you one of my wagons, and it full of goods?"

"No," he answered. "I wanted to make love simply because I wanted to make love to you. Because I—"

"Spare me," Brenna snapped as she turned to glower at him.

"All right," Logan replied calmly. Her words goaded him to lie outright, to give her the answer she thought she wanted to hear. "I wanted to make love to you because you're an available woman." He watched Brenna closely but saw no change in her demeanor. "Now that's out of the way," he said curtly, "will you sell me one of your wagons?"

Brenna slipped the buttons through the loops, starting at the neck of her gown and going down. "No. Armijo knows I brought five in with me, and—"

"You won't be losing any money," Logan told her. "I'll give you what they're worth."

"You can't possibly have enough money to pay me what I think the wagon's worth," Brenna snapped.

"Perhaps I don't, but I've got enough to pay you what they're really worth, what you can get for them out here in Santa Fe." Logan dug into his pocket, pulled out a roll of bills, and waved them through the air. "It's good," he said. "United States currency."

"I don't want it."

Logan moved to the chair, picked up his serape, and dropped it over his head. He scooped up his hat and put it on. The money he threw on the table as he walked by it to the door. "I'm leaving this as prepayment for the wagon that I'm going to take." He opened the door.

Brenna ran to the table, picked up the bills, and threw the currency at him. Logan watched the bills flutter through the air to land on the floor, scattered between him and Brenna. He said, "I've given you more than what the goods are worth. Much more than you'll get for them even here or in Mexico."

"You haven't given me one damn thing but a heartache, and I can't undo that," she shouted, "or I would. But you sure as hell aren't going to get my wagons as easily as you got me."

He stepped through the casement and closed the door. When he moved toward Brenna, she backed up.

"I have to have the wagon," he said. "Kirkwood and the Mexicans don't trust me and Thunder. We must prove ourselves. I could have stolen the wagon without your knowing who the culprit was. That was my first intention, but I couldn't do that to you. I know how

349

much this trip means to you and your business. That's why I'm buying the goods." He stepped forward; Brenna stepped backward.

"You're using me," she whispered.

"Yes." He took another step, but Brenna didn't move this time. "I'm using you," he admitted sadly. "Humans have a tendency to do that to one another." Fleetingly he thought about the way Houston was using him. "Sometimes we have no other alternatives."

His gray eyes captured hers, and Brenna was bound to him by the mesmerizing gaze. When his hands came out to catch her shoulders, she swayed toward him. Before they touched, however, a knock pierced the tension-filled room. Brenna looked at the door over her shoulder; she turned her head and looked at Logan.

"Señora Allen!" Doña Anna called.

Reluctantly Brenna pulled away from Logan; he dropped his hands. Brenna walked across the room, her hand clasping the huge wrought-iron bolt. She slid it, but she did not have time to open the door before Jonesey's voice boomed out.

"Miss Brenna! Come quick! One of our wagons has been stolen!"

Brenna's hand dropped from the bar. She turned her back to the door and stared across the distance at Logan.

"Wait for me in the patio, Jonesey," she said calmly. "I'll be out as soon as I dress." She pushed away from the door and walked to the low chest at the foot of the bed on which her valise sat. "With no regards to my interests whatsoever," she said to Logan, "you stole my wagon." Her back to him, she moved her trousers and shirt aside.

"I explained to you that I had to—" He stopped in mid-sentence. Brenna turned around, her revolvers in hand, both of them pointed at him.

350

Brenna's eyes were flames of anger. "I despise you, Logan MacDougald, for what you've done to me. I hate myself even more because I allowed you to do it. You're despicable and undoubtedly the lowest and vilest scoundrel I've ever met. Nothing but a vulture." She cocked the revolver. "You deserve to be dead."

"I told you once, Brenna Allen, never to point a gun unless you're going to shoot," Logan said.

"I never point a gun unless I intend to shoot," Brenna said, and pulled the trigger.

A bullet whizzed by, barely missing Logan's head. "Are you crazy!" he exclaimed, instinctively ducking. "You could kill me."

"If I wanted to badly enough, I would." She moved closer to Logan and fired at his feet, making him hop from one foot to the other. "Now get out of here, and don't ever come near me again. This time I mean it, Logan. Don't come back for any reason whatsoever. Your kind of love I can do without."

"Miss Brenna!" Jonesey shouted. "Are you all right?"

"What is wrong, Señora Allen?" Doña Anna called out. "What is going on in your room?"

"Brenna—" Logan began.

Brenna lifted the gun and shot Logan's hat off his head. "Get out, you varmint, and remember, I don't ever want to see you again."

"I don't believe that."

"Then believe this." She peppered the air with shots.

A barrage of bullets chased Logan through the small garden, Brenna behind him. He scaled the adobe fence, calling over his shoulder, "Just you wait, Brenna Allen; there's going to be a reckoning day for sure." As he disappeared, the door to Brenna's room opened and Joaquin burst in.

"Brenna, what is wrong?" the *vaquero* called, his

spurs jingling as he ran across the room into the garden.

Brenna dropped her hands to her side. "Nothing," she calmly replied. "Just a varmint—the two-legged kind."

Joaquin started to brush past her. He searched through the garden.

"It's all right now," she said. "I frightened him away."

"I am so sorry," Doña Anna exclaimed, wringing her hands together. "I would not have this happen to my guests."

"Miss Brenna," Jonesey said, his eyes narrowed as he watched Brenna, "are you all right?"

Brenna nodded and cast her driver a trembling smile. "I'm fine." She returned to the room and laid her revolvers on the chest. "Now if you'll excuse me, I'll get dressed, and we'll go check out my remaining wagons."

A frown of concern on his face, Jonesey backed out of the room, but Doña Anna hesitated. Her troubled gaze bounced back and forth between Brenna and Joaquin.

"Doña Anna," a maid called from the patio. "Please come quickly. I need your help with the mutton."

Doña Anna cast a furtive gaze over her shoulder, then peered back into the room.

"It's all right, Doña Anna," Brenna assured the older woman. "I'm fine." She looked at the man who stood immediately to her side. "And Joaquin is leaving."

"Doña Anna," the servant called again. "Please come."

With a nod of her head Doña Anna turned and moved away from Brenna's room, but Joaquin did not budge. He reached out and caught her face tenderly.

"You're shaking."

She was—from anger, not fear!

Joaquin pulled her into his arms. "I'm so sorry you were frightened." He opened his mouth to say more, but then he closed it without saying a word.

Thankful for his strength, Brenna rested against him for a moment. Then she straightened and pushed out of the embrace. "I thought you were riding with Francisca and Roger."

Joaquin smiled. "We were, but I soon tired of being nothing more than a chaperon. I escorted them home, and they are now under the watchful eye of Francisca's nanny."

"Speaking of chaperon," Brenna said, "I think perhaps you better leave before your mother returns to find you yet in my room."

"I'm not worried about what my mother thinks."

"I am," Brenna said. "I don't want to do anything that would offend her. She's been very gracious to me since I've arrived here."

"Governor Armijo sent his apologies that he cannot meet us for lunch today; he'll be joining us for dinner," Joaquin told her. "So I'll escort you to the La Fonda to check out your wagons." His ebony eyes danced with devilment. "And I'm yours for the remainder of the day."

Brenna laughed despite herself. "That sounds promising."

"I hope so."

"Now I think it's time for you to go."

Still Joaquin made no effort to move. "I'll be right outside your door if you need me."

"Thank you," Brenna said, "but I'll be fine." She heard a movement and lifted her head to gaze out the door that opened into the garden. There for a second she saw Logan, astraddle the fence. His face was a mask of fury, hard and indomitable. Then he was gone.

"Are you sure you're all right?" she heard Joaquin say as he walked out.

"Yes," she whispered.

The door closed, and the lock clicked into place. Brenna's heart knew that she had lied.

Chapter Twenty-One

"I am so sorry, Don Joaquin," the landlord apologized vociferously in Spanish, his hands waving through the air as eloquently and as rapidly as he spoke. "This morning when I came out to get fresh water, I found my guards tied and gagged. The lock had been forced on all the gates, and the wagon was gone." He lifted the large apron he wore and wiped his face. "I assure you, I posted my best men as guards. Aware that this could happen, I tried to prevent it."

"Do not be overly concerned about it, Señor Gonzales." Joaquin calmed the man. "Señora Allen is naturally concerned about the theft of her property, but she does not blame you."

"Thank you, señora," Gonzales repeated several times to Brenna even though she didn't understand a word he said. A weak, but relieved, smile crooked his lips. He pointed to one of the tables beneath the portico. "Please, have a seat, Don Joaquin, and I will give you and the Señora Wagon Captain a glass of my finest wine."

Joaquin nodded. "We shall be delighted," he said, and as Joaquin led Brenna to a table in the shade of the portico, he repeated for her benefit his entire conversation with the host. "You cannot blame the poor man," Joaquin said. "He did his best toward you. Like everyone else in Santa Fe, he is a victim of the whims of the governor."

"Why do you not do something about him then?" Brenna asked.

Brenna's question startled and angered Joaquin. He stopped walking and turned to look down at her. His eyes narrowed and his face set in disapproval. "Women should not become involved in politics," he said.

"I'm not," Brenna answered. "But I would like to know why you and your people tolerate a corrupt government rather than do something about it."

"We are not like you Texans," he said. "We do not feel that we must break ties with our mother country in order to have the kind of government which we desire. My father and I are working for change within the established government. We are happy being Mexicans, and we want to retain our ties with Mexico."

Brenna had been puzzled when Francisca made much the same declaration last night in Armijo's carriage; she was even more puzzled now. Joaquin made it sound as if the people of Santa Fe were happy with their status; they did not wish for liberation. The thought was so farfetched Brenna could hardly comprehend it. But it was something she had to report to Childers; it was something the Imperialists had to know before they based an entire political campaign on the empire premise.

He began walking again. "Soon Papa and I shall journey to Mexico and make a full report on Manuel Armijo's abasement of his office. We shall see a new governor appointed. But," he said with a dismissive smile, "back to what we were talking about."

"What we've never stopped talking about," Brenna said. "Manuel Armijo."

Joaquin ignored Brenna's sarcasm. "Whatever Armijo wants, he gets, and evidently he wanted more than

356

the tariff on your wagons." Joaquin's tone became more reflective. "I suspect it was one of his men who broke into your room today. I only wish you were a better shot."

That stung! "I am a good shot! I just wanted to scare the man away."

Joaquin pulled her chair out. "Then next time"—his voice hardened—"shoot to kill."

"Killing varmints is different from killing men," Brenna said. She watched Joaquin move to the other side of the table to sit opposite her. "I find I can do the first quite well. I find that I'm bound by a conscience when it comes to the killing of men."

"Believe me"—Joaquin seemed to spit the words—"Manuel Armijo is the lowest kind of varmint. None is lower."

"Here you are, Don Joaquin." Gonzales bustled to the table, a wide smile across his friendly face, a tray in hand. "My very best wine." After the host poured the wine, he departed. Joaquin leaned back in his chair and crossed one leg over the other. He took a swallow, then asked, "Do you know what you were carrying on the stolen wagon? Do you have any idea why someone would want to steal only one of your wagons and leave the remainder?"

"No," Brenna answered, lowering her eyes. She felt guilty because she was letting Joaquin think Armijo broke into her room and stole her wagon, but her guilt wasn't such that she felt the necessity to confess that Logan was the culprit. "Sam has my copy of the inventory lists."

"We shall soon find out." Joaquin lifted his hand and snapped his fingers, summoning one of the children who ran about the courtyard. "After we have them," Joaquin said, "we will go inspect the wagons to see what was stolen."

357

"It's not that important, Joaquin," Brenna said. "Please, don't go to any trouble on my account."

"It is no trouble." A little boy came running to their table, and Joaquin took a coin out of his pocket. Speaking to the child in Spanish, he asked, "Do you know Señor Roper?" When the boy nodded, Joaquin handed him the money and said, "Please ask Señor Roper and his wife to join Señora Allen and me in an hour for lunch."

Brenna took off the black hat Francisca had loaned her and laid it on the table. Next came her gloves. When she settled her hands in her lap, she felt the stiffness of the letter in her pocket; she heard the faint crackle of paper. She was reminded of her task. She didn't have time to worry about the wagon Logan had stolen. She had more important work to do, and the sooner she did it, the better.

She looked at Joaquin. "You said that you were mine for the remainder of the day?"

Joaquin's breath caught in his throat: Her words were so provocative. Her eyes were startlingly beautiful. He was never sure if they were going to be blue or green. Today they were blue—the same color as the jacket of the riding habit Doña Anna had borrowed from one of her friends to let Brenna use.

"I am."

"I would like to see about renting me a store," Brenna said, and immediately she saw the disappointment in Joaquin's eyes.

But he quickly collected himself. He was glad that Brenna was not forward, as so many of the Santa Fe women were. He admired her reserve. "It will be many days before you can open your shop. Your goods must first pass through customs, and this might require as much as a week of negotiations with Armijo."

"Oh, no," Brenna told him. "The governor has said

that if I pay a flat fee of one thousand dollars a wagon, I—"

Joaquin leaned across the table and took one of Brenna's hands in his. "The governor is playing with you. He will charge you the flat tariff, but he will also inform you that many of the goods which you bring are banned. Iron, lead, gunpowder, and candlewick, to name a few. Also a tax is levied for keeping a retail store. Even if you get the permit, you have so many more legalities to go through that it will take you days, perhaps weeks, before you actually start doing business."

"No," Brenna murmured, "that can't be true."

"But it is, *chiquita.*"

Brenna was pondering Joaquin's words so deeply she didn't immediately pull her hand from his. Absently she gazed around the courtyard at the people who were milling around. Some were coming out of their rooms; others were filing in through the gate. Her gaze strayed to a table beneath the portico on the far side of the court.

There sat a man, clad in billowing serape and sombrero. Indolently he reached up and with his forefinger tipped the brim of the hat back, so she could better see his face. Logan MacDougald! Brenna started and immediately jerked her hand out of Joaquin's clasp. Logan stared at her, his face still hard and set. He offered her no smile. With blatant arrogance he lifted his glass and saluted her; then he quaffed the whiskey in one swallow. Never taking his eyes from her, he set the glass down and mouthed one word: "Tonight." Then he stood, dropped several coins on the table, and walked away.

"Is something wrong?" Brenna heard Joaquin say as Logan disappeared through the gate.

She returned her gaze to Joaquin's worried face.

"What is wrong?" he asked.

"Nothing," she murmured. "I was . . . thinking about what you said."

"And you are worried, no?"

"A little," Brenna admitted, reluctantly dragging her wandering thoughts from Logan MacDougald to the problem at hand.

"Sometimes the traders consign their goods to one of the local merchants," Joaquin said, "but—"

Brenna's head jerked up. "—but that is marvelous. I could consign my goods to an established merchant."

"That could be done, but you wouldn't make as much money this way as you would if you retailed your own goods. Still, it would be a way around the language barrier."

Quite casually, as if it were a natural flowing of the conversation, Brenna said, "Last year while in Houston I met one of your local merchants. He's a naturalized citizen of Santa Fe. Mr. Peyton H. Alexander. Perhaps he would either buy my goods outright or sell them on consignment."

"I do not like Peyton Alexander," Joaquin said.

"We don't have to like him," Brenna argued. "I am merely using him. If he sells my goods, it's a simple business arrangement."

Eventually Joaquin acquiesced. "I will take you to see him. Perhaps this would be the best way for you to sell your goods. And," he added, "this way you can spend more time at the hacienda with my family."

Brenna liked Joaquin, but she knew his interest in her was more than friendly. She didn't want to hurt his feelings. "I think perhaps it will be best if I stay at the La Fonda."

"No! We will not let you do that!" Joaquin exclaimed. "You are a woman on your own with no one to protect you."

"I have been on my own for six months or more," Brenna answered. "Since I was widowed. I am well able to care for myself."

"That I will determine," Joaquin declared. "Now tell me about your husband."

Glad to be on such a safe emotional subject, Brenna complied readily with his wish. When she finished, Joaquin picked up her left hand and ran his fingers over the pale indentation on her fourth finger. "Is there no man in your life now?"

Brenna hesitated fractionally before she lowered her head and said, "No."

"What about the Señor MacDougald my sister is all the time chattering about?"

Brenna made no reply as she stared at her hand lying in Joaquin's. *What about Logan MacDougald?* her heart mocked. She closed her eyes, as if the action would stop the mocking words. Then she felt Joaquin's hand on her chin. He guided her face up.

"I think perhaps Señor MacDougald tugs at your heart, no?"

"No," Brenna whispered, "Señor MacDougald isn't really interested in me. He's out to avenge the death of his family, who were massacred by the Comanches. When it comes to a woman in his life, any one will do."

"Somehow, *chiquita,*" Joaquin said, using the endearment easily, "I do not think that is true."

"You think I'm lying."

"No," came the gentle answer, "but I think perhaps you do not understand men very well. I think despite your marriage, you are an innocent." He chuckled and closed his hand around Brenna's. "I shall take advantage of your lack of experience and of Señor MacDougald's absence to convince you that I should have a place in your heart—a permanent place."

"I don't want any man to have a permanent place in

my heart," Brenna said, pulling her hand from the warm clasp. "Please, let's just be friends."

"I will accept your friendship if that is all I can have," Joaquin told her, "but I cannot accept less if I can have more. I promise that I will not force myself on you, Brenna."

Brenna heard a door slam across the courtyard and looked up to see the Ropers coming out of their apartment. Billy waved to her as he and the little messenger boy ran to join several children who were playing across the patio. She smiled and waved back. When Sam and Gertrude joined them, Brenna made the introductions and they visited through lunch. Afterward Sam, much recovered from his respiratory ailment, gathered Jonesey and several of the teamsters, and all of them walked to the wagon sheds. With Sam checking off the items, the men quickly reviewed the remaining goods.

Sam folded the eyepieces of his glasses and dropped them into his coat pocket. "Well, Brenna, I guess you could call this a blessing in disguise." He had to stop for a moment and inhale deeply, but his breathing was no longer labored to the point that he gasped for air. "The only items stolen were those that were on the banned list. Way I see it, you shouldn't have much difficulty in getting through customs."

"Miss Brenna . . ." Jonesey tugged at Brenna's sleeve. "Come here a minute, will you?" When the two of them were standing off from the others, he said in an undertone, "Don't you think all of this is rather odd? Somebody was in that garden at the Sandovals' house earlier today. That somebody you was never able to hit! And whoever stole these here goods went through all the wagons."

Brenna knew what Jonesey was inferring. "Yes," she admitted, "whoever stole the goods knew what he was

362

doing. He stole only the most valuable—those that would bring the highest price!"

"Maybe so," Jonesey murmured, scratching his chin, "but whoever done it, Miss Brenna, went to all the trouble to repack your wagons. And"—his voice lowered even further—"don't you think it odd they didn't take all the wagons?"

Brenna stared at Jonesey for a full second before she said, "Let's be thankful that whoever stole our wagon didn't want all of them, Dwight Jones, and do not—*absolutely do not*—speak of this to anyone else."

Jonesey returned the stare. Finally he nodded his head, a small grin tugging his mouth. "Miss Brenna, this here is one time you can count on me to keep my mouth shut."

When Brenna returned to Joaquin, he said, "I think perhaps our first stop should be at the Governor's Palace to report the theft. Then we shall call on the local merchants."

"I'll report the theft for you," Sam offered. "Gertrude and I are going that way. The governor sent word that he would see me this afternoon."

"I would appreciate it, Sam," Brenna replied. She didn't want to have to be around Manuel Armijo any more than was necessary. "I would like to make arrangements for the sale of my goods as soon as possible."

"That is settled," Joaquin said. "I would offer to give you and your wife a ride, Señor Roper, but the señora and I are on horseback."

"Thank you anyway," Sam said. "Mrs. Roper and I will enjoy the walk."

"Then we shall see you and Señora Roper at dinner tonight?"

"Until dinner," Sam answered.

After Brenna and Joaquin left La Fonda they rode

through the plaza and stopped in front of one of the small adobe buildings. On the door was a sign in Spanish, *Comercio de Alexander*. They dismounted and entered. The store had only one room with a floor made of adobe bricks, and since there were no windows, the only light came through the door and from the candles hanging in holders on the wall. On rough shelves that lined the back wall were all sorts of goods, ranging from bolts of cloth to spices.

Brenna and Joaquin trod through the maze of open barrels until they reached the counter, a large, unfinished piece of flat wood balanced on two barrels, behind which stood the proprietor. He was a tall, thin man with graying hair. Dressed in faded shirts and baggy trousers tucked into worn black boots, he was totally unassuming.

"What can I help you folks with?" he asked in Spanish.

"Mr. Alexander?" Brenna asked, speaking English.

"Yes, ma'am," the man replied, also in English. A little surprised, he squinted his eyes to look at her better. "Don't believe I know who you are, ma'am."

"I'm Brenna Garvey Allen, Mr. Alexander," she said. "My father and I met you last year when you were traveling through Texas." She waited a moment.

Giving them their privacy, Joaquin meandered through the store, finally to stop at the door.

When Alexander's brow remained furrowed in thought, Brenna added, "Mr. Clarence Childers introduced us, and speaking of Mr. Childers"—she dug into her pocket and withdrew the letter—"he asked me to give you this."

"Ah, yes," Alexander murmured as he turned the piece of paper over to stare at the scrawled handwriting. "Now I remember. Childers and I discussed the opening of trade between Texas and Santa Fe at the dinner at the hotel. Your father is the Irishman from Martin DeLeon's Colony?"

"Was, Mr. Alexander."

The man peered at her a moment before he nodded his head. "I'm so sorry, Miss . . . uh . . . you said your name was Allen?"

"Yes, I married shortly after my father and I met you."

Alexander dropped the letter into the pocket of his trousers, and his lean features relaxed into a smile. "Did I meet the fortunate young man?"

Brenna nodded. "Shawn Allen. Remember, he talked to you about amassing a trade caravan between Texas and Santa Fe, and you told him that if ever he was out this way, to be sure to look you up."

Alexander's eyes darted furtively to the front of the store. "Yes," he nodded, his gaze returning to Brenna, "I do remember. Congratulations on having married such a fine, enterprising young man. I suppose the wagon train that came into town yesterday belongs to him?"

"No, Mr. Alexander, it belongs to me. You see, Shawn was killed by the Comanches six months ago."

"Mrs. Allen," Alexander said with true-felt regret, "I'm so sorry on your losses."

"Thank you," Brenna replied. "Now I've come to ask a favor of you."

"What's that?" Alexander asked.

"I would like to know if you'd sell my goods on consignment."

Again Alexander looked at the front door. "Yes, ma'am, I'd be delighted to do that for you. I'll need an inventory of your goods; then we'll have to get the arrangement approved by the governor."

Always the governor! Brenna sighed. "How long will that take?"

"Can't really say," he replied. "Depends on the

365

governor." His lean features eased into a smile. "Tell you what; I'll come by this afternoon and look at the goods to see what condition they're in. Have a copy of the inventory lists prepared for me."

"Thank you, Mr. Alexander," Brenna said. "I really do appreciate your helping me."

"Don't mind at all," Alexander returned. "Now, where are the wagons?"

"They're at the wagon sheds at the La Fonda Inn," Brenna told him, "and you may ask for either Roger Hollis, my wagon boss, or Dwight Jones, my lead driver."

Alexander bobbed his head. "Good! Now, there's also the matter of the contract, Mrs. Allen. We need to have that signed before we petition the governor."

As Brenna stared into the man's colorless eyes she thought of what Logan had said about the man; she thought of Joaquin's distrust of him. A chill ran her spine. But, she hastily reminded herself, you don't have to like the man to work with him. The cause you're working for is greater than petty likes and dislikes.

She turned to the door. "Don Joaquin, would it be all right for Mr. Alexander to bring the contracts to your home this afternoon for me to sign?"

Joaquin turned and strode back into the room, his spurs jingling as he walked. "That will be fine. Will you come yourself, or will you send a servant, Señor Alexander?"

Alexander's gaze slowly moved from Joaquin to Brenna. Finally he said, "I'll be coming myself. I'll need to discuss the contract with Mrs. Allen."

Brenna smiled. "Thank you, Mr. Alexander. You don't know how much weight you've taken off my shoulders. I'll be awaiting your visit this afternoon."

"Yes, ma'am," he said.

Brenna turned and was walking out when she called

over her shoulder, "Oh, yes, Mr. Alexander, when I was at Bent's Fort, I met Colonel Warfield, the man who saved Doña Francisca's life. He wanted me to give you his regards."

"Yes," Alexander murmured, his eyes darting to Joaquin, "I met the man when he came through Santa Fe. Haven't seen him since. Don't have too much to do with men like him, though. He's a menace to *us* Mexicans."

"I agree," Joaquin said, and as he and Brenna walked out of the store, he asked, "Do you know this Colonel Warfield well?"

Something in Joaquin's tone warned Brenna to be cautious in her reply. "No," she said, "I just met him in passing." She said no more. She didn't want to have to go any deeper into explanations.

Joaquin and Brenna returned to the hacienda, where Francisca was waiting impatiently. Brenna visited shortly with Don Sebastian and Doña Anna; then all of them retired to their rooms for a siesta.

"I know you are tired," Francisca said as she led Brenna to the guest bedroom, "but I'm so full of curiosity I cannot leave until you tell me all about today."

Brenna took off her hat and hung it on a rack as she walked into her room. "Nothing of consequence really happened," she said, peeling off her gloves. They landed on the top of the table. Off came the jacket and the riding skirt.

"That's not what I heard," Francisca said, a mischievous glimmering on her lips. "Someone tried to come into your room and you shot at him. Joaquin went rushing into your bedroom, and you and he spent the day together." She rolled her eyes. "Tell me that nothing happened."

Francisca's questions brought visions of Logan back

367

to Brenna—visions and memories that she had successfully pushed to the back of her mind for the most part of the day. Now they returned in a rush to inundate her. Just as she would never forget the sweetness of Logan's touch, the wonder of his passion, she would never forget his using her or the anger on his face when he leaped over the fence. She owed him nothing.

"Did you recognize the man?" Francisca questioned.

Brenna sat on the bed and tugged her boots. "Should I have?" she grunted.

"Could it have been one of Armijo's men?"

Again Armijo was unjustly carrying the blame for Logan's actions. Brenna shrugged. "I . . ." Lying didn't come easy to her. "Francisca, I don't want to talk about it. It leaves a bitter taste in my mouth."

Francisca sat in the chair across the room and watched as Brenna took off her other boot and her socks. "You're in love with Logan, aren't you?"

Wordlessly Brenna moved to the dresser and lifted the pitcher above the basin. Her back to Francisca, she leaned over and splashed water on her face.

"I like Logan very much," Francisca said. "Next to Joaquin and Papa, he's one of my favorite people." She watched Brenna dry her face and neck. "I wish you had met Joaquin first, but I am not sorry that you love Logan."

"I haven't said that I love Logan," Brenna answered.

"You haven't said that you don't love him either."

The towel slung around her neck, Brenna walked to where Francisca sat. "I don't know how I feel about Logan. At the moment he's not very high in my graces."

Francisca chuckled. "It was Logan this morning! You were shooting at him!"

"You're just guessing!"

"Don't you just wish," Francisca teased. "Roger was

so surprised when he found out the man had gotten away. He said you were a crack shot."

"Roger? Not Señor Roger?" Brenna asked, changing the subject. "How is your friendship developing with him?"

"Fine!" Francisca exclaimed. "Mama and Papa like him, so they gave me permission to address him by his given name."

Brenna grinned. "As if you haven't already been doing just that!"

"They've invited him to come to the house with us. Papa said he might have a place for Roger at the hacienda."

"I think it's time we took our siesta," Brenna said. "If we're going to be up as late tonight as we were last night, I'm going to need some rest. What time is dinner?"

"We shall eat at eight," Francisca said, "but we'll gather in the patio at seven. I'll see you then."

When the door closed behind Francisca, Brenna was finally alone, alone with thoughts of Logan. She remembered Logan's silent promise. Tonight! He was coming back tonight. For just a moment she allowed herself the delight of anticipation, but she quickly quelled it. Logan had no right to steal her possessions; no right whatsoever! He had no right to blatantly disregard her wishes by jumping in and out of her life and trampling on her heart. If only he had come because of her—that she could more easily forgive.

She moved to the door that opened into the garden—locked tightly since this morning's episode. She tested the bolt to see that it was secure. She didn't want to see him right away; she was still angry; she was still hurt.

Was loving always this bittersweet? she wondered. She marveled at the ease with which Logan cast her emotions from one extreme to the other, from sorrow to sheer ecstasy, from laughter to anger, from joy to tears. No matter what else the sensation, always she felt the pain. Always she felt the loneliness after he left her.

She was glad Logan had seen her with Joaquin. It would do him good to know that other men were interested in her! He wouldn't win her forgiveness any too easily or quickly.

She lay down and took a nap, awakening only when the maid knocked and said in broken English, "A Señor Alexander is here to see you."

Quickly Brenna re-dressed and combed her hair. Then she was out the door and across the patio to join Peyton. H. Alexander, who sat on one of the long benches in the shade of a small, squat tree. He rose to greet Brenna.

"I came as quickly as I could, Mrs. Allen," he said when both of them were seated. "I inventoried your wagons, and I brought the contract for you to read and sign."

"Thank you, Mr. Alexander," Brenna said. "This really takes a load off my shoulders."

She took the papers that Alexander handed her and began to read.

"Mrs. Allen"—Alexander lowered his voice, his eyes slowly circling the courtyard—"we must be careful in all that we say and do. The Mexicans are most distrustful of Texans."

Brenna unconsciously lowered her voice to say, "But I thought the Mexicans wanted to break away from Mexico and join Texas in her freedom."

Alexander's faded eyes landed on Brenna. What he had said was true, but he didn't want her to know it. He needed those guns. They would make him a wealthy man. Aware that he had slipped, he vigorously nodded his head. "The people want their freedom from

370

Mexico, Mrs. Allen. They sure do. But Don Sebastian isn't one of that number. He's very much against the Texas rebellion and swears his allegiance to the Mexican government. Anything that you and I discuss must be kept between us. Do you understand?" Again he lifted his head and glanced around the courtyard.

"Yes," Brenna replied.

"Rumor has it that one of your wagons was stolen from the wagon sheds at La Fonda."

"Yes," said Brenna. "A wagon which contained mostly items banned by the Mexican government."

"What was in the wagon?"

Brenna felt the tension emanating from the man who sat close to her. The answer to the question was most significant to him.

"Candlewicks," she enumerated, "iron products, gunpowder, and tobacco." She waited a moment before she asked, "Why are you interested, Mr. Alexander?"

In that same low voice he asked, "Are you aware of the contents of Childers's letter?"

"I haven't read the letter," Brenna answered, "and even if I had, I'm sure I would find it nothing but innocent and friendly. A letter from one merchant to another. Mr. Childers is an intelligent man."

Alexander nodded his head.

Brenna added, "I have an idea of its true significance."

"We cannot precipitate a revolution in Santa Fe and Taos without weapons. Childers promised me guns. Plenty of guns. The kind the rangers use. He also promised me ammunition and men."

Brenna lowered her head and looked at the document in her hand.

"Warfield came into Santa Fe with a group of straggly men whom he put together and calls his army."

371

Alexander didn't hide his disgust. "Hardly able to take care of themselves, much less come up against Armijo's soldiers."

"Houston knows about this?" Brenna asked.

Alexander looked at her blankly for a moment.

"President Houston," Brenna clarified. "He's the one who authorized Warfield to prey upon American and Mexican traders. Did Houston hire Warfield to help in the revolt of Santa Fe and Taos?"

Alexander's face cleared, and he laughed. "Heavens forbid! The man would bust his gut if he knew what we were planning. He doesn't want any more trouble with the Indians or the Mexicans. The United States wouldn't tolerate another rebellion against Mexico, and Sam Houston is going to try to please the good ole U.S. of A." Alexander laughed heartily. "Texas won't stand a chance of being admitted to the Union once we stir up trouble here in Santa Fe and in Taos."

"I don't think that's a good choice of words, Mr. Alexander," Brenna said. "We Imperialists are not trying to stir up trouble; we're trying—"

"Please forgive me, Mrs. Allen," Alexander interrupted her. "I assure you I did not mean to sound flippant."

Brenna did not like Alexander. She suspicioned he was all that Logan had said he was and more, but he was the man with whom she must deal. "How could Houston not know what you're planning to do?" she asked. "He commissioned Warfield. I read the commission myself."

"You're partly right," Alexander confirmed. "Warfield was commissioned indirectly by Houston, directly by Hockley, who was secretary of war at the time. Neither Houston nor Hockley knew that Warfield was working with Childers." Alexander balled his hand into a fist. "We can do nothing without more weapons, and we haven't seen a sign of them, nor have we received word of them." He turned to Brenna. "Do you know anything about the shipment?"

Brenna shook her head and said thoughtfully, "Perhaps Shawn was to have smuggled them in to you, but at his and Papa's death, plans were changed." When she looked into Alexander's disappointed face, she added, "But I'm sure Mr. Childers will send someone with them. When I reach Houston, Texas, I'll send word to Childers, and—"

"I want you to take a letter to Childers," Alexander interrupted the second time. "I have given him the names of men who are willing to work with him to start a rebellion here. Also I've given him important military information."

"Where is it?" Brenna asked, her heart thumping so fast she could hardly breathe.

Delivering Childers's letter to Alexander was one thing; taking the reply back to Texas was another. Although Texas considered Santa Fe and Taos to be a part of their republic, the Mexican government had yet to recognize the legitimacy of Texas. And Brenna suspicioned that the Santa Feans themselves were happy being a part of Mexico. The moment Brenna accepted the letter she ceased to be an innocent Texan visiting Santa Fe; she ceased to be a mere trader. She was a spy working for Texas to undermine the Mexican government.

But, she reminded herself, she wasn't encouraging insurrection. She was merely extending to the people of Santa Fe and Taos the freedom from Mexican tyranny that all Texans had fought for.

"It's the last three pages of the contract," Alexander said. "When you get to your room, separate it from the other papers and hide it. Hide it carefully. If the letter is found on your person, I do not have to tell you what your fate will be."

"Surely you wrote your answer in code," Brenna said.

"I didn't have time to use the phrases and words that Childers and I agreed upon. I'm being watched all the time, and my premises are continually searched. I had to take advantage of the time, and that demanded immediate action."

Alexander stood up. "Now I must go. Armijo's men follow me everywhere I go. After you have gotten approval from the governor for the sale of your goods through my store, he will affix the official seal to both copies of the contract. You will keep one; the other he will send to me." With those hasty words Alexander was gone.

Brenna hurried back to her room, separated the papers, and signed the contracts. These she left on the table. The letter she folded and inserted into the secret compartment of her luggage. She undressed once again, and clad only in her dressing gown, she lay down to ponder the enormity and danger of the situation in which she found herself.

What if someone slipped into her room unawares and searched through her belongings? A secret lining in the valise might be the first place they would look. She searched her mind, wondering where else she could hide the documents. A place so obvious no one would think to look.

Chapter Twenty-Two

Although she didn't sleep, Brenna lay in bed until she heard Lupe's call: "Are you ready for your bath, Señora Allen?"

"I am," Brenna answered as she stood, walked across the room, and opened the door.

After Lupe made several trips, Brenna was sitting in a tub of hot, sudsy water, leisurely bathing. She leaned her head against the back rim and closed her eyes as she listened to the noise and activity in the patio.

The door opened and Lupe entered with a beautiful gown in her arms. "Señora, Doña Anna asked me to bring this dress to you. It was purchased in Mexico City, and she has not had time to have alterations made so that it will fit Francisca. La señora thinks it should be long enough for you."

Later, fully clothed, Brenna stood in front of a floor-length mirror, gazing at herself. Lupe had combed her hair into a chignon atop her head, gentle curls wisping around her temples. While the dress was modestly cut, it was one of the most daring Brenna had ever worn. The colors—black and turquoise—were hot and sultry; they deepened the color of her eyes; they created a sense of mystery and promise. The high collar accented the slender beauty of her neck; the bodice was tight and low-cut. An inset of delicate black lace revealed, yet at the same time hid, the upper swell of her breasts.

Then came Francisca's call and entry. No sooner had the door closed behind her than she exclaimed, "Oh, Brenna, you are so beautiful. Your eyes are magnificent! Never have I seen such a color before." In her hands she held a beautiful, diaphanous scarf. "This is for you," she said. "It will go beautifully with your gown."

Brenna took the filmy piece of black material. Smooth and silky, it flowed through her hands. Imitating the women whom she'd seen in Santa Fe, she took the rebozo and wrapped it around head, neck, and shoulders. While it was too transparent to cover anything, its whisper of color hinted at sensuality. It was most provocative.

Francisca clasped her hands together and stared at Brenna. "You are so lovely, Brenna. Joaquin is going to be so proud of you tonight, and *verdad,* he will tell Mamacita, 'I told you so.'"

Brenna reached up to touch one of the springy curls. "Why should Joaquin say such a thing to your mother?"

Francisca's eyes danced with mischief. "He is the one who chose your dress."

Looking at Francisca's image in the mirror, Brenna slowly dropped her hand to her side. "Lupe said the dress was from your mother." She shook her head. "Surely you know I cannot accept such a gift from a man."

All mischief was wiped from Francisca's face; her eyes reflected her concern. "I am so sorry, my dear friend," she apologized. "I did not mean to imply that Joaquin had given you the dress. He only helped Mama choose the right one for you." Francisca thought quickly; she talked as rapidly. "He reminded her of the color of your eyes. That is why he chose this dress."

Brenna said nothing; she continued to look accusingly at the younger girl.

Francisca shrugged. "Besides, it is too late to change now. Our guests have begun arriving, and dinner will be served shortly. Afterwards we shall dance."

Lupe's knock and announcement confirmed Francisca's words. With one last look in the mirror, Brenna turned and followed her hostess out of the room into the brightly lit patio. She greeted Sam and Gertrude and was happy to see that they blended into Don Sebastian's household. While Sam talked with Don Sebastian and Gertrude visited with Doña Anna, Brenna mingled with the other guests, her eyes darting to the courtyard doors as she apprehensively awaited the governor's appearance. She didn't have long to wait.

Manuel Armijo, resplendent in a crisp new uniform, marched through the doors, a large, satisfied smile curving his lips. He greeted Don Sebastian and Doña Anna cordially and stayed to talk with them a long while before his gaze sought Brenna out of the crowd. His eyes appreciatively ran the length of her figure quickly to return and linger on the lace inset at the bodice.

Brenna had never used a fan in her life, but now she understood its function. She lifted the expensive black and ivory creation, and with a deft flick of her wrist she swished it open. She gently—defiantly—waved the fan below her chin; the lace inset she totally covered.

She felt a warm touch on her elbow, and she heard Joaquin's low voice. "Manuel Armijo is nothing but a lecherous old man."

"I agree," Brenna said, her eyes still on the governor. "I despise him."

"No one likes him," Joaquin returned. "We tolerate him because we have no option, but we do not like him.

377

Soon, though, we shall be rid of him."

Armijo began to walk toward Brenna. Joaquin felt her stiffen.

"Do not worry, *chiquita*," he said, inadvertently addressing her with the endearment. "I will stay by your side."

Armijo bowed low in front of them, but Brenna did not extend her hand in greeting. The governor straightened, his eyes gleaming dangerously. "Bid the señora good evening," he instructed Joaquin, "and tell her that she is indeed a lovely woman."

Brenna nodded and smiled after Joaquin interpreted the words.

"I have given much thought to providing her with a vendor's license," he continued. "At first I thought perhaps I would give permission, but now I'm not so sure."

Joaquin's voice had hardly ceased the translations when Brenna asked, "Why has he changed his mind?"

Armijo gladly complied when he heard Joaquin repeat the question. "I am not sure of Señora Allen's purpose in coming to Santa Fe. I have cause to believe that she is working with the illegal government of the Texans."

"Although you are the governor, Manuel Armijo," Joaquin Roman Sandoval said in his hardest tone, "you had better have evidence to substantiate such a charge before you accuse one of our guests of such a crime in our own home."

Armijo slipped his hand into his jacket and withdrew a crinkled sheet of paper. "I have evidence, Don Joaquin." The ebony eyes were filled with hatred. "A letter which Señora Allen delivered to Peyton H. Alexander earlier today."

Brenna didn't understand what the two men were saying, but she did recognize Childers's letter. She had carried it long and far enough. After what Alexander had told her earlier today about his being under suspicion, it took little imagination for her to guess Armijo's words. But she had to remain calm and controlled. She kept her expression bland, her eyes innocent. Whatever else Childers was, he was no fool. She was sure he wouldn't have written anything incriminating in the letter. Armijo was bluffing.

"Is that the letter I delivered to Mr. Alexander today?" she asked Joaquin. She smiled. Two could play this game.

"I was with the señora when she delivered the letter," Joaquin answered Armijo.

Brenna gave Armijo an icy smile. "You may also tell the governor that I am personally acquainted with Clarence Childers, who is a leading merchant in Houston, Texas. And he certainly is not a member of the government. Because Mr. Childers had met Mr. Alexander when he journeyed through Texas last year, Mr. Childers sent his regards. Is that a crime, señor?"

Brenna watched Armijo's face as Joaquin translated her words. The expression never changed. The cold black eyes settled on her. "The letter sounds innocent enough," the governor replied, "but I should like to see the papers which Alexander left with Señora Allen. I happen to know that this man named Childers is the leader of a movement that wishes to see Texas become an empire, its boundary to stop only when the Texans reach the Pacific Ocean."

By now Don Sebastian was standing beside his son. "That may be true, sir," the father agreed, "but you do not have proof that Señora Allen is working with such a man or that she is conspiring to overthrow our legitimate government. As long as Señora Allen is our guest, she will not be harassed by our government."

"I can only surmise then," Armijo said, "that you are

in this insurrection attempt with Alexander."

"You may surmise anything you wish. You always have," the elder Sandoval said, "but you will not come to my home for dinner and pull your military antics. I'm not afraid of you, Manuel. I'm not afraid of your soldiers."

Doña Anna ran to her husband's side and caught his arm. Her face was ashen; fright shadowed her eyes.

Brenna tugged Joaquin's *chaqueta* sleeve. "What did Armijo want?"

Joaquin quickly explained Armijo's request to Brenna; then he asked, "What papers is he talking about?"

"The contract which Alexander drew up for the selling of my products on consignment."

Brenna glanced at Doña Anna; then she looked at Don Sebastian. Guilt settled heavily on her. Involving herself in this plot to overthrow the Mexican government was her prerogative, but her involving people like the Sandovals was wrong. No matter how she looked at the situation, she could draw only one conclusion: She was using them. But she had gone too far to turn back now. She must do her duty, but she must also manage to keep them out of it at all costs.

She said, "I don't mind the governor looking at the contracts, Don Sebastian."

"You do not have to do so," the elder Sandoval said. "If I accept your word, so shall he."

"I'll go get them," she said.

Before she had taken more than two steps, Armijo's voice rang out. Brenna didn't understand the command, but she knew it was a command nevertheless. She recognized the authority behind the words. She stopped and waited for Joaquin to speak.

"Because of the delicate situation in which he finds himself," Joaquin said stiffly, his fists clenched to his side, "the governor would like to accompany you to your rooms."

Brenna spun around.

"Absolutely not!" Don Sebastian exclaimed. "My allegiance to my government is not in question, and neither is my guest's."

Brenna was becoming more deeply entangled in the web of deceit. To Joaquin she said, "Please tell your governor that I have done nothing wrong, and I will not subjugate myself to such humiliation. It is not fitting or proper for a gentleman to come into a lady's bedroom."

She heard Armijo's mocking words; she heard Joaquin's interpretation. "He wants to know if you have something to hide."

Brenna glared at the man. She knew Armijo planned to do more than look at the contracts. She looked beyond him to the soldiers who had entered the courtyard and stood at attention on either side of the gate. He was prepared to search her luggage and to arrest her. He was prepared to involve the Sandovals in the conspiracy charges. Somehow Manuel Armijo had learned of the letter she was to take back to Childers—and that letter was incriminating.

"Get out of my house," Don Sebastian ordered in a low voice. "Get out right now."

"No, Don Sebastian," Brenna said. "I do not wish to cause you any harm or undue embarrassment. I have nothing to hide; therefore, I have nothing to fear. If Doña Anna will accompany me, I shall be more than happy to let the governor enter my room."

Armijo was temporarily taken aback. This was not the reaction he had planned. Still he was glad that his plans were unfolding so smoothly and effortlessly. Not only would he incriminate Peyton Alexander and Brenna Allen, but he would charge the Sandovals as conspirators. He would also learn the whereabouts of the weapons and intercept them from Lattimer.

Brenna turned and led the way to her room, where she threw open the door. As soon as she had lit the candles, she pointed the fan to the table on which rested the two copies of the contract. Armijo's boots snapped against the tile as he moved toward the table. He picked up the contracts and he read each. He laid them back down, and his eyes carefully ran around the room to light on the valise.

I was right, Brenna thought. *The valise is too obvious!*

Armijo looked at the piece of luggage a long time, then leveled a long, searching gaze at Brenna. Her head held high, she returned the stare, she refused to quail. She forced herself to remain composed.

"Well?" Don Sebastian asked.

The governor looked toward the owner of the townhouse. "It seems, Don Sebastian, that I owe Señora Allen an apology. These papers are nothing but contracts for the selling of her goods on consignment." Again Armijo's glance went to the valise.

"Perhaps, sir," Brenna said daringly, "you'd like to search through my personal belongings."

"That is not necessary!" Don Sebastian's voice whipped through the room.

"I don't mind," Brenna contended. "I can understand the position he's in, and now that I've had time to think about it, I would like to convince him of my innocence." She was shaking so badly inwardly, she didn't know if she could take the few steps to her valise or not.

Brenna didn't have to worry about it; Joaquin moved for her. He picked up the piece of luggage and slapped it on the table in front of Armijo. "Señora Brenna wishes to proclaim her innocence. She wishes you to seach through her personal belongings."

Armijo took the valise and opened it. He dug
through the clothes. Doña Anna's face flamed with
color as he dropped Brenna's undergarments piece by
piece on the table. He ran his hands around the sides
and over the bottom, not once but twice. A third time.
His nail caught on something.

He set the bag down and he leaned over, his eyes
peering into the depths. The room was quiet—too quiet
for Brenna. Perspiration beaded in the palm of her
hand; it rolled down the valley between her breasts. He
had located the secret compartment.

"Ah," Armijo sighed, a smile on his face as he lifted a
packet of papers from Brenna's valise. He turned
around and waved them through the air. "And what
are these?"

As soon as Joaquin translated, Brenna said, "Those
are my bills of lading, sir, and personal papers that
belonged to my father."

"You don't mind my taking them to the Palacio to
have them translated, do you?"

Armijo didn't care if she had a communication from
Alexander to Childers among the papers or not. With
these in his possession he could falsify charges against
her. He would have Roberto Onega claim that such a
letter was found among them.

The interpretation over, Brenna said, "I do mind
your taking them. They are my private papers.
However, if you'll bring Mr. Onega here, he and Mr.
Roper can translate the papers together for you. You
trust Mr. Onega; I trust Sam Roper."

Even after Joaquin repeated her words in Spanish,
the governor stared uncomprehendingly at her.

"Mr. Roberto Onega," Brenna said. "Isn't he the
soldier who does the governor's translating? Señor

383

Armijo does trust Onega, does he not?"

Armijo's affirmation was long in coming, but once he nodded his head, Don Sebastian said, "Come, everyone. Let's go back to the patio. There's no need for us to delay our dinner or fiesta because of this." As soon as all were out of the room, he addressed Brenna. "Señora Allen, you and I shall stay in the study with Señor Roper and Roberto while they are translating these papers."

Brenna sat in one of the straight chairs, upholstered in black leather, as Roberto read her papers aloud. Sam peered over his shoulder, correcting him on a word or phrase several times.

"There now," Don Sebastian declared when the reading was done. He turned to Brenna. "Here are your papers, my dear. Shall we leave them here for the time being, or do you wish to return them to your valise?"

"I'll get them later," Brenna said. "Now we should return to the party. I'm sure your guests are hungry."

Armijo smiled tightly. "Tell Señora Allen that I deeply apologize. But in my position I cannot be overly cautious."

Brenna allowed Don Sebastian to lead her back to the patio, where she was caught up in the gaiety of celebration. She allowed Joaquin to teach her several of the Mexican dances, and she was soon spinning around the courtyard from partner to partner. The earlier ordeal forgotten, she laughed aloud and her eyes sparkled.

The beat of the music quickened; it was hot and sultry. Because the steps of the dance were so quick and complicated, Brenna looked down at her feet to make sure she made the correct movements. She glided around the circle to change partners. As his hand clasped hers warmly, she looked up the splendid male

384

body that was clothed in the tight-fitting garments of the *caballero*.

Brenna's laughing sea-green eyes clashed with eyes that were cold as steel.

"Logan," she murmured, missing her step and stumbling against him, "what are you doing here?"

Chapter Twenty-Three

"I never break a promise," Logan told Brenna. "I said that I would be here tonight, and I am." In time to the music, he caught her wrist with both hands and pulled her against him blatantly for a moment before he twirled her about. "I don't enjoy watching someone encroach on my property."

"I'm not property."

His voice was low, and only she could hear him. His words were sharp. "You're mine, and I'm keeping you."

"Hardly yours," Brenna said. "I'm not an animal that one brands and keeps, nor am I a possession."

"A tigress for sure," Logan disagreed as they dipped and swayed around one another. "You hiss and scratch when you're angry. But I've seen the other side of you, too. I've made you purr, my darling, and I've felt your claws as they ripped my back in a fit of passion."

"Hardly something you should brag about," she retorted. "I'm a passionate woman. Any man could have done as much."

"No man better have done it!"

"You should know by now I'm mistress of my own destiny. I do whatever I choose to do with whomever I choose to do it." She ducked under his arm and whirled around him. She could tell that he was angry. Perversely, she was glad.

With fluid motion Logan swayed to the sultry rhythm, his body an extension of the music. Around Brenna he deftly moved, his feet never missing a step. Closely he came to her, his arms once again closing around her waist. He pulled her against his long, hard form, never quite touching her anywhere but at the waist.

In public for all to see he deliberately bent her over, his eyes mocking her, his hands making love as they gently feathered up her arms in the barest of touches. Underlying his movements was still the fire of anger. He caught her hands, and the two of them spun around and around. As suddenly as he began the pirouette, he stopped. He danced away from her, his red sash flowing through the air.

Brenna had known that Logan was graceful, but she was surprised that he was so well versed in Mexican dances. She knew so little about him. "How do you know so much about Spanish culture?" she asked.

Logan swept his body close to hers. "San Antonio and her lovely señoritas taught me." He smiled. "The language, the dance, and the customs."

"Which customs?"

Logan laughed. "Do you really want me to tell you all the details?" He moved away.

Brenna couldn't take her eyes off him; they held her an unwilling captive. In front of everyone he deliberately seduced her. And her traitorous body wanted to give in. Valiantly she fought the feelings that assaulted her. She wouldn't be seduced. Yet her breasts tingled to life when she felt the heat of his gaze as it seared through the delicate black lace.

Logan couldn't take his eyes off Brenna. Never had she looked more provocative or more tantalizing! But her state of attire only served to bank the fire of his anger even higher. She hadn't known he would be at the fandango; therefore, she hadn't dressed to please him. She had worn this revealing dress to pleasure the Mexican *hacendado*.

Logan's eyes, hot and lustful, rested on Brenna. Beneath the lace he saw the creamy smoothness of her skin—skin he wanted to touch and caress until she was moaning in his arms. Skin he wanted to taste. But none of this did he admit by word or deed. He still tasted the bitter gall of her having shot at him earlier in the day. Now he would teach her a lesson!

Brenna shivered. This night held more for her, and while she didn't willingly admit it, neither was she going to run from it. She would beat Logan at his own game. She wouldn't allow him to embarrass or insult her in front of these people. Pushing convention aside—that convention that had required such decorous behavior in the Sandoval household—she smiled brightly at Logan. Her feet began to move to the beat of the music.

Before she knew what was happening, Logan reached out and caught an end of the scarf in one hand and twirled her about with the other. As if she were a top, he unwound the scarf, a wolfish smile on his face.

"I see you." His eyes lowered to her breasts and lingered. "All of you."

Although he had taken off her only a transparent scarf, Brenna felt naked—totally naked. More, she was totally vulnerable. For just a moment she was furious that Logan would do this to her. She had stood by and allowed Shawn to strip her of her integrity, but she wouldn't allow another man to do that to her. She may not win, but she would go down fighting.

She caught the *rebozo*, pulled it through his loose clasp, and defiantly wound it around shoulders, neck, and head. She threw back her head arrogantly and laughed. Holding her hands above her head, she clapped her hands in imitation of the Mexican dancers she had seen, and she began to move her feet. She twirled around Logan and tapped her feet to the beat.

When she mesmerized him—and mesmerize him she did—she slowly unwrapped the diaphanous scarf to reveal first her shoulders, then her neck, and finally her head. She undressed herself! As blatant as Logan's action had been earlier, Brenna's movements were seductive. They stimulated the imagination.

Logan was burning with anger that fought with desire. Never had he wanted a woman as much as he wanted Brenna.

Joaquin, standing beneath the portico, sucked in his breath as the flimsy material sailed through the air. He knew Brenna loved Logan, but he wasn't ready to concede her to the Texan yet. He would do his best during their days at the hacienda to replace Logan MacDougald in her heart.

Manuel Armijo moved farther into the shadows to hide the telltale bulge in his trousers as he felt his loins tighten. Brenna Allen was one of the most sensuous women he'd ever seen, and he would have her! He wanted her so badly, he ached. Before he was through, he would bed the Texan.

The scarf floated through the air to slide down Logan's cheek. Brenna danced closer, caught the other end of the *rebozo,* and wrapped it around his throat. The touch of silk was so caressive that against all his resistance, desire rippled through Logan's body. Brenna tugged; Logan readily complied with her silent command. He swayed closer to her.

"You're so beautiful," he said, his lips moving toward hers. "So utterly lovely that I'm going to kiss you."

"In front of all these people?"

"In front of all these people."

"We'll see about that." Before he could touch her, Brenna drew back. She was so exhilarated she laughed; so sure of herself and of her ability to arouse Logan, her eyes sparkled their victory.

"Yes, we'll see about that."

His hands banded around her waist; he threw her into the air, then brought her against him. He arched, molding her body to his, melding her body to his. His fingers wove into her hair, and he guided her face to his. He would take the kiss. She had been tantalizing him all day. He could stand the torment no longer.

"I will take my reward."

The music stopped. The spectators clapped and cheered. Breathing deeply, a sheen of perspiration on his face, Logan gently set Brenna down, but he didn't immediately turn her loose. His arms slid around her waist and he pulled her against him. She insinuated her hands between their chests and shoved, but to no avail. Logan clamped her to him.

She lifted her face. "Don't, Lo—"

His head angled and lowered; his lips covered hers in a hot, lingering kiss to silence the protest. His hands moved up and down her back, and the kiss deepened. Finally, when he had plundered her lips and the recesses of her mouth, he pulled back.

Oblivious to everyone standing around them, they stared into one another's eyes. All arguments, all disagreements fled in the face of love. And both knew, both admitted they loved one another.

Joaquin was the first to break the silence. He moved from the portico to the patio. "You must be Logan MacDougald," he said, breaking the mesmeric bonding between Logan and Brenna. "I have heard so much about you from Francisca."

Slowly Logan released Brenna, turned to the Mexican, and shook hands.

"I am Joaquin Roman Sandoval, Francisca's brother."

And the man who wants Brenna! Logan thought. *The man who will get her if I'm not careful!*

"Señor Logan!" Francisca rushed up to throw her arms around Logan's neck and give him a big hug. "What a wonderful surprise. I did not expect you, but I am so glad that you could come. And"—she backed off to gaze at him—"you do look stunning in your *caballero* costume."

Logan bowed with a flourish and laughed into Francisca's face. "Thank you, Doña Francisca. You are quite charming yourself."

By this time the members of the wagon train who were present thronged around Logan.

"Logan"—Sam pumped Logan's arm enthusiastically—"I'm so glad to see you." He paused only long enough to draw air into his lungs. "Gertrude and I have been so worried about you." Sam draped an arm around his wife and drew her closer.

"How's your health, Mr. Roper?"

"Splendid," Sam said, thumping his chest proudly. "I haven't had a single spell since we arrived in Santa Fe. I can speak several sentences before I must stop for breath."

"I'm glad to hear that."

"Where's Thunder?" Gertrude asked.

"He doesn't like towns," Logan replied evasively, his eyes searching for and finding Brenna. "He's camped out a ways."

"Hello, Mr. MacDougald." Roger pressed to the front to shake hands with Logan. "Glad to see you."

Logan smiled easily. "Well, Hollis, how's life treating you?" The gray eyes twinkled with devilment. "Got yourself a pretty señorita yet?"

Roger's face turned a dull red. "I'm sure hoping

so, sir."

Logan looked beyond Roger to Gertrude Roper. "Well, Mrs. Dawkins—I mean, Mrs. Roper—how is Billy doing?"

"Just fine. Growing like a weed. Took to Santa Fe right off. Why," Gertrude declared with the pride of a mother, "he's already starting to talk Spanish. Right now he's with the people who own the La Fonda Inn. He wanted to stay so he could play with the Gonzaleses' children." She paused a minute and her eyes darkened. "I don't know what I'm going to do if his mother— when his mother gets here and takes him away from us." She looked up at Logan. "You haven't heard anything about her coming, have you?"

"I have," Logan said. "Her wagon train arrived several days ago. It fell to me to tell her about the deaths—her husband's and brother-in-law's—and I also let her know Billy was safe and sound with you and Sam."

"How did she take it?" Gertrude asked, her eyes dark with sympathy for Lilly Ellington.

"Pretty bad," Logan replied. "She has no one left but Billy."

"No," Gertrude said softly, shaking her head, "that's not true. She has me and Sam for as long as she wants and needs us." A sudden smile spanned her face. "I'll have Sam send her a letter to that effect. Why, if Lilly Ellington wants to, she can stay with us for a while."

Logan smiled with the woman. "She sent word that she'll be coming on the next wagon train."

"Billy will be so happy to hear this. I can hardly wait to tell him."

Manuel Armijo walked up to Logan, and the circle of friends melted away. "I don't think I've had the opportunity to meet you, señor." The greeting wasn't an introduction; it was an accusation. "I like to know everyone who comes to Santa Fe."

Don Sebastian stepped to Logan's side. "This is Logan MacDougald. He is Señora Allen's wagon boss."

"He did not come into town with the train," Armijo pointed out. "And a Señor Hollis was introduced as her wagon boss."

Although Logan spoke Spanish, he waited for the interpretation, and he gave his answer in English for Brenna's benefit. "All the governor says is true," he answered Don Sebastian. "I couldn't come with her at the time because I had business at Bent's Fort."

"What kind of business?" Armijo asked.

"My business," Logan answered in Spanish, surprising Brenna and Armijo.

"Would it be of interest to me, señor?"

"I don't know," Logan answered. "I don't intend to tell you to find out."

"Perhaps I already know," Armijo suggested.

The two men sized each other.

"I understand that you are a horse dealer, señor."

Logan's eyes narrowed. "Why would you think that?"

Armijo laughed. "Word gets around, señor. You'd be surprised at how much we know about the happenings in Texas. As much as you, maybe more. We get your newspapers, and they are quite informative!"

"Don't believe all you read, señor," Logan said.

"I don't. You should come see me at the Palacio during the day, señor. I'm sure we can do a lot for each other."

"I'll think about it, Governor," Logan replied.

Don Sebastian motioned to the musicians, and they began to play again.

"Is he also one of your house guests, Don Sebastian?" the governor asked, nodding his head toward Logan.

"Yes, he is," Don Sebastian replied before Logan had a chance to speak. "Now let's enjoy the fiesta."

Manuel nodded curtly. "When are you returning to your hacienda, Don Sebastian?"

"Tomorrow."

"Is the señora going with you?"

"Why do you ask?"

"Merely curious," Manuel replied, lacing his hands together behind his back. "Is she not curious about her permit? Has she so soon forgotten her purpose in coming to Santa Fe?"

"The ride to my hacienda is not so far that you cannot send us word when you've made your decision. In the meantime we'll take her wagons with us."

Again Manuel nodded. "What about Señor Mac-Dougald? Will he be traveling with you?"

"Yes. Also Señor and Señora Roper, their grandson, and Señor Hollis."

"I understand that you have employed Señor Roper as your personal secretary."

Don Sebastian nodded his head. "I have. He and his wife are coming to live at the hacienda with us."

Armijo didn't stay much longer. He had many things on his mind. Riddles that needed solving. Plans that needed to be finalized.

Brenna was happy and slightly inebriated when the last guest finally left. Exhausted, she murmured her goodbyes and hugged and kissed Doña Anna and Francisca good night. She hummed as she walked to her room. Leaving the door ajar so torch light would flicker into the room, she crossed to the table and lit the candle. Then she lit those which hung suspended on

394

wall holders. When she returned to the table to set the matches down, she felt the early morning breeze as it blew into the room to send the flame dancing through the air.

She slowly pivoted to see her room torn up. Her hand flew to her mouth, and she gasped. Someone had searched her room. What if they— She rushed to the bed and fell to her knees. She groped until she found her boots. With shaking hands she examined them. The right one. The left one.

"No," she cried, when she saw the heel was missing. "Oh, my God!"

The door slammed. The bolt slid into place; the lock clicked. Brenna whirled around to see Logan standing there.

"Are you by any chance looking for this?" he asked, pulling several folded sheets of paper out of his pocket and holding them in the air.

Brenna leaped to her feet and sailed across the room. She grabbed for the letter. "Give me that," she demanded. "That's my personal property."

"How much do you think your life would have been worth," he asked, "if Armijo had found this letter?"

"Well, he didn't," Brenna answered. "I had him fooled. He thought he'd found the letter when he discovered the hidden compartment in my valise."

"If you're going to become a spy, dear heart," Logan said, walking to the outside wall to check the lock on the door, "you're going to have to be just a little smarter. The hollow heel is an old trick." He pulled the curtains over the opened window, the breeze gently brushing against them.

Brenna laughed. "Looking at the mess, I wouldn't think it was quite that old. It evidently took you quite a while to find them."

"I didn't leave the mess," Logan told her as he

stripped off the cravat and dropped it to the floor. "Armijo's men did it after I left."

"How did you know about the letter?" Brenna asked.

"Just like Armijo, I figured it out," Logan answered, the jacket coming off to land on the chair. "Alexander made a trip to Texas last year to see Childers. Both of them espouse the idea of an empire, and what better place to start than Santa Fe and Taos? And who's a better go-between than you—an innocent woman leading a caravan to Santa Fe?"

"You make it sound like I'm stupid," Brenna said. In the candlelight that flickered across Logan's face, she saw his smile.

"No," he replied, "I don't think you're stupid." He moved closer to her. "I think you're so caught up in your cause that you're blinded and deafened to reason. I think you're naive when it comes to spying."

"What are you going to do about the letter?" she asked.

"Nothing," he said.

"You're going to let me deliver it to Childers?" She was astonished.

"If that's what you wish," he replied.

"I can't believe this." Brenna planted her hands on her hips. "You know what Childers is going to do with the information, yet you're saying you'll let me take this to him."

"I've made a copy," Logan told her, "and I'll take that to the president. So he'll know as much as Childers. I'm not worried about Childers. By the time he can do something, Texas' future will have been decided."

"You know something," Brenna said.

"I know a lot," he admitted. "I know that I'm going to make love to you."

"That's not what I mean!"

"I do." He moved so that he was standing directly in front of her, looking down into her upturned face. "I've always thought you were beautiful." He grinned. "Even in those baggy trousers and that shirt." As quickly his face sobered. "Even this morning when you were shooting bullets at me and chasing me away. But tonight you were more than beautiful. You were extraordinarily desirable." He lifted his hand and traced the outline of the lace inset. "All covered up except for this little diamond of lace, yet you had all those men panting after you."

"Hardly all the men." Brenna seemed to breathe the words.

"Armijo."

"He's not a man."

"Joaquin."

"Perhaps Joaquin," Brenna agreed jauntily. She was pleased when she saw Logan's mouth firm into a line of disapproval. "No one else."

"The dashing young *caballero* is interested in you." Logan clasped her waist with both hands and tugged her closer. His whiskey-scented breath was warm against her skin.

"He likes me."

"No." Logan's fingers tightened. "He more than likes you. He's well on his way to being in love with you."

Brenna didn't deny it.

"And you're leading him on."

She chuckled. "You're jealous."

"Jealous as hell," Logan admitted frankly.

"You didn't have to follow us."

"No," Logan admitted, "I didn't have to follow you, but I did. The idea of your spending all day with him was tough, but I could hardly stand the thought of your enjoying the time you spent with him."

"I do enjoy being with him," Brenna admitted. "He's

a wonderful person."

"What am I?" Logan asked.

For the first time Brenna heard a note of uncertainty in Logan's voice and knew that he was the one in need of reassurance; he needed to be reassured of her love. She had known for a long time that he loved her, but at this moment she knew he loved her . . . unconditionally. More, Brenna realized if she were to insist that Logan abandon the search for his sister at this moment, if she were to insist that he abandon his search for the Comancheros, he would.

That she wouldn't make this demand of him was her most startling self-discovery. She had fallen in love with Logan for what he was—the man who loved his sister so much that he hadn't given up hope; the man who loved his country and his people enough that he was willing to make the necessary sacrifices to ensure their safety. Yes, she loved Logan MacDougald just as he was. She accepted him as he was.

Now she must love him unconditionally!

"Brenna"—Logan was almost pleading—"what am I to you?"

A sweet smile curling her lips, Brenna reached up to work the first button of his shirt loose. "According to a source whom I trust implicitly, you're Logan Andrew MacDougald." The second button. "You're a man who works for Sam Houston, and you wish Texas to become a state in the Union." The third. "You're a man with a purpose in life. You want to avenge your family their cruel, barbarous death at the hands of the Comanches." The fourth. "You're a man who has deep emotions and who loves unconditionally."

She worked the last button loose and swept the material aside. She wound her arms around him and pressed her face against his chest. She felt his accelerated heartbeat. "You're the first man who ever made love to me, and the only man to whom I ever made love." Her breath was warm against his skin. "And no matter what happens, Logan, no matter how many times you must leave me to go in search of your past or your future, I'll still love you." Her voice was husky with tears.

Logan captured her chin in his hand and guided her face up.

"I'll either be at your side, or I'll be home waiting for you when you return."

His lips touched hers in a hot, consuming kiss that set both of them on fire. Like a prairie fire in a drought, they burned out of control, and neither cared.

She felt his hands brush down her back, his rough palms rasping against the texture of her dress. Her breasts tightened with desire and throbbed against the constraining material. When she felt his hands slip under her arms to cup the swollen fullness, she pulled her mouth from Logan's and moaned.

Her hands glided up Logan's back, caressing the muscles along his spine and across his shoulders. Her fingers tangled in the mop of thick brown hair. Complying with her every demand, following each loving injunction, Logan captured her lips again and again. Each kiss grew deeper; they were hungry and devastating. Anticipation, excitement, and pleasure swept through both of them.

Eventually the kisses were not enough; they had been apart too long. They separated and undressed. Then they were together on the bed, he on his side, she on her back. Propped on his elbow, lying beside her, Logan ran his hand over her hip. He marveled at the silken texture of Brenna's skin beneath his rough palm. As if he had never seen her naked before, he looked at her.

She was so lovely. The uptilted breasts, the small waist, the gentle flare of rounded hips, and the delicate brown triangle. Bringing his gaze back up to her face, Logan saw the passion-glazed eyes. He ran his hand through the silky curls that framed her face; his hand moved again, his fingers tracing her mouth.

Then his warm fingers, so strong and callused from work, lightly kneaded her nipples until they were hard and throbbing under his touch. She sat up; he shifted his weight, and both hands slipped beneath her breasts. He delighted in the feel of the satin-smooth weight in his palms. His mouth trailed a fiery path over the gentle swell until his lips closed over a tempting crest.

Brenna, leaning back against the pillows, writhed beneath the love strokes, and her stomach contracted with the sweet ache of desire. As if it were the first time she had made love to him, she caught her breath and moaned softly. Instinctively she arched, thrusting her breast more fully into his mouth. She wove her fingers through his hair.

Brenna was more aware of Logan than she had ever been. She was acutely attuned to his touch, to his every command. She felt his fevered warmth; she saw the perspiration that glistened on his body. She saw the passion that blazed in his eyes. His clean, masculine scent blended with the sweet fragrance of the burning candles to fill her nostrils.

"You're mine, Brenna. All mine. Joaquin Sandoval will never have you. That I promise." His voice was muffled against her stomach. "No other man will ever have you!"

Brenna didn't take exception to his possessive words. She understood his need to be reassured. Everything—everyone—he had ever loved had been forcibly taken from him, and he was afraid that would happen again.

"I'm yours," she assured him, "because I want to be yours. Because I love you, no one can take me from you."

Brenna was in the throes of deep passion, aware only of the stirring and demands of her body. Yielding to this primitive urging, she gave herself up to him eagerly, freely. She held nothing back. Her fingers pleasurably furrowed in the crisp golden waves of his hair, and she guided his mouth back to hers. She wanted to know again the sweet fierceness of his kiss; she wanted every inch of her body possessed by the man she loved.

Logan's mouth devoured hers hungrily. His hand left her breast to travel down the flat stomach to the brown mound of femininity between her thighs. His hand slid through the downy softness, unerringly seeking the place he hungered for. With consummate skill, with a confidence tempered with love, his fingers entered and lovingly explored the most intimate part of her.

When Brenna felt his touch, she slid down on the mattress, going hot and cold all over. Her eyes closed, faint sighs whispered through her lips, and her head rolled from side to side in sheer pleasure. Her delight was Logan's. Intent on giving her pleasure, his whole body joined in the amorous assault. As his hand probed, as his fingers moved inside her, his teeth teasingly grazed around the fullness of her breasts to the throbbing nipples and back again. So ecstatic was her pleasure, Brenna cried aloud.

But still he hadn't given her enough; she wanted more. *She had to have more!* The tormenting longing for more seared through her blood to pound in her head and drum in her heart. Her hips began to undulate in that dance as old as time itself. She lifted her buttocks, straining against Logan's hand. Her body trembled with the force of the emotions that he had unleashed in her. She begged for release.

His body clamored for release yet he deliberately held back. He fought against losing himself in the pleasure of her hot, velvety sheath. He concentrated on loving Brenna; his primary concern was for her to know the wonderful release his hands could give. Slowly he caressed her, whispering endearments in her ears when he wasn't kissing her.

Brenna continued to writhe under his loving ministrations. At the very moment when she thought she could stand the torment no longer, her blood turned to molten passion to surge madly through her veins. Her heart drummed frantically; her breath shortened. Every nerve in her body screamed for relief. Paradoxically, all her feeling was centered in hte pleasure point immediately beneath Logan's hand. Suddenly it exploded, and she involuntarily contracted. Moans of pure delight escaped her slightly parted lips. She was dizzy with the pleasure that winged through her body. Dazed by the intensity of her climax, Brenna lay on the bed, staring into Logan's face.

"Thank you, my love," she whispered. "Now I shall give you pleasure."

"I've already had pleasure." Logan gasped as her fingers gently curled around his masculinity.

"Not like I'm going to give you."

But Logan could not endure more foreplay. Now was the time for his release. Gracefully smooth, he moved so that she was beneath him. Brenna welcomed his weight; she was astonished but delighted at the alacrity with which her body responded to him. He eased his knee between her legs and spread them apart. His hands slipped beneath her hips to lift her up to him. Brenna sucked in her breath when she felt his hardness sink into her femininity. Both sighed as her body welcomed his most penetrating touch.

Their bodies were locked together. Their souls were

bound together in love. Her fingers gripped into the flexed muscle of his buttocks. As he thrust deeply, more rapidly, more fiercely, Brenna's body once more burst into an uncontrollable blaze of passion. His mouth caught hers, and their lips joined as his manhood filled her.

Lying beneath him, Brenna was unbearably conscious of the heat of his chest as it pressed against her breasts, of his warm hands as they cupped her buttocks. Conscious of the seductive movements of his body, of the strokes within her, Brenna slowly, rhythmically moved her hips. Logan moaned his pleasure, pressing more urgently. The deeper he thrust, the higher Brenna soared. Then her breath caught in her throat, her heartbeat accelerated, and that same knot of pleasure formed in her stomach again. She was propelled to that highest pinnacle of love; then her body shuddered in Logan's arms.

"I love you," she sobbed. "I love you, my darling." Her lips caught his in a deep kiss of gratification.

No longer did Logan have to control or restrain himself. Lost in a world where nothing existed except him and Brenna, his entire body ached with the need to release the pent-up desire that surged through him. When Brenna gasped, tensed, then shuddered her pleasure another time, he no longer held back. Turning her kiss of gratification into one of deep passion, one of ultimate promise for himself, his hand tightened around her hips. His last anticipatory movements verged on savagery and violence, but tempered with love, they merged into supreme ecstasy.

Their eyes closed, Brenna and Logan drifted hazily in and out of the sensual world they had created with their love. Vaguely Brenna was aware of Logan lying next to her, of his hands still lightly caressing and touching her. She was acutely aware of the deep satisfaction of her body. She smiled and stretched, a sigh of contentment escaping her lips.

"I'm glad Doña Anna moved you out of Francisca's room," he said.

Brenna laughed. "That would have put a damper on tonight, wouldn't it?"

"No," Logan replied. "I would have kidnapped you if it had been necessary. I was determined to make love to you tonight."

"What did you go with my wagon?"

"I don't have your wagon."

"Logan," she drawled impatiently, pushing up on an elbow to look down at him.

"I bought it, so it's mine."

"What did you do with it, Logan?"

"I scrapped the metal—"

"You what!" she exclaimed.

"I scrapped the metal," he repeated. "Makes good arrowheads. Furthermore, Indians don't have any use for metal stoves."

"Arrowheads for the Indians?"

"Arrowheads for the Comanches," he said. "Thunder and I shall soon be dealing with them. We have a meeting set up. Hopefully we'll take enough trade away from the Comancheros that they'll—"

"—come after you."

"Hopefully they'll invite us to join rather than let us compete with them."

"Don Sebastian said you were coming to the hacienda."

"I am." He brushed his hand up and down her arm. "I'm not about to leave you out there alone with Joaquin Sandoval. That man has determined to make you his. I think he's heard the tinkle of wedding bells."

"I think I like the tinkle of wedding bells."

"You want to get married?"

"Yes," Brenna answered. "I want to get married. I want a home and a family."

"A husband like Sandoval?" He spread his fingers through her hair and tugged her face down to his.

"No," she whispered as she looked into the warm gray eyes—eyes fraught with anxiety and uncertainty, "I want a husband like you."

"I've never been a husband before," he muttered. "I don't know that I'll be any good at it."

"But you'd like to try."

"Yes," he whispered fervently. "Dear God, yes, Brenna, I want to give it my best shot."

"That's all I'm asking for."

"I couldn't stand it if you wanted Sandoval." Logan gathered her into his arms roughly and hugged her. "I swear to you, I wouldn't have let that man have you."

"No," she murmured, stretching out, her hand moving to the pleasure points on his body, "I don't intend to let Sandoval have me. Now hush being so arrogant and so possessive, and make love to me."

"Yes, ma'am." The answer was docile; his hands moving over her body were anything but. They were arrogant and sure and possessive.

Chapter Twenty-Four

Wearing a light morning gown, one of the many which Doña Anna had supplied for her and which Brenna had insisted upon paying for, Brenna sat in the shade beneath the portico at the hacienda, sipping a cup of chocolate. Her black hair, hanging loosely, was pulled back from her face and secured with a length of ecru ribbon that matched the piping on her gown. Although the lifestyle at the hacienda was filled with gaiety and activity—fiestas that lasted long into the night—Brenna was rested. She savored the gracious life enjoyed by those who lived on this baronial estate.

"Come, lazybones. Get your clothes on," Francisca chided as she darted out of her bedroom into the courtyard. "We will go to the corral and watch the vaqueros."

Brenna made no attempt to move. She was thoroughly enjoying her laziness. "Watch the vaqueros, Francisca, or the vaquero?" When Francisca playfully pulled a face, Brenna laughed.

Enjoying the joke at her expense, Francisca joined in the laughter. "*Vaqueros, mi amiga.* Roger, Joaquin, and Logan. They are competing against one another."

"That sounds interesting." Still Brenna didn't move. She picked up her cup and took another swallow of hot chocolate.

"Exciting, not interesting!" Francisca corrected. "Joaquin is one of the best *vaqueros* in the country. He has won many, many times at the rodeos. He is the very best. No one can outride, outrope, or—"

"I think Logan will give him pretty stiff competition," Brenna interrupted with a grin.

Francisca's eyes flashed with exhilaration. "Oh, Brenna, I will love this. We shall see who is best, shall we not?"

After the two of them had chatted for a while and had drunk another cup of chocolate, Francisca went to check with her mother to see if there were any chores for her to do, and Brenna disappeared inside her room to dress. First she combed her hair and swirled it atop her head in a coil. Then she chose to wear a brilliant green riding habit. The bodice was tight, deliberately styled so that it molded her breasts and midriff; the gored skirt flared from her waist to swirl around her ankles. She sat in the nearby chair and pulled on her embossed leather boots, complete with silver spurs which she had purchased from a silversmith in Santa Fe.

Her dressing complete, she stood in front of the mirror and pirouetted. She smiled to herself; she loved the bright colors with which the Mexicans clothed themselves. Quite frankly, she was caught up with life in Santa Fe. Although the people were of Spanish and Mexican descent, they had their own culture and attitude about life that was separate from the people in Texas or Mexico or even California.

Their life was simple, and most of their wealth was worn on their backs, yet the citizens of Santa Fe were extremely happy. The song that they sang, Brenna learned, came from their heart and souls. These people were as uninhibited in their dress as they were in their spirit. Brenna found them to be far more unconventional than Americans or even the Mexicans with whom she was acquainted in Texas.

Since coming here she had changed her mind about many things. No longer did it seem so important for her to impose her political beliefs on these people. She would love for them to enjoy the freedom that Texans enjoyed, but she had begun to see that the majority of the people did not wish this for themselves. Until they did, any overtures by any government would be an intrusion on their rights. She would have to tell Childers this when she returned to Texas; she would have to convince him of this.

She didn't like Sam Houston any better; she didn't respect his politics, but she had to concede he knew what he was talking about when he insisted on making Texas a state in the union. Grudgingly she admitted this was for the best interests of all concerned—Mexico, Texas, and the United States.

Perhaps Alexander had been right when he used the phrase "stirring up trouble." Rather than assisting the people in establishing their own government, Texans who espoused an insurrection in Santa Fe and Taos would simply be creating trouble—more trouble than they could handle. She would deliver Alexander's letter, but she would also address the Imperialists. She would tell them all she had learned.

When she made her decision, a burden lifted from Brenna's shoulders, and she smiled. No longer did she feel guilty about staying with the Sandovals and enjoying their warm hospitality.

"Brenna!" Francisca pounded on the door. "Are you not ready yet? We'll miss all the excitement if you don't hurry. My, but you take a long time to dress."

Brenna's smile turned into soft laughter at Francisca's incessant chatter as she donned her black hat, trimmed in silver braid, and adjusted it at a jaunty angle. When she was satisfied with the way she looked, she walked to the door and swept it open. "I'm ready," she said. "What do you think?"

Francisca bobbed her head energetically. "As always, you look lovely. I can hardly wait to see the dark looks Joaquin and Logan give to each other when you arrive." She lowered her voice. "And I wonder which one of them will win your heart and your hand in marriage, mi amiga."

Brenna made no reply. She was both complimented and irritated by this competitive jealousy between the two men. Although she repeatedly told Joaquin that she wanted only friendship, he continually pressed for more. Although she assured Logan time and again that she was not romantically interested in the Mexican hacendado, Logan still set out to prove himself. Today's contest was no different.

"You are indeed a fortunate woman," Francisca said, "to have two such men fighting for your love."

"I'm not sure they are competing for my love." She sighed. "Or if they're competing for the sake of competing. I happen to be the prize which both of them want."

Francisca thought a minute, then shrugged. "That is what I said, Brenna. Both of them love you, and only one can have you for his wife. You do not like?"

"I'm not sure I enjoy being courted this way."

Soon Brenna and Francisca had covered the distance between the house and the corrals. The first to see them was Roger. He broke away from the vaqueros who lined the fence and ran toward them.

"Francisca," he called, "I'm so glad you came. I rode the wild mustang longer today than I have ever done."

Francisca's face fell. "I missed seeing you ride, *querido?*" She turned accusing eyes on Brenna. "Because you took your time in dressing, Brenna, I missed seeing Roger ride the mustang."

"But now that you are here"—Roger's eyes danced—"I shall ride yet another. You will be so proud of me. I am learning fast."

Brenna smiled and walked away, leaving the two lovers to enjoy their bantering. She climbed atop the corral fence and looked above the milling herd of mustangs and through the cloud of dust at Logan and Joaquin, who straddled the opposite fence. Neither man saw her yet. Both were concentrating on the mounted *vaquero* who was separating a white mustang from the herd.

"Is this the one you wanted?" the man called in Spanish.

"That's the one," Logan replied in the same language.

"This one is going to be hard to break, señor," the *vaquero* informed him. "He has a mind of his own."

Brenna watched as several of the *vaqueros* wrestled with the horse, holding him in place with ropes while others put the saddle on him. Pulling the ropes, they forced the mustang against the fence and yelled for Logan to mount.

"Hurry, Señor Logan," one of the *vaqueros* yelled. "This one is mean; he's the devil himself. He will break loose in a minute."

"Not mean," Logan corrected. "He's just full of spirit." Logan pushed himself up. Before he climbed into the saddle, his gaze caught Brenna's. Across the corral they stared at one another. "That's the way I like 'em."

Brenna saw the glint of determination in his eyes. She smiled and raised her hand to her lips. She blew him a kiss. The chiseled features of Logan's face relaxed into that familiar quicksilver smile. With two fingers he tipped the brim of his hat; then he lowered himself on the mustang. He eased his hand under the grip, tightened his fingers, flexed them, and tightened them again. The *vaqueros* loosened all but one rope.

"Let him go," Logan yelled.

The last rope came off, and the mustang was free.

Exhilaration winged through Brenna as she watched the mustang run around the corral. But his freedom was short-lived. He realized he had an unwanted burden on his back. He stopped short, lowered his head, and kicked up his rear legs. Logan held on, his left hand swinging behind. Up came the front legs; the rider stayed on. The horse bucked and snorted and leaped into the air, bowing his back. Logan's hat flew off, but he fought to stay on, his right hand tightly banded around the cinch.

Long, tense minutes passed, and at times Brenna was sure Logan was going to be thrown. He seemed to go in one direction, the mustang in another, but through it all he managed to stay in the saddle. Then the horse quietened, and Logan relaxed. Too soon! The horse pawed the ground with its front hooves, then reared in the air. Higher and higher it seemed to climb; still Logan hung on.

Brenna caught her breath. The horse was winning. Logan slipped. His hand bit into the leather strap. He was still in the saddle. When the front hooves hit the ground, the back ones flew up. Again and again, like a seesaw. Still the rider remained the mustang's burden. One last snort. A shake of his head. The mane flying through the air. The horse pranced around the pen. Gently Logan nudged with his knees. At a full gallop they headed through the opening in the fence.

"Logan is truly a *vaquero*."

Francisca's murmur startled Brenna. She had been so caught up in Logan she didn't realize anyone was sitting beside her.

Francisca was in awe of the man. "He rides as if he were born to the saddle."

By the time Logan returned with the gentled mustang, Joaquin was standing with Brenna and Francisca. Logan dismounted, caught the horse's head in his arms, and murmured in his ear. He brushed his hand along his neck and shoulders. Then he patted him. With a few words of instructions, Logan left the horse with one of the *vaqueros*. When he saw the young don talking with Brenna, his eyes narrowed and his lips tightened.

"You are good, Logan," Joaquin praised. "I have seen few men who can ride so well." He handed Logan his hat. "Even fewer who could best me . . . as you have done this day."

Logan accepted the compliment with a quick nod of his head. "You're pretty good yourself, Joaquin. Another minute or two, and I'd have been sprawling in the dust with my hat."

When the laughter died out, Joaquin asked, "Have you ever tried *el coleo* before?"

Francisca cut her eyes at Joaquin.

Logan shook his head.

"Would you like to try it?"

"No, Joaquin," Francisca exclaimed, "you cannot challenge Señor Logan to bullbaiting. It is too dangerous for one who is inexperienced."

Joaquin's ebony eyes never moved from Logan's face. "The decision is yours, Logan. If you decide to indulge me, I shall promise to protect you from harm."

Logan's eyes narrowed. "Explain the game to me."

"As many *vaqueros* as want may participate. On horseback we pursue a wild bull, and the vaquero who wins the race seizes the animal by the tail and tries to overturn it by a twist of the wrist."

"No, Logan," Brenna cried, rushing to his side.

Logan wrapped his arm around her waist and pulled her to him.

"The decision is yours," Joaquin said quietly, his eyes flickering over Logan and Brenna. "It is a game that requires great bravery."

The insinuation didn't go unnoticed. "I'll play on condition," Logan answered.

"What condition?"

"First, I'd like to see a demonstration."

"Fair enough," Joaquin conceded.

"And after, we'll play a game of my choosing."

Joaquin nodded his head. "As you will." He walked off, yelling instructions in Spanish to the *vaqueros*. He sent them to get a wild bull and to bring it back to the pen.

Francisca and Roger ran behind Joaquin, Francisca berating her brother in Spanish for insisting on having the game.

"You don't have to do this for me," Brenna said to Logan, turning so that she was facing him and he was holding her in a loose embrace. "You don't have to prove your love to me."

"I know. You look pretty," Logan said. "Where'd you get this riding habit?"

"From Doña Anna."

"She's given you a lot of new clothes," Logan said, jealousy burning inside him. He felt as if the force behind Doña Anna's generosity was as much Joaquin as friendship for Brenna.

"She didn't give them to me," Brenna said. "She selected them, but I paid for them." She laughed. "I'm not accepting gifts from Joaquin."

A smile broke loose on Logan's face. "I've enjoyed being at the hacienda with the Sandovals, but I've missed spending my nights with you," he said, smiling even more when he saw the faint color tinge Brenna's

413

cheeks. "Guess if I intend to spend any more with you, we're going to have to follow convention and get married."

Brenna lowered her face and played with one of the buttons on his shirt. "Does that bother you?"

"Not in the least," Logan admitted. "The sooner I get my ring on your finger, the quicker Joaquin Sandoval will leave you alone."

"That's not the only reason you're marrying me?"

"No," he said. "I love you."

She raised her head to look imploringly into his eyes. "Logan, you don't have to take part in this . . . game. You don't have to chase a wild bull to prove your masculinity to me."

"I hope not," he murmured, leaning down to place a kiss on the tip of her nose. "If I haven't demonstrated my masculinity to you by now, I don't think I ever will."

"Then why?"

"If I back down, I will lose the respect of Joaquin and his *vaqueros*. To them this is a test of manhood. I want to do it, and I want to pass with high marks," he confessed. When she nodded, he said, "Will you give me something for luck?" He lowered his face to hers. After a long, leisurely kiss, he pulled away. "And this?" he asked, taking the scarf from her neck and tying it around his. Another quick kiss; then he was gone.

Brenna and Francisca climbed on the fence again and watched as the *vaqueros* returned with a wild bull in tow. As soon as they had him in the pen, they closed the gate. Amidst excited yells, the *vaqueros* lined up and chased the bull. Joaquin, of course, won and, with a quick twist of the wrist, flipped the bull.

He rode up to where Logan stood, his legs apart, hands on hips. "See, Logan?" he mocked. "The game is simple."

"Quite simple," Logan returned.

The contest began in earnest. Logan moved to his roan, mounted, and rode to the gate to join the other *vaqueros*. Joaquin took off his hat and tied a brightly colored handkerchief around the top of his head to keep his hair from tumbling into his face and obscuring his vision. Then he took his place at the gate.

Joaquin turned his head and looked at Brenna. "You will give us the signal to go, Brenna."

She nodded and waited for the *vaqueros* to line their horses in the opening. The second she yelled, "Go," they charged after the bull—a huge, ferocious creature. Soon no one was in the race but Logan and Joaquin, and Joaquin was the leader. He grabbed the bull's tail and gave a dexterous twist. The bull stopped short, but he did not turn over. He snorted, dug his heels into the dirt, and braced. Joaquin came flying off the horse to land in front of the angered animal.

His head down, his front hooves pawing the dirt, the snorting bull glared angrily at the dazed man. Joaquin quickly rolled over to get out of the way and tried to get to his feet. He winced and groaned and leaved over, grabbing his ankle with both hands.

"My leg," he called to Logan, "it is broken. I can't move."

Logan turned his horse and raced back to Joaquin. When he reached the *hacendado*, Logan leaped out of the saddle and placed himself between Joaquin and the bull.

"Get Don Joaquin out of here," he called in Spanish to the *vaqueros*, "while I keep this bull occupied." He stripped Brenna's scarf from his neck and dangled it in front of the snorting bull.

The bull, momentarily distracted by the activity, continued to paw the dirt with his front hooves. His eyes darted from Logan to the flash of brilliant material. Logan didn't move; he watched the animal's eyes. When the bull lunged, Logan jumped aside just in time to keep from being gored. For an animal so large, the bull turned sharply and quickly and was bearing down on Logan again. He ran, hoping to reach the fence and safety before the bull reached him. His heel caught on an exposed root; he fell.

All he could see coming at him were those horns—and they were the most ferocious-looking weapons he'd ever seen. Somewhere he heard Brenna's scream. The bull snorted, showering Logan with spittle. His nose was so close, Logan could feel it. Blood spurted all over him. It was all over.

Logan heard the bull squall, run back, and finally drop to the ground, a sword extended from his chest. Pushing up on his elbows, Logan saw the horse standing next to him. Joaquin was in the saddle. Although his eyes were dark with pain, he was smiling.

"You saved my life, *mi amigo;* I could do no less than save yours. But"—his grin widened—"I do not think we shall be able to play your game today. Some other time perhaps?"

Before Logan could respond, Brenna was in the dirt beside him. "How could you?" she cried, tears running down her cheeks. "How could you do this to me?"

"Baby, baby," he soothed her as he wrapped his arms around her. "Everything's going to be all right."

"But not because of you two," Francisca shouted, her irate face swinging back and forth between Logan and Joaquin. "You are two foolish men, and both of you could have ended up dead." She marched to Joaquin. "Now, you go directly home, so we can take care of your leg."

"Little sister," Joaquin said, "I love you dearly, and I appreciate your attention and ministrations, but I absolutely forbid you to talk to me in that tone of voice." He lowered his voice. "Especially in front of the *vaqueros.*" He smiled at Francisca, then turned the horse and headed for the house.

Arm in arm, Brenna and Logan walked back by themselves, glad for the opportunity to be alone. They had shared few of these moments during the past three days that they had been at the Sandovals' hacienda.

"Tonight," Logan said when they reached Brenna's room, "no matter what happens, I'm coming here."

"To my room?" When he nodded, she asked pertly, "What for?"

"You know what for, woman!"

"Yes! I know what for."

A smile on her face, a purr of contentment coming through parted lips, Brenna leaned against the door once she was inside the room and anticipated the night with Logan. No matter how many times they made love, she never had enough. She always wanted more.

Once Logan was in his room he closed the door and leaned against it, a smile on his face as he anticipated his night with Brenna. Of all the women he'd made love to in his life, Brenna was special. He never tired of her. Always he wanted more . . . and more . . . and more. . . .

"Hello, my brother."

Logan jerked his head up to see Thunder standing by the window.

"You look like a man truly bemused by a woman."

Logan moved farther into the room. "I am, my brother, I am."

Reverting to Cherokee in case they should be overheard, Thunder said, "It is time. Kirkwood has arranged a meeting between you and one of the Comanche chiefs."

417

"When?" Logan asked. He took his hat off and tossed it on the small chest at the foot of the bed. "Where?"

"Tonight," Thunder replied. "Kirkwood would not say where. He will take us to the meeting place."

"Did he say which chief we were to meet with?"

Thunder shook his head. "I have told you all that I know."

"Neither Kirkwood nor the Mexican traders know where our wagon is stashed, do they?"

Again the Cherokee shook his head.

"I'll meet you about eleven o'clock tonight," Logan said. "That will give me time to tell Brenna goodby."

"That kind of goodby will have to wait," Thunder quietly returned. "We have a long ride ahead of us before we meet Kirkwood; therefore, we must leave at once."

Pensively Logan nodded. Already he was imagining Brenna's reaction to his departure. "Does anyone know you're here?"

"No. I will go the same way I came. I will wait for you at the large boulder near the creek." He walked to the door, and again with that uncanny ability he had to read Logan's mind, he asked, "Are you thinking of giving up the mission for the woman, my brother?"

"I love her," was Logan's simple answer.

"Then you must consider her. Perhaps you need time to think." Thunder's fingers closed over the doorknob. "In making your decision consider that we are one step closer to the men who killed your parents. For nineteen years you have lived for this moment. I would hate for you to let it pass you by. If you do, you will add more regret to your life."

"I no longer feel the compulsion to find the man who killed my parents," Logan returned quietly. "But I will finish the job I began for Houston and for Texas. Give

418

me an hour."

When Thunder was gone, Logan moved across the room to stand in front of the opened window. He gazed at the rolling hills around him, the mountains in the distance. The Sandovals had carved an empire out for themselves by shedding a lot of sweat and blood. They worked hard, and they had much to show for it.

Logan was surprised to find himself thinking of settling down, of marrying and raising a family—his and Brenna's children. He dreaded telling Brenna that he was leaving again, and not necessarily because he dreaded her tearful, perhaps angry reaction. He didn't want to leave her because he loved her; he wanted to be with her. He wanted to hold her close in his arms—never to let her go.

For just a moment he had contemplated telling Thunder that he didn't want to meet with the Comanches; he didn't want to infiltrate the Comancheros. They knew where the hideout was located. He could tell Houston and let him dispatch a band of rangers. But he had gone too far to turn back now. He also had Thunder to think about. And he had promised Houston!

Logan quickly packed his gear and slapped his hat on his head. His bedroll and saddlebags over his shoulder, he strode down the hall to Brenna's room.

When she opened the door, she took one look at him and said, "You're leaving?"

He saw pain darken her eyes; he saw the forced smile. Moving into the room, he closed the door and slung his belongings to the floor. As he reached for her, he said, "I must go."

"I know," Brenna whispered. "I'd just hoped that it would be later, not sooner."

They clutched each other tightly.

"I want you to understand," Logan said, "I'm not

going in search of ghosts from the past. Your love has washed all bitterness and hatred from me."

He felt her fingers as they dug into his back; he knew her pain and anguish; he felt them, too. "I can't bear to leave you again, my darling. You're more precious to me than anything or anyone. But I must finish this job for Houston. So much is at stake. If there were any other way, I wouldn't go."

Brenna pulled her head back and looked into his face. Tears welling in her eyes, a smile on her trembling lips, she said, "I do understand, my darling. If you didn't go, you wouldn't be the man I love. If you didn't, you'd hate yourself one day and may come to hate me." Her lips trembled as she smiled. "All of Texas—in fact, the whole United States—is depending on you, Mr. MacDougald."

"Right now, Brenna Garvey Allen," he said, "you're the only one who counts. You're the one who fills my life with meaning; you give me reason for doing what I must do."

This was the confession Brenna had long awaited. Joy sang through Brenna's veins. "We'll have tonight, my darling."

She lifted her face as he lowered his, their lips meeting in an urgent kiss. When the kiss ended, he picked her up in his arms and carried her to the bed. He knew Thunder was waiting, but for one time in his life without qualms he pushed duty aside for his own pleasure . . . and for Brenna's.

Chapter Twenty-Five

Late that same afternoon as they sat in the patio, Don Sebastian said, "I'm sorry Señor MacDougald had to leave so suddenly. He is a fine man."

"I shall miss him," Francisca lamented. "It is nice to have someone around who can best Joaquin at a few things. Keeps him from being so arrogant."

Joaquin pulled a face at his sister, then truly grimaced as he moved his leg the wrong way.

Francisca laughed. "You won't be baiting a bull for a good while, Joaquin Roman."

Doña Anna laughed and joined with her daughter in teasing Joaquin. "He won't be baiting anyone with that broken leg."

"Since I have to sit around and keep my foot propped up, Papa," Joaquin said, "I think I shall request a seller's permit from the governor for myself, and I can sell Brenna's goods."

Don Sebastian thought for a moment before he nodded his head. "You could do that," he agreed. "You won't be any use to us around the hacienda until you can walk and ride again."

"Are you going to use Roger, Papa?" Francisca asked.

Don Sebastian smiled fondly at his daughter. *"Sí, mi hija,* I shall train Roger to be a *vaquero.* He is a quick learner."

Lupe raced onto the patio. "You have a visitor, Don Sebastian. Roberto Onega. Many soldiers came with him."

"Does Vicente know?" Don Sebastian asked.

"Sí," Lupe answered, *"el gran vaquero* knows. He is with Señor Roberto now."

Don Sebastian nodded. "Bring Roberto out here," he instructed. "He shall join us for dinner." When Lupe disappeared, Don Sebastian turned to Brenna. "Now we shall know if you are going to be able to sell your goods or not. I'm sure Roberto brings word from the governor."

His hat under his arm, Roberto soon appeared in the courtyard. He greeted Doña Anna first, then Don Sebastian. Next he flashed Francisca a large smile. "Hello, Francisca," he said. "How are you doing today?" Brenna he ignored altogether.

"I'm doing fine, Roberto," Francisca answered with a smile. "Joaquin is the one who is not doing so fine."

Roberto looked at the splints on his leg. "What happened?" he asked.

"El coleo," Francisca murmured, her eyes laughing.

"Sit down, Roberto," Don Sebastian said in English, so Brenna could understand the conversation. "Would you care for a glass of wine?"

"I would love to have a glass of wine, Don Sebastian," Roberto replied in Spanish, pointedly ignoring Don Sebastian's example, "but I cannot. I'm afraid that I have bad news for you."

"What kind of news?" Don Sebastian asked. "And please, Roberto, answer in English. I wish Señora Allen to understand all that we say. There is no need for the endless waste of time in translating."

Roberto wasn't pleased with the request, but he nodded as he laid his hat in the nearby chair.

"I have come to arrest Señora Allen and take her into custody."

"What?" Brenna leaped to her feet.

"What is the meaning of this?" Don Sebastian asked. "I thought we had settled this issue the other night."

"Señor Peyton Alexander has suddenly departed Santa Fe," Roberto announced. "However, before he left, he signed a document in which he confessed that he and Señora Allen were conspiring to lead a rebellion against the authorized government of Santa Fe."

"I don't believe this!" Don Sebastian exclaimed. He turned to Brenna. "Tell me this is not so."

Roberto unbuttoned his jacket and reached into an inner pocket. He withdrew a small leather pouch, which he opened to extract several papers. "This is a letter from Clarence Childers, a merchant in Houston, Texas," he said as he spread the letter on the table and thumped it with his forefinger. "If you will look, you can see that it was written in coded phrases. Alexander has translated it in the margin."

Brenna rushed to the table to stand beside Don Sebastian; Joaquin pushed to his feet and limped behind her. The three of them looked at the paper.

"This is a trick," Brenna insisted. "Mr. Alexander would not do such a thing to me."

"To save his own hide, he did," Roberto said. "The governor promised him amnesty if he confessed, and he did. He told us the entire story. He also admitted to the governor," Roberto went on, "that he had given Señora Allen a letter to take back to her government in Texas."

Logan and Joaquin were right. Alexander was worse than a scoundrel, and she was caught in a trap of her own making. Would she never cease placing trust in the wrong people?

"Can you prove that Childers's letter was really

written in coded language?" Brenna asked.

"We do not have to prove that, Señora," Roberto returned. "We have Alexander's word for it."

"That's all you have, and that is not enough evidence to convict me of a crime," Brenna challenged.

"Ah," Roberto droned, "but there is the matter of Alexander's reply. According to him, his letter was not written in the agreed-upon code."

"Is there such a letter?" Brenna taunted daringly. "You certainly found nothing of the kind the other night when you thoroughly searched my room."

"No," the soldier answered, "we didn't. But that is of little consequence now. We have Alexander's written confession and the letter which you delivered to him. That is evidence enough for the governor. You are under arrest, Señora. I am to take you back to Santa Fe, and from there you will be taken to Mexico City to stand trial. Your goods will be confiscated and will become property of the government."

Don Sebastian looked across the table at Brenna. "Did you deliver such a letter to Alexander?" he demanded.

Brenna nodded, but Joaquin answered. "I was with her when she carried it to him, Papa. But she's innocent. She had no idea what the coded content was ... if the content was indeed coded as Armijo suggests." Joaquin turned to her. "Were you aware of any hidden message, *chiquita?*"

Brenna didn't want to lie, but neither did she wish to implicate the Sandovals. "I did not read the letter," she answered. "I was told that it was a letter of introduction from Childers to Alexander."

"See!" Joaquin exclaimed. "She is innocent."

"Roberto, you and your soldiers may leave. I will bring the señora in to Santa Fe," Don Sebastian said.

"I wish I could, sir," Roberto answered, but his tone

424

of voice and his expression declared otherwise, "but I cannot. Governor Armijo gave me explicit orders to return with both the señora and her property." Roberto extracted more papers from the pouch. "Here are the official papers of arrest, Don Sebastian."

Joaquin jerked the papers from Roberto's hands. He read the charges, and he looked at the official seal on the bottom of the sheet. "Is there nothing we can do?" he asked his father.

Don Sebastian took the papers from Joaquin and read them. "At the present there is nothing. Our only recourse is to appeal the case in Mexico City."

"Then we shall," Joaquin declared. "I'll not let Manuel Armijo get his slimy hands on Brenna."

"Don Joaquin"—Roberto drew to his full height and reverted to Spanish—"you are forgetting that I am a soldier of Governor Manuel Armijo, a duly appointed official of the government of Mexico."

"I am forgetting nothing," Joaquin said. "Now you and your soldiers ride back to town and tell Manuel Armijo that we are not turning Brenna Allen over to him."

"You are defying an order of your government, sir?"

"I am defying the order of Manuel Armijo. I'm not convinced yet, sir, that Manuel Armijo is an official of my government, and rest assured my government has its seat in Mexico City." Joaquin was so angry he forgot his injured leg and rested his weight on it. He howled with pain and quickly fell into the nearest chair.

"You will leave, Roberto," Don Sebastian said quietly. "Tell Manuel that I will come to the Palacio tomorrow to discuss the charges against Señora Allen. You may also tell him that I am appealing the case to a higher authority in Mexico City."

"I will not leave without the Texan or her wagons."

Don Sebastian clapped his hands, and a dozen

vaqueros rushed into the patio. The *gran vaquero* walked up to Roberto. In Spanish the *hacendado* issued the command: "Escort Roberto Onega and the soldiers back to town. Forcibly if you must, and see that no one returns tonight to disturb me. Señora Allen's wagons are to be guarded."

Vicente caught Roberto by the upper arm, but the soldier jerked himself loose. "I shall leave," he said, his eyes smoldering with hatred, "but I shall return, gentlemen. All of you are interfering with the working of the government."

"Roberto," Don Sebastian said, "you try so hard to bark like a dog, but you yap like a puppy. Now get out of here and give me no more of your idle threats."

"We shall see, Don Sebastian, if they are idle."

"Come in," Don Sebastian called.

Brenna opened the door and walked into the candlelit room. She was glad to see that the *hacendado* was by himself. Hoping to find him alone, she had waited until after everyone else had retired for the night to come to his study.

When Don Sebastian saw Brenna, he laid his pencil down and immediately stood. "Señora Allen," he said, "why are you up so late?"

"I need to talk with you," Brenna said as she closed the door.

Don Sebastian moved from behind his desk. "You are worried, no?"

"I am worried," she admitted, "but I also have a confession to make."

"Sit down, please," he said. He walked to a table near the window and poured both of them a glass of wine. "So you wish to make a confession, do you?" His smile and soft tone were indulgent.

426

Brenna nodded and gratefully took the glass that he held out to her.

"Perhaps I already know what you wish to say to me," he said.

Brenna jerked her head up and stared at him.

"You knew, or at least you suspected, that the letter you delivered to Señor Alexander was more than a mere introduction of one merchant to another."

"Not quite as strong as I knew, and not as weak as I suspected," Brenna admitted.

Don Sebastian nodded. "What you did was wrong, but I understand your motives. Because of your education in citizenship and freedom, you Texans are an impulsive lot. You wish to spread your good tidings of liberty across the continent whether the inhabitants are ready for it or not. You are not content to wait and to work within an institution. You must create your own institutions."

"Do you not want liberty for yourself and your people, Don Sebastian?" Brenna asked.

He walked to the window and stood, looking into the shadowed garden. "Yes, I desire it with all my heart, but I wish to use other methods than those employed by the Texans. All I am is of Mexico, my heritage, my language, my culture. I do not wish to sever my life-string. I wish to work through the institution to bring the same political changes to my people." He turned to her. "I suppose that is hard for you to understand."

"It is," she answered, "but now that I've met you and been around your people, I understand that the decision is yours to make. I can't force liberty on you; I can only hope that our example can influence you to have the same thing . . . to fight for it if necessary."

"You think us cowards?" he asked.

"No, I just can't understand your being content with an antiquated government manipulated by the few to serve them, and not the many."

"I'm not content, señora, and I am working to bring about the necessary change. Now"—he swallowed the last of his wine—"I think all of us should be in bed. I am riding to Santa Fe tomorrow to discuss your arrest with Armijo. With God's blessing I shall settle this matter before it reaches the higher courts in Mexico City."

"Please, Don Sebastian," Brenna said, "sit down. I have something else I wish to discuss with you."

"Can it not wait until tomorrow?"

Brenna reached into her pocket. "No, I want you to know it now. It may influence your actions tomorrow." She held the letter out to him. "I accepted a letter from Alexander and agreed to deliver it to Clarence Childers in Houston, Texas." Brenna looked closely at the elder Sandoval, but she saw no censure or condemnation on his countenance.

Without a word, he set the glass on his desk and reached for the letter. While he unfolded it, Brenna continued to talk.

"As you can see," she said, "it's military in nature and advocates the overthrow of the present authorities in Santa Fe and Taos. Names, dates, and places are listed."

"You are a spy!" Don Sebastian exclaimed. "You are working with the government of Texas!"

Don Sebastian's accusations hurt Brenna. She had come to love and respect him; she didn't wish him or his family harm. Neither did she wish to lower herself in his estimations. But in order to live with herself, she had to be truthful with him.

"In the beginning, when I first decided to come to Santa Fe and to deliver Childers's letter," she said, "I didn't think of myself as a spy. I, like all Texans, believed Santa Fe and Taos to be part of our republic. I also believed it was my duty to undermine foreign authority in these cities, which in this case was the Mexican government as symbolized by Armijo."

"And now?" the elder Sandoval asked. He dropped Alexander's letter on his desk.

"Now I feel like a spy without a country for which she is spying. I have taken advantage of your friendship; I've betrayed your trust and confidence in me, and I may have endangered my country's future."

Don Sebastian studied the woman sitting in front of his desk. Her face was pale, her eyes dark with worry.

"What did you propose to tell your president when you arrived in Texas?" he asked kindly.

Brenna laughed bitterly. "I'm not working for the president, Don Sebastian. He has no idea that I'm here or what my ulterior motive for coming was. To be honest, I'm not working for anyone. Childers wrote the letter, but he didn't send me. Originally he gave it to my husband to deliver."

"Then you are not duly authorized by your government to engage in spying?"

"No, I took it upon myself to bring the letter after my husband died. I guess I thought I would singlehandedly bring about a revolution of independence in Santa Fe!"

"What do you think now?"

"I think you and your people must decide what you want out of your government and work toward that end. I was prepared to say this to the Imperialists when I returned home."

The *hacendado* picked up the letter and handed it to Brenna. "This is yours, Señora Allen. Do with it as you wish."

Brenna took the paper and looked at it; she raised her head and looked at Don Sebastian. "I don't understand."

"You were misinformed when you came to our city;

now you know. I trust you to take the correct report back to your people." He pushed away from the desk. "Now we must go to bed. I have many things to do before I leave for Santa Fe."

"After I've confessed, you're still going to defend me?"

"Sí," he said, "I am going to defend you. You are not a spy, and your government is not plotting the overthrow of our government." He laughed. "At least, not that you know of." He laid his arm over her shoulder. "Will you go to bed now?"

Brenna smiled and nodded her head. "I will, but first I must do something." She walked to the desk and held the edge of the letter over the candle. A flame burst into the air as the paper caught on fire, and soon nothing remained but the curled-up ashes, which Brenna brushed into a wastebasket.

"Now there is no letter," Don Sebastian announced.

"How do you know that I am not playing a game with you?" Brenna asked. "I could have copied the letter."

Don Sebastian blew out the candles on one candelabra; the other he picked up. "I know and understand people, Brenna Allen. You are not a deceitful person. Misguided by your passions perhaps, but not willfully deceitful. You're honest, and I trust you."

"Thank you, Don Sebastian." Then she asked, "What will your family think of me?"

"This is our secret, my dear." He caught her elbow in his hand and guided her to the door. "Now, let's get some sleep, shall we?"

Chapter Twenty-Six

No one would believe it was only June, Brenna thought as she looked at the dry, desolate country that lay between Santa Fe and Mexico City. Miles of rugged terrain; death and desolation more frequent than water. She caught the wet material of her blouse between her fingers and pulled it from her body; her riding jacket had long been discarded because of the oppressive heat. Although the Mexican riding skirt was comfortable and allowed her more freedom of movement than a dress, Brenna longed for her trousers. They were cooler and less cumbersome. She untied the bandanna around her neck and wiped the perspiration from her face; then she plunged the linen scarf into her opened neckline and daubed at the moistness.

Her greatest desire for years had been to make the lucrative trade circle: Texas to Santa Fe to Chihuahua to Durango and back to San Antonio. Soon she would have reached all her destinations except San Antonio. She wondered if she'd ever see Texas again. Armijo had been unrelenting in his charges; he had shown no mercy; he had granted no leniency. Her only hope lay in Mexico City—and she didn't hope for justice, only mercy and the influence of a powerful family.

Ahead she saw Joaquin astride his Arabian. His leg

431

was still in splints, but that had not kept him from traveling with her. Huberto Botello, one of his *vaqueros,* rode scout, and Roger Hollis was captain of the dragoons—a military unit made up of *vaqueros* and Hollis's men. Behind her trundled eight freight haulers—five of them hers; three of them belonging to Don Sebastian—and the large, ornate carriage belonging to the Sandovals, but no one rode inside. Brenna and Francisca much preferred their horses.

"Do not look so glum," Francisca said as she pulled her horse abreast Brenna's. "The Sandoval de Josefina y Mariano de Madrid family is influential in Mexico; my father and Joaquin shall have these charges against you dismissed. I promise."

"I'm not worried about myself," Brenna replied. "I'm concerned because I have involved your family in this. This is my problem, not yours."

"No, it is ours also," Francisca returned. She had no idea that Brenna had ever received a letter from Alexander. Don Sebastian had been true to his word; he told no one of Brenna's confession. "Armijo is a servant of our government, and he is the one who is pressing charges on the basis of little evidence. Our honor demands that my father and Joaquin exonerate you." Francisca laid a hand on Brenna's lower arm. "Please do not worry. Everything will be all right."

Brenna could not restrain the bittersweet smile that tugged her lips. "I'm doing what I always dreamed of doing," she said, "but the circumstances have changed."

"We will have fun in Mexico City," Francisca said, and proceeded to regale Brenna with delightful stories of the capital.

Brenna only half listened; the other part of her scanned the horizon. She pondered her destiny; she pondered Logan's destiny. She could only hope that he

432

had been more successful in completing his task than she had hers. If he knew her fate, surely he would come to her rescue. Surely!

"Indians!" Huberto Botello shouted as he crested the hill, his horse at full gallop. "Hundreds of them, Don Joaquin."

Brenna didn't speak Spanish, but she understood the warning, as did everyone else on the wagon train. Before Joaquin yelled the command, the teamsters were turning the vehicles into the circle; soon everyone was cloistered within the wagon fort. Before Brenna knew what was happening, hundreds of Indians converged to surround them. It seemed that for each one she killed, two more appeared. Men dropped to the ground all around her. The attackers relentlessly circled the wagon, their shouts filling the air, their arrows volleying through the wagons. Finally they withdrew.

The sudden quiet was as disconcerting to the travelers as had been the attack. Brenna and Francisca tended the wounded; Roger raced around the compound and gathered the ammunition. Joaquin assessed the damages and determined their status.

"Not enough ammunition to stay another attack," Roger reported.

Joaquin muttered expletives under his breath. Because of his leg, he was practically immobile, and he was angry and frustrated. Brenna and Francisca were his responsibility, and he was ineffective as their protector. His men lay dead around him.

"I have never seen so many Indians at one time," Roger said. "They seem to be everywhere. What are we going to do?"

As if in answer to Roger's questions, a brave crested the ridge, a white cloth dangling from the end of the lance he held up. In answer Joaquin hobbled through the wagons and stood outside the circle of protection. He tied a handkerchief to the end of his rifle and waved it through the air several times.

The brave slowly approached and, when he was within hearing distance, said in Spanish, "We will bargain with you, *Mexicano*. We want the women, the wagons, and all the animals. The men can go free."

"I hear you," Joaquin said. "I will think about it."

The Indian drew a line in the dirt; then he threw his spear. The blade sank into the earth with a thud, and the shaft vibrated. "You have until the shadow touches the line. If we do not have your answer before then, we promise all of you death." He turned and rode off.

As soon as Joaquin was inside the fort, he repeated the conversation to Roger, then said, "We must get the women out of this. I do not want either of them to become prisoners of the Comanches." Joaquin smiled thinly and pointed. "I want you to take three horses and the women and hide in those boulders. When the battle is over—long after the battle is over—take them back to the hacienda. My father will know what to do."

"I can't leave you out here to face them," Roger said. "Let someone else do it."

"You have no alternative, *mi amigo*," Joaquin returned. "I am the wagon master, and I have the authority. I trust the women only to you. Now get Brenna and Francisca, and bring them to me."

Neither Brenna nor Francisca were happy with Joaquin's plan. Both of them protested.

"You need us, Joaquin," Brenna argued. "I can fight as good as any of the men whom you have."

"I do not deny that, *chiquita*," Joaquin agreed. "I will even go further and say that you outfight many of my men, but without ammunition, none of us is going to do much fighting. And we soon will be out of

434

ammunition. Please, don't make me resort to force. Go with Roger."

"I'm not going," Brenna said.

"Nor me," Francisca chimed in.

"Yes," Joaquin answered, "both of you are going! Without you I have a chance of bartering with the Indians and saving the lives of my men. Perhaps the Indians will take the animals and wagons and let us go free. It's evident they don't want prisoners."

"You don't have a chance," Brenna said.

"I probably don't," Joaquin returned, "but the men have a slim one without you; none with you and Francisca here."

Thirty minutes later, Roger, the women, and horses were hidden in the boulders. When the Indians topped the ridge later, they watched Joaquin raise a white flag and wave it through the air. Slowly the line of braves moved toward the wagons, finally to stop within speaking distance.

"We wish to surrender," Joaquin called out. "We will give you all our animals and wagons."

One of the braves, who wore a buffalo headdress, rode in close. "What are you called?" he asked in Spanish.

Joaquin hobbled across the wagon tongue. "Joaquin Roman Sandoval. Who are you?"

"You are the chief?" the Indian asked.

Joaquin nodded.

The Indian stared at him for a long while before he identified himself as Animal Talker. He looked inside the compound. "What about the women?"

"I have no women," Joaquin answered.

"You lie!" Animal Talker exclaimed. "You have two women with you. I want them." He nudged his horse so that he pushed Joaquin against the wagon; he pressed his lance into Joaquin's chest. "I will kill you a slow, tortuous death, *Mexicano,* unless you let me have the women."

"I don't have any women," Joaquin said the second time.

Animal Talker yanked his lance back, raised it in the air, and swished the front of Joaquin's shirt to leave a long red slash across his chest. "Where are the women?"

"No," Francisca cried and lunged forward, "I cannot let them do this to Joaquin. I must go to him." She started to run out of the rocks, but Roger caught and held her. "You can't go," he said. "Joaquin knows what he's doing."

"That murdering beast won't stop until he has killed Joaquin," Francisca sobbed. "He knows that Brenna and I are traveling with the train, and he wants us. He said he would let all of you go free if he could have us."

"He's lying," Roger said. "You can't believe him."

"Where are the women?" Again Animal Talker dragged his lance over Joaquin's chest, crisscrossing the other cut. "The sign of your god," he mocked. "Perhaps you better start calling on him for help, *Mexicano.* He is the only one who can save you . . . if even he can!"

"Please let me go," Francisca whimpered. "Please." Francisca fought against Roger, but he refused to let her go. Tears ran down her cheeks as she begged.

Brenna didn't know how much more she could take of this. Logan's word rang in her ears to mock her: *The price of trailblazing is high!* How many were going to die because of her?

"I will ask you one more time, *Mexicano:* Where are the women? If you do not tell me, I shall kill you."

"He's going to kill Joaquin," Francisca cried. "You must save him, Roger!"

Animal Talker pulled his lance back. Before he could release it, Brenna raced from her hiding place, screaming as she ran, "Don't kill him! Dear God, please don't kill him." She threw herself across Joaquin and begged the chief. "Take me, but let him go."

"Go get the other woman," Animal Talker commanded several of his braves, and pointed in the direction from which Brenna had just come. When the braves dragged Francisca and Roger out of the rocks, Animal Talker said to other of his warriors, "Tie the men together. We will take them with us." The Comanche chief then looked at Joaquin. "I am a man of honor, and I would have let you and your men go free, *Mexicano,* but now I must take you with us."

"No!" Joaquin lunged at the chief, but his leg threw him off balance and he fell. He pushed up and braced on his elbows. "You cannot do that. I am the one who lied. Take me, but set my men free. They are warriors, like the men who follow you. They take my orders and do my bidding. They have committed no wrong, Animal Talker, but have a chief who made an error in judgment."

"You are a brave leader, Joaquin Roman Sandoval," Animal Talker said, "but I do not listen to your words."

Balancing his weight on his uninjured side, Joaquin rose to his feet to lunge again at Animal Talker. The chief pulled back his lance and with all his strength struck the *Mexicano* on the head, knocking him unconscious.

Brenna's and Francisca's screams merged into one; they struggled with their captors, but the Comanches held them. Animal Talker urged his horse to where the two women stood. "Tie them up," he commanded in Comanche, "and put them in a wagon. Make sure they are not harmed. Put the *Mexicano* in another wagon. Tie the men together. They shall walk." He smiled at his warriors. "Today the Great Spirit has been good to us. We have captured many prizes, and we can buy many guns."

Bound and gagged, Brenna and Francisca were shoved into one of the wagons. Looking out the back, they saw two braves toss Joaquin into another wagon. They bound Roger and the other men together with thongs and herded them as if they were animals. Roger looked up, smiled at Francisca, and winked. A brave who saw the silent communication knocked Roger to his knees and raced to the wagon to lower the flap.

As they traveled into West Texas deep into Comanchería, Brenna lost count of time. Days merged together as one long ordeal. The Indians did them no physical harm, but they leered at them and tore their clothing to expose their bodies. Roughly they hauled them out of the wagons when it was time to eat or relieve themselves; as roughly they returned them at travel time. Never did they see Joaquin and the men only at a distance.

Early one morning they eventually arrived at the village. Comanche women ran out to greet the returning braves and to inspect the prisoners. Joaquin was jerked out of the wagon, no thought given to his head wound or his broken leg. When he could not move fast enough to join his companions, the Comanches jabbed him with their lances. The men were herded to a large tepee and put under guard; Brenna and Francisca were pulled out of the freight haulers and shoved aside as the women inspected the goods. Then the wagons were routed to the other side of the village, near a large platform.

The women concentrated on Brenna and Francisca. They walked around the two, touching and poking at them as if they were pieces of meat to be selected for a meal. They talked and laughed; they spat on them; they

438

tore at their clothing. Brenna had never suffered such humiliation in all her life, but she refused to give the Indians the satisfaction of knowing it. Tears ran down Brenna's cheeks, but she didn't cry. She stood erect and squared her shoulders; she glared into their mocking visages.

"Don't cry," she commanded Francisca. "Don't let them know they're upsetting you."

"How can you act as if nothing is happening?" Francisca cried. "We are standing here, our clothes torn into shreds, our bodies more exposed than covered, and all of these . . . these Indians are gaping at us."

"I don't think," said Brenna, striving for a calmness that she really didn't feel at the moment, "our state of undress affects them the way it does us."

One Comanche woman grabbed Brenna's braid and tugged on it. She motioned for the white woman to follow her. Another Indian shoved Francisca in the opposite direction.

"Brenna," Francisca screamed as they hauled her away, "make them take me with you. Don't leave me alone!"

Brenna turned, but several more women circled around her. Grasping her arms and shoulders, they dragged her through the village and finally threw her into a tepee. Dazed, Brenna lay on the floor for a few minutes; then she moved to the door and pushed the flap aside. Planted outside was an Indian guard. He kicked at her and growled something in Comanche. She dropped the piece of leather and crawled back into the shadowed interior.

The next few hours seemed longer than a lifetime to Brenna. Exhausted and weak, she finally lay down and closed her eyes, but her thoughts were too troubled for sleep. The same questions—questions that had no answers—plagued her. What were the Comanches going to do with Joaquin and Roger and the rest of the men?

She remembered Gabby's words: *"What they can do to a man ain't a pretty sight, Brendy gal!"*

Torture them!

Logan had warned her! *The price of trailblazing is high! The price of trailblazing is high!* Louder and louder the words grew until Brenna thought she would scream; they tormented her; they haunted her. She alone was responsible for what was happening. She had endangered the lives of Joaquin and Roger and Francisca and the men who had traveled with them.

She must save them. She must!

She didn't ponder hers and Francisca's fate. She knew what would happen to them. Logan had told her long ago what was happening to women prisoners, and since the Indians had not violated their bodies, she could only assume they were to be traded to the Comancheros and then sold into prostitution in Mexico.

Brenna wanted to, but she couldn't cry; she had no tears. She thought about escaping, but she didn't know where to go. Furthermore, she couldn't leave Francisca. Brenna wanted to be brave, but courage had deserted her.

She wanted Logan!

Eventually the guard set a bowl of food and a pouch of water inside the door. Using her fingers, Brenna ate the bits of meat and mush. Then she drank the water. Afterward she lay down again and finally fell into a fitful sleep.

She was awakened in late afternoon—judging by the position of the sun—when a woman came into the tepee and shook her shoulder. Brenna sat up and looked into a face that was filled with hatred. The woman motioned for Brenna to follow. Again she was led up the main street, only to be vilified and abused. Some of the women and children spat on her; others threw dirt and pebbles at her.

In a clearing on the outskirts of the village, she saw hundreds of braves seated on the ground around a large platform. She lifted her head and saw Francisca standing in the center of the stage, her tangled hair hanging loose about her shoulders. The sleeves of her dress were ripped from the bodice, hanging only by threads; her gown was dirty and rumpled. Her head was bowed. Even though she and Francisca were in the same predicament, Brenna's grief was for the other woman rather than herself.

The Comanche led Brenna through the crowd, up the steps, and onto the platform. Then she turned and walked away, leaving the two women alone. They turned to each other and embraced.

"Brenna," Francisca said, clinging tightly, "I am so happy to see you. I didn't know what is going to happen to us." Her eyes brimming with tears, she pulled back and looked into Brenna's face. "I am so frightened."

"Don't cry," Brenna commanded rather sharply.

"You are not afraid?" Francisca whispered.

"Yes," Brenna answered, "I am so frightened that I'm quaking, but we mustn't let the Comanches know it. To know they can manipulate the emotions of their prisoners gives them a sense of power." She smiled thinly. "Now put on a brave front."

"I can't," Francisca said.

"Of course you can," Brenna returned impatiently. "They enjoy seeing us whimper and beg. Don't give them an ounce of pleasure. Think of how proud Roger will be of you."

"What will they do to Roger and Joaquin?" Francisca asked, fresh tears spilling down her cheeks.

"I cannot begin to guess the reasoning of the Comanches," Brenna replied. "We must wait and see."

"The waiting is hard, mi amiga. I can imagine all sorts of things, horrible punishments—"

Kindly, Brenna interrupted. "Think only on good things," she said. "Think about your wedding with Roger. The celebration. The eggs filled with cologne which you break over the guests' heads."

"Is that the way you do it, Brenna?" Francisca asked. "You think of Logan, and these thoughts give you strength to do that which you think you cannot do?"

"Yes"—Brenna's voice was rough—"I think of Logan."

If only he were here, he would rescue them. He would know what to do. He could handle the Comanches; Logan MacDougald could handle anything.

Chapter Twenty-Seven

As Brenna looked over the sea of faces, her gaze swept beyond the Comanches to a group of approaching riders. For the most part, they were a hardened and coarse lot. Their clothes were dirty and worn, their hair and beards unkempt.

One of them, apparently the leader, was different. He was clean and refined. He was distinguished-looking—tall and lean. His graying hair was cut short and combed back from his face; he was dressed in black from the hat he held in his hand to the highly polished boots he wore. The bandanna around his neck was black silk, the material shimmering in the morning sunlight.

He turned, and Brenna saw the puffy scar that zigzagged down the side of his face. Inadvertently she gasped. The man's eyes, a dark, filmy brown, collided with hers in time to see her shock. He stared for a second; then his lips stretched into a thin, sinister smile. He lifted his hand and lightly ran his forefinger down the scar; then he swept his hand through the air and donned his hat.

He walked to the platform and ascended the steps. When he stood in front of Brenna and Francisca, he swept his hat off and bowed low. "Good morning, ladies," he said in English.

"Who are you?" Brenna demanded.

"Oswald Lattimer," the man replied as he straightened and replaced his hat, "at your service, madam."

"Have you come to rescue us, señor?" Francisca asked in a teary voice.

Lattimer turned his attention to the lovely mexicana. "Sí, señorita, I have come to rescue you." He reached out and lightly outlined Francisca's face. When she jerked her head away from his touch, he laughed.

The sound wasn't warm and humorous; it was dark and chilling.

"You are feisty, little one. I like that. I have never liked docile, complacent women."

"My father is Don Sebastian Sandoval de Josefina y Mariano de Madrid," Francisca sputtered indignantly. "He is a wealthy man, señor. He will pay you well to return me unharmed to him. And if anything should happen to me, he will kill you."

Again the man laughed. Again he ran his finger over the scar on his cheek. "I know who your father is, my dear," he replied. "I also know who you are. You are Doña Francisca Marina Sandoval de Josefina y Mariano de Madrid. I am not a mercenary man, señorita; therefore, I do not wish to be recompensed by your father for returning you. Also I must confess that your good governor has paid me well to see that none of you Sandovals arrive in Mexico with your reports of his corruption."

"What are you saying?" Francisca demanded. "Are you going to kill us?"

"Alas," he sighed, "I must. His hand moved toward her face a second time; again Francisca dodged the touch.

"What are you, señor? A murderer?"

"I am a trader."

"You're a Comanchero!" Francisca's exclamation

444

was barely a whisper.

"Sí"—he shrugged expressive—"I'm a Comanchero." His obscure eyes raked over her young, beautiful body. "I trade with the Comanches." He moved his hand and captured her chin. "And I am trading with them for you, Francisca. I want you. I want to taste every inch of your luscious body."

Both women reacted at the same time.

Francisca jerked her head and whimpered, "No."

Brenna lunged at Lattimer and pounded his chest with her fists. "Leave her alone!"

Lattimer turned Francisca loose only long enough to knock Brenna to the floor. "If you know what is good for you, Mrs. Allen," he grunted as he kicked her in the ribs, "you will refrain from making me angry."

"Please, señor," Francisca cried, "do not hurt her. Please return us to my father."

Lattimer's hand flew to Francisca's face again, and his fingers painfully bit into her tender flesh. "It's either me or these Comanches, my dear, and I should think I'm the one you would choose."

Brenna was dizzy with pain as she struggled to her knees. She folded her arms across her midriff and clutched her ribs. "Why not take an experienced woman instead of a mere girl?" she goaded.

Lattimer laughed and looked down at Brenna. "You are a courageous woman, Mrs. Allen. I must admire your spunk and tenacity. But I have other plans for you. I want this ripe little plum who has never been taken by a man. I want to enjoy all her virginal delights."

Francisca's face flamed with mortification, and she twisted her head, but Lattimer wouldn't release her chin. He leaned over and planted hot, wet lips on hers. When he finally released her, Francisca spit in his face. Lattimer drew back his hand and slung it with all his might. He slapped her so hard, she fell to the floor and blood trickled from the corner of her mouth.

"You will learn how to please me, señorita," he hissed through narrowed lips. "I promise you!" He turned and walked down the steps and disappeared into the crowd.

Brenna moved to where Francisca lay. "Are you all right?" she asked.

"I'm fine," Francisca replied, her voice strong and even. "How are you, *mi amiga?*"

Brenna managed a weak smile. "I hurt bad. I don't know if he broke the ribs or just bruised me."

Dimly, as the two consoled and encouraged one another, they heard a Comanche—Animal Talker—talking in the background. He and Lattimer were together, engaged in deep, serious conversation.

Brenna moved so that she could see the men. Although they spoke Comanche, she could tell they were arguing. Lattimer talked; Animal Talker shook his head vigorously, the polished horns of the headdress gleaming in the firelight. Soon Lattimer gestured and shouted. Animal Talker smiled smugly. The more Lattimer shouted, the wider the Comanche smiled until he threw back his head and guffawed. When he caught his breath, he yelled something to his braves, and they joined him in raucous laughter. The chief turned and walked away to leave an angry Comanchero standing behind him. The scar, puffy and pink, stood out in relief against Lattimer's furious, ashen face.

Animal Talker turned to his people and spoke. A flurry of activity beset the village. Braves scattered in all directions, soon to return with the eight freight haulers in tow. Some pulled the wagons, while others pushed. Soon the vehicles stood in a circle in front of the platform. Corralled in the center were all the animals the Indians had taken from Brenna and Joaquin.

Brenna and Francisca huddled together in the middle of the platform, wondering what was going to happen next. Night quickly fell, but Animal Talker was in no hurry to begin his trading with the Comancheros. He sat down on a large buffalo blanket and shouted more commands. Brenna watched as the braves built a huge bonfire, the light arcing over the platform and the wagons.

Eventually he rose and walked to the platform. He stood, his back to the women. He spoke in Spanish for the Comancheros and gestured in sign language for his people. "Tonight, my brothers, the Comanches, we have gathered to trade with the Comancheros. The Great Spirit has been good to us. The winds have blown in our direction. We have many white warriors and two women." He turned and swept his hand toward Brenna and Francisca. "Wagons filled with goods and many horses and mules and oxen. All these things the *Mexicanos* want. The Comancheros are willing to give us what we wish in return because they wish to trade with the mexicanos. Scar-Face has promised us the guns like the Texas Rangers use—the ones that shoot six times without having to be reloaded or broken apart for the reloading."

As Animal Talker spoke, Francisca quietly interpreted for Brenna. The two of them saw the Comanches nod their heads at their chief's words; they heard the murmurs of agreement.

"Have you brought the guns as you promised, Scar-Face?" Animal Talker asked.

Lattimer stood and walked to the platform to stand beside the Comanche chief. He followed Animal Talker's example; he talked both in Spanish and sign language. "I have traded with you, my Comanche

447

brothers, for many seasons. Always I have kept my word. I told you that I would give you guns for women and trade goods. I have spoken. So be it. But first, I must know: What have you done with Don Joaquin Sandoval?"

"I have him," Animal Talker said. "His fate rests in your hands."

"Good," Lattimer murmured. "If I have both him and the girl as hostages and bait, I can lure the good don and doña from their stronghold in Santa Fe. Killing them will be no problem." Lattimer smiled and nodded his head; then he clapped his hands. "Bring the guns."

Even as Lattimer spoke, a horse galloped up to the platform; the rider stopped short, dismounted, and rushed up the steps to where the Comanchero stood. He leaned his head close to Lattimer's and spoke in an undertone—so low that neither woman could hear.

"We don't have the guns," the man said.

"What do you mean?" Lattimer demanded.

"Shipment has been delayed."

"When can I expect them?"

The man shrugged. Lattimer's face twisted, and his hands slowly fell to his side.

"Is something wrong, my friend?" Animal Talker asked, a sarcastic tinge to his voice.

"I have to wait for my guns," Lattimer said. "We will feast and celebrate tonight. We will deal when the guns arrive."

"I say we deal tonight," a male voice called from the shadows.

Lattimer jerked around; Animal Talker slowly turned.

Brenna straightened up, grimacing as she flexed her bruised ribs. "Logan," she whispered.

448

He emerged from the darkness and walked to the platform.

"Logan!" Brenna ran and threw herself against him. Logan drew back, his hands whipping up to catch her shoulders. "My God, woman," he exclaimed, "don't you think you've caused me enough trouble for one lifetime? Will you never learn your place? Had you stayed home, none of this would be happening. I could be getting on with my business." He pushed her away. "Get over there and leave me alone."

Brenna had borne her shame; she had fought against tears and hysteria; she had consoled herself with thoughts of Logan. But his actions this moment broke the thin thread that held her feelings intact. Reason abandoned her; emotions rules. Hurt, grief-stricken, she stumbled back and fell to her knees, slowly crumbling to the floor. She caught her side and moaned with pain.

Francisca crawled to Brenna. "It's all right," she murmured as she wrapped her arms around her friend. "He is only doing this to protect us."

Ignoring Brenna and Francisca, Logan turned to Animal Talker. He signed and spoke in Spanish simultaneously. "I am Logan MacDougald, son of He-Who-Hunted-the-Antelope, a Cherokee chieftain."

"You are white," Animal Talker said.

"I was born white," Logan clarified, "but when I was nine the Comanches killed my parents and kidnapped my sister. I was taken in and reared by the Cherokees."

Animal Talker measured the man who stood in front of him. "You do not hate the Comanches for what they did to you?"

"I hate the man who did it to me," Logan replied. "I have sworn that one day I shall kill him." *And you!* Logan's gaze included Oswald Lattimer.

449

"Who is the Comanche whom you hunt, MacDougald?"

"White-Hair."

A small smile tugged the young chief's lips. "Some say that White-Hair is a legend."

"I say he's a man like you and me, and I say that one day I shall kill him for the shame he has brought upon me and my family."

"You are either a fool or an extremely wise man."

"My father, Antelope Hunter, said that I am a mixture of both," Logan answered. "On some days I'm more the fool, on others more the wise man."

Animal Talker laughed quietly. "I like you, Logan MacDougald. I think I should have liked your father, He-Who-Hunted-the-Antelope. I am He-Who-Talks-To-Animals. I should like to trade with you." He turned, sweeping his hand as he pivoted. "You see what we have. Two white women, wagons of trade goods, and animals."

"You can't do this!" Lattimer shouted in Spanish. He was so disconcerted he forgot to sign. He had known from the beginning that dealing with this young buck was going to be difficult. "I'm the one who informed you of the wagon train. I want the Sandovals. You have always traded with me."

"For many seasons, Oswald Lattimer," Animal Talker said, "my father and my uncle traded only with you. But when Buffalo Horn was killed, you severed the honor that bound us together in trade. You are the one who opened the way for us to trade with others." The Comanche chief smiled; patiently he had waited for this day. He found revenge extremely sweet and satisfying. "We displeased you because we chose to return to our camp and bury our dead chief. In your anger you promised that you would trade guns to any Indians who came to you first, be they Comanches,

Apaches, or whomever. Now I, Animal Talker, wish to trade with the man called MacDougald."

The firelight played over Lattimer's face, the features harsh and unyielding. The eyes were still muddy and dull; they were like a stagnant pool, breeding stench and destruction. "Don't you think you should find out what he has to trade first?"

"I have not seen forty or fifty winters, as you have, Scar-Face," Animal Talker returned, "but I know how to conduct my affairs." The Comanche chief concentrated on Logan again. "You see what I have to trade you. Do you wish any of these goods?"

"Women are good to have," Logan said, his eyes raking over Francisca and Brenna. "They have their place in a man's life." He grinned at the chief. "Or should I say in his bed. But for my purposes one is as good as another. I will take them, but they are not my primary interest."

Animal Talker wasn't sure if MacDougald was lying or not. He strained through the flickering light; he tried to read the eyes and the face, but they were expressionless.

"We have wagons and horses."

"I have horses." Logan waited a moment, then asked, "How about the men whom you took as prisoners?"

"You want them?"

"Yes," Logan replied, "I want them."

"Nothing else."

Again Logan's gaze strayed to the women; a wolfish grin touched his lips. "I will take the women. I think they can give me many hours of pleasure."

"No," Lattimer shouted, "do not let him have the women, Animal Talker. Give me some time and I shall have the guns for you."

"What are you willing to trade me for these people?"

"I have a wagon full of scrap metal," Logan replied.

"Scrap metal." Animal Talker wrinkled his face in contempt. "What will we do with scrap metal?"

Logan grinned. "You will make arrowheads, my chief. The most deadly and well-balanced arrowheads in all Comanche Land. Your braves will be feared above all other braves."

"I prefer the guns like the Texas Rangers use," Animal Talker said. "Why should I agree to accept anything less?"

"Because I can bring you the scrap metal now, and I did not make you any promises. Lattimer cannot bring you the kind of guns he has promised."

"You know this to be true," Animal Talker said.

"I know this to be true."

"You son of a bitch," Lattimer swore under his breath. "How do you know what I can or cannot do?" He closed the distance between him and Logan. About the same height as Logan, Lattimer looked him square in the eyes. "I could kill you with my own bare hands."

"I wouldn't suggest you try it," Logan said in a low voice. He swallowed his hatred for a moment. Now was not the time to kill Lattimer; he had to learn who was supplying him with information and with weapons for the Comanches. Reverting to English, he said, "And if you'll be little more hospitable, Mr. Lattimer, I'll discuss working with you."

"Why should I discuss working with you?" Lattimer hissed. "I have successfully traded with the Comanches for more than twenty-five years, and no one, especially not some young upstart like you, is going to demand entrance into my organization. You remind me of this cocky little buck. Both of you wearing trousers and pretending to be men."

Logan cut his eyes at the breechclout Animal Talker wore. "I don't think both of us are wearing trousers," he said on quiet laughter. "And neither of us is pretending to be men. Now, I think you ought to reconsider, Lattimer." Logan's voice was low and hard and mocking. "I'm not asking for, nor am I demanding, entrance into your organization. I'm cutting myself in. I have what you want, and you're going to have to bargain with me to get it." He smiled coldly. "I have Joaquin and Francisca Sandoval."

Lattimer looked at Logan a full minute before he threw back his head and laughed. "For a horse thief, you talk pretty big, MacDougald. Where's the Cherokee that you ride with?"

"How do you know that I ride with a Cherokee?" Logan asked, evading the question. Lattimer thought Thunder was dead, and that was the way Logan wanted to keep it.

"Newspaper," Lattimer drawled. "We get them out here, you know. Had a picture of you and the Indian." The Comanchero smiled smugly. "Old Sam was offering a mighty big reward for the two of you. Somebody might be tempted to take you in."

"It'll take a bigger man than you or any of them who work for you," Logan said. "Now, what's it going to be?"

"I've got to admit, MacDougald, you've got guts, and you call a good bluff. I have to admire that in any man."

"No bluff," Logan returned. "You've heard my deal. If you want the Sandovals, you'll deal with me."

"I'm not beaten yet," Lattimer said. "I have contacts in Texas. I can get more guns."

"Not soon enough. The longer you wait to give them to Animal Talker, the less inclined he is to trust you. You wouldn't want an Indian war on your hands, would you?"

Lattimer lifted his arm and slowly drew his finger down his scar. "You'll let me have the Sandovals?"

"I'll think about it," Logan replied. "Of course, she's the one I'm most interested in."

"She's the one I want," Lattimer said. "Her and that brother of hers."

Logan shrugged. "We'll probably be able to make a deal. Until then I'll keep Francisca by my side at all times. If I so much as think you're about to trick me, I shall take her. She's a virgin, you know."

"What about the Allen woman? I thought you cared about her."

Logan laughed. "I care about no one but myself, Lattimer. She was an available woman when I needed one the most. I used her."

Francisca gasped. She could hardly utter the translation for Brenna. When she did, Brenna said nothing. She tilted her head and stared defiantly at Logan. No matter what his expressions said, no matter how void his eyes were of emotion, Brenna knew Logan loved her. As surely as if he had spoken the words, she felt them wrap around her warmly to bind her soul and body to him. Hard had been the path their hearts had trodden to love, but she and Logan now shared it unconditionally. Her heart loudly proclaimed her absolute faith in him. He understood his adversary well; he would rescue her! That's the kind of man Logan Andrew MacDougald was.

Chapter Twenty-Eight

Anxiously Brenna paced back and forth. For three days she had been locked up in this two-room house—the door bolted from the outside and the two windows barred—her only visitor an elderly servant woman who spoke no English and who delivered food and picked up the empty dishes.

She didn't know where Logan was; she didn't know what had happened to him . . . or Francisca . . . or Joaquin. Her heart heavy, she moved to the only window at the back of the room and gazed on the dry, parched village that spread around her prison like spokes on a wheel. Hard, callused men and women slowly ambled in the streets, but Brenna recognized none of them.

Footfalls on the wooden veranda surprised her. It was mealtime, but the steps were too heavy for a woman. Brenna slowly turned around but didn't move. She heard the bolt grind through the bars; she saw the knob turn and the door open. In walked a man.

"Logan," she whispered.

He was devastatingly handsome. His hair was brushed back from his face, an errant wave lopping over his forehead. His bronzed neck rose from the opened vee of a dark blue shirt. The sleeves were cuffed several times so that his lower arms were exposed. His hands rested lightly on his hips, slightly above the two revolvers. His black pants molded his legs perfectly, and Brenna found it hard to tell where material ended and the polished leather of boots began.

With compassion Logan looked at Brenna. His beautiful, fiery lover was tattered and bruised. Her hair hung in tangles around her face and over her shoulders. The blouse was torn and dirty, the riding skirt rumpled from her having worn it day and night for days. Her face was streaked with dirt, and anxiety colored dark semicircles beneath her eyes.

"I'm sorry," he murmured, stepping into the room and holding his arms out.

"Oh, Logan," she sobbed—the small sound carrying such a deep wave of love. She flung herself into the protective warmth of his embrace and buried her face in the soft, clean material of his shirt; she saw the silver chain and the talisman. She felt his chest rise and fall with his breathing.

"Forgive me, baby," he whispered. "I did the only thing I could do to save you. I couldn't let Lattimer or Animal Talker know how much you meant to me; I couldn't have saved you any other way. Lattimer's not a sane, logical man; he's a murderer. Life means nothing to him."

Brenna pulled back to look into his face. "I know why you did it, my darling." She smiled through her tears of joy.

Laying his cheek on top of her head, Logan breathed deeply and held her. He didn't want to let her go for fear he would lose her . . . this time for good. "You don't know the hours I've spent at night walking back and forth across the floor, wondering how you were, wishing I could be with you. I love you."

"I know you do." Her voice was barely audible.

He lowered his head and kissed her forehead—the

touch infinitely gentle and reassuring. Brenna returned her head to his chest and listened to the steady beat of his heart; she felt the rhythmic motion of his chest as he breathed; she smelled the good, clean odor of him. She rubbed her palms against the fabric of his shirt.

"How is Francisca?" she asked.

"She's fine."

"She's in the big house with you?"

As Logan thought of the large two-storied house at the end of the street—the most beautiful building in the town and Lattimer's home—guilt stabbed his heart anew. The hours he had spent pacing the bedroom floor at night were not even the beginning of penance. While he had been enjoying all the luxuries of the big house, Brenna had been locked in this two-room prison.

"I would have come sooner," he said; he had to explain. "But I couldn't. Although you were locked up out here, I knew you were safe, but Francisca is not. I must keep Lattimer from touching her. I don't dare leave her alone with him."

Brenna pulled back and lifted her hands to cup his face. "Please stop punishing yourself on my account," she said. "I don't blame you for what happened. I can only thank you for saving me. Really, I understand."

A smile tugged at the corners of Logan's mouth. "Calming Francisca and keeping her out of Lattimer's clutches is a full-time chore."

Brenna laughed. "Knowing Francisca, I can imagine."

"This is the first opportunity I have had to slip away from the house. Lattimer left for the day. He won't be back until suppertime."

"How are Joaquin and Roger and the others?"

"Safe for the time being," Logan said, moving to look out the window to make sure no one was coming

457

toward the building. "I've got to get them out of here before Lattimer kills them." He paused and turned from the window. "Kirkwood's dead. Following Lattimer's orders, he tried to kill Thunder. Thunder had to kill him in self-defense, but I don't want Lattimer to know it yet, so I've allowed him to believe the reverse happened."

"Where do we go from here?" she asked.

"Tonight we're all having supper in the big house."

"Part of your plan for our escape?" she asked quizzically.

Logan shook his head. "Right now, I don't have one. This place is a veritable fort, and guards are posted everywhere with orders to shoot anything that looks suspicious."

Brenna heard the anxiety in Logan's voice. "What about Thunder?"

"I don't know where he is or what he's doing." Logan brushed his hand through his hair. "I can only hope he has been able to trail me and has devised a way of penetrating this place."

Logan didn't tell Brenna about his strange alliance with Mario Laguna Jamarillo. One, she had enough on her mind now. Two, he didn't think she would understand. He wasn't sure himself he could trust his swarthy little companion and his followers—but they were all he had.

Brenna caught the tattered riding habit in her hands and said, "Am I to come to dinner in this?"

Logan smiled lamely at her joke. "No, I'll have your trunk brought to you, and anything else you need."

"I want to bathe and clean up," she answered. "What time shall I be ready?"

"Six," he returned, and added regretfully, "I must leave now." He caught her into his arms one more time and kissed her thoroughly.

458

When he left, Brenna heard the sound of the bolt as he slid it into place. This time it didn't frighten her; she didn't feel like a prisoner anymore. She didn't feel alone.

Not long afterward the dour little woman and two scaly men brought in a tub and plenty of water, towels, washrags, and soap. When they were gone and the door was again closed and locked, Brenna pulled the shutters and shed her clothes. She thoroughly enjoyed the next few hours. She bathed; she washed her hair and brushed it dry; then she coiled it atop her head. She slipped into a clean white chemise and dug through her chest until she found the appropriate gown—the turquoise and black one she had worn at the fandango, the one that brought back wonderful memories. This she had the woman iron for her.

At nightfall when Logan arrived, Brenna was dressed. Cleaning up and changing clothes had been therapeutic; her emotions were sharp again. She was excited and eagerly anticipated her evening. She smiled when she heard his footfalls on the veranda. She moved into the bedroom and listened as he opened the door.

Logan paused a minute, looking around the deserted room, before he called, "Brenna, are you here?"

She stepped through the door into the candlelit room. "I am." She held the diaphanous black scarf loosely in her hands.

Logan, still wearing the clothes he had on earlier in the day, stopped short. His gaze flickered over the dress to the scarf, finally coming to rest on the lace inset. Memories of that evening long ago in Santa Fe resurrected so strongly, Logan felt the physical response of his body—a response he had to deny at the present because he had to be aware of and on guard around Lattimer at all times.

Brenna stepped through the door, the material

rustling with each step she took. "What do you think?" she asked.

Slowly, deliberately Logan closed the distance between them. He clasped her shoulders and pulled her into his arms.

"This is what I think." His lips came down on hers in a hard, searing kiss that was tinged with a savage desperation born of concern, anxiety, and fear. As his mouth possessed hers, his hands began to claim her back. Up and down they moved, until finally they cupped her hips. He pressured her against him.

As savage as the kiss had begun, it soon mellowed into tenderness and desire. When Logan finally lifted his head, he and Brenna were clinging together, their breathing harsh and irregular.

"I love you," he whispered, burying his face in the sweet hollow of neck and shoulder. "I love you, my darling."

"I love you," Brenna whispered.

Short minutes later, Logan led Brenna down the street toward the big house, the shutters flung open, brilliant candlelight flowing from the windows. They walked into the parlor, a huge, comfortable room richly furnished—most of which was European in design. The adobe floors and walls had been paneled with the same timbers that formed the ceiling.

Francisca sat on the sofa, nervously twisting her hands in her lap. When she saw Brenna, her face brightened, but she didn't move. Her gaze darted furtively back and forth between the sinister man and the couple who had entered the room. Lattimer stood in front of a large table, a cigarette in one hand, a glass of liquor in the other. He smiled and bowed from the waist.

"Good evening, Mrs. Allen. I'm so glad you could join us for dinner this evening."

"Why, thank you, Mr. Lattimer, for thinking to invite me," she said with a dazzling smile. "I had many more pressing things to do, but Mr. MacDougald wouldn't take no for an answer."

"You'll be glad that he persuaded you to come, Mrs. Allen," Lattimer said, a strange smile playing his thin lips. "I wanted you to see that although we're nestled out here in the middle of Comancheria, we Comancheros enjoy all the amenities of civilization. I have a surprise planned for all of you this evening."

Footsteps in the hall caused all of them to turn toward the door. Francisca turned white and gasped; Brenna stiffened. Joaquin, resplendent in his caballero costume, hobbled into the room. The wound on his head was healing nicely; it was still slightly discolored, but the swelling had gone down. Immediately behind Joaquin came his jailer, who brandished a revolver. The *Mexicano* looked at his sister and smiled; then he turned his head toward Brenna, his smile encompassing her as well.

Lattimer dismissed his man with a wave of his hand and smiled at Joaquin. "Don Joaquin, I am so glad that you were able to make dinner also."

Joaquin bowed deeply. "Although I had no say in the matter, I am happy to be here."

Lattimer raised his glass in acknowledgment. "Never have such illustrious people graced my home. Now we shall go to dinner." He led the way into the dining room.

Something about the table puzzled Brenna.

Lattimer laughed softly. "The table is set for six of us, and we are only five in number," he said. "We are shy one guest, but he'll be here as soon as possible." Lattimer sat himself at the head of the table. "Doña Francisca, you will sit here beside me on the left. Don Joaquin, please sit next to her." Lattimer looked at

Brenna. "As much as I would like for you to sit next to me, my dear, I'm going to let Mr. MacDougald have that honor. He and I have some business which we must discuss. You will sit across from Don Joaquin."

The meal began, and course after course was served. Lattimer ate and drank heartily; he engaged in desultory conversation. Logan and Joaquin joined freely in the discussion; for the most part Francisca and Brenna were quiet.

Brenna's eyes kept darting to the empty place at the head of the table next to her. A trick of Lattimer's, she knew. But what? Why?

"Now," Lattimer announced as he produced a pouch of tobacco, "I think it's time for us to do some serious talking." After he rolled his cigarette, he placed it in the corner of his mouth. He reached for the nearest candelabra and brought it close to his face, the light flickering over the scar. "I shall use you, Don Joaquin and Doña Francisca, to lure your mother and father away from the hacienda. I shall also demand a large ransom for your release."

"But you are not planning on releasing us, are you?" Joaquin said. As if they were discussing such a safe, mundane subject as the weather, Joaquin picked up his wine and sipped it. "I must commend you on your excellent taste, Señor Lattimer. This is truly one of the finest wines I have ever sampled."

"Thank you, Don Joaquin," Lattimer said. "Your friend, Manuel Armijo, gave it to me." He lifted his glass and held it in front of the candle, the light playing through the golden liquid. "It's part of my payment for ridding him of the Sandovals."

"If this is all he paid you," Joaquin said, "then you have been underpaid. I promise you that getting rid of the Sandovals is going to be a difficult if not impossible task indeed."

462

"Difficult but altogether within the realm of reason and probability." Lattimer took a sip of the wine. "You, Doña Francisca, shall remain here at the big house with me. If you behave yourself, I shall probably marry you; otherwise, I'm afraid that you will share the same fate as Señora Allen." For the first time Brenna saw the muddy eyes clear up. "You'll be sent to one of my best bordellos in Mexico."

"Aren't you forgetting that these people are my property?" Logan asked.

"No, my young fool," Lattimer said, "I am forgetting nothing. I lured you here to my hideout because this is my territory; I'm as familiar with it as I am the back of my hand. The people out here are mine; their complete allegiance belongs to me and the order of the Comancheros. All of you are my prisoners." He lifted the decanter and poured himself another glass of wine. "Before I turn you over to Animal Talker and his people to kill, I have decided to settle your curiosity. You know that I haven't planned my raids without inside help."

Excitement pumped through Logan's body in such proportions, he could barely restrain himself. He reached for the decanter and was surprised his hand wasn't shaking. He, too, refilled his glass.

"How do you know that Animal Talker will kill me?" Logan asked. "He and I have a business arrangement that is suitable to both of us."

"While Animal Talker took your scrap metal, he will as quickly turn against you. You are expendable. Animal Talker is an intelligent man who knows that bows and arrows will not stand up to the new six-shooting revolver the rangers are using. When I tell him the cost of the guns, he will gladly pay."

"You're confident of this?"

"I am," Lattimer quickly replied, ending with a peal

of laughter. "By the way, the shipment arrived thi
afternoon. That's why I was called away from the fort
So you see, MacDougald, I have no need for you after
all. Before you die, however, I decided that I would
introduce you to my informant, the man who also sees
that I get whatever it is the Indians want."

Lattimer took a large swallow of his drink, held it in
his mouth, savored it, then swallowed. He looked at
Brenna and spoke. "You're an Imperialist, aren't you
Mrs. Allen, working with Clarence Childers?"
Brenna's evident surprise pleased him. "Childers is a
poor, misguided soul who is so consumed with his
cause that he's willing to do anything to keep the
Comanches stirred up so Sam Houston can't get Texas
annexed to the union."

"Clarence Childers?" Brenna asked, her heartbeat
slowing with disappointment. Surely one of Texas'
foremost political leaders wasn't involved with murderers like these.

Lattimer nodded. "The same. But you're very much
like Mr. Childers, are you not, Mrs. Allen? You, too,
want to see an empire of Texas."

"Yes," Brenna admitted, "I am an advocate of
Imperialism, but I draw a line on the extremes to which
I'll go to have an empire, Mr. Lattimer. I won't steal
from my government to give to thieves and murderers;
I won't work with the likes of you and your
Comancheros."

"Such harsh judgment coming from a woman who is
a guest of the people under discussion."

Everyone at the table was tense and apprehensive.
All looked from Lattimer to Brenna and back again.

"How did you feel when you learned that the citizens
of Santa Fe weren't interested in your revolution?" he
asked.

"They have a right to their own feelings. I can't fault

464

them for their beliefs, whether they oppose mine or not."

Lattimer's eyes landed on Brenna's left hand. "Armijo told me that you are a widow?"

They were playing cat and mouse, Brenna thought. He was the cat, she the mouse. "Yes, I am."

"Your husband?" he questioned by inflection.

"Shawn Allen."

"He was also an Imperialist?"

"Yes."

"Did he die for the cause?"

Brenna felt as if her nerves couldn't be pulled another inch without breaking. Then she felt the gentle and reassuring pressure of Logan's hand on her thigh. "No, he didn't die for a cause save his own. He was killed by Comanches when he was hauling freight from Lattimer, Texas, to Refugio and San Patricio."

"I'm sorry, Mrs. Allen," Lattimer said. "Such a loss for a young woman like yourself."

"Can we move on?" Logan asked. "There's no need for all this trivia."

Lattimer smiled; he lifted his hand and lightly patted his scar with his index finger. "Let me have the pleasure of being a good host, MacDougald. It's seldom that I have this honor." His gaze swept from Logan to Brenna and back to Logan. "You love Mrs. Allen, do you not? You try not to show it, but I think you do."

Brenna stiffened, but she as quickly relaxed when she felt Logan's hand squeeze her leg.

"Armijo seemed convinced that you two did," Lattimer continued. Now the dull, brackish eyes landed on Brenna. "I know you love him. Kirkwood told me so. Abbott Kirkwood, Mrs. Allen, your hunter and guide."

"You don't have to tell me, Mr. Lattimer; I know who Kirkwood is. By the way, where is he?" Brenna

465

asked, although Logan had already told her that the scout was dead.

"He's taking care of some business for me," Lattimer replied. "But enough of business. Evidently our guest will not be arriving for dinner." He stood. "Shall we adjourn to the parlor?"

"I would prefer to return to my rooms," Brenna said.

"Not so soon, Mrs. Allen," Lattimer said. "I have provided entertainment for all of you. I wanted to show you that we do enjoy some amenities of civilization."

Once the group was in the parlor, Francisca and Brenna sat on the sofa. Logan and Joaquin remained standing. Lattimer walked to the liquor table across the room.

"Would you care for another drink?" he asked Logan.

"No." Logan needed to be clearheaded tonight. Constantly he must be on guard around Lattimer, outguessing and outbluffing him.

"You, Don Joaquin?"

"Not I," Joaquin declined, sitting down in the chair next to the sofa.

"Then I shall drink by myself," Lattimer announced. A knock sounded, and he looked toward the door, where his manservant stood nodding his head. "Good," Lattimer said. "Our entertainers have arrived."

The servant withdrew, and three men, their musical instruments in hand, filed into the room. Soon they were playing soft Spanish songs. Then the tempo changed; it was hot and lusty. A dancer glided into the room, her arms weaving above her head, her fingers deftly clicking castanets.

Her dress molded her body from her shoulders to her knees, where it flared out in rows of ruffles. The bodice was low-cut, revealing the swell of cinnamon-colored breasts. Her black hair, parted in the center and hanging loose, swirled around her body like a curtain as she danced. Deliberately, effectively she spun a sensuous web and totally ensnared her audience.

When the music suddenly stopped, she gracefully melted to the floor and lay there as if in a trance. Perspiration glistened on her face and breasts; her breathing was deep and ragged. The audience didn't move or speak; they couldn't take their eyes off her. They were afraid to break the spell that she had cast over all of them.

"Ah." Lattimer's harsh voice echoed through the room. "I see that you've arrived at last. We'd almost given you up."

Heads turned and eyes focused on the door.

All the blood drained from Brenna's face; she was ashen. "It can't be!" she whispered. "You're dead!" The room began to spin around her, faster and faster. She grasped the arm of the sofa and held on; she didn't want to faint.

The woman on the floor lithely sprang to her feet and raced across the room to throw herself in the newcomer's arms. "Shawn!" the dancer exclaimed. "What a wonderful surprise. I did not know you were coming tonight. Lattimer did not tell me."

467

Chapter Twenty-Nine

Logan spared the man in the door a fleeting glance; then he was on his knees beside Brenna. By the time he rose with her in his arms, the stranger had flung the dancer aside and was beside him.

"I'll take her," Shawn said. "She's my wife."

"The hell you will," Logan said. "Now, get out of my way." In a matter of minutes Logan was in the hall, up the stairs, and in his room. The others followed him, Shawn Allen in the lead, Joaquin hobbling behind. Logan crossed to the huge four-poster bed and laid Brenna down. "Light some candles," he ordered, and since Francisca was immediately behind him, she complied. Logan sat down on the side of the bed and caught Brenna's hands in his.

Joaquin moved to the other side of the bed and looked down at the ashen woman. As soon as Francisca had lit the candles, she joined her brother. Shawn walked to the table and poured himself a whiskey, which he quaffed down in one swallow. Enjoying the scenario, Lattimer stood in the doorway.

"I promised you an entertaining evening," Lattimer said. "And nothing could be more dramatic than this."

"Why didn't you tell me she was here?" Shawn asked while he refilled his glass.

"Same reason I didn't tell her you were alive,"

Lattimer answered. "I wanted to surprise the both of you."

"Get some smelling salts," Logan ordered.

"Don't worry," Lattimer said. "She'll come around soon. She's just shocked."

"And why shouldn't she be?" Logan exclaimed, coming to his feet. "She thought her husband was dead." He strode to the table and poured a glass of brandy. After he returned to the bed, he lifted Brenna in his arms and tried to force some of the fiery liquid down her throat. She sputtered, but she didn't regain consciousness.

"Why in the hell didn't you let her know you were alive?" Logan demanded of Shawn. "Why did you let her think you were dead?"

Shawn's fingers tightened around the glass he was holding. "She was better off," he replied, gulping his third glass. "She would have found out sooner or later what I was doing, and she wouldn't have stood for it."

"I can't believe for a minute that you had her concern at heart," Logan said.

"Brenna's not a greedy person like her husband is," Lattimer supplied. "I found Shawn Allen extremely easy to buy, and he's the one who persuaded Clarence Childers to enlist my help in furthering the cause of the Texas empire."

"Childers is the one supplying you with guns?" Logan asked. He didn't like the man, but he found it hard to believe that he was in cahoots with hardened criminals like the Comancheros.

"Childers is stupid," Shawn answered. "He's all caught up in his empire movement and in grandiose dreams of becoming the emperor of Texas. He thinks we're using the guns for an insurrection in Santa Fe and Taos. He has no idea that we're going to give them to the Comanches."

"How can you do this?" Joaquin asked. His ebony eyes raked contemptuously over Shawn. "Go against your own people and provide weapons for your enemies! Not only your people but the citizens of Santa Fe and Taos."

"When you like money, it's quite easy." Lattimer walked farther into the room and hiked his foot on one of the chairs, disregarding the expensive upholstering.

Logan raised Brenna, turned her over, and began to unhook her gown.

"What do you think you're doing?" Shawn shouted, dropping the empty glass to the floor.

"You've got eyes," Logan answered. "Use them."

"Get out of here," Shawn ordered. "I'll take care of her. She's my wife."

"You've already said that." Logan's hands worked down the back of her dress, and he pulled the waist open so she could breathe better. "And you've already proved the kind of care you can give her. Now, all of you get out of here."

"If you think I'm going to leave her alone with you," Shawn said, "you're—"

"I'm better than nothing," Logan said, "and that's what you left her with when you faked your death. Now, get out of here before I kill you with my own bare hands."

"Although I wouldn't enjoy anything more," Lattimer said, "I don't think this is the time or place for such a contest." He laughed. "Come to think of it, it wouldn't be a contest at all. Come, Shawn," he said as if speaking to a pet animal, "let's go to the study."

Shawn looked from Logan to Lattimer. He was undecided.

"Mr. MacDougald, why don't you join us as soon as you have Mrs. Allen in bed?" Lattimer ordered.

"I will," Logan answered. "I have some questions I

want answered."

"Don Joaquin," Lattimer said, "you will spend the night in the house with us, but as I told Mr. MacDougald the night we arrived, escape is impossible." While they walked down the hall, Lattimer continued to talk. "I have guards posted throughout the interior and exterior. If you should attempt to leave, they have orders to shoot first and ask questions later."

"I will take care of her for you," Francisca said to Logan when they were alone.

"Thank you," Logan said, "but I'd like to be here when she awakens."

Knowing that he wished to be alone with Brenna, Francisca nodded. "I'll be in my room. Come get me when you leave." She quietly withdrew.

Logan stripped Brenna's dress off and laid it across the foot of the bed. Then he walked to the chair across the room and sat down to wait. He hadn't counted on Shawn's miraculous resurrection. Brenna hadn't either. Had Shawn planned his own death, or was it an accident of which he took advantage? Logan proposed to learn the answer to this question before the night was over.

Brenna opened her eyes and turned her head to gaze at the candle on the table next to her. As her vision cleared, she focused on the flame that leaped and danced into the air. Then she remembered; she bolted up.

"Shawn!" she cried.

"He's not here." Logan was on the bed beside her. He gathered her into his arms. "I'm here, sweetheart."

"Oh, God, Logan, he's dead," she sobbed. "Shawn's dead. Gabby identified the body. He buried him."

"Gabby thought he was dead." Logan rubbed his hand down the back of her head in soothing motion and held her until her crying ceased. Then he picked up the glass of brandy and handed it to her. "Drink this."

She took a swallow, then another. "I have to talk with Shawn," she said.

Logan shook his head. "Not tonight. You need some time by yourself to think." He took the glass from her hands. "Lie down, and I'll get Francisca to come sit with you. I'm going down to talk with Lattimer and Shawn."

Brenna allowed him to move her and pull down the bedspread. When she was under the sheet, she said, "You have the information Houston needs, don't you? Lattimer is leading the Comancheros, Shawn is the middleman, and Childers is the supplier."

Logan nodded.

"Now we've got to get out of here." She burrowed the back of her head in the feather pillow. "That's going to be the problem, isn't it?"

Logan couldn't resist sitting down beside her. He placed a palm on either side of her and lowered her face, his lips capturing hers in a long, sweet kiss. "I don't think it's going to be a real big problem," he said. "Generally a job this size only calls for one half a ranger, and we have two. One and a half more than we need."

Brenna smiled and lifted a hand to touch the talisman that swung from the chain. "I didn't think you were a ranger."

"Not officially, but I still think and act like one."

"You're not afraid of Lattimer?"

"Yes."

"You know I'm going to have to talk with Shawn," she said. "He's my husband."

Logan's eyes darkened. "I know, but I'd like for that to be tomorrow."

"All right," Brenna answered.

472

They looked at each other; for now this was all they ould do. Never had either of them yearned more for he tenderness and love of the other. But Shawn stood etween them.

"Legally I belong to Shawn," she told Logan, "but ightfully and morally I belong to you."

"Brenna," Logan murmured, and her name on his ips became the most intimate of caresses. He caught er in an embrace.

They held each other until a knock resounded in the oom. The manservant called out in Spanish. "Señor Lattimer wishes to see you in his study, Señor MacDougald."

"Tell him that I'll be down," Logan replied. Then to Brenna he said, "I must go; Lattimer wants to see me."

"Please be careful," Brenna whispered.

"I will." Logan stood and walked to the door; he urned and smiled at her. "I'll get Francisca to stay with ou until I return."

"We . . . we can't . . ."

"I know." His smile was full of understanding. "I just vant to say good night."

With that promise Logan stood and moved to the loor. When he stopped and turned to wave at Brenna, e saw a movement at the window. A man. One of Lattimer's guards. He looked closer and smiled. Then e was gone. Before he walked into Lattimer's office, Logan made two stops. He sent Francisca to Brenna nd visited with Joaquin.

"MacDougald," Lattimer said when Logan entered he room, "I'm glad you finally decided to come. Did ou have to tell everyone good night?"

"Didn't have to," Logan answered, "but I wanted o."

"And you always do what you want to do?"

"So far."

473

"Whiskey?" Lattimer offered.

"No, thanks." Logan looked at Shawn, who slumped on the sofa, guzzling another drink.

"Guess you're wondering about Allen," Lattimer said.

"I am," Logan replied.

"Want to tell him, Shawn, or shall I?" the Comanchero asked. When Shawn waved his hand, Lattimer laughed. "I shall be more than happy to tell your story." He rolled a cigarette and lit it; then he inhaled deeply and exhaled. "Shawn was going nowhere fast when he met my man Kirkwood. Through Kirkwood I employed Shawn to keep abreast of the news in the new republic. I paid him good money. When I learned of this empire movement and I saw how their minds were working, I saw an opportunity to expand my territory. You see"—he tapped the cigarette over the ashtray—"I have no desire to see the United States annex Texas. If they do, our base of operation will be endangered."

"Was Brenna's father in on this?" Logan asked.

"No," Shawn said, surging to his feet and weaving across the room to the liquor table.

"Much to Shawn's regret, Nolan Garvey found out that Shawn and Childers were working with me, and he threatened to go to Houston with it."

"So you killed Garvey."

"I had to," Shawn shouted, balling his hands into fists. "I didn't want to, but I had no other choice. He threatened to expose me and Childers. He was going to see Houston. We would have been hanged without a trial."

"You're a poor excuse for a man," Logan said. "You killed Brenna's father and messed up her life. Did you also set up the Comanche attack on your wagon train?"

"With a little prodding from me," Lattimer put in. "As you've pointed out, Shawn is a weak man. His

474

conscience was getting a little too heavy for him to bear, so I figured I needed to get him out of Texas, but I didn't want him dead. I needed him. So we planned the massacre."

"The men who were skinned," Logan said.

"My men did it," Lattimer said. "Disguised as Indians." He laughed. "A work of genius, wouldn't you say?"

"Butchery is more like it," Logan said. "Your men were responsible for the death of Brenna's scout and the hide hunters."

Lattimer nodded. "Through Kirkwood also for the death of your Indian friend, and soon I can take the credit for your death, Logan MacDougald."

Out of the corner of his eye, Logan saw Shawn refill his glass with whiskey. "Are you really planning on sending Brenna to one of your brothels, Lattimer?"

Shawn's movements stopped.

"No," Lattimer replied, his eyes mere slits, "I won't use her in one of mine."

"One of your friend's perhaps?" Logan suggested.

Shawn's hand was shaking so badly that liquor sloshed from the glass onto the table. "You're not sending Brenna to any whorehouse," he screamed, and spun around.

"Be reasonable, Shawn," Lattimer said, his voice extremely quiet and patient. "We've been able to handle Childers because he's all caught up in his political scheme, but Brenna's different. She's trouble; we have to get rid of her."

"But to sell her, Lattimer," Shawn argued.

"It's either that or kill her, Shawn." Lattimer waited a moment, then said, "Selling her is better for all concerned, Shawn. She lives, and you make some money. We're talking about money, and lots of it. She's young and comely; some rich fellow will probably want to buy her for himself. He might even set her up as his own mistress."

Shawn turned back to the table and picked up his glass.

"I'm thinking she'll bring at least a thousand dollars." A pleased smile pulling his lips, Lattimer watched Shawn take a swallow of whiskey. "All of which you may have, Shawn."

"I don't know," Shawn finally said, shaking his head.

"If she behaves," Lattimer argued, his voice still low and pacifying, "she'll be all right."

Logan was angry and disgusted. Lattimer had been correct in his assessment of Shawn Allen: The man was weak, totally guided by greed. "If she doesn't *behave*," Logan softly interjected, "she won't be all right, Shawn. Just think about it for a minute: You're selling your wife into slavery."

Shawn quaffed down the last swallow of liquor. "Lattimer," he said, "I've done a lot of bloody things for you, but I'm not going to let you send Brenna to a Mexican whorehouse."

"I am, and there's nothing you can do about it," Lattimer announced.

"Oh, yeah?" Shawn pulled his revolver from the holster as he staggered across the room. "I'll kill you—"

A shot rang through the room. Shawn dropped his weapon and clutched his chest. Blood oozed through his fingers. As he crumpled to his knees he muttered, "—first." He fell over.

Logan ran to him and touched the pulse at the base of his neck. He looked up at Lattimer.

"I don't know if credit is given for killing worms," the Comanchero said. "But sooner or later they all get squashed."

Brenna and Francisca came rushing into the room, Joaquin right behind them.

476

"What happened?" Brenna cried. She clutched Francisca's robe more closely around her body.

Logan was on his feet before Brenna could reach Shawn. Catching her in his arms, he said, "He's dead."

Brenna pulled away and knelt beside Shawn. She pushed a lock of hair from his face and folded his hands over his stomach. For the briefest of moments, she cupped his chin with her hand. "Yes," she murmured, "he's dead. He has been for a long time now."

Lattimer clapped his hands, and his servant entered the room. "Dispose of the body," he ordered coldly. "The rest of you can go to bed and have sweet dreams."

The four of them, Logan, Brenna, Francisca, and Joaquin, walked out of the room, never once looking back. They said little when they parted for their bedrooms; each wondered what the morrow would bring.

The candle had burned down in the bedroom Logan used, but it cast enough light for them to see. Brenna walked to the window and stared at the moonlit village, which was not very different from Santa Fe.

Logan pulled a large chest across the door; then he unfastened his gun belt and laid it on the table next to the bed; he slipped off his boots and socks.

Brenna turned around in time to see him return to the trunk and pull out two blankets. "What are you doing?" she asked.

"Making me a pallet," Logan answered as he spread the cover on the floor, "so I can sleep in here with you."

"Why not the bed?" A smile touched her face.

Logan slowly straightened, his eyes fastened to hers. "I thought you might prefer to sleep by yourself."

"No, I don't want to be alone tonight."

Silently Logan walked across the room and caught Brenna in his arms; she laid her head on his chest.

"I had accepted his death," she said. "Now I've . . .

477

got to go through it again."

"I wish I could bear it for you, my darling," Logan murmured. "I would gladly carry your burden."

"I'm more shocked than sorry," she confessed. "I don't have any grief left. Maybe I ought to, but I don't."

"No," Logan told her, "you shouldn't. Shawn Allan wasn't worth it." Logan knew he would never tell Brenna exactly how low Shawn had stooped. The knowledge would only hurt her more, and she had enough grief with which to live. "I love you."

Brenna lifted her face. "I love you, my darling, and I want you to love me. Nothing stands between us now."

Their lips met, and Brenna, swept with an intense yearning, clung to him and enjoyed his kisses. Laced with tenderness, they were different from the ones they had shared earlier. His lips pursued a breathy path to her throat, and she heard herself moan, the sound dim and faraway. Logan's light beard abraded her skin, and he whispered her name over and over. His lips sought for and covered hers again. He gave; he took. He drew her soul within himself. Brenna's hands swept upward and tangled in his silky hair. Finally Logan swooped her into his arms and carried her to the bed. He undressed her first, then himself. He was on the bed with her.

He covered her body with his own, and she sank deeper into the soft mattress. For endless minutes they lay there, Logan comforting her with his presence, Brenna accepting his gift. The only sounds in the room were those of their breathing and the slow, rhythmic beating of their hearts.

Brenna could feel Logan, hard and aroused, against her leg, but he made no move other than to cup her face between his massive hands. She knew that he would not take her; he would offer only solace. She must make love to him.

Desire burned inside her, yet it was tempered by a fierce, unexpected tenderness for this man whom she loved more than life. She felt as if it had been an eternity since she'd touched and been touched with such sweet tenderness, such infinite joy. She must show Logan how she felt; she must let him know how much she loved him. He was willing to share her grief and sorrow; she would share with him the intense pleasure that coursed through her veins.

Her hands slid over his shoulders and down his arms. His breath drew in sharply when she traced a pattern across his flat stomach, along the juncture of thigh and groin.

"Are you sure?" he whispered, his hand moving down her throat, over her breasts, and lower.

"Yes," she whispered in return, "I'm sure."

Brenna closed her arms about him, gently pulling his body close to hers. She held him, savoring the comfort and love he so willingly gave to her. Her hands moved up his back, her fingers spreading through the mop of golden-brown hair. He lifted his face; she lowered hers, and they kissed.

In between kisses, Brenna murmured, "I love you."

Logan stroked her with slow deliberation, easing his hand over her body. Finally his hand closed over her breast; he held and savored its fullness, its beauty. He coaxed the delicate mound to an aching arousal. His thumb teased the nipples with light brushes that made them stiffen with yearning. When Brenna thought she could stand the sensual torment no longer, Logan moved his hands, lifted his face, and pressed ardent kisses along her chin, down her neck, to her breasts. He nipped at her flesh and kissed her stomach, his tongue drawing erotic designs as he continued his journey.

When Brenna could stand the erotic torment no longer, he levered himself over her, and she opened her body to the virile thrust of his need. She began to move her hips around his hardness, and he slowly moved within her, gently at first, then more urgently as their desire mounted and carried them to the realm of ultimate fulfillment.

Logan's lovemaking was gentle and unselfish. His thoughts were for Brenna first, himself second.

Chapter Thirty

"What's happening?" Brenna asked when she heard the shouts in the square and the gate open. She was off the bed and at the window before Logan answered. She watched a large group of Comanches ride into the Comanchero city.

"Animal Talker and his braves," Logan said. "They're here for the guns."

Brenna saw two wagons on the other side of the plaza. "Shawn brought them in last night."

"I'm going down," Logan said. "I'll send your chest right over."

"No," Brenna said, "I'm going down with you." When Logan opened his mouth to protest, she said, "Please, Logan."

He nodded. As he stood and watched the activity in the square, Brenna quickly dressed, putting on the turquoise and black dress, and combed her hair. When she was finished, the two of them walked downstairs and out of the house. They stood, arm in arm on the veranda.

"Hello, Chief Animal Talker," Logan called in Spanish. "Why are you here?"

Animal Talker dismounted and joined Logan and Brenna. "The Scar-Faced One finally has guns for me. I have come to get them."

"Good morning, MacDougald," Lattimer said in English as he walked out of the house onto the veranda. "I wish you were the kind of man I could trust in my organization; I'm going to miss you."

"Am I going somewhere?" Logan asked.

Lattimer laughed. "The way of all flesh, Logan MacDougald."

Joaquin and Francisca walked out of the house about that time.

"Both you and Joaquin Sandoval," Lattimer added. "But the two of you can rest assured that I will take good care of the ladies."

Logan felt Brenna shiver.

"Now, my Comanche friend," Lattimer said, reverting to Spanish, "let's barter for the guns."

"What do you wish to exchange for them?" the chief asked.

"White women."

"I have no white women."

"Then, Animal Talker, I want you to kill all the men whom you captured the other day."

"Logan MacDougald?" the chief asked.

"Logan MacDougald."

The Comanche studied Logan a long time before he nodded his head and said, "I do not wish to kill a brave man such as Logan MacDougald, but my people need the guns."

"Aren't you going to ask to inspect them first?" Logan questioned.

Lattimer laughed. "You may inspect them if you wish, Animal Talker, but MacDougald is stalling for time."

Animal Talker looked at both men for a minute; then he looked at the wagon. "I will inspect the guns."

"As you wish," Lattimer said impatiently, leading the way to the freight hauler.

"I want you and Francisca to move into the house," Logan said as soon as the Comanchero was out of earshot. "When the ruckus starts out here, I want you to go into Lattimer's office and look in that chest against the wall. You'll find weapons and ammunition."

"You're sure that something is going to happen?" Brenna asked.

"Sure," Logan replied.

When the women returned to the house, Joaquin moved closer to Logan, and both of them stared at the retreating figures of Lattimer and Animal Talker.

"It will be soon, *mi amigo?*"

Logan looked around the square at the serape- and sombrero-garbed men. "Soon." His gaze returned to Lattimer's men as they rolled up the canvas and unloaded two crates. They levered up the top. Animal Talker knelt and picked up one of the revolvers. He looked at it closely.

"These are not the guns!" the Indian brave shouted.

His words wiped the smug satisfaction from Lattimer's face. He knelt beside the box and picked up the six-shooter.

"No!" He shook his head disbelievingly. "These are the ones that have to be broken down in three parts. This can't be!"

"You have tricked me, Scar-Face," Animal Talker accused. "You were going to give me these guns that are no good to the white men or to my people." He slung the gun to the ground. "I will not forgive you for this!"

"No," Lattimer shouted, "this is a trick! Someone tricked me!" The Comanchero turned around and looked at Logan. "Somehow," he accused, "it had to be you. Allen didn't have that much sense or guts. Only you would have brought me the wrong kind of guns."

"We were worried about your shipment of guns,"

Logan admitted, "but when Thunder went back to Sam Houston to make his report"—Logan grinned—"in case we didn't survive with the Comancheros, he learned that Samuel Colt, the designer and manufacturer for the Colt six-shooter, went broke. He can't get enough orders to produce his forty-four six-shooter. What we own is all we can get."

"You're lying about the guns and the Indian," Lattimer shouted. "That Cherokee is dead. Kirkwood killed him."

"I'm not lying about either," Logan replied. "Thunder isn't dead. Kirkwood is. The rangers have a few of the six-shooters, but even they can't get more. Anyone who has one treasures it." Logan looked at Animal Talker. "Lattimer will never be able to get you the kind of guns the Texas Rangers use because they aren't making it anymore."

Animal Talker nodded. "You speak with straight tongue, son of He-Who-Hunted-the-Antelope. I trust you." The Comanche turned without a word and walked to his horse.

"Where are you going?" Lattimer shouted.

"I leave, Scar-Face. We trade with you no more. Now you will have to kill and rob for yourself."

Lattimer's face twisted in anger. He pulled his revolver from the holster and aimed it at the chief's back. A shot rang out. Animal Talker spun around to see Lattimer's gun fly from his fingers.

"He was going to shoot you in the back," Logan said, dropping his revolver into his holster.

"I will kill him," Animal Talker said.

"No," Logan replied, "he is mine."

"Why?"

Logan reached into his pocket and pulled out the locket which he dangled from his fingers, the gold glinting in the sunshine. "Twenty years ago," he said, "this man, White-Hair, and his braves attacked my home."

Animal Talker nodded, an odd gleam in his eyes as he stared at the locket.

"Oswald Lattimer raped my mother and killed both my parents."

"How do you know this, MacDougald?" the Comanche asked.

"My father was scalped and left for dead, but he was still alive," Logan answered. "He is the one who cut Lattimer down the face and throat. I saw it all from a clump of bushes near the house where I was hiding."

Lattimer snarled. "Given the chance, MacDougald, I'll kill you."

"You're going to have the chance," Logan said. "Choose the weapon."

A rifle in one hand, a knife in the other, Brenna was standing inside the door, listening to the men talk. Because they spoke in Spanish, Francisca translated.

"Hacha pequeña!" Lattimer said.

"Oh, no," Francisca whispered, "not the hatchet!"

Logan returned to the veranda, unfastened his gun belt, and handed it to Joaquin. "The men in those red and yellow striped serapes," he said quickly, "are our men. That one over there is Thunder. If he's had time and opportunity, he's released Hollis, Jonesey, and the other drivers. Watch the Comancheros. If Lattimer gives the order or if I kill him, they will try to kill me."

"I will watch them, *mi amigo.*"

Laying her weapons aside, Brenna was out of the house in Logan's arms. "I love you."

"I love you."

"I hope I'm with child," she said.

Logan chuckled. "It'll be a miracle if you're not."

She mustered a smile. "I want you to live long enough to give me your name. I don't want to go

485

through the rest of my life named Allen."

"That's the first thing we'll do when we return to civilization," he promised. He caught her hand in his and pressed the locket into hers. "Keep this for me."

Brenna nodded.

"I have the hatchets, MacDougald. Are you ready?" Lattimer called.

"I'm ready," Logan replied.

He gave Brenna a long kiss before he returned to the center of the plaza. He picked up several, flexing his hand around the handles and swinging each through the air. Finally he chose one. Then he and Lattimer faced one another.

Lattimer had heard Logan tell Animal Talker that he had been reared by Cherokees, but the Comanchero didn't know the extent of self-control Logan could exert. His first play was to agitate him. "Even though it happened about twenty years ago, I remember your maw," he taunted. "Had pretty red hair she did, and pretty green eyes." He started to move in a circle. "Right good lay she was. Often wish I had carried her off with me rather than kill her."

Logan remembered all that Antelope Hunter had taught him. He closed out the taunts and retreated to the Silence. With steely gray eyes he watched the Comanchero, and when the hatchet sliced through the air, Logan easily swayed out of range. Again and again Lattimer wielded his weapon; as many times Logan dodged it.

"I'm going to tear your face in two, like your paw did mine," Lattimer promised. He gained new wind and moved in closer.

When Logan backed up, his foot caught on a root and he stumbled. Lattimer swung, his blade slicing Logan. A thin red line of pure fire crossed Logan's chest. Thunder jumped off the wagon and moved closer to the fighting men. His eyes darted around the square, where he had Mario and the other *Mexicanos* strategically posted. He nodded to Roger and Jonesey, disguised in Mexican serapes. Tense, poised, they all awaited his order.

Logan breathed deeply and looked down at the blood oozing out of the cut. He moved suddenly, and his arm swished back and forth through the air. His blade licked Lattimer's upper arm; it sliced across his stomach. Lattimer dropped his hatchet and caught his stomach with both hands, blood spurting through his fingers. He fell to his knees. Logan came in for the kill. He raised the hatchet.

"Don't," Lattimer begged. "Don't kill me. I'll do anything you ask of me." Even without the man's begging, Logan knew he couldn't kill Lattimer. He discovered that his hatred had diminished; his purpose dimmed. "Where's White-Hair?" he asked.

"We don't have time to talk," Lattimer wheezed. "I'm bleeding to death."

"You'll get no medical attention until you answer my questions," Logan replied.

"I don't know," Lattimer yelled. "I don't know."

"Not good enough."

"I haven't seen him since that raid," Lattimer said. "We never rode together again."

"Likely story."

"It's true," Lattimer insisted. "He and your sister fell in love, and he changed for the worse. His whole world was that woman."

"You're lying!" Logan charged. He couldn't believe that Flanna had fallen in love with one of the men responsible for killing their parents. "Flanna would have come back to me."

"Well, she didn't, and she did marry the Indian and bore him a son. Rumor has it that she died in

487

childbirth, and White-Hair has grieved ever since. Now, for God's sake, man, help me."

Logan reached down, grasped one of Lattimer's hands in his, and helped him to his feet.

"What are you going to do with me?" Lattimer asked.

"Take you back to Texas to stand trial." Logan turned and walked away.

"Watch out, Mr. MacDougald!" Roger Hollis yelled when he saw Lattimer pick up the hatchet and draw back to hurl it at Logan.

As soon as Logan heard the cry, he whirled around. Brenna was faster; her knife sailed through the air; the blade plunged into Lattimer's heart. He gasped, blood gurgled through his mouth, and he fell down, his weapon thudding to the ground beside him to lay in a pool of his blood.

At the same time Thunder threw the serape from his shoulders and waved his hand through the air. Pandemonium broke loose. Gunfire blazed across the plaza; men were running everywhere, but the Comancheros were surrounded. Strangely, the Comanches did not join the fracas. Animal Talker personally owed Logan a debt of gratitude for having saved his life, but his braves owed nothing to the Comancheros or to Logan. They sought cover, coming out only when the battle was soon over.

When Logan walked across the courtyard, Brenna threw herself into his arms. She laid her head against his chest and held him tightly. "I thought he was going to kill you."

"Your woman is a warrior," Animal Talker said, moving from behind the porch column.

Logan smiled. "My woman is a warrior."

"My braves and I leave now," the chief said. "We return to our village. You may return to your village in peace. My people will not harm you."

Standing arm in arm, Brenna and Logan watched the young chief move across the plaza to mount his horse. He rode to the gate of the village, turned, and looked at Logan for a long time. Then he returned to the porch of the big house.

"MacDougald," he said, "you asked Lattimer about the one called White-Hair."

Logan stepped nearer. "I did."

"He lives." The Comanche chief waited a minute before he said, "He had a child by a white woman. This son was called Man-of-the-Gold-Talisman because of the necklace which he wore."

"The locket which I showed you?"

Animal Talker nodded.

"Does the white woman yet live?"

Animal Talker did not answer Logan's question; rather he said, "She did not know any of her family lived; she thought all of them had been killed. She and White-Hair loved each other very much. When she died at childbirth, White-Hair mourned her death. Some of my people say she is still alive. They still see the woman with the flaming hair riding beside her chief and husband."

"Have they really seen her?" Logan asked, tenaciously clinging to the hope that Flanna was still alive.

"Yes, Logan MacDougald, they have seen her because they wish to see her. She was loved and honored by my people."

"She is dead."

Animal Talker nodded. "She died giving birth to her son, the one who wore her talisman."

Flanna had a son. He had a nephew. "Is he alive?"

"Yes."

"I would like to see him."

"He is a Comanche, Logan MacDougald. He claims

489

no white blood. He will not want to see you."

"He's not all Comanche," Logan blazed. "He's half-white. He's Flanna's son and my nephew."

Animal Talker reached up and took his buffalo headdress off. Brenna gasped; even Logan was momentarily taken aback.

"I have the white hair like my father," Animal Talker said.

"You are my sister's son?" Logan asked.

Animal Talker hesitated momentarily before he said, "No, I am White-Hair's second son by his Indian wife. Gold Talisman, my brother, is the eldest son. He is a medicine man—a man of peace."

"Why was he raiding into our settlements?"

"He came because he had a vision that I would be killed if he did not protect me with his medicine. While he was saving my life, the white man ripped his talisman from his neck."

"Will you take me to see him?"

Animal Talker shook his head. "I will return to my village and tell my father and brother all I have heard and seen. If they wish to see you, they will send word. Then you will come."

"I have his locket which I will keep for him," Logan answered. "If he wants his talisman, he'll have to come get it."

Animal Talker stared at Logan for length; then without another word, he settled his headdress over his head and rode off.

"What did he say?" Brenna questioned.

"White-Hair is still alive," he said.

"What about your sister?"

"She is dead, but her son lives. He's Animal Talker's half brother."

Before Brenna could say more, Joaquin said, "*Mi amigo,* you and Brenna are welcome to travel back to

490

Santa Fe with us."

"Thanks," Logan said, his eyes locking with Brenna's, "but I think I'll be heading back to Texas. I want to return these guns to the rightful owners, and I need to make a report to the president."

"What about you, Brenna?" Joaquin asked.

"My work isn't finished yet," she replied. "I'll be going on to Chihuahua and Durango." When she saw the disappointment in Logan's eyes, she said, "I have to sell my goods. You don't know how deep in debt I am. Everything I could beg, borrow, or mortgage has gone into saving my company."

"I think I've worked something out," Logan said. "I have some money which I'm willing to invest in a freight hauling company." He reached out to catch her hands in his. "Furthermore, Brenna Allen, I want to go home, so I can change your name from Allen to MacDougald before our son or daughter decides to join us."

"Oh, Logan," Brenna breathed ecstatically.

About that time Mario swaggered up, a smile spanning his face, his black eyes dancing. "Ah, Señor MacDougald, we have done good, yes?"

Logan laughed. "We have done good, yes."

"And we get our reward?"

"You certainly will. You've earned it. Señor Jamarillo," Logan said, "I'd like to introduce you to my bride-to-be, Señora Brenna Allen."

Brenna looked up at Logan, a bright smile radiating her face. "I like the sound of that, Mr. MacDougald."

Mario swept his sombrero off and flourished a deep bow. "I am delighted to meet you, señora. I wish you all the happiness in the world."

"Thank you, señor," Brenna returned.

"Now, Señor MacDougald," Mario announced, "I think it is time for me and my *compadres* to be leaving.

Our women are expecting us."

"More like they're waiting for the booty," Logan said.

Mario grinned. "They will get some of the reward, señor, but not all of it."

"What will you do with the remainder?"

Mario laughed. "Trade, señor. What else?"

"You saw what happens to outlaws," Logan said.

"Ah, señor," Mario drawled, "I'm no *bandido,* just a trader." He swung up on his horse and touched his fingers to the edge of his sombrero. "Adiós, *mi amigo. Hasta luego."*

"He's nice," Brenna said. "What did you give him as a reward?"

Logan drew Brenna into a tight embrace and rested his head on the crown of her head. "Not much."

Brenna heard a rumble and turned around. Her eyes opened wide and she exclaimed, "You gave him my wagons!"

Logan threw back his head and laughed.

"You gave him my wagons!" Brenna pummeled his chest with her fists.

Tears of happiness misting his eyes, Logan caught her hands in his. "No, my little wildcat, I didn't give him your wagons. I gave him the wagon of scrap metal only."

"That's all?" Brenna asked skeptically.

"No, as payment for helping me apprehend the Comancheros, I promised him some of Lattimer's spoils." He pointed in the opposite direction. "If you'll look over there, you'll see your wagons."

Brenna turned.

"You'll also see your wagon master and lead driver."

In amazement Brenna listened as Roger—truly transformed from a tenderfoot into an experienced frontiersman—yelled the orders, and saw Jonesey lead